CW00351342

Douglas Lindsay was born in Scotland in 1964. He is currently continuing his tour of eastern Europe, living in Warsaw, Poland, with his wife and two children.

Also by Douglas Lindsay,
available from Long Midnight Publishing:

The Long Midnight of Barney Thomson

The Cutting Edge of Barney Thomson

A Prayer For Barney Thomson

Barney Thomson & The Face of Death

The King Was In His Counting House

THE LAST FISH SUPPER

Douglas Lindsay

LMP

This edition published in Great Britain in 2006 by
Long Midnight Publishing
Suite 433
24 Station Square
Inverness IV1 1LD
e-mail: info@barney-thomson.com

www.barney-thomson.com

*A catalogue record for this book is available
from the British Library*

ISBN 0 9541 387 5 9

Printed and bound in Great Britain by
Mackays of Chatham plc, Chatham, Kent

for Kathryn

Prologue

2 Deaths

Jonah Harrison was the kind of guy who twisted the seatbelt every time he sat in a car.

The town of Millport on the island of Cumbrae in the Firth of Clyde. 2:46 on a grey and bleak Monday afternoon in April. Jonah had been sitting at his laptop for three hours. On-line, fingers tapping. Awaiting the outcome of the 2.40 at Kempton Park. He was two thousand down on the day, nearly thirty thousand down on the year. January had been good, but he'd lost all his gains in one abysmal afternoon at Taunton in late February, and the six weeks since had been increasingly ugly. He was out of control, and the time he didn't spend at his computer was generally used to complete credit card applications. A few months earlier he'd had no interest in the horses whatsoever, but he'd been given a copy of *Seabiscuit: An American Legend* for Christmas, he'd devoured the book, and he'd immersed himself in horse racing ever since, uncovering a gambling addiction along the way. It's good to discover new interests in your later years, other than drooling and shouting at teenagers.

Jonah was also unhappily married, his wife was having an affair with the local Church of Scotland minister, and he had a small malignant tumour in his colon which was still some vicious wasting months short of making itself known.

However, none of that actually mattered as he was about to die on his way to taking a pish.

1

His legs were shaking under the desk; from the waist down he looked like Elvis. In fact, from the waist up he looked like Elvis. Circa '77, serious contender for the lead role in the upcoming Hollywood action flic, *Fat Bastardman*. No stranger to the buffet table, no alien at the fish and chip shop, doughnut poster child for the new millennium, it was Jonah who had eaten all the pies. He had been needing to go to the bathroom for over an hour, but had continually put if off, such was his obsession.

At 7-1, *Brother's Leap* had seemed a decent bet. He had placed well in a couple of previous outings at Goodwood Park and Thatcham, the ground suited him. So Jonah had gone for a clear thousand on the bet, in the hope of wiping off a quarter of the year's losses in one swoop.

He rose hurriedly from the desk, pushing the laptop away from him and finally logging off, as *Brother's Leap* trailed in ninth of ten. A month earlier the loss of a grand in one go would've had his insides curling up like a snake, but now it was nothing. Forget about it and get back on with the business. Only ever one click away from the next big score.

He walked briskly up the hall and pushed on the bathroom door. Locked. No surprise, as Ruth more or less lived in there. He knocked loudly.

'Ruthie, come on!'

Ruthie, however, was not about to escape the enslavement of the bathroom mirror, to which she was as much beholden as was he to the heirs of Seabiscuit.

'I'm still doing this,' she replied calmly, although she could tell from the peculiar quality of his voice that he must be desperate.

'Ruthie!' he ejaculated.

'You bursting?' she asked calmly, while applying Duraglut Face Cement to the canyons in her cheeks.

'Aye!' he called, hopping pathetically from one leg to the next, 'I am bursting. Are you done?'

She paused, keeping Jonah at his barn dance shindig for another few seconds, while her mind drifted to the Reverend Dreyfus, a delicious man of upstanding character.

'No,' she said eventually. 'Go and pee in the kitchen sink.'

2

He banged his fist against the door to accompany the heartfelt exasperated grunt. Leant his head against it for a second, before quickly accepting his fate.

He turned hurriedly and broke into a run over the five yards of the upstairs landing. The stairs were steep, not to be taken in a rush and certainly not by the man who'd eaten all the curry. On top of which Jonah had his weak ankles to think about.

He blundered down the first few steps much too quickly. His ankle gave way – didn't break or anything, just twisted round as if someone was ringing water from it – and he pitched forward. Twenty-two and a half stones of unsightly animal blubber flew through the air. He landed on his head on the step fifth from the bottom. Ought, at least, to have stopped himself with his arms, but they were too busy flailing around trying to grab at banisters. And while his ankle had survived the twist without breaking, his neck was not so fortunate. Sudden rupture of the top of the spinal cord, the neck buckled and snapped, slight crunching of bone, and less than a second later his full weight thundered onto the bottom of the steps and down onto the floor.

The house shook.

In the bathroom, Ruth Harrison watched the gin ripple in her glass. She glanced at the door, waiting for the tyrannosaur. When it didn't appear, she looked back at the mirror and continued her in-depth study of the latest blackhead in the collection.

In death, Jonah Harrison's bladder held firm and there was a certain serene beauty about his squashed and pudgy cheeks.

✂

The other death occurred not on that day, but on a Monday afternoon almost thirty years previously, during the long, hot summer of '76. Water shortages, ice cream wars and grass parched a very pale brown.

Azarael Corinthian was the kind of man who had been bred for great things, his entire life pointing in one direction, to one great end. A life that involved many secrets and a lot of waiting. And so, naturally, he had rebelled through most of his life and had reached his mid-thirties with none of the required poise and maturity which had been expected of him.

He had been brought up in Millport and had a robust contempt for the place. Yet even though both of his parents were dead by that summer and he had no other family on the island, something brought him back there every year. Some dedication to duty perhaps, which found its way out, no matter how deeply buried it was in his subconscious.

That summer he returned to Millport after having spent the better part of seven months in Las Vegas. Too much gambling, although it had surprisingly all but evened itself out over the piece, too many women, too much alcohol, too much junk food, too many nights spent in luxurious hotel rooms with expensive drugs and prostitutes.

He had come to Millport to dry out and reconnect with his past. Unfortunately his immediate past of cocaine and burgers and cigarettes and vodka had more of a connection. After three days on the island he had decided that he was feeling good enough about himself to take some light exercise. He had started with the time honoured Millport tradition of cycling leisurely around the island, which had been straightforward. However, he had then made the unsound judgement call that he could go for a short run in the afternoon up to the top of the hill at the centre of the island, from where one can look west down over the golf course to the hills of Bute and Arran, and north back up the firth to the mountains of Argyll, and east and south to the mainland.

He never made it to the top of the hill, instead suffering a severe heart attack on the way up. It was at least twenty minutes before a car passed by to stop for a look at the prone body and by the time he had been taken to the small hospital at the foot of the hill, it had been too late. Azarael Corinthian was dead at the age of thirty-six, and the unhappy world of at least a few other people would be thrown into turmoil.

1

Dead Original

'Think of a new way to commit murder.'

Everything was new in the room although it had the appearance of senescence. The dark brown leather had been sprayed to give mustiness, the books had been coated in dust. Out of town visitors to the house thought it early Victorian. James Randolph knew better, having seen the house grow stone by stone, but he was impressed with the feel of it. Why build in today's style, which would be outdated in a decade, when you could create a house which looked like it had been part of the landscape for a hundred and fifty years?

But a new method of murder? That was far more interesting.

'Define new?' said Randolph. 'A new implement of death or a new way to extinguish life?'

Bartholomew Ephesian stood with his back to Randolph, looking out over the Clyde. The Isle of Bute was dull and grey across the water, the mountains of Arran mostly shrouded in cloud. The sea was restless and for the moment there wasn't a single boat to be seen. Ephesian glanced at the small clock on the mantleshelf. Quarter to three. Quarter to eleven in Hong Kong, and he wondered how many women Ping Phat would be in bed with at that moment.

'A new implement means nothing,' he said, making a small gesture with his glass. 'You could kill someone with a candy bar. I'm talking about something much more fundamental, something far more intrinsic to human life. A cardinal death.'

'You'd need to know medicine,' said Randolph.

5

Ephesian turned for the first time in ten minutes, gave Randolph the benefit of his eyebrow, and looked away. Never actually looked Randolph straight in the eye.

Had Bartholomew Ephesian been born in the 1990's, he would have been taken to a psychologist and would have been quickly diagnosed as having some condition which had recently come into vogue in the United States. However, he'd been born into a wealthy family in the west end of Glasgow just after the second war, and so he'd just been marked down as another gifted but spoiled kid. Couldn't relate to his classmates, got into too many fights, and could multiply one thousand three hundred and forty-one by eight hundred and seventy-six in under a second. However, much more than most, his personality and behavioural patterns had dominated and shaped his life. From his need to self-employment from an early age, to a total inability to relate to the one woman who had ever loved him, his existence had been dominated by a continuing effort to find a space in amongst everyone else in the world.

'And how would you know it was entirely original?' Randolph added. 'You have access to Scotland Yard files? FBI? Interpol?'

This time Ephesian didn't turn. Randolph had felt amused by his own question but he found the silence disconcerting. He could see the gulls circling above the water, could hear their doleful cries; the sound of the sea, waves on the shore far below. Intimidation by silence, against the weakness of spirit which allowed one to be thus intimidated; the polarisation between the two men. Ephesian had power, even if, to those in the town, it did not seem to extend much beyond the small bays and the shops along the shorefront of Millport. Randolph was a man who lived in a house by the boatyard, with little else to define him.

'Yes,' said Ephesian, looking out to sea, 'as a matter of fact I do.'

Randolph felt a dryness in his mouth. He should have known better than to try and engage Ephesian in any kind of verbal exchange. A discussion about garden weeds was likely to leave him feeling as if he had a death threat hanging over him.

6

'Imagination,' said Ephesian coldly. 'That's what's required.'

'How long do I have?' Randolph asked quickly. Get it over with, abrupt retreat, and he could be back in the sanctuary of his own garden in five minutes.

Ephesian turned slowly. He swallowed the remnants of the glass and placed it carefully on the desk.

'Midnight Wednesday,' he said, looking at a point somewhere to Randolph's right, his eyes falling on a copy of Robert Louis Stevenson's *The Merry Men*.

'Two days?' said Randolph, weakly.

'I'm glad you can count.'

Ephesian sat down behind the desk and leant forward.

'You know who, now you have the when. The how is entirely up to you.'

Randolph didn't reply. Generally this was how conversations with Ephesian were completed, with him in wretched silence.

'Of course, I'm just toying with you. I'm not actually expecting you to have any imagination whatsoever. There probably is no such thing as a new way to commit murder. Just try and be a little different if you can. Try to surprise me for once, James. And if you can't, a knife in the back.'

Randolph nodded. Forced the words, 'Yes, sir.'

Interview over. Ephesian had humoured him for fifteen minutes, but he tired quickly of Randolph and his type. It wasn't as if he had to practice good management of any sort. He wasn't accountable to anyone.

'I have an appointment,' he said brusquely.

Randolph didn't hesitate. Stood up, looked into Ephesian's distracted eyes and then walked quickly from the room, closing the door behind him. Ephesian stared at the door, tried to let the muscles in his back relax, then he let his head fall forward and placed his face into his hands.

It was almost over.

2

The Last Barber

Barney Thomson, barber, stopped outside the door of the shop. He turned and looked out over Millport bay, at the view he would have for the next few years of his working life should he choose to become the owner of the establishment he was about to visit.

The shop looked out on a three foot high white sea wall across the road. To the right was a tiny harbour and a short pier; to the left, the main road around the island running along the front of the town, along to Kames Bay and the old Victorian houses, before disappearing around the far corner. In the bay, seventy yards out, there were a couple of small islands. A few boats rustled in the agitated water. Half a mile out to sea was the green bulk of the island of Lesser Cumbrae. Across the sea to the left, the shore of the mainland and the portentous grey buildings of Hunterston B nuclear power station. To the right, past the edge of the town and the old George Hotel which stood at the end of the pier, Barney could see the cloud-shrouded hills of Arran.

He turned and let his eyes wander along the front of the town. There were a few people abroad, well wrapped against the cold, but not many. The town had the feel of an out of season English seaside resort in miniature, cold and grey, and Barney wondered that if in these days of cheap flights to Europe, it ever lost that feel, even in July and August. Did anyone come to Millport on holiday anymore, as he had done for so many years?

There was nothing depressing about it for him, however. He loved this place, and if anywhere felt like home to him now, it

8

was here, even though he hadn't stood on this seafront for almost twenty years.

He turned, he opened the door to the shop and walked in to a light tinkle of the bell. The bell will be the first thing to go, he thought, as he closed the door behind him, and looked around the familiar surroundings of a barbershop that could've been in any small town in the world. Three seats, large wall of mirrors, a bench along the opposite wall, walls in need of a paint.

The middle chair was occupied, the other two pushed in against the counter. The one nearest the window had obviously not been used in a couple of decades, the seat at the far end was beside the sink.

Barney was surprised to see the barber was a young man of about twenty. His customer was an old fellow, who was slumped in his chair, noisily sucking up slobber. At the back of the shop there was another man in a white coat, a broom in his hand, deliberately sweeping up, taking great care with every stroke. With his gnarled features and his hunchback it was hard to guess his age, but Barney could tell that whoever he was, whatever he did, he wasn't a barber.

The barber and the hunchback looked round. The old bloke festered in his own armpits, slurped at a line of saliva on his chin and subsided further into his seat.

'Hi,' said Barney.

'Dude!' said the young guy, in that totally assured way of the young to imitate American culture in a west of Scotland accent with complete confidence.

'Barney Thomson,' said Barney, his accent broadening.

'Totally,' said the barber. He laid down the scissors and extended his hand. 'Tony Ephesian. People call me 2Tone.'

Of course they did.

'This cat is Igor,' said 2Tone, indicating the hunchback.

Barney looked quizzically at him. Igor the Hunchback. A face from the past? It had been a few years, another time another dark episode in his life. But Barney's life had been strange, and he wasn't sure if he really did recognise him. And how was it that Igor had come to this place? The same Igor, or was there a

9

great hunchbacked collective, liberally dispersed through the barbershops of Scotland?

Barney nodded and said, 'Igor.'

Igor glared at him, said something incoherent that sounded like 'Arf', then went back to sweeping up. Barney glanced at the clean floor and wondered what it was exactly that he was sweeping. Maybe he spent his entire day brushing at the same spot, like some deranged obsessive.

'Igor's like this, you know, totally mute kinda guy, you know? That means he can't speak,' said 2Tone. 'And he's like completely deaf as well, which is cool, 'cause it means you can like talk about him and stuff and he doesn't hear.'

Barney nodded, unable to take his eyes off the brush. Maybe some years previously Igor had killed someone at that very spot, and was destined forever to spend his days brushing compulsively, chained by guilt and the eternal need for penitence. He shook his head to lose the image.

'I'm just gonna finish off Mr Watson's *Ben Affleck* cut, Dude, then we can talk. You just want to like, look around and I'll come hang in a minute?'

'Aye,' said Barney, and 2Tone went back about his business, snipping carefully around the ageing napper of Mr Watson.

Mr Watson dribbled some more onto his chin, 2Tone ducked into his next manoeuvre and Igor swept slowly, glancing occasionally up at Barney with great suspicion, as if expecting him to suddenly grab a flaming torch, round up a mob of angry villagers and chase him off into the woods.

Barney stared at the three strange inhabitants of the shop, took another look around the limited surroundings, which presented nothing of any greater interest on second inspection, then walked behind 2Tone to the back of the shop. Igor stopped sweeping, looking distrustfully at Barney as he stepped across his work site. Barney opened the door at the back and stuck his head round. A small kitchen, brightly decorated, window onto a short stretch of garden. Nothing much else to see, he turned and walked back past Igor and stood at the front window of the shop, looking across the road and the sea wall, out across the water.

He shivered, wondering at how odd it was that somewhere he had not visited in so long could be so familiar. It was as if he had never been away.

The door to the shop opened, Barney turned, hauled from the stupor of his melancholic reflections. 2Tone ushered Mr Watson from the shop and the old man doddered out into the cold, barely able to stand up straight.

'Hang loose, Mr Watson,' said 2Tone, closing the door. Igor glanced up, muttered something under his breath, and started sweeping around the chair at the paltry clippings from Mr Watson's *Ben Affleck*.

2Tone came and stood beside Barney and then, much to Barney's consternation, he put his arm around his shoulders.

'You know what I like?' said 2Tone, and Barney glanced at him uncomfortably.

'Not yet,' he said.

'I like that really dudey sound a spoon makes when you're stirring a cup of hot chocolate, you know? It's got a much richer tone to it than when you're stirring tea or coffee.'

Barney stared out to sea. Hot chocolate?

'So, Dude,' said 2Tone, 'what d'you think of the whole setuparooni? Like totally cool, or what?'

'This is your shop?' asked Barney.

'Like, yeah, totally,' said 2Tone, then he sniggered in an irritating manner. 'You know, it was like my dad who bought it for me and everything, you know? I saw that movie *Barbershop*. Did you see it? I totally dug that film and I thought, wow, like, you know, what an awesome thing, to own a barbershop. To like cut hair, isn't it totally awesome? I thought, wow, I'm just going to be like totally humbled by that as an experience. Cutting hair, you know, like wow.'

He smiled at Barney, nodding sagely, his arm still around him in lifelong fraternal barbershop camaraderie.

'So why are you selling?' asked Barney.

'It's a load of shite,' said 2Tone. 'It totally bums me out. I hate cutting hair, man. How do you, like, do it all day?'

Barney smiled.

11

'My dad owns most of the shops along here, but he's totally pissed at me about this, so he just wants to sell it. It's like, you know, fair enough. An eye for an eye and all that.'

'That's not really an eye for an eye,' said Barney.

'Yeah, cool,' said 2Tone. 'You going to buy it, man?'

Barney nudged at his arm until he took it from his shoulders, then 2Tone took a step back, folded his arms and smiled at Barney as if they were all in it together.

'Aye,' said Barney.

'Dude!' said 2Tone smiling and nodding his head. 'So, like you know, I know there's like paperwork and stuff to be totally done, but like, I am so outta here man. You don't mind taking over?'

Barney stared at him for a second, not entirely getting his meaning until 2Tone started putting on his jacket.

'You mean, right now, don't you?' said Barney.

'Are you cool with that?'

Barney looked at the shop, laughed ruefully. Why not? He glanced at Igor, wondering if he would be taking such immediate leave as 2Tone but knowing he wouldn't.

'Sure,' said Barney.

'Awesome,' said 2Tone. 'My dad'll be along in a minute. Wants to have a word with you. I'm gone. See you around, dude.' Then 2Tone glanced at Igor and turned back to Barney, his voice lowered only slightly. 'Be nice to the wee fella, you know. He's got a hunchback.'

Igor looked up, shook his head, and returned to his sweeping.

'I'm guessing he'll stay with the shop,' said Barney.

'Part of the furniture,' said 2Tone. 'Apparently he's been working here since like the 20's or something, you know. I think he like fled from a village in Bavaria, some shit like that, though not before the villagers cut his tongue out. Totally shocking, you know. The madness of intolerance.'

Igor didn't look up this time, but he could tell they were talking about him and he knew that it would be complete nonsense.

'Dude,' said 2Tone, holding out his knuckles so that Barney could do a thing.

12

'2Tone,' said Barney, declining the knuckle knock.

'Solid,' said 2Tone, making it look like the clenched fist knuckle gesture had been just that.

And then 2Tone was gone. Barney watched him go, glanced up at the bell as it tinkled for what was destined to be the last time, then looked round at Igor.

Igor looked up from a dustpan and brush, his stooped position exacerbating the hunch. The two men stared at one another for a short while, a look that was enough to indicate there would be far more respect between them than had existed between Igor and 2Tone. Barney nodded, Igor did a thing with his head. Then Barney turned and pointed at the bell over the door, looked back at Igor and dragged his finger across his neck.

The most meagre of smiles came to Igor's face. He couldn't hear the bell but the vibration of it got into his soul every time the door opened. The bell was history.

'Thanks,' said Barney, and Igor went to the back of the shop to find the toolkit. Barney watched him go, then turned and looked back out across the sea.

So, here he was again. Back in a barber's shop, and this time, hopefully, he would get to stay. Settle down, a few years of mundane existence and at some stage he would get his life into order, or else he would slowly grow old and die here and that would be the end of it.

Yet the sea was grim and dark this afternoon and, as with everything he looked upon these days, it seemed to hold dark portents. Was anywhere he ever visited free of death and murder? Was there anywhere sleepy enough that he could rely on it to lie down and be dull for the rest of his days?

He shivered and turned as Igor came up behind him, carrying a small step ladder and a screwdriver.

'Thanks, Igor,' said Barney, shaking off the shiver.

'Arf,' said Igor.

13

3

I'd Sooner Chew
My Leg Off

Ruth Harrison tentatively opened the bathroom door in the wake
of the enormous thud at the bottom of the stairs. She had waited
for a couple of minutes for Jonah to come and tell her what little
accident had befallen him, before, unusually for her, some sixth
sense had kicked.

'Jonah!' she called. 'You all right, love?'

Nothing. After all, the dead don't speak.

'Jonah!'

Scowling at the thought of having to leave the bathroom an
hour earlier than intended, but feeling the first blight of nerves
at what she was going to find, she hesitantly walked along the
upper landing until she could see the bottom of the stairs. She
stopped in her stride, her mouth dropped open. Suddenly
confronted by the sight of the giant bulk of her husband piled
high in a heap of dead blubber, her heart thumped, her throat
turned dry.

'Aw, Christ,' she muttered. She began to walk gingerly down
the stairs, getting more circumspect as she approached the
corpse. She stopped just short of him, closed her eyes, took a
deep breath. Her head spun. Opened her eyes again before she
fainted, got to the bottom of the stairs, stepped over the gigantic
weight of Jonah's thighs and knelt down beside his head.
Gingerly she placed her fingers under his nose to check for
breath, although she already knew that there wouldn't be any.
Yet the stillness of the air drew a small gasp from her and she

14

sat back against the wall, shuffling an extra foot or two away from him.

'Christ, Jonah,' she said. 'If you hadn't spent so bloody long sitting at the computer, you wouldn't have been in such a rush.'

Not now, not ever in her life, would it occur to her that if she'd allowed him entry into the bathroom he wouldn't have died.

She heard a noise and looked upstairs. Heavy footsteps along the hall. Hurried yet laboured, away from the stairs towards the bathroom. The bathroom door closed, there was silence.

A moment and then her heart suddenly started thrashing wildly. She stood, looked nervously up.

'Is anybody there?'

She waited. Nothing.

'Hello?'

Neck straining, the sound of her heart in her ears, beginning to panic. Deep breath, last look at Jonah, then she turned and ran towards the front door and out into the small cul-de-sac which led off the road down into Kames Bay.

'Nature or nurture?' asked Bartholomew Ephesian.

'Nature,' said Barney quickly.

Ephesian stared at himself in the mirror. Barney glanced out to sea. He'd been in the shop for twenty minutes and already he was at home, already it was like he'd worked here all his life. The shop felt familiar, the view of the cold, grey ominous sea felt familiar, the edgy waves, ill at ease with the day, felt familiar. He could stand at this window all day, transfixed. And he would work here every day. Cold, disturbing seas in the winter, occasional warm, hazy flat calms in the summer.

Ephesian had arrived soon after his son had left and had said he would discuss the deal while Barney gave him a haircut. Almost as if he only wanted to sell the premises to someone who was a competent hairdresser. He had requested a straightforward *Alec Guiness*, taken his seat with not even the formality of a handshake, and had set about asking a series of quick-fire questions determined to get to the bottom of Barney's id. Deciding whether or not Barney was worthy of buying

15

something from him. That he had yet to look Barney directly in the eye, Barney assumed was part of the game. He did not yet have a handle on the man's personality, but could recognise the jeopardy inherent in him. Igor did not like Bartholomew Ephesian and had found something to do in the backroom which would take however long Ephesian was out front.

'Frankenstein or Dracula. More likely?'

'Dracula,' said Barney.

'More dangerous?'

'Dracula,' said Barney.

'More intrinsic?

'Dracula.'

'Godfather I or II?'

'I.'

'Madonna or Britney?'

'You're kidding me?' said Barney.

'There is no such thing as low culture, Mr Thomson,' came the quick reply. 'We must embrace human life in all its manifestations.'

'Madonna,' said Barney, without much enthusiasm.

'Italy or Switzerland?'

'I need parameters.'

'There aren't any.'

'Italy.'

'John or Paul?'

'George.'

'You're going to kill someone. Hands on or off?'

'Bullet in the back of the head from two feet.'

Not that he'd been thinking about it, although there were obviously occasions standing behind a seditious customer when exploding the head would be the option of choice.

'Nice,' said Ephesian. 'China or Taiwan?'

'China.'

'China or Tibet?'

'Tibet.'

'Red or brown?'

Barney tried to attract his gaze in the mirror but Ephesian looked steadfastly into the dark wells of his own eyes.

16

'Red,' said Barney.

Ephesian paused. Barney felt the slight twitch in the head, although the face remained expressionless. Mind on the job. He stood back to check he'd nailed the sides. The *Alec Guiness*, despite the obvious pitfalls, was a walk in the park, but a good barber always keeps his eye on the napper.

'The Turin Shroud. Fact or fake?'

Barney gave this one some thought.

'Fake,' he said after the gap.

'Why?'

A departure. Had been waiting for the question where he would have to explain the answer.

'For belief that the Shroud is genuine, that the chemical reaction which created it was actually able to take place, implies faith. I have none.'

'You believe that the sun will rise in the morning?'

'Not on the east coast of Scotland I don't,' said Barney, smiling, to counter.

Ephesian ignored the smile. He had been able to smile and laugh as a child, but years of being battered by life as an adult had stripped him of even that social ability.

'Everyone has faith, Mr Thomson.'

Barney put his scissors in his top pocket – ignoring the story he'd read in the previous month's *Barbopolitan*, where a barber in Redundant Falls, North Dakota, had stabbed himself in the heart – and ran a final comb through Ephesian's hair.

'Be a sinner and sin strongly, but more strongly have faith and rejoice in Christ,' said Ephesian.

Barney smiled again. 'Have haircut, will quote,' he said.

'We are each nothing without faith,' said Ephesian. 'You believe that the sun will rise in the morning?' he asked again.

Barney didn't answer. Slipped the comb into his pocket beside the scissors.

The door to the shop opened and a middle-aged man entered. He hesitated, avoided looking Ephesian in the eye, although he needn't have bothered, then took his seat. There were no magazines to pick up, so he looked out of the window at the grey sea and placed his hands uncomfortably on his knees. Most

17

people in Millport did not like to be in the presence of Bartholomew Ephesian any more than they had to.

'Can I see to the next customer?' asked Barney.

Ephesian examined his hair in the mirror for perfection, found it, and gestured with his eyebrows for Barney to remove the cape.

Still studying himself in the mirror, he rose, accepted Barney's help to put on his jacket, then finally turned to face him.

'An adequate job,' he said, looking at Barney's shirt. 'You can have the shop. I'll have my solicitor finalise the papers this evening, we should be able to sign in the next couple of days.'

They shook on it and then Ephesian turned and walked briskly from the small shop. The door closed and immediately the atmosphere lifted, so that it seemed as if the room had been exorcised of some presence, a demon, which the others had not previously really been aware of. Barney looked out to sea, felt an unusual chill as he looked across the troubled bay, then turned round to face his first customer in the latest establishment which he was to grace in his career. The door at the rear of the shop opened and Igor appeared, broom in hand.

'You're on,' said Barney to the customer.

The man, looking every inch very, very shaggy around the head, removed his jacket and took his place in the big chair.

'What'll it be?' asked Barney, trying to guess, and deciding this would be a man who'd ask for something frivolous. A Barney Rubble or a Batfink.

'I'll have a Tony Blair, please.'

Right enough.

18

4

The Full Robbie Range

Police Constable Thaddæus Gainsborough, the sole representative of the Millport constabulary, answered Ruth Harrison's call in under five minutes, arriving a few seconds before the ambulance. Gainsborough checked out Jonah's body to establish death and began a rudimentary attempt at reviving him. He was soon interrupted by the paramedic Luciens, who muttered, 'Oh, you're doing that all wrong,' took over, and made an equally futile attempt at resuscitation. Gainsborough left him to it, directed Ruth Harrison away from the sight of her husband's prone body and took her across the street to Brenda The Muppet's house. He placed the two of them together, squirmed with discomfiture at the initial outpouring of grief from both women, then left them to their cups of tea and grandma-soft biscuits. He returned to the house to complete a thorough check of the premises, establishing that there was no one else present. The noise must have been the wind, he would later say to Ruth, and Ruth would believe him and forget about the footsteps on the hallway and forget that the wind never wears shoes.

Then Gainsborough and Luciens tried to move Jonah's body to the ambulance, something they were completely unable to achieve until they called in the assistance of a couple of neighbours. Eventually Jonah Harrison left his house for the final time and Luciens made a joke about it being just as well that they'd had the ambulance's suspension looked at recently. Ruth Harrison stood across the road watching him go, a cup of

PG Tips in her right hand, her left hand dabbing at the corner of her eyes, taking away tears which weren't quite crocodile but which were at the very least fairly large lizard. And then she stumped up the courage to return to her house. Declining Brenda The Muppet's offer of company, she walked back in through the front door and stood in the hallway feeling the stillness and silence, which was so much more than it had ever been when Jonah had just been down at the pub.

✂

Five o'clock, late afternoon mincing coldly into early evening. The rain had started just after four, coming sullenly in from the sea and smearing the window, so that the view which so beguiled Barney was veiled. Nevertheless, he was still standing at the window, watching the grey day become black early evening, dark well before its time, with Igor standing beside him leaning on his brush, when the door to the shop opened and a woman entered.

Barney had had a reasonably solid afternoon. Four haircuts, not including Ephesian at the start of his stint. The *Tony Blair* had been followed by a regulation short back and sides, a *Brendan Fraser* and a mullet, by God!

Igor glanced at the woman and grimaced. She smiled at him, he abruptly turned away, trailing his brush behind him and retreated to the back of the shop. She watched him go and then turned to Barney. She extended her hand and smiled. A natural smile, not something you'd get on the back of a packet of breakfast cereal.

'Hi, Garrett Carmichael,' she said.

Barney took her hand and said, 'You're called Garrett?'

'Yeah. You'll get used to it. I'm Mr Ephesian's solicitor. One of them at any rate. Thought I'd come in and say hello.'

It's her mouth, thought Barney. A perfect mouth. Everything else is sweet but the mouth is perfection. Full lips but not Hollywood-bloated, no lipstick, beautiful.

'You're looking at my lips,' she said.

'Aye,' said Barney, and he looked her in the eye. 'Sorry.'

'That's all right,' she said. 'I haven't had them done.'

'I know,' said Barney.

20

'I like popping caviar on them,' she said. 'And between my tongue and the roof of my mouth. Great sensation, don't you think?'

'Aye,' said Barney, slightly entranced, although knowing that this was not a woman for him.

The door opened behind him, popping the moment like a fish egg on your tongue, and a lumpen old man entered.

'Mrs Carmichael,' said the man, then he looked at Barney with suspicion. 'Stranger,' he said, 'you the new barber?'

'Aye,' said Barney.

'Can you do a 'Robbie Williams *Somethin' Stupid*'?'

'I can do the full Robbie range,' said Barney, 'although that one's a little five years ago.'

'I'm eighty-seven.'

'Take your point.'

'Cool,' said the old geezer, and he sat down. Barney looked at the clock above the mirror, then decided that he didn't care about the time anyway. It was his shop, or at least it was about to be, and he could work whatever hours he felt like. He nodded at Garrett Carmichael, then started going about his business. Cape round the old fella – he was already aware of the exorbitant average age of his customers – picked up a razor, clipped on a number four head and paused.

'Where are you staying?' asked Garrett Carmichael, having settled onto the bench behind him.

Barney didn't turn. Where was he staying? The door at the back of the shop opened and Igor emerged, coat on and buttoned up to the neck. He glanced at Carmichael then looked at Barney.

'Igor,' said the customer. Igor caught his eye and acknowledged him. 'New coat?' said the old guy. 'It's a good fit.'

Igor ignored him or didn't hear him, looked quickly again at Barney and was gone out the door, which opened and closed in comforting silence. Barney watched him go, then turned back to the head in front of him.

Where was he staying? He rarely knew the answer to that.

'Maybe try the hotel along the road.'

'My mother's got a room,' said Carmichael. 'Sea view, en suite, five minutes' walk.'

He hesitated. Finally turned and glanced at her, then quickly turned back and flicked the switch on the razor, letting it plunge down onto the old fella's neck, like a host of swooping nazgul descending upon a meadow of sleeping hobbits.

'Aye, all right,' he said quickly, over the buzz of the razor.

'Cool,' she said. 'I'll wait, take you over there when you're done. She's doing steak pie tonight.'

'I'll find somewhere else to eat. It's a bit short notice.'

'I already told her you're coming.'

He paused with the razor, took a pace back to examine what he'd done so far, then laid it down on the counter and lifted the scissors and comb.

'You know what I like?' said the customer. 'I like leaving my falsers in the freezer for twenty minutes, then slipping them in and drinking a glass of neat Lagavulin. Oh aye.'

Barney caught the man's eye, until he was distracted by Garrett Carmichael's face in the mirror and those great lips smiling at the image of a pair of false teeth tucked in beside the ice cream.

✄

James Randolph sat in his small house down by the boatyard, looking out over the Clyde to Bute and the clouded hills of Arran. He was on-line, idly trudging through Google, putting in death and murder. A new kind of murder? Not a hope in hell. How could he, a man of so limited imagination, come up with a new kind of murder? It was just another of Ephesian's games.

A new kind of murder. The phrase played in Randolph's head, a mantra to his lack of wit. And he searched Google for any old kind of murder, from real life or literature. For all his hubris and bombast, Ephesian could not know of every murder that had been committed in the last hundred years, in real life and in fiction.

A new kind of murder. And yet, that wasn't the most interesting part of it. The victim, that was the interesting thing. Why Ephesian should want this particular person dead, Randolph had no idea whatsoever.

22

He rested his chin in the palm of his hand and looked out at the channel, where one of the nuclear submarines out of Faslane was slowly inching its way out past Bute on its way to the Irish Sea, and his mind drifted with the vessel until *a new kind of murder* became a playfully repetitive tune in his head.

5

Force of Nature

The table had been set for five. Barney viewed it with some suspicion but was automatically drawn to the window to look out at the water. It was an old house at the west end of the town. Up Cardiff Street from Shore Road, take a left down the hill to the playing field and the small park, then along to near the end of the older houses. Three along, as the weird old hand of fate should have it, from James Randolph.

Barney turned at the flurry of too many clothes behind him, as Miranda Donaldson, Garrett Carmichael's mother, bustled into the room, a five year-old boy at her heels, a younger girl in Garrett's arms. Barney was suddenly confronted by an entire family. With the exception of Mr Carmichael. He felt like a sheep walking into a wolf convention.

Stay cool, Barn, he thought. Don't let the children phase you.

'Hello,' he said.

'I'll be looking for £90 a week, an extra £3.50 a night if you want a hot meal. I can do you a packed lunch for £2.50, but only if you give me plenty of notice. I'll be looking for the first month up front and prompt payment in the future.'

'Mother! God, let him in the door, will you?'

Barney said nothing, although he did feel his cheeks rippling with the G-forces of the woman's presence.

'Don't take food to your room, I deadbolt the front door at eleven, there's no smoking, no coming in drunk from the pub, and you're out the door the first time I hear language that the

Lord did not intend. Shoes off at the door, I'll let you off this time, although Garrett ought to have told you. Don't leave clothes lying around any other part of the house, I expect tidiness and order. That particularly applies to the bathroom. No toothpaste on the sink, no urine on the floor or the rim of the bowl, no faecal matter left attached in the bowl after a bowel movement.'

'I should've said,' said Garrett behind her, apologetically.

'There's only one television and the reception's not very good, so I don't want you watching it. No loud music. If you actually manage to make any friends in this town, don't bring them back here without my clearance, and under no circumstances will there be fornication of any description.'

'You'll have to come back to my place then,' Garrett threw into the mix, then shrugged an apology at the joke.

Her mother gave the appropriate look at the remark then turned back to Barney.

'Are you content with that or will you be taking your leave?'

'Content,' he said.

'Good. You can remove your shoes now. Your tea's ready. Steak pie. That's all there is, so too bad if you don't like it.'

With that she left for the kitchen. Garrett smiled; the children stared expectantly at Barney, as they had done throughout his interview, waiting their turn.

'She's a little intense,' said Garrett.

'I didn't really pick up on that,' replied Barney.

Garrett shrugged it off. There was, after all, just plain nothing she could do about her mother. She put the girl down next to her brother and knelt down beside them.

'Guys, this is Mr Thomson who's going to be staying as a guest at Gran's for a while.'

'Hello,' said Barney. 'What are your names?'

'I'm Hoagy,' said the boy. 'This is Ella. She's a gobshite.'

'Hoagy!' said his mum.

'That's what you said!'

Barney held out his hand and Hoagy Carmichael took it importantly. Then he put his hand out to Ella and she retreated

25

behind her mum, giggling. Barney poked his finger under her armpit and the giggle increased.

'Do that to me!' said Hoagy, and Barney reached out for him.

Rosa Kleb appeared at the door.

'It's on the table,' she said snippily.

'Right guys,' said Garrett, 'hands washed!'

'I washed my hands last morning.'

'Get to the sink.'

'Did you hear about Jonah Harrison?' said Miranda Donaldson.

'What about him?' asked Garrett.

'Fell down the stairs, banged his head.'

'Shit, is he all right?'

As they talked, Barney suddenly found himself leading the children off to the bathroom. Basic instinct.

'You're out of nappies, right?' he said to Ella, who looked at him big-eyed.

'She is,' answered Hoagy, 'but she still poos in her pants sometimes. Mum says she does it just to annoy her, because it never happens when she's at Gran's.'

They got into the bathroom, Hoagy pulled out a small stool to help him stand at the sink.

Barney lowered the toilet lid and sat down; Hoagy splatted water around the place, Ella stood in the middle of the bathroom and stared at Barney.

'Where's your father?' asked Barney.

'He's dead,' said Hoagy, in the matter-of-fact manner of the too young to grasp the concept. 'Mum says we'll see him when we die, but that won't be until after I'm a dad and Ella's a mum.'

'Long time to wait yet,' said Barney.

He turned, aware that there was someone behind him.

'How are you getting on?' asked Garrett.

'Fine,' said Hoagy.

'Your boy is scrubbing up for open heart surgery. We should be done in an hour or so.'

Garrett pounced on him and started rinsing the half gallon of liquid soap from his hands.

26

'Had a death in the town today,' she said.

Barney felt his heart sink. A tangible feeling, where his insides dropped and rearranged themselves in some new squirming order. Was it not inevitable? The curse that pursued him. Death. Everywhere he went.

'What happened?' he asked, looking up. Don't let it be a murder, he thought. Leave me in peace. Let me walk into a new town and let it be ordinary. I'm not looking for Brigadoon, no Utopia on earth, no Eden where the sun always shines and there is always fruit on the trees. Just a normal town, with the good and the bad of town life, but most importantly, where people don't get murdered the minute I walk into the damned place.

'Jonah Harrison,' she said, moving onto Ella, and quickly washing her hands, 'big fella lived round at that wee scheme behind Kames Bay. Fell down the stairs, banged his head. Died instantly.'

'Was he pushed?' asked Barney, assuming the inevitable.

'Pushed?' said Hoagy.

'No one was pushed,' snapped Garrett.

'Sorry,' said Barney. 'Just an assumption.'

'He just fell down the stairs. Big guy, must've been twenty-five stone. God knows the crack he must've hit his head with.'

'Why was he pushed?' asked Hoagy.

'I didn't push him,' said Ella, contributing to the general conversational confusion for the first time.

'No one pushed anyone,' said Barney. 'Come on, let's go and get dinner.'

'Yeah!' said Hoagy, suddenly excited by the thought of food that he had no intention of eating.

'Yeah!' said Ella, with even less reason to rejoice.

'All right, I'm sorry about the pushed thing,' said Barney.

'Just don't do it again,' said Garrett, and they walked off together, like a microwaveable instant mum and dad, to the dinner table.

27

6

Red, Red Is The Rose...

Bartholomew Ephesian sat alone at the large dining table. His soup plate had been cleared, he was waiting for roast pork, roast potatoes and several other perfectly cut and steamed vegetables. He liked his dinner plates to be full and an array of colour, as long as there was no red. In silence, bar the crunch of the fire and the jabber of the rain against the window. Drinking a caustic French Chardonnay, a little resentful and petulant, but playful around the mouth, extraordinarily well lengthed, hinting at summer fruits, icecap meltdown and eight out of ten cat owners.

He invariably dined alone. Food was too much of a pleasure to be wasted on company.

The door opened, Jacobs walked silently into the room. Three and a half minutes ahead of schedule. Ephesian liked exactly twelve minutes between courses. He did not, however, look askance at Jacobs in any way, knowing that if his man had chosen to enter sooner than expected, there would be a good reason for it. He regarded him with his eyebrow raised, the international symbol of the curious, his gaze as ever directed at the knot in Jacobs' black bow tie.

'There is a call, sir,' said Jacobs. 'Mr Phat.'

Ephesian tried to mask his surprise. He looked at the clock. 6:05pm. 2:05am in Hong Kong. Phat never worked this late. His every working day was the same. He would play two rounds of golf in the morning, stop at the club for a large lunch, arrive at the office at two o'clock in the afternoon and leave at seven-thirty in the evening. The rest of his day would then be divided between his principal pleasures of cinema, food, and sex with at least three women at the same time. He went to sleep at three o'clock in the morning and was back on the golf course by seven. A life by clockwork.

'I'll take it in here, Jacobs,' Ephesian said. Jacobs nodded and began his retreat.

'You'll listen, of course,' said Ephesian.

'As you wish, sir,' said Jacobs, before closing the door.

Jacobs had been in Ephesian's family for as long as either of them could remember. He was Ephesian's contact with the outside world, the bridge between his condition and the rest of humanity. After so long in his service, Jacobs understood everything about his employer, understood that all the quirks and the madness and the rudeness and intolerance were all part of who he was, his behaviour always prosaically justifiable in his own mind. It had been through Jacobs that Ephesian's mathematical genius had been channelled into an ability to make money. Without him he would have remained on the sidelines, his talents used and abused by misunderstanding employers. Through Jacobs, Ephesian had become much richer than any of his forebears. And it was one of the bizarre obsessions which had dominated his teenage years and had never left him, which had brought the two men to Millport and now to the defining moment of their lives.

Ephesian waited a few seconds, aware that the palms of his hands were suddenly clammy. He was close to his dream and every little thing that could affect it from now on was going to have this effect on him. He lifted the phone, hands uncertain.

'Ping!' he said, with the level of enthusiasm which he knew Ping Phat liked to conduct all his conversations.

'Bartholomew,' said Ping Phat, 'you are well? Have I interrupted as pig grease cooked in cow fat and batter you eat?'

Ephesian paused and then answered, 'I did but taste a little honey with the end of the rod that was in mine hand, and, lo, I must die.'

Ping barked out a laugh.

'Just so long as happen that does not before arrive I do,' said Phat.

29

Ephesian closed his eyes. Jesus! Why couldn't the man just leave him alone?

'You're coming to Scotland?' said Ephesian, attempting to keep the surprise and annoyance out of his voice and wondering suddenly where Ping Phat was. If he was calling now it wouldn't be because his working hours had changed, it would be because he was in a different time zone. God, was he already here?

'Absodefinitely,' said Ping Phat. 'You are good man, Bartholomew. In you one hundred per cent confidence I have, that you know my fat friend.'

The fat friend remark at least took away some of Ephesian's nervousness. He stopped himself on the brink of an acerbic, *well why are you coming then?* choosing instead not to fill the silence.

'But a long wait it has been for myself as well as for you. To be there at the end I wish.'

Stop sounding like fucking Yoda, you stupid Chinese twat! Ephesian wanted to shout down the phone. He bristled in silence. Ping Phat could speak English perfectly well. Getting sentences the wrong way round was an entirely elective process.

'That's wonderful,' said Ephesian, the enthusiasm long since departed from his voice.

'Bullshit!' exploded Phat, laughing loudly. 'But let's not our friendship ruin now with honesty.'

Ephesian grimaced bitterly.

'Paris I am in,' said Phat. 'France,' he added, as if he was an American.

Ephesian clenched his fist tightly round the phone. Direct flight to Glasgow and the man would probably get a helicopter to the coast. He could be in Millport tonight.

'When are you coming?' he asked, his voice full of contempt, wholly displaying his complete inability to hide his feelings or to manipulate any other member of humanity by artifice and sophistry rather than strength of will.

'Wednesday evening I will be there,' said Phat. 'The road has been long, my fat friend, and present I shall be when we all coffee drink at the café of light eternal.'

30

Ephesian had wondered if Phat would feel the need to be there at the denouement to all Ephesian's work. For that was how Ephesian viewed it. It was his work and the prize should be his. Phat had provided the financing all these years. Ephesian was wealthy by old Scottish money standards. Phat was wealthy in an Asian or Middle Eastern way, with investments and bank accounts and businesses to make Ephesian look like East Stirling. But just because Sharp or Vodafone or whoever sponsored Manchester United, it didn't mean that they took the glory when United won anything.

'You will stay as my guest, of course,' said Ephesian formally, already beginning to wonder if this was someone else who might need to be taken care of.

'Kind that would most be,' said Phat. 'Thank you. I will a little entourage be bringing. Room you have, no?'

Ephesian stared at his desk, blood pressure shooting through the stratosphere. He had plenty of room. His house was ridiculously huge for such a small town and for the fact that he lived alone. Accommodating an entourage would not be a problem. It might make it more difficult to murder him, however.

'Certainly, Ping,' said Ephesian.

'Delightful,' said Phat. 'Wednesday I will call, let you let know the time, I will.'

Oh, for crying out loud, shut up.

'Very good, my friend,' said Ephesian.

The line went dead. Ephesian gripped the receiver then placed it back in the cradle. He stared at the Moroccan rug he had picked up in Rabat ten years previously. His eyes always fell on the same orange camel in the row of ten. Well, why wouldn't Ping Phat want to be here? They had uncovered the whereabouts of the most sought after relic of these times. They were about to be present at the biggest event in two thousand years of history. Was there anyone on the planet who would not want to be there, given the chance?

The door opened, Jacobs entered carrying a tray, Ephesian's dinner covered by a large silver lid. Jacobs laid down the tray and began to rearrange the table.

31

'Well?' said Ephesian.

Jacobs placed the dinner plate in front of him and lifted the lid, so that the roast pork steamed out at them, then he poured some more wine into Ephesian's glass and put the bottle back in its small rack at the side of the table.

'Clearly,' said Jacobs, his voice measured, 'something requires to be done about Mr Phat.'

'Yes,' said Ephesian, nodding. Then he added, 'Bullet in the back of the head he needs,' although he could not manage the accompanying rueful smile.

The expression on Jacob's face flickered and then he turned and left the room, leaving Ephesian alone with his roast dinner and a new decision to be taken.

✂

Late at night, Ruth Harrison lay in bed watching the streetlights on the ceiling. Twenty-eight years of marriage had ended and with it nearly three decades of arguments over whether or not to sleep with the curtains closed. Now she had the decision to herself, yet she felt suddenly bound to do as Jonah would have wished. So she lay with the curtains open, as he had liked and she had always hated. Had she been self-aware to any level, she would have realised she was only doing it to compensate in some way for her ambivalence over her husband's death.

As she lay she wondered what she could do with her future, and what she could do with the insurance money which she assumed, wrongly, she would have coming. And at the same time she felt guilty that she was contemplating the life of the merry widow so soon after his unfortunate demise. However, as the delicious Jane Austin once wrote; *Let other pens dwell on guilt and misery. I quit such odious subjects as soon as I can.* And talking of guilt, she no longer had to feel guilty about the Reverend Dreyfus.

She smiled. Sure, he hadn't come round this evening, not even in the moment of her distress, but she knew he'd had the Bible Study Group to lead, and he always worked on the following week's sermon starting on a Monday night. He would be round the next day to discuss Jonah's funeral arrangements and their new life could begin. He was one man who would not be living up to his Christian name.

There was a noise in the hall outside her bedroom door. She gasped, immediately her body tensed, she felt the fear and surprise in every bone, she gripped the bedclothes and looked at the door. Another sound, another footfall, closer to the door.

She held her breath, she wondered if she should pick up something with which to defend herself. Yet she couldn't release her grip on the bedclothes, no matter the meagre protection they provided.

Another footfall, this time slightly beyond the door. Her eyes were wide. Another, then another and then she heard the bathroom door open and close, the bolt hurriedly placed over. Head pressed back against the wall, bolt upright with fear, she listened. Toilet seat up and then the long stream into the bowl of water, trickling to a conclusion.

The flush of the toilet. Silence.

She waited for someone to emerge but the footfalls had stopped and there were no further sounds of bathroom activity.

She waited. And she waited. And Ruth Harrison was still sitting bolt upright in bed waiting, when the sun came up and began to flood her bedroom with light at just before six o'clock the following morning.

7

The Eager Nature
Fit For A Great Crisis

Barney was standing at the window watching the rain sweep
across the main street. A chill north-easterly was bringing it
from behind, so that the window of the shop was clear and he
had a good view of the agitated sea and the few moored boats
bubbling nervously about on the water. Igor stood behind him,
one eye on the window and Barney's back, the other paying
scant attention to dusting the rail around the middle of the shop.
Having dusted it the day before, it required little attention.

Igor was thinking about toast and marmalade and bacon
sandwiches and a good muesli and the first cup of tea of the day
which is always the best. Barney stared out to sea, thinking of
the guy who set out to row across the Pacific, realising a few
hours in that he'd forgotten his tin opener.

Maybe that's what he needed. Some grand adventure to
answer his continuing mid-life crisis. He had wandered
restlessly for some years, encountering absurd murder and death
wherever he went. Always thought that what he needed was to
settle somewhere, a quiet town where nothing ever happened
and where one sleepy day blended seamlessly into the next. But
had he not found that already, only for it to prove equally
unsatisfactory? From Helmsdale to Annan and others in
between. Nowhere seemed right, and though he now felt happy
enough standing looking out over a view that felt new and
familiar at the same time, how long would it last? He clung to

the barbershop as some continuing certainty in his life but maybe that was what he needed to get rid of.

He needed to get out there, do something grand. It didn't have to be something that had never been done before, just some great final act of magnificent stupidity. Row the Atlantic. Walk the Silk Road. Climb all those peaks in China that no one's ever heard of before. Invade Poland. Visit all the Scottish football grounds in one season. Something big and illustrious, something that he could write a book about and appear on Parkinson to discuss.

He turned and looked at Igor who was running a silk cloth along the top of a dusty picture of George Hamilton III, hair as immaculate as ever.

'Igor,' said Barney.

Igor turned, picking up the vibration.

Barney gestured to the picture and ran his thumb across his neck. Igor nodded.

'Arf,' he said, and he lifted the picture from the wall, took it into the back room and popped it into the bin.

Barney looked back out to sea. For all the murder and ludicrous adventure that his life had entailed, here he was arriving mundanely at cliché and conformity. Hitting middle age with his legs encased in concrete and nowhere to go, contemplating rowing across the Atlantic in a preposterous attempt to give his life some meaning. He wondered how many thousands, how many millions of men were standing or sitting or lying at that very second, thoughts mincing through the mud, lost in middle-aged gloom and contemplating some huge act of audacious folly to compensate for a complete lack of self-value.

He imagined making the big decision to row across the Atlantic; making all his plans, fixing up corporate sponsorship, remembering his tin opener and some tins, doing months of training up and down Loch Lomond in bad weather, before heading off down to the Canary Islands to set off. Then he'd get to Playa San Juan on Tenerife, first thing in the morning, feeling brave and bold and decent and courageous, a man alone with his destiny, and he'd look along the beach and there he'd see the fifty other middle-aged British blokes who were having a mid-

35

life crisis that day, all nodding to each other and saying 'Morning, Gerald, nice day for it'. Flask of tea and off they'd go to redeem their existence.

When the Spanish or Italians have a mid-life crisis they get an eighteen year-old girlfriend and start driving a Ferrari. It's much more British do something really grand and stupid like run marathons, climb mountains or sit in the basement trying to build your own spaceship. At some point you wake up and you realise you've achieved fuck all, and the only thing for it is an act of monstrous and supreme folly.

'Arf,' said the voice behind him and Barney turned. They looked at each other. Barney felt as if Igor had been reading every one of his thoughts.

'Aye,' he said, 'I know.' Igor nodded.

The shop door opened to the first customer of the day. Barney moved away from the window and a ninety-three year-old great grandpa minced into the shop, looking for a Snoop Dog cut, and more than willing to tell Barney about the time he'd climbed Mont Blanc naked in December in his 50's, that his two favourite things in the whole world were the feel of an empty wine bottle and the way snow falls off branches in clumps during a thaw, and that the thing which annoyed him more than anything on the planet was the way it was completely impossible to get a Weetabix from the packet without covering the kitchen in crumbs.

8

The Silence Of The
Uncomfortable Biscuit

Ruth Harrison nervously fiddled with the cafétière, squirting hot liquid over the kitchen work surface beside the kettle as she pushed the plunger down over the Tesco's own, Columbian grade A, strength 6 filter coffee. She twitched, she muttered a low curse at the mess and the fact that this happened every single time she made herself a cup. It so annoyed her that she usually went for the more mundane pleasures of instant but this morning she needed a much higher dosage of caffeine. Even if it did serve as a diuretic, which she could have done without at that juncture. She looked over her shoulder, shivered, bit her bottom lip.

Her first full day as a widow. The first day of the rest of her life. The Reverend Dreyfus would be stopping by, although she had already called him and he had said he was running late. Maybe it was just because she was feeling a bit shaky after the night she'd had, but the insecurity which hadn't come despite his non-appearance the previous evening, had now arrived in droves. This was it, she had become instantly and permanently accessible to him and Dreyfus was absent. If any of his other parishioners had died, he would have been on the doorstep of the bereaved in minutes.

Fridge, milk, cupboard, biscuits. The great wealth of mince pies and cakes and chocolate that greeted her on opening the cupboard door brought Jonah back into her head and she turned on the lights under the kitchen unit, even though the room was already bright. She sat at the breakfast bar facing the door, a point from which she could see the place where Jonah had died, and took her first sip of coffee. It was still too hot, but she let it burn her mouth. In her general state of mental flux and disorder she imagined she could feel the caffeine hit her bloodstream the instant it stung the inside of her lips.

The doorbell rang, Ruth Harrison jumped at the sound, strained nerves, then she quickly collected herself, shook off the feeling, and then instant calm. She'd been wrong about Dreyfus. She took another sip of coffee, then a longer one, even though it burned, so that her breath would at least smell of it. Rather that than the stale scent of a night of worry, especially since she hadn't been able to clean her teeth that morning.

She rose, quick check in the hall mirror, everything as it should be, bit of a pointless dab at the hair and she was ready. Deep breath, could taste the coffee, straightened her shoulders then she opened the door.

Bartholomew Ephesian stared at her with a look of sympathy and compassion, his eyes resting on her chin.

'Mrs Harrison,' he said from behind a large bouquet of flowers, 'I'm sorry about Jonah.'

She stared at Ephesian, wondering who he was for a second, her feelings of confusion mixed with the ruin of her optimism.

'Mr Ephesian,' she said finally, the surprise in her voice betraying the fact that she had only just realised who he was.

'Mrs Harrison,' he said, 'it really was a terrible tragedy.'

'What was?' said Ruth, still confused.

'Your husband,' said Ephesian, as if understanding her emotional turmoil, although he had no concept of what might be going through her head, and neither did he care.

She had never spoken to Ephesian before and, as far as she was aware, he was not known for his spontaneous acts of compassion.

'Yes,' she said. 'So sudden.'

'May I come in?' he asked brusquely, thinking it was possible he could end up standing on the doorstep for the rest of his life.

She looked at him strangely, wondering why he would want to do such a thing, then she glanced unthinkingly past him, looking to see if anyone was watching, looking to see if the Reverend Dreyfus was about to arrive, then she nodded and stood aside for him to enter.

✄

Half an hour in and things were a little uncomfortable. Beyond the introductory offer of a cup of coffee, which had been accepted by Ephesian as a means by which a minute or two could be killed, there had been barely two sentences strung together. This was death by social nicety and Ruth Harrison had no idea what he was doing there. Minutes would seem to pass without either of them saying anything. They would listen to the old clock ticking and every now and again their eyes would almost meet and she would smile while he grimaced. She wondered if she could just ask him to leave. She also wondered if she should tell him why she hadn't slept all night but Bartholomew Ephesian wasn't a man to be interested in something like that. Ephesian lifted another biscuit, just as the words 'have another biscuit' were about to leave her mouth. *I wish the Reverend Dreyfus would come,* she thought. *I wish anyone would come. I even wish...* She stopped the thought. It wasn't that bad.

'Jonah never went to church,' said Ephesian.

She look vaguely in the direction of his face, shook her head. Lifted her coffee cup and drained it for the eighth time.

'You'll have the Reverend Dreyfus give the service?' he asked.

Slight catch of breath at the name, she looked up again but there was nothing in his face. No insinuation. Why should there be? Reasonable question.

'I think so,' she said. If he ever turned up.

'A good man,' said Ephesian, then he added unthinkingly, 'though they say that at any given time he might be having affairs with three women in his congregation.' He knew that Ruth Harrison was one of them but as usual with him the words were not intended to manipulate, they were all he could think of to say at that particular moment. He felt as awkward in this

39

situation as did she but completely lacked the conversational skills to bring this chat over tea and biscuits around to the reason that had brought him here in the first place.

Ruth had just been punched in the stomach. Three women! She'd never heard it before and she had no idea if Bartholomew Ephesian was just toying with her. But then, did it not have a ring of authenticity to it? It felt like it could be true. Like when Luke tells Leia that Darth's her father.

'Jonah wasn't a religious man,' said Ephesian.

This time there was something in Ephesian's voice, a slight change in quality from the false sincerity and the painful attempts at conversation. This was him finally getting to the point of the visit, although he now sounded awkward in a different way. That they were actually going to get to the nub had her feeling relief as well as curiosity, although both feelings were overwhelmed by the painful moment of realisation about the Reverend Dreyfus.

'Hadn't been in church in years,' she said.

'No,' said Ephesian. 'I know.'

She glanced back and then away again, disconcerted. That Bartholomew Ephesian should know anything about her husband at all seemed strange.

'He went out on a Tuesday evening,' said Ephesian. She glanced up quickly again, worried now. Didn't like the fact that Ephesian should know about Jonah's social engagements. Maybe that was what bothered her, as she'd been mostly unaware herself what Jonah had done on all those Tuesdays. Ought to have known, as there'd been plenty of gossip around the village about it, but it demonstrated how uninterested she'd been in her husband's life.

'I think maybe you should leave now,' she said suddenly, voice betraying her lack of confidence.

Ephesian's face contorted briefly then grimly relaxed.

'I'm sorry,' he said, 'of course, of course. This is a very difficult time for you and I'm sitting here making inane small talk. Thoughtless of me. I should leave you in peace.'

She glanced at him, felt a shiver worm its way down her back. Suddenly Ephesian looked like the dangerous man that everyone

40

said he was, he was the ominous presence that hung over the town from the big house on the hill.

Ephesian rose and straightened his jacket, Ruth Harrison got to her feet, staring at the floor. She could feel his discomfort, he was completely unaware of hers.

'Take care of yourself, Mrs Harrison,' he said and he stepped away. She couldn't look at him. 'I'll see myself out.'

He turned and left the sitting room, she couldn't bear to even watch him go. The front door opened and Bartholomew Ephesian stepped back out into the cold morning. He closed the door behind him and only then did his face change.

He stopped on the steps, he stared at the hill in front of him, rising above Kames Bay.

'There might just have to be another death in the family,' he muttered to himself, then he walked on quickly down the steps and climbed into his BMW.

Inside the house Ruth Harrison twitched the curtain as the car drove off, then she retreated into the middle of the room and looked down at the remnants of coffee and biscuits.

What had all that been about? Jonah and Bartholomew Ephesian? Had they ever even spoken to each other? As if she didn't have enough to worry about. Shaking herself out of it and deciding it was time to start fretting and getting annoyed about the Reverend Dreyfus, she placed the detritus from the most uncomfortable half hour she'd had in years onto a tray and headed into the kitchen.

A tray which she suddenly dropped as she heard the first of the familiar footfalls on the upstairs landing, heading in the direction of the bathroom.

9

The Evil Succubus
of Doom

'So, we go for a walk, beautiful, beautiful day. Warm and hazy, no clouds, the buzz of insects, the burble of a small river, just the slight breath of wind. All the live murmur of a summer's day, as Arnold wrote, you know. Perfect. May 1941, remember it like it was yesterday. Birds in the trees, that delicious warmth that gets under your skin. Only one problem…'

'The girl was mingin'?' ventured Barney.

'Crustaceous,' said the old guy beneath his scissors. 'Don't know what was going on. I was with the Engineers, stationed down in the south of England. She was the sister of one of the other guys. Set me up totally. Got a weekend off, came up for a few days with her in Callandar, thought I was in luck. She meets me off the train. I'll be wearing pink, she says, and that should have been the warning shot across the old bows straight off. Pink, for God's sake. I takes one look at her and I think, you must be flippin' kidding me, darlin'. I'm not touching you with a stick. Should have just walked right past her and gone to the boozer, got one of the other guys to write to her saying I'd been shot and killed in North Africa. But no, I'm a decent bloke, couldn't completely blank her, so I go up, hold out my hand, I'm Rusty Brown, I say, and off we go for two nights in a hotel, and by jings was I glad we'd booked separate rooms. By jings!'

Barney stood back and checked the sides of the head. He was cutting the hair of another old fella in his early 90's who'd come in looking for a Kobe Bryant. He was amongst strange people, but his gloom of early morning had lifted with his parade of pensioners with their stories and strange haircut requests. And it was almost as if they'd worked out the appointments between themselves, as they only ever came in one at a time.

'So, where was I?' said the old fella, who still called himself Rusty, even though he hadn't been in the army since 1946, his given name Matthew was a perfectly acceptable name for anyone, and he was under no requirement whatsoever to have a schoolboy nickname. Like Midge Ure and Sting.

'Beautiful summer's day,' said Barney. 'Insects buzzing, trees and grass and a river running through it.'

'Aye,' said Rusty, 'that was it. Postcard perfect. The war seemed a hundred miles away. Well, to be fair, it was actually about eight hundred miles away, but you know what I'm saying, it was like there was no war.'

'I hear you,' said Barney.

Igor swept and wished that Rusty Brown would get on with his story as he'd heard it before, and knew, as Barney did not, that he would tell it every time he came into the shop.

'We sit by the river, side by side on the grassy bank. Watch the insects buzzing on the surface of the water, could even see a couple of fish. Not a soul in the world except me and the bogmonster from Inverary.'

'So what happened?' asked Barney.

Igor glanced up. You'll only encourage him by asking questions, he thought, then he mouthed the answer in time with Rusty Brown's reply.

'I kissed her,' he said, ruefully. '*I* kissed *her*! I mean, what was I thinking? In the name of God!' He looked wide-eyed at Barney, Barney smiled. Igor's timing had been perfect. He too looked wide-eyed and then he made the appropriate gestures with his hands as Rusty said, 'How does that happen? Seriously. What is it that makes a sane man do something like that?'

'How did you get out of it?' asked Barney.

'Ah,' said Rusty and he looked sly. 'I got one of the lads to send me a telegram telling me I was needed in Gallipoli.'

'Right. Didn't she know you'd got the wrong war?'

43

'Ach,' said Rusty, 'she was a woman. She didn't know the difference.'

Barney laid down the scissors, checked once more over the hair, then lifted the hand mirror to show Rusty the back of his head. Rusty nodded his appreciation, Barney went about the mop-up business, brushing off, removing the towel and cape.

'Gave her brother a right bollocking when I got back,' said Rusty. 'Still, the eejit got a bullet in the face when he stepped off the boat in Normandy, so he got what was coming to him.'

Rusty straightened up, checked himself in the mirror, fished in his pocket for a fiver, handed it over, nodded at Barney, looked at Igor and said, 'I've got a hunch you'll be here the next time,' then walked to the door laughing quietly to himself. Igor and Barney exchanged a look. And, as Rusty left, right on cue another old fella walked in, he and Rusty knocking knuckles as they passed. The door closed, the new customer looked from Igor to Barney.

'You're the new barber,' he said to Barney, showing remarkable insight. 'I'm Ginger Rogers.'

'What can I do for you, Ginger?' asked Barney.

Ginger removed his jacket and took his place.

'I'll have a Kiefer Sutherland, please, my man. *24.*'

'No problem,' said Barney.

'Aye,' said Ginger Rogers. 'It isn't that they can't see the solution, it's that they can't see the problem,' he added, quoting GK Chesterton for no apparent reason.

'Arf,' said Igor from behind his broom.

Ruth Harrison had cleaned her teeth and was feeling a little happier. She'd had to visit the local grocers to buy a new toothbrush, thereby avoiding the need to go to her bathroom, also taking the opportunity to use their toilet, but at least now her mouth was fresh should there be any need for kissing.

She looked at the clock. 12.17. The Reverend Dreyfus should have been here an hour ago. Maybe he could have lunch when he finally came. Lunch and a glass of wine.

She looked in the fridge and found a bottle of white. A velvety Montenegrin Chardonnay, persuasive yet hardworking, somewhat brutal on the nostrils, sadistic on the tongue and venomous on the throat, but gentle on the stomach and lower intestines and a positive boon to your rectal passage.

What to eat? She looked around the fridge, didn't encounter anything that would pass for a lunch dish. She straightened up, closed the fridge door. She hadn't cooked since she'd been married. Jonah had done all the food shopping and all the cooking. Ruth hadn't been near a meal in its pre-ready-to-eat stage for more than two decades.

'Maybe there'll be something in the freezer,' she mumbled.

The freezer was outside in the garden shed, somewhere else she never went, partly because of the spider issue.

She opened the back door, pulled her cardigan tightly across her chest, two yards, then she tentatively opened the door to the shed, expecting to immediately find herself covered in garden tarantulas.

The shed was immaculately clean, which was how Jonah had liked to keep it. Not a cobweb in sight. With trepidation she flicked the light switch and, hunching over to reduce her overall body size so that the spiders would have less of an area to land upon, she leant in and opened the freezer door.

She had no idea what sorts of things Jonah kept in there, or indeed, whether he ever did any freezer shopping. Discovered, for the first time in her life, that the freezer had drawers and she had to inch her way further into the shed to pull them out.

Top drawer, ice cream. Five flavours, all involving chocolate.

Second drawer, vegetables. Peas, corn, carrots, peppers, chips. All right, thought Ruth, we can have something with chips and peas, with ice cream for dessert.

The third drawer was large and taken up completely by a turkey. Obviously he'd bought that before she'd forced him to take the family out for Christmas lunch at the George.

Fourth drawer. Bread. Four loaves. Could she give the Reverend Dreyfus a chip butty?

She bent down, opened the bottom drawer. There was only one item, a freezer bag, frosted white, closed with a small white plastic tie-up. Maybe it was some kind of meat she could defrost in the microwave. She lifted it out to see what was inside. Hard to tell, and she had to press against the bag to make out what it was.

Suddenly she realised what she was holding. She dropped it on the floor, her body tensing instantly with the shock. She staggered back, smacking her head on the shed entrance, dislodging a large garden spider which then fell onto her face. She screamed and stumbled out into the garden, flapping frantically at her cheeks. She ran into the centre of the garden, whisked off her cardigan and threw it on the grass, then started scrabbling at her hair in case the spider had fled upwards. Hands all over her head, then over her neck and back, all breathlessly accompanied by a frenzied jig.

Eventually, after a full minute, the panic of having had an actual spider land on her face subsided, and she stood nervously in the middle of the lawn, staring at the ground, her hands on her hips. And only then, once she had assured herself that there were no spiders anywhere near her, did she start to think about what she'd just discovered in the freezer. She stared at the door to the shed.

And the thing that bothered her most about it, she suddenly realised, was that she was going to have to go back in there to put the bag back inside the freezer and close the door, because there was no way that she could let anyone find out about it.

'That was a bit of a performance, darlin',' said a voice from the other side of the garden fence. 'Been at the waccy baccy again?'

She looked round at Romeo McGhee. Felt a little stupid, but her feelings of embarrassment were nothing compared to the anxiety produced by her freezer find.

'Spider,' she said.

'Cool,' said McGhee.

'Not really,' said Ruth Harrison.

And she looked down at her cardigan and wondered if it was safe to pick it up, or whether she should stand all over it first.

46

10

The Vulture Flock

James Randolph was being chased down a dark alleyway by a pack of slabbering wolves. The walls of the alley were closing in, and as he ran he could feel his legs becoming heavier and heavier. Then there was the flock of vultures circling overhead, the squadron of Meschersmitts coming in for the attack, streams of bullets already kicking up dust all around his feet, the lions prowling the roofs of the buildings above, their teeth stained red with blood, and the volley of thunderbolts being sent down by the god Titan. And that was not to mention the nagging doubts he had at the back of his mind that he'd left the oven on, the bath tap running, the freezer door open and toast under the grill.

Classic anxiety dream.

He awoke with a start, was immediately aware of the awful taste in his mouth. Sat upright too quickly, felt terribly dizzy and immediately let his head back down on the pillow.

'Shit,' he said, as the room swirled above him. He closed his eyes and instantly his head began to spin and churn. When he opened them again to lose the feeling, the room was still in a tailspin. Focus. He needed to focus. He looked at the clock. 12.31. He never slept that late. He kept his eyes focused on the red numbers, hoping to keep the nausea at bay. His head was pounding, throat dry, horribly dehydrated. Water, he hadn't drunk enough water. Never did. What had he been drinking anyway? Red wine. Three bottles, maybe four. Four bottles of red wine!

47

Murder! It came back to him. He was supposed to be thinking of an interesting way to commit murder. He'd thought he would find something on the web and he must have spent seven hours on there. And as he'd surfed, he'd drunk red wine. And as his frustration had grown, the more he had drunk. Elaborate methods were everywhere but when it came to it the deaths would usually be through loss of blood or lack of air or poison or fluid in the lungs. But thinking of a genuinely original way to end life? He wasn't a doctor or a scientist. He was nobody. And so he had gone to bed at just after one in the morning, at least three bottles of red wine inside him. Which explained the spinning room.

The doorbell rang again, as it had done half a minute earlier, which was the reason he had woken up in the first place.

'Shit,' he muttered, but there was no way he was even going to begin trying to get out of bed. Head back on the pillow and he stared at the ceiling. Felt marginally better. He would lie still for another ten minutes, then get up very, very slowly. Pop three *Nurofen On The Piss Extra-Strength* and drink several pints of water. Sit in front of the TV. Maybe venture some toast in an hour or so. Go out for a walk in mid-afternoon. Think of a new way to kill someone. He groaned.

The phone rang, the sound penetrating viciously into his head. He groaned again, reached out.

'Hello,' he mumbled.

'James!' barked Ephesian. 'Get out of bed. Answer the door!'

'What?' said Randolph, not entirely able to keep abreast of what was happening.

'The door!'

'How d'you know there's someone at the door?' he asked stupidly.

'Because it's me who's there,' snapped Ephesian.

'Oh,' said Randolph. 'Oh, shit, I'll be right there.'

He hung up and staggered down the stairs, his head bouncing off the walls. He opened the door in his jogging bottoms and 1982 New England Patriots top, with an unshaven, sleep-ravaged face and absolutely minging of alcohol. Ephesian swept past him.

48

'For God's sake, James, you're disgusting. Take five minutes to have a shower and swallow a bottle of mouthwash. We need to talk. I'm going to make myself some coffee.'

Ephesian marched into the kitchen and James Randolph minced pathetically back upstairs.

><

From his bedroom window, Romeo McGhee could see down into Ruth Harrison's kitchen. She was standing with her back to the sink, clutching a small glass in her hands. He'd had a good laugh at her performance with the spider in her hair, but he had also seen the genesis of it.

Romeo McGhee had been watching Ruth Harrison from his bedroom window for years. Fancied her in a strange kind of way. He also had a vantage point on her bathroom window, although the frosted glass meant that whilst he was aware of how much of her life she spent in there, he could never actually see what she was doing. He could use his imagination, however.

He also knew about the Reverend Dreyfus. And he knew that Ruth Harrison had stumbled out of the garden shed after picking something up out of the bottom drawer of the freezer. And he also knew what she'd done with it after she'd convinced herself that there were no more spiders about her person.

><

'We have a problem,' said Ephesian.

'Of course,' replied Randolph.

'What d'you mean, of course? Have you the faintest idea what I'm talking about?'

Randolph took another sip from his hot cup of milky coffee, five sugars, not enough caffeine. He now smelled of shower gel, toothpaste and alcohol, his hair was still wet and spiky and he was wearing a dark blue Lacoste polo shirt.

'What?' he said.

'Jonah Harrison,' said Ephesian.

'What about him?' asked Randolph. He hadn't spoken to anyone the previous day after leaving Ephesian's house.

'He died going to the bathroom.'

'Jesus,' said Randolph.

'Fell on the stairs, smacked his head off the wall.'

49

Randolph nodded, Ephesian stared at Randolph's chin across the divide. Still waiting for him to catch up with the conversation.

'And how's that a problem?' asked Randolph eventually.

'Because,' answered Ephesian, 'of the contents of his freezer.'

He glowered at the crocodile on Randolph's top, anticipating the penny dropping at any moment, which finally it did.

'Ah,' he said, looking for all the world like a man who'd been waiting all his life to drink three or four bottles of wine in order to turn into one of the lower invertebrates. 'And Ruthie doesn't know anything about it?'

'Of course she doesn't,' said Ephesian. 'You need to go round there and get it back. Today.'

'And how exactly am I going to get to look in her freezer?'

Ephesian's head twitched.

'She's not going to be there. I'm about to call her and inform her that the Reverend Dreyfus has just left my house. I will say that he requested I contact her and ask her to meet him at the Manse in twenty minutes time. Ruth, obviously, will find this a little strange, but nevertheless will take the opportunity to go round there to see him.'

'Won't she call him to check?'

'No,' said Ephesian coldly. That, of course, was exactly what he had said to Jacobs when his man had suggested the idea.

'You don't know women,' Ephesian continued, as if he himself did. 'If she calls to check then she runs the risk of him cancelling. She will just go, at which point you go to her house, you don't even have to break in, you just go to the back garden, into the shed and retrieve the goods.'

Randolph nodded, his head bobbing up and down above his coffee cup.

'What can go wrong?' said Randolph, thinking that this task was a lot easier than the kind of thing Ephesian usually threw at him to keep him busy.

'Quite,' said Ephesian, with suitable acknowledgement to all the things which could go wrong.

50

11

Little Italy

Barney walked into a small office situated not far along Stuart Street from the barbershop, its window looking out on the same grey and blustery day. Closed the door behind him to the happy tinkle of the bell and shook off the cold. Garrett Carmichael looked up and smiled.

'Hi,' said Carmichael.

'Hello,' said Barney, determined not to rise to any flirtations that might come his way. Not that he was being presumptuous, but he did recognise that quality in himself these days, the quality which got under the skin of women. That whole Clint Eastwood *Man With No Name* vibe. Even though, of course, he had more of a Steve Buscemi *Man Called Barney* vibe going on, but there was still something about that to get the ladies talking. 'How are the kids?' he added, because he thought he should.

'They're fine,' said Carmichael. 'Course Hoagy asked me this morning if I was pregnant which made me feel really good about myself, but I whacked him one and he's promised not to do it again.' She flashed her smile.

Still unsure what to say, Barney blundered, 'You're not pregnant then?'

'No!' she said. 'God, you're as bad as the kids!'

Barney felt suitably contrite and took a place at the other side of the desk from her. Don't say anything, he was thinking. Don't say anything! That was the real thing about *The Man With No Name*. He hardly ever opened his mouth and consequently never said anything stupid. Perfect. Igor has more chance of getting this woman, thought Barney. Then he realised he was thinking about getting her which was not what he wanted, so he closed his mind to it and concentrated on a small patch of wall two feet to the left of her head.

He was right about Igor, however.

Carmichael produced a couple of documents and passed them across the table.

'All you have to do is read those over, sign them where indicated and hand them back. Mr Ephesian will sign when the monies have been paid. I would advise you to get a solicitor to study them. There's no one else on the island but you should be able to get hold of someone in Largs. I can recommend a couple if needs be.'

'Sure,' said Barney, taking the papers and idly looking at them, in that way where he wasn't going to take any of it in. 'Who are you going to recommend?'

She looked in her drawer, fished around for a couple of cards, then handed them over. *MacKenzie, Berrie, Lee & Rosen* and *Medway, Nadel-Klein & Dance*.

'They're both cowboys, but what do you expect from the legal profession?' she quipped.

'Great,' said Barney.

They looked at one another. Neither really knowing what the other was thinking or what to say next. Barney battling the urge to speak because he knew it would be inane, knowing that he'd be better off back in the shop talking to old men about the war and how they liked the sound of aluminium foil scrunching or the feel of opposing magnets.

'How was my mum's?' asked Carmichael to extend the agony.

'Fine,' said Barney. And then finally he found the resolve to stand up, clutching the papers in his right hand.

'Should get back to the shop. There's bound to be some other octogenarian war hero looking for an Enrique Iglesias.'

'Sure,' said Carmichael. 'You want to have dinner tonight?'

Barney hesitated. Here we go. The first test. What was it he'd penned in for the night? Have dinner at the house, go for a walk along the front, listen to the waves coming up on the beach and the rocks, early to bed with an old adventure of Parlabane.

'I told your mother I'd eat at hers. I'm kind of scared to change that. She's probably killed a cow specially.'

'It's all right,' said Carmichael, 'I already took the liberty. She's going to look after the kids, we can go out.'

'Oh,' replied Barney. 'Right. Better come then.'

'Great,' said Carmichael. 'I'll call later.'

'Right.' A pause, wondered if there was anything else to say.

'Be sure to get the papers checked before you sign them.'

'Aye,' said Barney, and he turned awkwardly and left the office. Carmichael watched him go, kept her gaze up and out to the troubled sea for a short while, then once more buried her head in the minutiae of small time island property matters.

Barney breathed a sigh of relief as he returned to the shop. He entered just as Igor had finished sweeping up from the previous customer and a new customer was just removing his coat. The two men looked up at Barney as he entered.

'The new barber?' said the customer, an old chap in a cloth cap.

'Aye,' said Barney. 'Take a seat.'

Cap off and hung up, the old fella muddled into the seat.

'Tremendous,' he said. 'I'll have a *Ricky Martin*, and while you're doing it I'll tell you about the time I met a lovely American girl in Bali.'

'That sounds interesting,' said Barney.

'Arf,' mumbled Igor bitterly.

✄

There have been various ways to get to the Isle of Cumbrae from the mainland over the years. Various sizes of passenger ferries to the main pier in Millport, car ferries to the same destination, a briefly operated hovercraft in the mid-60's. They all evolved into a car and passenger ferry which runs, out of season, once an hour from Largs – more regularly summer and weekends – directly across the water to a landing slip on the far side of the island from the town, from where a bus completes the passenger journey.

As Barney settled down into the straightforward fluff and pamper of the *Ricky Martin*, a black Audi drove slowly up the Cumbrae slip, the last of only four cars on the 11:45 crossing. There are certain places where a black Audi A4 with reflective windows would not be out of place. Cumbrae was not one of them, however, and everyone noticed as the car slowly reached the top of the slope and then paused while the driver decided which way he should go.

'Which way d'you think, Luigi?' he asked.

The passenger in the front seat removed his sunglasses and looked at the driver. Then he pointed at the **Millport 5** sign right in front of them.

'I just can't work it out,' said Luigi, sarcastically. 'Who knows what that sign means? I can't work it out.'

'I didn't see the sign,' said the driver starting to move off, the sound of the engine barely audible.

'What d'you mean, you didn't see the sign? It's right there in front of you. The three cars in front all went this way. The stinkin' bus is pointed this way. How many stinkin' signs are you looking for? There are more signs here than the blessed St Paul got on the road to Damascus, for Chrissake's.'

They drove on in silence, smoothly coming up behind an old Ford in front.

'I didn't see the sign,' muttered the driver after a while.

'Tony,' said Luigi, 'sometimes you're just a fucking idiot. Me, I drive halfway across Europe and I don't miss a sign. You, you need left and right written on your stinkin' socks.'

Shortly after making the call to James Randolph, Bartholomew Ephesian stood in the library of his large house on the hill. This was one of the rooms with its back to the view of Bute and Arran, but still the view up the hill of Cumbrae towards the highest point in the centre of the island and the far reaches of the golf course, was more than enough to regularly hold him there. Many a rainy day had been spent sitting in one of the large comfy chairs by the window, a book in his lap, looking out over the grass and rocks and sheep and the grey skies, so that he'd be lucky if he read a page. And always his thoughts were

54

the same, always thinking about the one great day which lay in the future and the part which he would have to play in it.

Now, at last, the time had come. For years he and the rest of the group had been searching, working on the clues that had been left by their forebears, to establish the location of the final clue in the game. The intended time of revelation, the coming of the third millennium, had been missed. Now, however, the breakthrough had been made – a breakthrough which had been inevitably simple and had been staring them all in the face for years – and he had quickly put into action the plan to bring his years of work to fruition. The short notice had partly been an attempt to wrong-foot Ping Phat but the fat Chinaman had still managed to get himself on a plane. Now that he was coming it was just another problem to be added to the list. It was regrettable that he knew about it at all but once that fool Lawton had felt the need to broadcast his discovery it had been inevitable. Still, Ping Phat could be taken care of, along with anyone else whom he felt it necessary to remove from the picture.

He lifted his arm to the sixth shelf on the east wall of the library and pulled gently at an old copy of Robert Louis Stevenson *Virginibus Puerisque*. With a mellow hum the shelves adjacent to this one slid slowly back, revealing a doorway leading to a dark, steep stairwell. With a glance over his shoulder, Ephesian flicked on the old brass light switch, stepped onto the top of the stairs and pressed the button to close over the door.

12

The Judas Tree

Ephesian had been right about Ruth Harrison's reaction to his phone call. She was very sceptical but she so desperately wanted to believe that the Reverend Dreyfus was calling her to him that she was prepared to accept it. And there was no way she was phoning first to check. When there's the slightest ray of light at the end of the tunnel, there's no point in trying the nearest switch to see if it'll turn it off.

She left her house at a little before one, having recovered from her experience with the spider and mostly managing to ignore any thoughts of what she had found in the bottom drawer of her husband's freezer.

She swung open the garden gate and looked up at the blue door of the manse. Mouth a little dry, heart pounding, insecurities bubbling to the surface. Walked up the path and stood on the threshold of her future. He had been busy, there were always many things to do for a minister and he had wanted the time to be right before calling her to see him. Now, at last, they would be able to be together.

She studied her vague reflection in the frosted glass of the door. Smiled. Dabbed at her hair. Rang the doorbell. This was the first minute of the rest of her life.

✂

James Randolph had watched Ruth Harrison leave her house, he had followed her for a couple of blocks as she'd walked back

56

towards the centre of town and up the hill, and then he had run back to the small housing estate just behind Kames Bay.

Now he walked slowly up her garden path, the odd glance over his shoulder to make sure that no one was watching. Quickly down the side of the house, put his hand through the slat in the gate to open the lock from the inside, stepped into the back garden and closed the gate over. He looked around at the neighbouring houses. He was overlooked by only one and he tried to remember who lived there. McGhee maybe. Not sure, but there was no one watching in any case.

He walked purposefully to the shed, opened the door, stepped in and, without turning on the light, started looking through the drawers of the freezer. Top, ice cream, then vegetables, then a turkey, then bread, then... Then nothing. The bottom drawer was empty.

He stepped back, not too concerned. He had probably just missed it higher up. This time he turned the light on and started checking more slowly. Each item was taken out and studied. He opened up the ice cream tubs and the unopened packets of frozen peas. Got to the bottom of the freezer, still a blank.

Back over it again, this time with more urgency, beginning to realise that he was once more about to fail his employer. If it wasn't here it wouldn't be his fault but that wouldn't stop Ephesian blaming him all the same.

He pulled out all the drawers, spreading the contents over the floor, to see if there were any hidden compartments behind. That would also make sense for such a sensitive item. Still nothing.

'Fuck,' he said, the single syllable delivered with a thespian amount of drama and exasperation. 'Shitting fuck.'

Looked around the shed to see if there was another freezer but it was a small shed. A quick, frantic yet thorough search, over in half a minute. He straightened up and looked down at the floor, strewn with frozen peas.

'Shit,' he said this time and then began to clean up, putting peas that he'd trodden on back into the packet.

Freezer loaded up again, drawers shoved back in, door closed, he stood back and took a last look at the shed. Still breathing

57

heavily, decided he was clear. It would take CSI to know he'd been there. He stepped back, narrowly avoided clunking his head on the doorway and thereby bringing down the same old spider who had now found his way home, and then back out into the garden. Closed the shed door and then he was gone, back up the garden path, through the gate and on his way.

It was like he'd been a ghost.

Except for the fact that Romeo McGhee had watched it all through the small telescope he had rigged up at his bedroom window. He had expected to see Randolph coming, he had known what he was looking for and he had known exactly why he hadn't found it.

✂

The Reverend Judas Dreyfus closed the lid of his freezer, turned and walked away through the basement of the manse. He never failed to make the walk back to the stairs and up into the large house without being aware of the pounding of his heart and a tangible nervousness about what the future held.

He rubbed the palm of his hand and turned back to glance at the freezer as he reached the door to the stairs. He hesitated, as if drawn to once more lift the lid and look at the contents, and then he turned finally, stepped onto the stairs and closed the door behind him.

The doorbell rang, he nodded slowly and climbed upwards. He emerged from the cupboard under the stairs and walked down the short hallway to the front door. He paused, he straightened the sleeves of his sky blue shirt, ran a finger around the dog collar and felt ready. Whatever little personal disaster awaited him outside, he was prepared. He opened the door.

Ruth Harrison smiled, Judas Dreyfus struggled to keep the instinctive expression off his face. This situation wrote the book on *The Last Person You Wanted To See*. Dreyfus hadn't thought that she would have had the nerve to turn up uninvited and he'd had no intention of going to visit her himself. He'd already arranged for the session clerk to pay her a visit later that evening. Jonah's funeral was a possibility but it wasn't as if there weren't alternatives on the island. He didn't have to do it.

58

'Mrs Harrison,' he began, 'how are you? I was sorry to hear about your loss.'

He knew the effect his words would have on her but had made the instant decision to be brutal. If she was going to have the neck to turn up here uninvited, then he was going to have the neck to call someone who he had slept with fifty-three times in the last year, Mrs Harrison. No use of the first name and certainly no use of any of the sweet affections such as Sugar Lump, Schnookie Pie or Buttercrush, which had peppered the vast majority of their illicit liaisons over the past twelve months.

Ruth Harrison swallowed.

'Fine,' she said, uncertainly. 'You know, fine I think. You're fine? How about you?'

'Very busy,' he said abruptly. Short and nasty.

'You wanted to see me?' she said.

'Why would you think that?' said Dreyfus. No let up. Prepared to be in complete denial about their affair. It had been fine while it'd lasted but it wasn't as if he didn't have two or three others in the congregation to keep him going. Ruthie had been on her way out in any case. 'I understand that this must be a very difficult time for you, Mrs Harrison and, of course, you have my sympathy, but you know how much work falls under my remit. I've arranged for Mr Rowlands to pay you a visit tonight.'

None of it went in. The individual words and sentences were unimportant. The affair was at an end.

'You wanted to see me?' she repeated plaintively.

'No,' said Dreyfus defiantly, 'I did not.'

'But Mr Ephesian,' said Ruth, 'he said. He called. To say. To say you wanted to see me.'

Dreyfus' gaze burrowed through her. A set-up?

'Well,' he said brutally, 'I don't.' And he slammed the door.

And so Ruth Harrison had a moment of blinding epiphany. The Reverend Judas Dreyfus was a complete and utter bastard. He was a Judas right enough. Had his parents known the second he popped out of the birth canal? Had he appeared in the world, looked at his mother, flicked her the bird, said 'Fuck you,' and made a mad lunge for the mid-wife's breasts to have his

59

breakfast? Had they been able to tell from the first moment he'd looked at them? Or maybe he had changed his own name in later years because he had known the true nature of the beast, the black core at the centre of his heart.

As her world turned upside down far more than it had done the previous day with the death of her husband, she turned away from the door and walked back down the long path of the Manse front garden.

As she reached the front gate to go back out onto Hope Street she bumped into old Mr Wallace, who was sporting a very tasty *Ronan Keating*.

'William,' she said absent-mindedly, barely able to think, all her functions automatic.

'Ruthie,' said William Wallace. 'Funny weather.'

'Aye,' said Ruth.

Wallace laid a brief hand on her shoulder as he walked past her.

'I dare say that that's you just been fucked for one last time by the Reverend Dreyfus,' he said lightly.

She stared at him, eyes wide, unable to speak.

'Judas by name, darlin', you know what they say,' he added, then he smiled some consolation and went on his way.

Ruth Harrison turned and watched him go, keeping her eyes on him until he had turned down the hill but never for a second did she take in anything about the scene. Her universe had just been altered forever.

13

Seeing Over My Hump

'Frankly speaking, it's the equal and opposite of all things,' said the old fella under Barney's scissors. Must have been the twentieth old guy of the day and his ability to talk was no less than any of the others.

'The whole yin-yang thing,' said Barney.

Tao produced the One; the One produced the Two; the Two produced the Three; and the Three produced the ten thousand things; the ten thousand things carry the yin and embrace the yang, and through the blending of the material force they achieve harmony, thought Igor, internally quoting Lao Tzu. *But no*, he thought, *I can't say it. I just have to stand here with my brush listening to old muppets talk shite*. Such is the way of the warrior.

'Exactly,' said Hugh Fraser, who was only just getting started on his dissertation on the exact nature of the female of the species, just as Barney was completing his Colin Firth 'Love Actually'.

'Think about it,' Fraser continued. 'Women are smashing to have sex with, they're usually quite happy to clean up and stuff, they give birth to your kids, they change nappies, they do all sorts. They're nice to look at, they have breasts... You know what I'm saying about breasts?'

Barney nodded.

'Breasts,' continued Fraser, even though he had already established that Barney knew what he was saying, 'are God's gift to man. Big breasts, small breasts, breasts that have been digitally altered, sagging breasts, breasts that can fit into a champagne cup, breasts that overhang a double D, breasts that cry out to you from across the street, breasts that cry out in the night, waiting to be loved. Big thumping breasts forged by the dwarf kings in the bowels of Middle Earth, beautiful breasts, ugly breasts, breasts with more than one nipple each, eccentric breasts, breasts created by the ancient god-kings of Indonesia! Thy two breasts are like two young roes that are twins, which feed among the lilies!'

Are you finished? thought Barney.

Song of Solomon pish! thought Igor. Fraser's quote was from the same verse that contains the bizarre romantic entreaties of *thy teeth are like a flock of sheep*, *thy hair is as a flock of goats* and *thy temples are like a piece of a pomegranate*. On one memorable occasion immediately prior to losing his speech, Igor had used that very verse as a chat-up line in a bar in Riddrie and, as a matter of fact, such was the violent disdain with which he had been treated by Lucile Lewis, 17, he hadn't been able to speak since.

'Aye, there's plenty more to be said about breasts,' said Fraser.

'You were making a point about women in general?'

Fraser paused, as if giving one last pleasant thought to breasts, and then continued with his thesis.

'Women,' he began again. 'They know how to cook every single vegetable known to man. I mean, some women I've met even know what kohlrabi is without going anywhere near Jamie Oliver. And frankly speaking, they're far more careful drivers than men, say what you like about them. I'm telling you, you want to get from A to B without any trouble, no word of a lie, I'd take a woman every time.'

Igor raised his eyes. *Some days I have trouble seeing over my hump*, he thought, *but I can still drive better than any woman.*

'Sewing, knitting all that stuff. Patience, they've got patience. And even though they look great in a nurse's uniform, they make good doctors too. I'm telling you, sonny, if I need to go to see some high-falutin' doctor with more degrees on the wall

62

than shite because I've got a problem with the old waterworks, you know, so that I've got to pop the old Johnson out on the table, I'd rather I was seeing a woman, you getting me?'

Barney acknowledged him and made another swift movement with the razor to further expedite proceedings.

'And frankly speaking, most of them, at least most of the ones I've known, have been completely understanding about the male need to watch football, golf and a whole variety of other sports. I was shagging this bird once who used to sit with me to watch the darts on the tele. I mean, frankly, that is outstanding.'

Fraser looked at Barney in the mirror, took a couple of seconds to catch his eye. Barney's barber sense made him look at the customer and say, 'But?' as the yang part had obviously been dealt with and it was time for the yin.

'But,' said Fraser, 'they are the most conniving, devious, scheming, underhand, calculating, sneaky, Machiavellian, conspiratorial, surreptitious, clandestine, furtive bastards known to man. If we were wild animals they'd eat us after sex. They're mean, merciless, callous, malicious, cold-hearted, pitiless, cruel, spiteful, vindictive and downright naughty. They're the human equivalent of those whales that come up onto beaches, catch seals and then take them back out into the sea and toss them about like a rugby ball, just for a bit of a laugh.'

Barney stood back and stared at the rounded contours and the perilous abandon of the crown of the head that is a Colin Firth and decided that the little haste at the end there had pretty much brought everything to a satisfactory conclusion.

'We're done,' he said suddenly.

Igor looked up quickly. Thank God! he thought. Barney glanced at him and smiled.

'I'm only just getting started!' wailed Fraser.

The door opened and another old fella came in, right on schedule, wearing a hat. As he removed the completely inappropriate fedora, Barney's eyes were immediately drawn to his hair and it was obvious that here was a man who had recently been given a very, very poor *Felix Leiter* by the lad 2Tone.

'Bit of an emergency,' said the old guy, looking at Barney.

63

'I'm done here,' said Barney and he started to brush away the hair from around Fraser's shoulders.

'Perry,' said Fraser, nodding at the *Felix Leiter*.

'Hugh,' said the *Felix Leiter*, nodding at the *Colin Firth*.

'I should leave you to it, right enough,' said Fraser, turning back to Barney. 'Perry's need is greater than mine and I am spent on the subject of women for the moment.'

Barney smiled but didn't encourage him any further. Fraser rose, brushed himself off, handed over the cash, nodded at Igor who grimaced in return and then was on his way.

Perry Liebowitz took his seat and glanced at Barney in the mirror.

'You'll be wanting me to perform a Felixectomy?' said Barney.

'Aye,' said Liebowitz.

'Shouldn't be a problem,' said Barney.

'Fine,' said Liebowitz. Then he said, 'You're new?' as if there was a possibility that Barney might not be.

'Aye,' said Barney.

'I was in the war, you know,' said Liebowitz ominously, 'a sapper. Took a hit helping the Yanks cross the Rhine. Long story, but I suspect we've got the time.'

Barney hit the off button.

'Arf,' said Igor.

✂

Bartholomew Ephesian was beginning to feel the cold. He had been sitting in the chamber, deep beneath his house on the hill, for over half an hour. Taking it all in, the exquisite joy of silence. This room had the dual purpose of serving the brotherhood and of serving his need for solitude and complete calm. When he was younger he had loved to be underwater, his ears filled, every sound blocked out. He had learned to hold his breath for minutes, so that he could disappear into swimming pools and the darkness of lochs. Now he was too old for that, though he had no doubt that he still required the escape. This room, this sanctuary, was to him now what the lochs around his family's holiday home in Perthshire had once been.

64

So it was almost over, only the last rites left to be performed. How incensed the Catholic Church were going to be when the world awoke on Thursday morning to a new day. A new dawn. A new beginning for them all.

For almost one hundred and thirty years now the *Prieure de Millport*, the most underground of secret societies, had been operated out of a house on this site, recently re-built by Ephesian, on the west side of Cumbrae, overlooking Bute and Arran. The *Prieure de Millport* was an institution so clandestine it didn't even allow any of Hugh Fraser's clandestine women to be members, an organisation so enigmatic and underground it made the CIA look like a bunch of brash Americans sticking their noses into other country's political problems.

In 1876 the *Prieure de Millport* had taken over from the more famous *Prieure de Sion*, in keeping alive an ancient legacy. The most important secret of the last two thousand years had been placed in their hands, to safekeep for the benefit of the entire world, until the time was right. Even then, parts of the secret had been hidden, so that the members of the society had been left guarding clues as well as the legacy itself. Now, however, Augustus Lawton had made the discovery that his fellows had sought for thirty years.

Many people, since the mid-nineteenth century, had wondered why a small church on an inconsequential island in the Clyde had been designated a cathedral. The answer was known only to the members of the *Prieure*. These men only ever numbered twelve at one time. Only upon death would they be replaced and an outsider would be invited to take the rigorous tests which would allow them to take the part of the recently deceased.

Ephesian heard footsteps on the steep stone stairs leading down to the chamber. As usual he felt an awkward discomfort at the sudden interruption of the peace but he knew that it would be Jacobs come to intrude on his glorious thoughts.

Ephesian lifted himself out of the chair at the head of the table, the chair that was not intended for him. He may have been Grand Master of the *Prieure* but that seat was for another and he didn't want to let Jacobs find him there. Straightened his jacket, leant on the table and surveyed the intricate stonework around

65

the room. The table and chairs and one small cabinet were the only objects of furniture placed in the room but the floor and the walls and the ceiling had each been beautifully created by the most gifted of stonemasons, every square inch replete with an eccentric mix of pagan and early Christian symbolism. The house above may have been modern but the chamber beneath had been here for the same length of time as the cathedral. Had the room been known of, it would have been one of the most fascinating tourist sites in Scotland. But now only eleven men alive knew that it even existed. Even Ping Phat, the man who had put so much money behind the organisation in recent years, had no knowledge of this room.

Jacobs emerged from the last corner of the winding one hundred and twenty-six step stairwell.

'Yes?' said Ephesian, looking up.

'Sir,' said Jacobs. 'You were going to place one last call to each of the other members of the party.'

Ephesian nodded.

'You're right,' he said. He looked at his watch. Early afternoon on the day before the world would forever change.

'And there is the matter of replacing Jonah,' said Jacobs.

It wasn't just the business of retrieving what Jonah Harrison had kept in the bottom drawer of his freezer. The *Prieure* had to have the full twelve members. On average, in Ephesian's time, one of the twelve would die every three or four years, and it had yet to be a huge problem finding someone of the right calibre on the island to take their place. However, there had never before been a rush to find a replacement. Everything in its time and eventually they would sort the wheat from the chaff and their man would be found. Sometimes it would take weeks, sometimes it would take months, but they always knew they'd get the right man to satisfy their requirements.

Now, however, they had a little over 24 hours. There would be no way to educate him in the ways of the society, there would be no way of testing him to establish his credibility as a keeper of the faith. The difference this time was that the man in question need only keep the secret until tomorrow evening.

After that there wasn't a person in the whole world who would not learn the truth.

'We have two options,' said Ephesian, 'neither of which fills me with pleasure or confidence, but given the circumstances...'

Jacobs nodded, accepting that the Grand Master of the Priory was about to take his counsel, as he did on most matters.

'Firstly, Mr Randolph, who would clearly not be one to rely upon under normal circumstances but whom I think we can trust given the truncated timeframe.'

Jacobs pursed his lips.

'The only other, I'm afraid,' Ephesian continued, 'is my son, Anthony. I realise that we are some decades short of being able to have implicit faith in his abilities in this respect but again I believe circumstances render the main objections to his candidature irrelevant.'

Jacobs nodded. Anthony Ephesian, 2Tone to everyone he could get to say it, was amongst the most unlikely candidates in the town. However, Ephesian was right about the situation and he was right about there being no other plausible alternatives. He was wrong, Jacobs thought, to even consider that idiot Randolph.

'It must be Anthony,' said Jacobs sombrely.

Ephesian nodded. He was expecting Randolph back any minute from his latest errand but it did not mean that he had to introduce him into the fold.

'Very good, Jacobs,' said Ephesian. 'I will have a preliminary talk with the boy tonight.'

'And now,' said Jacobs, 'it is time for you to place the calls to the brothers, to ensure that everyone is ready.'

Ephesian looked Jacobs in the chin, Jacobs held the slightly-off gaze, turned slowly, and then began to mince back up the stairs to the library.

14

Flowers In the Window

Luigi and Tony stood inside the Cathedral of the Isles, which stands hidden in the trees up the hill behind the town of Millport. Designed by William Butterfield, an architect more famous for Keeble College, Oxford and All Saints, Margaret Street, London, in the mid-19th century, the building is small, seating barely a hundred people, but is joined by college buildings to increase the overall effect of the structure. The nave of the cathedral is only forty feet by twenty feet but the one hundred and twenty-three foot steeple and tall pointed roofs make it seem much larger than it actually is. Kind of a Tardis in reverse.

While the nave is comparatively plain, the chancel and sanctuary are lush with colour and detail, with brightly coloured tiles and rich stained glass windows. Originally it had been very dull but early on in the 1860's the vicar at the time had managed to get the church, which was yet to be elevated to the status of cathedral, a place on the hit BBC series, *Changing Churches*. The famed designer of his day, Lawrence Llewelyn McGlumpha, duly arrived and used constructional polychrome on the floors and walls, as well as extensive stencil work on the beams, pillars and the exquisitely painted ceiling, which depicted the great variety of wild flowers that were found on the island. Of course, he went eight million pounds over budget.

'St. Peter's pisses all over this,' said Tony lightly.

Luigi raised an eyebrow at him then turned away and started to walk around the interior, running his hand along panels of wood, touching candlesticks. There would be something here, some basic piece of simplistic art, from which they would be able to derive the clue. Nothing the Episcopalians ever did was very complicated. That no one had ever found it before was because they hadn't known where to look. There were so many other sites in Europe where people had been searching in vain for years. No one other than those idiots at the *Prieure de Millport* had known to look here, until the previous week when Cardinal Salvatori had been given a sign. Or, more precisely, had been given a tip-off from one of his agents who had intercepted a telephone call between Ping Phat and Bartholomew Ephesian. Such had been the excitement of the situation for Ping Phat, he had neglected to take the usual security precautions; Ephesian, at the time, seething with anger at Lawton for divulging the information, had been too off-guard, too incandescent with rage to think properly. They had openly discussed something on an insecure line that should not have been discussed and the subject of the conversation had been passed up the chain of command.

'Look at this, it's so stinkin' small,' grumbled Tony. 'Don't these people realise that size matters?' He giggled.

'You're so stupid you're a bug, you know that?' said Tony. 'In fact, you're not a bug, you're an amoeba. You've got one cell, and you know what, it's not a brain cell. It's a stinkin' faecal cell. You're a single cell stupid shit, that's you.'

'Hey, well how many cells do you need? And what's with all this flower crap going on? It's a church, for crying out loud, not a garden centre.'

'The flower symbolism around this stinkin' cathedral is nothin' to do with stinkin' flowers and all to do with religious rites and the holiest of holies that we're going to find here. There ain't nothing ever done in the name of religion, my stupid amigo, that don't mean something other than what it looks like it's supposed to mean. You understand that or were there too many words in the sentence for you?'

'You know your trouble, Luigi?' began Tony, before he was halted by footsteps entering the cathedral behind them. The door to the college buildings, leading off from the chancel, closed and Father Andrew Roosevelt, Episcopal priest of the Cathedral of the Isles, stood before them. He smiled and walked forward, hands clasped together. His heart was still beating strongly, having just come from the administration room of the college, where he had taken a phone call from Ephesian. He hadn't been expecting everything to happen so fast but suddenly it was all going to fall into place. If he was honest with himself, he hadn't been expecting it to happen at all, never mind quickly. Now, suddenly, he was faced with being part of the most unique moment in history. His mouth was dry, his hands were clammy. He was scared.

'Good afternoon,' he said, trying to keep the uncertainty from his voice. 'You are visiting?'

Tony raised an eyebrow, all diplomacy foreign to him. Thinking, as always on these occasions, that he was looking at the enemy. Luigi stepped forward, smiling broadly.

'My brother and I are in Scotland for a few days. My parents, they met here just after the war. We were born in Glasgow but we moved back to Italy in the sixties. We are visiting some of the places they used to take us as small children. Largs, Millport, you know, the Clyde coast. We loved it. Did we not, Tony?'

Tony, being a single cell stupid shit, was about to get into a discussion on their respective parentage when, strangely for him, the penny dropped with a surprising clunk and he turned smiling to the priest.

'I love everything about Scotland,' he said. 'The weather, the ice cream, the football.'

'Yes,' said Father Roosevelt, 'well the ice cream I believe we got from you. You are clearly lying about the football, despite Celtic's defeat of Inter Milan in the European Cup Final of 1967...'

One stinkin' game and they're still talking about it, thought Tony. And Luigi.

70

'...and the weather, well, the levels of your diplomacy are legion and multi-layered. You know, last year there were over three hundred and fifty-seven different types of dreich weather recorded on the west coast of Scotland.'

'But the ice cream!' said Tony, concentrating on something that he'd said right.

'The cathedral,' said Luigi, looking to get Tony away from the subject of ice cream before he started talking about his favourite flavours. 'It is very impressive for such a small building, no?'

Roosevelt nodded, turned and looked round at the small area of the nave and chancel.

'Yes,' he said, head still going. 'The Cathedral's founder was the 6th Earl of Glasgow. Got quite carried away with the religious controversies of the day, bless him, and fortunately for all of us, I think, he was determined to revive the Episcopalian movement in Scotland. He commissioned William Butterfield to design the church and the adjoining college buildings.'

Let's talk about all the times Italian teams have knocked Scottish teams out of Europe, thought Tony. Let's talk about Juventus beating Rangers 4-1 at Ibrox in 1995. Let's talk about Celtic getting knocked out of the first round of the European Cup by Juve 1981. Let's talk about Dundee losing 5-1 to AC Milan in the 1963 European Cup semi-final. Or Dundee United losing 3-0 to Juve, or Hearts losing 4-0 to Inter, or Hibs getting spanked 6-0 by Roma.

'In 1876 it became the seat of the Bishop of The Isles and thus the church was elevated to the status of Cathedral of The Isles. It's a most fascinating history.'

Roosevelt smiled but he could tell he had sufficiently bored them that they wouldn't be asking any more questions.

The authorised version, thought Luigi, and he joined the priest in a bout of vigorous nodding. It wasn't the real reason this cathedral had been built and given such a special place in the church but he knew Roosevelt was not about to divulge that information.

'Thank you, Father,' said Luigi, 'you are right, this is a fascinating place. It is fine if we take a look around?'

71

Roosevelt smiled but for the first time thought he detected something in Luigi's eyes. The thrill of his conversation with Ephesian having died away, he now felt more attuned to his conversation with the two Italians. He smiled again at Luigi while he quickly went back over in his head what they'd said to him. It was odd though, this encounter coming so soon after his conversation with Ephesian. The Lord moved in mysterious ways indeed.

'Where did you say your parents met?' he asked, hoping not to give away his sudden interest.

'Scotland,' said Luigi. 'You don't mind if we look around?'

'Where abouts, exactly? It's always interesting to me where our Italian friends settled after the war.'

It may have been intended as an innocent question but it stuck out a mile as an attempted subtle act of interrogation. Immediately everyone knew that everyone else was suspicious and they were all on the defensive. Tony decided to put his extensive knowledge of Scottish football to its fullest use.

'Albion,' he said. 'Albion Rovers. Lovely place.'

Luigi, none the wiser, nodded. Father Roosevelt clasped his hands together and smiled.

'You are welcome to look around,' he said abruptly. 'There is much here that is beautiful. I have some business to which I must attend, I do hope you can excuse me.'

'Of course,' said Luigi. 'We have already taken up enough of your time.'

'Good day,' said Roosevelt.

Luigi nodded, Tony said, 'Your Grace,' because he was used to talking to men of the cloth like that. Luigi gave him a kick and Father Andrew Roosevelt turned and walked slowly away from the chancel and back into the college buildings.

Tony waited until he was gone and then said, 'Albion Rovers, eh? Check it out. Who's a single cell stupid shit now?'

'Yeah, well, let's not get carried away with your stinkin' genius and help me find something peculiar.'

Tony shrugged, sniffed, clutched at his groin and then began a not particularly close examination of the winged bull of St Luke, carved into the font.

Bartholomew Ephesian placed the red phone back in the cradle, then stood and looked out of the window. The nine calls had been made, the brotherhood had been alerted. The time had been set, the location was ready, as it had been for over a century, and now it was just a matter of waiting. This week there would be no Tuesday meeting; the Priory would meet on Wednesday, and under much more auspicious circumstances. He took out a small notepad and scribbled down the few things that needed taking care of before midnight the following evening.

James Randolph needed to recover the necessary item from Jonah Harrison's freezer; he himself had to speak to his boy and give him an induction into the ways of the brotherhood; there was the small matter of taking the appropriate artefact from amongst the decorative whims of the inside of the cathedral; and he and Jacobs had to come up with some means of dealing with Ping Phat upon his arrival. That would not be the least of his problems.

There was a knock at the door and Jacobs entered. Ephesian did not turn, his gaze staying where it was, locked on the grey waters of the firth, the hills of Arran as ever shrouded in mist and clouds.

'Mr Randolph is here,' said Jacobs. Ephesian nodded. That was one of the items off the list.

'Send him in,' he said coldly. It would be nice to be able to get rid of Randolph now but he needed him for his last piece of dirty work the following evening. And once he had completed the small task which he'd been set, then it would probably be time for him to be dispatched in a small car accident.

If only he himself had not been so discomfited by the sight of flowing blood. Red, red is the rose...

Jacobs retreated and a short time later James Randolph appeared. Had Ephesian turned to look at him he would have noticed that he was even more pale and nervous than normal, he would have recognised the agitated working of the hands, fingers locking and unlocking in a constant movement.

'You have it?' he asked coldly.

73

Randolph swallowed. His stomach was cramped with fear. Ephesian turned finally and looked at him, knew immediately from his posture that things had not gone according to plan. His eyes stared at a book on a shelf just to Randolph's right.

'What happened?' he asked.

Randolph still couldn't speak. Throat so dry he could've been stuck in a desert for forty days and forty nights.

'James,' said Ephesian, 'talk to me. If there's a problem, I'm sure it's not your fault.'

Randolph swallowed. His throat hurt.

Ephesian rose quickly from his seat. Wasn't yet annoyed, just wanted to get on with it. Peculiarly for him he was aware of Randolph's anxiety, as usually the feelings of others went quite over his head. He went to the drinks cabinet, poured out a glass of Bunnahabhain, handed it to Randolph. Randolph swallowed it quickly, enjoyed the ache of the flavour against his throat, coughed suddenly, wiped away a little spillage on his chin.

'Speak to me,' said Ephesian.

'It wasn't there,' said Randolph quickly, unable to look Ephesian in the eye.

Ephesian breathed heavily, stared at the rug and then turned away and went to the window. Looked down on the firth, eyes wide, watched a small sailing boat battling with the winds in the middle of the channel.

It wasn't there. Randolph was an idiot but he wasn't that much of an idiot. Either Jonah hadn't kept it where he'd said he did or else Ruth Harrison had already found it and moved it.

Jonah Harrison, despite the gambling and the insane credit card debt about which Ephesian well knew, had been a trustworthy man. A sad loss to the fellowship, particularly now with the fruits of their labours about to be harvested. He'd trusted Harrison completely. So if it had been moved, there was only one explanation. He turned back to Randolph, could see immediately that the man had relaxed.

'The wife must have found it but we know she hasn't gone to the police. Might have been better if she had. Go round there, speak to her, find out what she's done with it.'

Randolph nodded. More responsibility.

'Take Jacobs,' Ephesian added. 'Better take Jacobs.'
And Randolph felt relieved and annoyed at the same time.

15

Maggots Of Melancholy

There's a saying amongst aurally-challenged, mute hunchbacks, and it goes like this: just because you're deaf, doesn't mean you can't hear.

Igor had a reputation amongst the ladies as a good listener. None of them knew whether it was because he could lip-read or if it was because he instinctively knew what you were saying, but not one of his many confidantes in town doubted for a second that he understood everything they said to him. They could tell him what they liked and Igor was never judgemental. That was one of the many beauties of the man.

Ruth Harrison had returned home from her devastating meeting with the Reverend Judas Dreyfus, her heart broken. Perhaps the townsfolk would think she mourned for her dead husband and that might be no bad thing. She was shattered and broken and she did not care. She'd gone home, she had opened the fridge door and she had determined that she would spend her days sitting in front of the television, watching awful confrontational chat shows about men who were bastards, and she would drink wine at such a lovely steady pace that she would always be drunk. And then she had heard the footsteps padding heavily on the upstairs landing, she had heard the bathroom door open and close, she had heard the stream of urine and then the toilet flush, and she had immediately run out of the house, nerves shredded, in desperate need of someone to talk to. Someone she could trust.

She opened the door to the barber shop. For the first time that day Barney was inactive, the seemingly endless stream of old men looking for young haircuts having finally dried up. He raised an eyebrow, knowing that this woman was not here for a bouffant hair-do and a tonne of product.

She looked at Igor, Igor returned the look from where he swept. Igor's face automatically showed compassion for her loss, although he knew that she had long since tired of Jonah, his financial whims and his repellent personal habits.

'I need to talk, Igor,' she said.

Igor smiled and ushered her to the bench. Ruth looked at Barney. Igor shrugged sympathetically, as if to say, we're all in it together. He's one of us. She looked at Barney with uncertainty but was swayed by Igor's expression. If Igor trusted this man, then so would she.

She sat down, looking from barber to barber's hunchbacked assistant and back again.

'Barney Thomson,' said Barney, putting her at ease.

'Ruth Harrison,' she said.

'Ah,' said Barney. 'I'm sorry.'

She nodded in that way that you do, then turned back to Igor. Some day she would need to talk to him about the Reverend Dreyfus but not yet. Not while the wound was open and bloody and sore and being feasted upon by the maggots of melancholy.

'This is going to sound strange, so I'll just say it.' She hesitated, she steeled herself. 'Jonah's still in the house.'

Igor look surprised. Barney immediately thought of the prosaic and wondered if the ambulance had still to come to remove the body. That happens in today's Britain.

'How d'you mean?' he asked.

She turned to Barney, wondering if she should give him the whole story. His eyes were trusting and, whilst telling herself that all men were bastards, she decided that she would take him into her confidence.

'I was in the bathroom yesterday, really needed to go. Jonah comes to the door hammering to get in, I said, well to be honest, I said, go and pee in the kitchen sink. He must have been desperate, you know, I didn't realise. Else, you know, I would have let him in and everything.'

Igor knew that that was a whopperooni of a fib.

'So he thumped down the stairs and that's when he tripped and banged his head. That's how he died.'

Both Barney and Igor had already heard the story but they both shook their head sympathetically as if hearing it for the first time.

Igor did a thing with his hands.

'Oh aye,' said Ruth, 'they came and took him away really quickly. Even cleared up, you know. Luciens was very helpful, wouldn't even take a cup of tea.' *Of course, he's a man, and therefore a complete shite of the highest degree.* 'It's not that.' *It's the fact that Dreyfus dumped me, it's the fact that Jonah is going to haunt me for the rest of my friggin' life because I wouldn't let him go to the toilet. It's the fact that the stupid bastard kept something unmentionable wrapped in a small bag in the bottom drawer of the freezer.*

'What is it?' asked Barney.

'He's still in the house,' she repeated after another pause, another bite at the bottom lip of uncertainty.

Barney and Igor waited.

'He's haunting me. Or something. I don't know how many times I've heard it since yesterday afternoon. He was in his office before he died. Came out of there up to the bathroom door. Now there are footsteps coming out his office door, they pad up to the bathroom, the door opens and shuts, he takes a pee and then flushes the toilet.'

She looked wide-eyed at them. Igor looked wide-eyed back, very impressed with this bathroom tale of the paranormal.

'You think Jonah is stuck for eternity taking a pish?' asked Barney, trying to keep the doubt from his voice.

She looked sombrely at them.

'Aye,' she said, 'that's exactly what I think.'

Barney shrugged. There are stranger things in life than that.

'So would you like us to come round and check it out for you?'

At this Ruth Harrison dissolved into a liquefied pile of mush, looking with huge relief from Barney to Igor and back.

'Would you?' she breathed. 'Would you?'

'Sure,' said Barney. He and Igor exchanged a glance. Kind of a Steve McQueen/Yul Bryner *Magnificent 7* kind of thing, although had they acknowledged that that was what they were doing, they would probably have fought over which of them got to be Steve McQueen. 'Igor,' he continued, 'let's saddle up the horses and move on out.'

Igor smiled, although it emerged as a grimace, and the men set about their business. The *Magnificent 2*. Hired hands, sent out into the world to fight the paranormal. So in fact, it was more like *Ghostbusters* really. But then, who dreams of being Dan Ackroyd or Bill Murray?

✂

Fifteen minutes later Barney and Igor followed Ruth Harrison into her house. They had come to sit with the traumatised woman, to allow the house itself to bear witness to this bizarre tale of the supernatural.

Almost four o'clock and Barney had easily taken the decision to close early. He removed his jacket, Igor removed a variety of rough garments he wore to exacerbate his natural hump and stoop, Ruth put her coat over the banister and turned on the lights.

'Cup of tea?' she asked.

'That'd be lovely,' said Barney. 'Hardly any milk, no sugar.'

She looked at Igor who made his request for tea with a slight nod. Everyone in the town knew how Igor took his tea.

'You want me to go upstairs and have a look?' asked Barney.

She turned, kettle in her sticky little paws, and stared at Barney with amazement, wonder, surprise and incredulity.

'You'd do that?' she said.

Barney shrugged.

'Didn't come here to just drink tea,' he said. 'Igor, you stay with Mrs Harrison, she shouldn't be alone.'

'Arf.'

'Oh, thanks, Igor,' she said.

Barney got a sense, as he left the room, that there was something between Igor and Ruth Harrison, and he smiled at the thought. Bless 'em. Had no idea of the existence of the Reverend Dreyfus or of the mental torture that Jonah's widow was currently having to endure, but when you're broken, defeated, humiliated and crushed you are at your most vulnerable, and Ruth Harrison had always had a bit of a soft spot for Igor.

Barney slowly climbed the stairs. This was new. It wasn't like he hadn't encountered a killing field's worth of death in his time, but none of it had ever come back to haunt him.

Top of the stairs and he stopped, took a look around the landing. A couple of pictures on the walls, oddly tasteful. Imagined, correctly, they must have been Jonah's choices. A large chest of drawers, which he assumed would be filled with all the junk and pillows and sheets and duvets and clothes that they never used but didn't like to throw out.

He stepped into the room that Jonah used as an office. Suddenly he remembered something from long ago, a memory subverted or forgotten. When he and Agnes had been house-hunting before they'd married. An old house in Cambuslang not far from a school. A quiet road, big Victorian houses set back, with large front gardens. Hadn't had a hope of being able to afford it but they'd enjoyed themselves looking. They had gone up the stairs with the estate agent showing them round. There had been a small middle landing with a couple of bedrooms off. The estate agent had pointed them out but had not gone in. Agnes had stood back. Barney could feel it but had been curious.

He'd walked into the first room, a blue bedroom stripped bare. A couple of alcoves, carpet taken away, the floor stripped down to the wood. There'd been another door directly opposite and it had drawn him on. Slowly he'd walked across the room and opened the door.

The sun had been shining brightly into the room. The window was opened slightly and the light net curtain was moving softly. Wooden floor but this one was polished. The walls were spartan, a creamy off-white, no pictures or other decoration, yet

80

they had not looked bare. In the warmth of the sun, the room had almost had a Mediterranean feel to it. There'd been a small table with a sewing box, with an unfinished small crocheted blanket lying next to it. An old rocking chair had sat next to the table, positioned so that whoever sat in it could look out of the window at the orchard in the garden across the high wall next door. In the slight breeze coming in through the window, it had almost seemed like the chair had been slowly rocking.

And, standing there in that room in the warmth of the sun, Barney had felt a great weight of sadness and a sure and certain knowledge that he was not alone. The hairs had risen on the back of his neck, he could feel the fright in every cell in his body and he had quickly turned, closed the door and walked back through the blue bedroom. The estate agent and Agnes had been waiting for him on the landing, heads down, no conversation.

'She's still in there,' Barney had said.

The estate agent had nodded, Barney had looked at Agnes and the two of them had walked back down the stairs and out of the house and had never looked back. And slowly, over the years, the memory of that uncomfortable feeling had faded away, until it had completely vanished. Until now and Barney was standing looking at the empty chair from which, a little more than twenty-four hours earlier, Jonah Harrison had risen in a hurry and walked out to his death.

And yet, while the memory had returned, that same feeling was not there. No hairs springing to attention on the back of his neck, no feeling of fear or discomfort, no awareness of there being another presence in the room.

He walked back out into the hall and into the bathroom. A small narrow room, toilet, sink and bath all crammed together like commuters on a train. A lot of feminine products, no sign whatsoever that there had ever been a man in the house.

Still nothing. No sense of anything unearthly, anything that wasn't meant to be part of this world. Not that Barney felt he had any sixth sense for the undead but when there's something present, usually it works its way into your head. There was nothing. Decided that Ruth Harrison must be suffering from shock. An instant judgement.

He looked at himself in the bathroom mirror. Tired eyes, seen too much, in need of a long rest. Sleep, a lot of sleep. Maybe death, maybe that was all they needed.

'Jesus, Barney,' he muttered at his reflection, 'get a grip.'

He heard footsteps outside on the landing. Igor must have torn himself away from the Widow Twanky and come up to investigate the ghost himself. Ruth must be confident that old Jonah wasn't suddenly going to try and get a beer from the fridge.

The footsteps approached the bathroom, then Barney heard the door open and close, the lock placed hurriedly across. He was standing two feet from the door staring at it. It hadn't moved.

Now he felt it. The extra presence in the room. Every sense was heightened, he felt cold and hot at the same time. He shivered, a great wracking of his body. He heard the toilet seat raised, although it did not move, and then the sound of a long stream of pee into the centre of the bowl. He pressed himself back against the sink, staring down at the toilet. There was nothing in front of him but he could sense it and hear it and he was as sure of it as he had been of anything he'd ever felt in his life. Jonah Harrison was in the room with him.

The sound of the water dribbled to a halt and was followed by the toilet flushing and a long and relieved sigh. And then, as soon as it had come, the feeling was gone. Jonah was gone and Barney was alone. The tension in his muscles and on his skin relaxed, he was imbued with a feeling of overwhelming relief, the feeling that Jonah Harrison had just left behind. He relaxed.

The doorbell rang. Barney was juddered from the good feeling in which he had allowed himself to wallow, the moment had passed. Jonah Harrison had visited the toilet and the instance of micturition was gone. Barney walked out of the bathroom and back onto the upstairs landing, only vaguely curious as to who the visitor might be and how much sympathy they were about to heap upon the weeping widow; unaware that one of the two men

82

currently standing outside the door had come armed not with condolences but with implements of torture.

16

No One Will Survive

'I mean, really,' said Romeo McGhee. 'She's this super-
neurotic, highly-strung, constantly pre-menstrual, malicious,
vicious, irrational, over-stressed uber-bitch, and all you women
have her up there as, like, this icon or something. A feminist
icon. And that just sums it up, man. Feminism in a flippin'
nutshell. It's like you pick the weirdest, freaked out Loony Tune
of a woman and make her your role model. Women are so
screwed.'

Chardonnay Deluth took her eye away from the periscope and
looked at McGhee. She was lying on the floor, resting her head
in her hand. He was sitting on the carpet a few feet away, his
back against the wall, reading the blurb of a 70's compilation
CD.

'Why d'you say that?' she asked. 'What kind of icons would
you like us to have? She's making a statement, she's saying
she'll get on in the world without a man, she's saying she
doesn't need a man to lean on. You know, it was coming after
centuries of women being tied to either the kitchen sink or the
bed. So what if it's a little dated, it helped pave the way. It's
awesome and it's still going to be awesome three hundred years
from now.'

'All right, I get the whole *I Will Survive* thing,' said McGhee,
'I'm not dissing that, you know? But can she not give the guy a
break, it's not like he's left her? He's just doing his job, for
crying out loud.'

'What d'you mean?'

84

'Well, like the guy's an astronaut and everything. What, is he supposed to phone home every day? Is he supposed to be writing her flippin' love letters? Where the heck are you going to find a post box at seven hundred thousand feet? And how many times a day would there be a collection?'

She looked at him in a certain way.

'What?' she said.

'A collection, you know, if you had a post box in outer space, how often would Postman Pat be able to shuffle by there in his little red van?'

'Not that,' she said, 'what are you talking about? The guy's not an astronaut, he's just some moron who dumped her, and now he thinks he can just walk back into her life?'

He did a thing with his hands.

'*Now you're back*,' he sang, '*from outer space*. The bloke's been on a moon mission for six months. Give him a flippin' break, you know.'

Deluth waited for him to smile, indicating that he'd been joking. He stared at her, recognised the look on her face. Suddenly he could feel the redness begin to rise in his cheeks, as he had a minor moment of epiphany. Gloria Gaynor wasn't a super-neurotic, highly-strung, constantly pre-menstrual, malicious, vicious, irrational, over-stressed uber-bitch after all. And her ex-boyfriend wasn't an astronaut.

Deluth burst out laughing, falling onto the floor – which was an achievement seeing as she was already down there – tears immediately coming to her face. Romeo McGhee felt very, very stupid. And Deluth was laughing so much she was completely unable to tell him that Ephesian's men, Simon Jacobs and James Randolph, had just arrived at Ruth Harrison's house.

✄

Barney walked down the stairs. Still feeling odd about the whole Jonah Harrison thing. Unsure how to take it all and surprised at the feeling of well-being with which he had been left. Two men had just entered the house as he came to the bottom of the stairs. One, weak eyes, supine around the jaw, nervous, a quite dreadful *Peter Lorre* cut, and Barney could instantly read that his purpose here was not one of condolence.

The other man looked much harder, had the guise of compassion about him; wrinkled face and greying hair, deep blue eyes, teeth that were well-acquainted with an expensive dental surgeon, bit of a *François Mitterand*.

Ruth Harrison was on the defensive. She'd seen Jacobs about, knew that he occasionally emerged from Ephesian's house to skulk around the town doing his dirty work. Ephesian had been here earlier and she had obviously sent him away before he had found what he was looking for. Jacobs must have been sent down for the same reason, the spineless Randolph in tow.

They looked at Barney with suspicion, while also noticing Igor lurking by the kitchen door with what looked like, to Barney's not entirely untrained eye, a touch of lipstick on the corner of his chops.

'I'm sorry if you're busy,' said Jacobs, eyes furtively shifting between Ruth and Barney. Ignoring Igor. 'We need to talk.'

Ruth Harrison, fortified by a bit of a smooch with Igor while Barney had investigated her late husband's ghoul, stuck out her chest and looked Jacobs firmly in the eye.

'Well, say what you have to say. These men are here for their tea and they won't be going anywhere before you do.'

Randolph nervously began to click the nails of his thumbs. Jacobs rubbed his hands slowly, knowing he had to quickly make the call.

It wasn't as if they needed to get hold of the package right now, there were still over thirty hours to go. But often problems left to fester just keep getting worse. This was one which needed to be sorted out straight away and the presence of the new barber and the deaf mute hunchback wouldn't be allowed to derail proceedings.

'Jonah left something in the freezer,' he said coldly.

Ruth Harrison tried not to let the dawning awareness show on her face. She hadn't been thinking. Hadn't put two and two together; not only had the penny not dropped, the penny hadn't even been there in the first place.

Jonah had gone out every Tuesday evening, that was what this was about. What manner of problems had he left her with?

'I'm sure you could get your own frozen peas at the Spar,' she said crisply.

There was a lot of crisp, cold, snappy, frosty talk, as if the mere mention of the freezer was forcing the tone of the debate.

'You know what I'm talking about,' said Jacobs grimly.

'I'm sure that I don't,' she replied.

'Arf,' growled Igor in the background. Barney raised an appreciative eyebrow at him and wished sometimes that he himself was unable to talk and had the ability to articulate everything he was thinking by the eloquent use of one syllable.

Jacobs glanced at Igor, then looked back to Ruth Harrison.

'What have you done with the bag?' asked Jacobs brusquely, this time his lips getting thinner, the facial equivalent of cocking the gun. You know that way they do in films, where they never cock the gun to begin with so they can do it half way through being mean, to indicate that they really really are just about to blow someone's head off if they don't hand over the girl. Or the money.

'I don't know what you're talking about,' chimed Ruth Harrison, warming to her subject, protected as she was by the brave Igor behind and the curious Barney to her left.

'Mr Randolph,' said Jacobs, voice low and full of menace, 'came round earlier to speak to you about it. Finding you out, he took the liberty of checking in the freezer himself for the required item. We know where Jonah kept it, we know it is no longer there. You must have moved it.'

This time Ruth just stood and stared. At last the menace in his voice was beginning to penetrate, Ruth was being intimidated.

'The contents of that bag did not belong to Jonah,' said Jacobs. 'They belonged to the Brotherhood.' He paused, he let the words sink in. He had intended coming to her house and forcing her to hand over the freezer bag. However, if all he did was scare her into going to the police, her first port of call would be PC Gainsborough, who would be very concerned, make all the right noises, inform her that the appropriate action would be taken, and would immediately take the evidence to Bartholomew Ephesian.

87

'Tell us where the bag is, we can take it and we can leave. No fuss, no one needs to get hurt, no big issues. Simple. You can move on, we get our bag, everyone's happy.'

Another pause. He was wearing her down. Even she was beginning to see the sense in it. What did she want with the contents of that bag? It wasn't as if she was protecting her husband's good name. He had been a member of some secret society that kept something illegal in his freezer and he'd never mentioned it. Was she supposed to be supportive?

'Fuck off.'

The blunt warning came from the stairs. Everyone looked at Barney.

'Arf!' said Igor in support.

Jacobs didn't reply. He stared at Barney for a few seconds then turned back to Ruth Harrison.

'Mrs Harrison,' he began. Voice had dropped another two or three notches down the coldness scale. If he'd had a gun, it would've been one which he could've cocked six or seven times. 'Choose your friends wisely. Give us the bag and the matter will be closed now. Any other course of action would be folly.'

She hesitated. She swallowed. She glanced sideways at Barney.

'What he said,' said Randolph, as if that contributed anything.

'The bag,' said Jacobs brutally, ignoring Randolph.

Ruth Harrison bit her bottom lip and looked over her shoulder. Back in the direction of where she had planted the bag in the garden. To defrost.

Barney Thomson didn't care. He was no natural hard man but if ever there was a person to define the been-there-done-that personality type, he was it. When you've had years of dead bodies and murder and pandemonium and a life defined by Chaos Theory, two hard men, one of whom was as hard as a one minute egg, meant nothing. He stepped down the stairs, he moved in between Jacobs and Ruth Harrison.

'Fuck off,' he repeated. Thought to add a variety of other insults but he didn't need to. Sparse was good.

Jacobs tried to stare him down but Barney Thomson was a man who had seen too much to be intimidated by the hired help of a small time crook on an island in the Clyde estuary. There was a brush of wind and Igor was standing beside him, so that Ruth Harrison now had the full wall of protection before her.

Barney crossed his arms, the appendage equivalent of cocking a gun. Igor crossed his arms. James Randolph, not entirely in tune with proceedings, crossed his arms. Jacobs took the mood of the situation. Was it worthwhile getting into a fight at this stage?

He looked through Barney and Igor, right into Ruth Harrison's eyes, right into her head. She swallowed, she knew he would be back. Jacobs twitched, the bitter spasm of unfulfilled rage. Teeth gritted, he turned, opened the door and stepped back out into the grey of a bleak afternoon. Randolph attempted to give the three others the similar treatment but fell woefully short, and then he followed Jacobs out into the day, closing the door behind him.

They watched them go and then, with the door shut, relief descended upon the house.

Ruth Harrison let out a long sigh and said, 'Thank God they're gone.'

'Arf,' said Igor.

Barney looked at Ruth and could see she was shaken. Would have held out a hand to her but Igor got there first, which was probably best.

'You're right about one thing,' said Barney, matter of factly.

'What?' she asked.

Igor looked quizzically at him, picking up the vibe.

'Your husband's still trying to take a piss.'

17

'Take Some More Tea!'

Police Constable Thaddæus Gainsborough laid down the copy of that afternoon's Evening Times. Took another glance at the back page banner headline – *Dog With Transplanted Head of Dead Ibrox Legend Is New Rangers Signing Target* – propped his feet on the desk and looked out of the window as the afternoon wound its way to an end. His was another office with a west facing window, although he was down at sea level, the small police station just across the road from the tiny bay which precedes the playpark, the football field and the boat yard at the far end of the town.

He reached for his cup of tea and took his first sip. The perfect cup. He always took the time to do the job properly. Warm the pot. One spoonful of Harrods loose leaf No.16 *Afternoon Blend Pure Ceylon* per person and one for the pot – he always made tea as if he was doing it for five or six, although he inevitably drank alone – brew for five minutes. Warm the cup. Milk in the cup first, just the merest drop, just enough to take the edge off the darkness, so that most people looking at the brew would think he was drinking coffee. Pour the tea in through the strainer. Different strainer for each type of tea, never wash the strainer in soapy water, just a quick rinse. No sugar. Let the cup stand for a minute and a half while you read the paper – his ritual was so particular that the taste of Harrods No.16 evoked the Evening Times, the taste of No.12 *Scottish Breakfast* evoked

The Scotsman, the taste of No.5 *Not Morning, But Not Quite Afternoon* evoked the lunchtime news on BBC1.

He always made the perfect cup, so this one was no different. Held it in both hands, feeling the stinging warmth of the tea on his fingertips through the thin china. He always drank tea from the same cup, which he washed thoroughly afterwards. It had been given to him upon leaving his previous position as clerk at the station in Lamlash on Arran, and bore the inscription, *To Thaddæus Gainsborough, Lamlash 2004*, with Samuel Johnson's '*A Hardened and Shameless Tea Drinker*' inscribed around the rim. Guests were given a selection of mugs, including a Tweetie Pie, an I _ New York, an NPR Morning Edition, a Cambuslang Old Parish Church, a Bart Simpson Role Model, a Grumpy Old Man he'd received on his thirtieth birthday, and a bull terrier with a description on what loveable dogs they are.

The door opened. He dragged his eyes away from the hills of Arran and another contemplation on the girl he had left across the water, Minnie McDonald, 27. Didn't bother to remove his feet from the desk, as the only person whom he would not wish to be caught by in this position was Bartholomew Ephesian, and Bartholomew Ephesian never came down to the police station. The police station always went to him.

Father Andrew Roosevelt entered the office and closed the door behind him. He nodded at Gainsborough, Gainsborough smiled.

'Father,' he said. The men stared at one another for a second. Only eleven men in the world knew what they knew – at least, they thought it was as little as eleven – and they shared the joy of the secret for a second, no words passing between them.

'A great day is nearly upon us,' said Roosevelt eventually. The moment of secret male bonding had passed and they could both feel comfortable again. There's a place for heterosexual male bonding, although no one is entirely sure when that is, but it's always a bonus when those moments pass without undue distress.

'Cup of tea?' asked Gainsborough, to ensure that the encounter was firmly established on solid ground.

Roosevelt was well aware of Gainsborough's addiction and of the fact that he would get a damn fine cup of tea.

'In a minute,' he said.

'The brew'll be past its peak,' said Gainsborough. 'You have to be careful.'

To be honest, I don't quite have your anally retentive obsessive weirdness about tea, Constable, and if I was to consider tea to have a peak, I'd think the peak lasted from the point that the water and the bag were put in the same cup until the water had gone cold, thought Roosevelt, but he merely nodded, sat down across from Gainsborough and leant forward.

'There are two Italians in town,' he said quickly, before Gainsborough could tell him that studies at the University of Durham have indicated that the first invisible microbes of mould begin to form on a cup of tea after less than eight and a half minutes, even while the tea is still hot.

Gainsborough glanced at the clock, checking how much time he had to finish his cup before the fungal spores began to multiply imperceptibly on the surface of his drink. He took another sip.

'Are they lost or on holiday?' he asked, looking out at the grey day and wondering why any Italian would want to come to Millport on holiday.

'Oh,' said Roosevelt, voice taking on a cautionary note, 'they know exactly where they are and they're not here on holiday.'

Gainsborough found himself a little intrigued by the priest's tone and he raised his eyebrows in question, while hiding the rest of his face behind the cup.

'They've just been to the cathedral,' said Roosevelt. 'Snooping around inside, very suspiciously.'

'This is Millport.' Gainsborough indicated the weather. 'What else are a couple of visitors going to do on a day like this? Visit the twenty-eight screen multiplex? Go bowling? Eat Thai or go to the swimming pool and sauna? You said yourself, they're Italian. Italians love all that religious stuff. Show them a church and they'll amuse themselves for the afternoon.'

'No, no!' exclaimed Roosevelt, once he'd been allowed a word in. 'It's much more than that. They're acting suspiciously.

There's something grievously amiss. They lied. There was no reason for them to lie, not if they were just on holiday.'

'So, what are you saying? You think they're here to, what exactly? Invade? Claim Millport as part of a greater Italian republic? That might not be so bad.'

'Constable!' said Roosevelt, exasperated by the policeman's lack of concern. 'You must have received the phone call!'

'Aye,' said Gainsborough.

'Then you know that there are some people, some organisations, who will not be happy with what will be revealed tomorrow evening?'

'Aye,' said Gainsborough.

Roosevelt stared, as if not wanting to spell it all out in case the room was bugged. Of course, the room *was* bugged, because all police stations are bugged by MI5, but it's not like that mob would be too interested in what this pair were talking about.

The light of wisdom suddenly started to dawn on Gainsborough's face.

'Ah,' he said. 'Ah.' And he pointed upwards, indicating a higher power.

'Well,' said Roosevelt, 'I don't know that I'd go that far, but yes, that is my inference. These men are Italians and, more specifically, from Rome.'

'You know this for a fact?' asked Gainsborough. 'An actual fact?' he added, as opposed to the facts he read in the sports pages of the Evening Times.

'Like I said,' Roosevelt began, 'they're just acting strangely, so I can't be absolutely sure, but I think they should be taken care of just in case.'

Gainsborough took another long drink of tea. Glanced at the clock.

'Right,' he said. 'So, have you spoken to Mr Ephesian? That would seem the obvious course of action.'

'No!' said Roosevelt with surprising force. 'No, we mustn't bother him. There are some things we should be able to take care of ourselves. These are very important days for the Grand Master, he doesn't need to be troubled by every little thing.'

'Well,' said Gainsborough, 'I don't know that being about to be shat upon by the largest religious organisation on the planet is all that little a thing, but if you think it's best that he doesn't know...'

'Definitely, definitely.'

'So, what d'you suggest?'

Gainsborough drained his cup with a glance at the clock. Finally removed his feet from the desk and sat forward.

'You understand that the very future of the planet depends upon us to take care of this matter,' said Roosevelt.

'Well, I believe that might be a bit of an exaggeration but we'll run with it at the moment and see how we get on,' said Gainsborough.

'Good,' said Roosevelt. He pulled the chair out, sat down, nodded at the teapot to indicate that he would now take a cup, and said, 'Right, here's what we need to do.'

✂

Barney, Igor and Ruth Harrison trooped dutifully into the back garden. Barney crossed his arms against the cold, Igor seemed to crouch down before his hump, Ruth pulled her cardigan tightly across her chest.

'I just put it in with these roses,' she said, the fifth time she'd mentioned putting it in with the roses. 'I really have no idea why I did it and it's not like I know what I'm going to do with the thing, is it? It's not like I'm this expert in anything, you know.'

'And what was in the bag?' asked Barney for the fifth time.

'I'll show you,' she said, and she bustled across the lawn. Barney and Igor exchanged a glance and walked after her.

She came to the rose patch at the back of the garden, up against the wall which separated her territory from that of Mr Margoyles, the local wine drinker. Walking behind, Barney could see the disturbed earth in the midst of the roses and wondered what exactly she had been thinking. Obviously she hadn't been concerned about the thing defrosting; obviously she hadn't been concerned about it being discovered either, or else why hide it in the middle of your garden under obviously disturbed earth?

She lifted the small trowel which she had left lying handily at the edge of the lawn.

'Arf,' muttered Igor, and she turned and smiled at him. She may have benefited from Igor's empathy but it was a one way street. She never had any idea what he actually meant by any of his *arfs*.

She put the trowel into the earth expecting to hit the soft package straight away, as she had not buried it deeply. She scooped out some earth, surprised that it wasn't there. Inserted the trowel once more but again nothing. She shovelled in again, this time more quickly, then another few times, expanding her scope of works. In her sudden panic, she almost started digging into the soil with her hands but she stopped herself on behalf of her fingernails.

She turned round to look at Barney and Igor, her face showing everything. She didn't need to say it. Being a woman, she said it anyway.

'It's gone!' she gasped.

Barney walked over and bent down beside the small patch of ground. He wasn't about to go digging his hands in either but he knew there was little point. The hiding of the item in the first place had obviously been so rudimentary that there would be little trouble in finding it had it still been there.

'What was it?' asked Barney, looking at her.

Ruth Harrison stood up, a growing look of panic on her face. She stared at Barney, she turned to Igor for some reassurance. Igor grimaced at her but it really didn't help from the relaxation point of view. She turned back to Barney, she swallowed. She looked big eyed and lost.

'Arf,' said Igor.

18

Nietzsche Ate My Hamster

Romeo McGhee opened up the fridge door, took out a Miller, popped the cap, took a long first drink, belched, dragged the sleeve of his Eminem sweat-shirt across his mouth, farted with a cock of the leg, took another drink, forced a small burp which wasn't really worth the effort, checked the fridge for cheese – there wasn't any – closed the door and then turned round.

'They are so putty in my hands,' he said. 'Putty. What are you smiling at?'

'Still laughing about the outer space thing.'

'Move on, girlfriend,' he said, genuinely shameless. 'We are so about to kick arse.'

'You don't want to offer me a beer, then?'

He humphed a little, passed her the one from which he'd already drunk and then returned to the fridge. Planked himself down at the table.

'What's the plan?' she asked.

Romeo McGhee glanced round at the freezer, then turned back, the beer bottle surgically attached to his lips.

'You know there's this weird thing in town?' he said.

'The Brotherhood?' she said. 'Yeah, so? It's just a joke. The Masons or something, isn't it? Who gives a shit?'

'Yeah, yeah,' said Romeo, 'whatever. No one really knows what it is but we all know it goes on. They skulk around the lot of them and we all think it's a joke and they think that that's what we think, so they don't care. They cover it up with talk of card games and charity and rolling up their bleedin' trouser legs all that shit but there's weirder stuff than that goes on up at the big house. Fuckin' weirder stuff than that.'

'Such as?'

'Well my old man was well involved, wasn't he? And when he died, old Ephesian was round here the first day, you know what I'm saying? Soon as my old geezer had pegged it, the guy was round here like a flash. Which is what he just did with Ruthie across the garden. So, I'm thinking, it might just be for the same reason. He had something to collect from my house. And you know, I left him alone with my dad's stuff and he walked out carrying a bag. I thought it was all the old Masons shit, didn't really care. Left him to it. Now, old Ruthie didn't let him away with it so easily. She goes and finds what it is that Jonah had stashed away and what Ephesian's looking for. She doesn't give it to him and she hides it.'

He was smiling. Chardonnay Deluth stared back at him, getting quite sucked into the conspiracy.

'Unfortunately for the old Ruthmeister, I'm watching through my little bag of tricks up there. She leaves, I go and dig it up and now the thing that Ephisimo is looking for t'ain't in Rutheramma's freezer, it's in mine. And he can send as many of his henchmen round to the Ruthsmeller Pursuivant's house as he likes but he ain't finding shit.'

Drained his beer in one long gulp, belched massively and smiled knowingly across the table.

'I'm impressed,' she said, because she was the sort of girl who would be impressed by that kind of talk.

'Course you are, darlin'.'

'And now,' she said, 'you're going to tell me what it is that Jonah had in his freezer. Aren't you?'

He smiled again. Looked a bit cheeky. She loved it, because she was strangely besotted with Romeo McGhee. Most other people would have been taking a baseball bat to his head.

He stood up, opened the freezer door, lifted out the small bag and placed it on the table.

Chardonnay Deluth stared at it, not entirely sure what she was looking at. She lifted the bag, turned it over in her fingers, suddenly realised what it was. Others might have dropped it in horror but a huge smile came to her face. She looked at McGhee with wonder, the smile on his face increased ten fold.

'A human hand,' she said. 'Fuck me.'

He took another beer from the fridge and turned back.

'I could do that,' he said, smiling.

✄

Barney Thomson walked along the sea front. Had just passed the Crocodile Rock – the crocodile shaped rock that has been painted as a red, white and black crocodile since 1903, and which provided Elton John and Bernie Taupin much inspiration after a holiday to Millport in 1971 – and was promenading by Newton beach, looking out to sea, enjoying the smell of the air, the breeze in his face. A couple of dogs about, their owners in their wake, not many other people abroad. Just before six, late afternoon turning to early evening, the last hour of daylight soon to be lost under a layer of dark, low cloud.

He had left Igor and Ruth Harrison to it. Didn't think that Jacobs and the absurd Randolph would be back soon but had armed Ruth with his mobile number in case they returned even more heavy-handed than before. Thought, however, that there would be a night's reflection on their part before they hit upon another plan. He knew she'd be safe in Igor's arms, which was where he thought she would end up, and was literally where she already was, now that Barney was ten minutes away.

Barney smiled at the thought of Igor and a woman. Any woman. Good on the lad. Short, hunched, mute, deaf and downright ugly but there's nothing to get in the way of a beautiful personality.

Pondered briefly the human hand in Ruth's freezer but just didn't want to think about it. More death and murder and dismemberment. And so he allowed his thoughts to drift to Garrett Carmichael even though he knew she wasn't for him. Just not fated, in some way. Perhaps Agnes, his long gone ex-wife had been his fate. A dull twenty year marriage, that was all he could expect. There had been a couple of women in his brief sojourn in Edinburgh but he'd never really known what he'd wanted.

98

So much of human action is based on trying to achieve something new, because it seems so empty to sit on what you have. Yet where do you stop when it comes to relationships? With everything else, there's always another challenge. There's always another mountain; if not higher, then more remote or less well climbed or more dangerous. There's always another sea or ocean to circumnavigate or to row across or to dive to the bottom of. There's always another jungle to explore – or at least there will be for about another twenty years - another lost city to spend decades searching for. But with relationships, you so quickly come to the crunch and once you've made the commitment there's no moving on. Ever. Not without hurt and heartache and losing your insides. How much had he hurt Agnes?

'Thinking about women, eh?' said a voice.

Barney, sucked through a straw from melancholic reflections, looked round. An old fella sitting on a bench, eating a cheese sandwich, bottle of Strongbow at his side, watching the waves in amongst the boats. Barney had given him a *Justin Timberlake Superbowl XXXVIII* cut that morning.

'Aye,' he said, smiling ruefully. 'You guys all given some special psychic implant when you hit old geezerdom?'

Justin Timberlake indicated the sea with his cheese sandwich.

'We're all wise in the ways of the souls of men, who live by the sea,' he said.

Barney nodded.

'You know who said that?'

'Nope.'

'I just did,' said Timberlake laughing, and he took another bite of sandwich. Barney shook his head.

'Feels like I've come into a town of Aristotles and Nietzsches,' he said.

'Nietzsche was an arsehole,' said Timberlake.

'Aye,' said Barney. Everyone thinks that.

'You'll be going out with Garrett for dinner tonight then?'

Barney shrugged. I expect, he thought, that he knows what I had for my lunch too.

'Aye,' he said.

99

'She's not for you, though, you know that. Then you've got the whole mid-life crisis thing, which isn't really a mid-life crisis, it's beyond mid-life. Really, you're not too far from old geezerdom yourself.'

He laughed quietly, took the last of his cheese sandwich.

'That makes me feel better,' said Barney.

Swig of cider and the old fella indicated the sea again.

'With the exception of a good woman, all a mid-life crisis amounts to is the realisation that whenever you get what you want in life, you find out that you didn't really want it after all. You know who said that?'

Barney smiled.

'René Descartes?' he asked, playing the game.

'One of mine,' said Timberlake with that cheeky smile.

Barney smiled and began to walk off. Old men talking mince, everywhere he went. Timberlake allowed him a pace or two.

'Get by that and you'll be fine,' he said. Barney stopped but didn't turn. 'There's always suicide of course. The thought of suicide is a great source of comfort; with it a calm passage is to be made across many a bad night.'

Barney turned, smile gone, the weight of melancholy returning much more heavily than before.

'Nietzsche,' he said flatly.

'Aye,' said Timberlake. He drained the cider and winked. Barney stared at him for a second and then turned and walked on.

Suicide? It wasn't that bad.

Not yet, at any rate

19

Bar Room Blitz

Tony and Luigi were sitting in the bar of the George Hotel by the old pier at the bottom of Cardiff Street. Strategy to discuss, although Luigi was wishing he had strategy to discuss with a strategist, rather than with a monkey. There had been nothing obvious in the cathedral, which was as much as could be expected, but there must have been a clue somewhere. What they needed to do, Luigi thought, was take a bulldozer to the place.

'This is a nice wine,' said Tony, holding up the glass and checking it for length. 'Can't beat a good Italian.'

Luigi shook his head.

'My mother's piss tastes better than this shit,' he said. 'You're such a moron. You've been out of Italy two stinkin' minutes and you're more misty-eyed than Pavarotti.'

'This is a good wine,' protested Tony.

Luigi lifted his glass, swished it around, sniffed at it contemptuously, then took a substantial taste.

'Smell it,' he said.

Tony smelled it.

'You getting that?' asked Luigi.

'What?'

'Horse shit, that's what this smells of. Stinkin' horse shit. You'd think you hadn't seen Italy in years the way you go on. We were there yesterday morning for Chrissake's, and with any luck we'll be there again tomorrow night. Get a grip of yourself.

101

This is Britain. You think we export any decent wine to this lot? Are you kidding me? Why waste it on an entire nation of tasteless morons? These people eat French fries with pasta for crying out loud! Taste it again and when you do it, think of the wine we shared with the cardinal on Saturday evening.'

Tony took another sip of low-grade exported petroleum extract that passed for wine in Safeways.

'Jesus,' he said. 'This is terrible.'

'Thank you. I wouldn't use this shit in my bolognaise sauce.'

'Me neither.'

Luigi mouthed Tony's reply, mocking him.

'Bolognaise sauce. You never made a stinkin' bolognaise sauce in your life.'

'Oh yeah? Well, what about that time I nearly died eating your stupid bolognaise sauce. I was sick for a week. I was sick like a dog. I was so sick I thought my stomach was going to come out through my fuckin' eyeballs.'

'That wasn't bolognaise sauce, that was dog food made out of uncooked chicken offal. You're such a stinkin' idi...'

'Fuckin' Eye-ties,' said a voice from across the bar. Strong Glasgow accent, not so rare in these parts anymore.

Tony and Luigi looked round. There was a lad at the bar. Big, lumbering, meat and two veg short of a main course. Holding a pint, staring at the two emissaries from the Vatican with scorn. Mid-20's, denim jacket, ripped jeans, a suspect *Ewan MacGregor Trainspotting* cut, executed by an inexperienced hairdresser called Wendolene. Had been christened Donald Gallagher by his unsuspecting parents but had been known as Donaldinho for a number of years, by his own insistence.

'What did you say?' said Tony.

Luigi prodded Tony's arm. They weren't here to get into fights with morons in bars. They didn't have to keep entirely in the shadows but there was no need to attract attention to themselves any more than the fact of being two Italians in a small town in Scotland would anyway.

'Fuckin' Italian bampots,' said the guy. The barman glanced at him and wondered if it was too early to put a call through to Police Constable Gainsborough. It wasn't as if, after all, PC

102

Gainsborough wasn't expecting the call. 'Did yese get intae a fight at home and yese had tae run away?' said the guy. 'Wis that it? Yese were prob'ly shaggin' some'dy's missus, knowin' you lot. Or maybe,' and he turned around fully to face them, to lay the accusation wholly on the table, 'you were shaggin' each other and had tae get away fi' the lynch mob.'

Straight over Luigi's head. Couldn't have cared less. Tony, being a simple man 'n all, was on the verge of crashing over the table and attacking him. Luigi put his hand on Tony's arm.

'Oh, very nice,' sneered Donaldinho from behind his pint. 'Yese'll be shaggin' each other up the arse next. Course, the minute you see someone's back you probably want to stab them in it.'

Tony made to move, Luigi grabbed his shoulder, pulled him back down into his seat. Luigi did not yet suspect that this was a set-up but only the simple man rises to simple bait.

'Tony, sit down, shut up. Barman, are you just going to let this guy talk to your other customers like this?'

Donaldinho took a long drink from the trough.

'He's got a point,' said Murray the barman. 'Tuck it in, mate. There's no need for that kind of thing in here.'

There were two other occupied tables. A bloke and his wife, who looked worried by the whole business and were on the point of leaving; and a couple of old women on their annual escape from Glasgow, who were excited by the thought of getting to watch an actual wrestling match, likely with real blood.

'Is that no' just typical,' said Donaldinho. 'Hidin' behind others. Fuckin' brave the pair o' ye. Fuckin' arse bandits.'

'Enough, mate, or I'll call the polis,' said the barkeep.

Donaldinho glanced at him, then turned back. Luigi was staring at the floor, concerned only that Tony did not do anything stupid. Tony was agitating to go on the rampage. He may have been an out and out idiot and he may have been much much smaller than his adversary but he was more than capable of killing him.

He had a gun in his jacket.

'Two bum-fluffs the gither,' said Donaldinho, 'too wee and scaredy tae dae anythin' but sit there. Nae wunner we shat a' o'er yese in the war.'

Luigi tugged at Tony's shoulder, Tony wriggled free and came at Donaldinho like a tank.

Donaldinho cracked his pint glass off the edge of the bar, spraying beer over the barman, the glass pinging around the room. He turned and met Tony full on. Fists and feet and glass met in a fantastic crunch. A looping parabola of blood spurted instantly into the air.

The couple, who had up until now been quietly enjoying their gin and tonics, left hurriedly. The old women leant forward, hands clapping with glee.

'My money's on the Italian lad, Marion,' said one.

'Ach, away and bile yer heid, Nella,' said the other.

Donaldinho and Tony's heads met with a crunch, blood was everywhere, although it was impossible to see whose it was. The barkeep stood well clear, Luigi knew he could not get involved. At least one of them had to stay out of trouble. In any case, he knew that Tony would not need help.

And, as he took another sip of disgusting wine, the obviousness of the set-up finally hit him. He smacked his hand off his forehead, then he rose, pushed the table away from him and, avoiding the brawling couple in the middle of the bar, walked hurriedly up the stairs to get his things from the room.

20

The Well Of Life

The sea front was quiet and although Barney was a good distance from the George Hotel, he was aware of the stramash as Tony, the Vatican's less than holy ambassador, was dragged out by Police Constable Gainsborough. Tony had been disarmed and Donaldinho had been allowed to skulk away into the shadows – or, more accurately, to skulk away to the hospital, as his broken beer glass had been turned against him by his more expertly brutal opponent. Tony had belatedly realised what had occurred earlier to Luigi but there was nothing to be done about it now other than sitting in his cell until the inevitable call came through from a higher authority to have him released.

Barney watched for a few seconds, vaguely curious, then turned back to the red door. Hesitated, then lifted the brass door knocker – a wonderfully hideous gargoyle with a double nose and a bit of a *Boris Johnson* – and let it drop. A moment's pause, then the sound of two pairs of scampering feet. The door was pulled open and Hoagy and Ella stood against the wall forming a line of two, backs straight, arms by their sides.

Hoagy saluted and said, 'You have permission to come aboard, sir!'

Barney smiled, returned the salute, then stooped to inspect the troops as he went by. He straightened Hoagy's shirt and tugged at Ella's collar, which had her in fits of giggles.

'All proper and correct,' said Barney. 'Stand down.'

They both saluted, Hoagy's accompanied by a lop-sided wink.

'Where's your mum?' asked Barney.

'Upstairs,' said Hoagy. 'In the bathroom doing girl's stuff. But there's no amount of make-up going to help her lose weight.'

Barney nodded. Five year-olds are bad enough, much worse when they're going on fifteen, as most of them seem to be now.

'I heard that!' shouted Garrett Carmichael from upstairs. 'I've had enough of your cheek.'

Hoagy looked innocent and shrugged his shoulders. Ella shook her head disapprovingly and said, 'He's just a little fuck.'

They're coming on faster these days, thought Barney.

Like the wind, Garrett Carmichael appeared at the top of the stairs. Towel wrapped turban-like around her hair, red trousers, nothing on top but a black bra. Barney turned away.

'What did you say?'

'I said he's a little fuck,' Ella replied. Very matter of fact.

Garrett came steaming down to the bottom of the stairs. Barney glanced at her, looked at Hoagy – who gave him a *you get everything in this house* look – then stared at the ceiling.

'That,' said Garrett, holding Ella's hand, 'was a very, very bad word to say. Don't let me ever hear that again. Where did you hear it? It's very, very naughty. Do you understand?'

Domestic bliss, thought Barney. Wherever you look in family life there's usually something to support the way of the wanderer.

Ella looked blameless and perplexed.

'I just said he was a little fuck,' she protested innocently.

'Right!' said Garrett angrily, 'I told you not to say it! It's bad! Go and stand in the bathroom until you're ready to say sorry.'

One and a half seconds, then the three year-old bottom lip appeared and she burst into tears. Garrett let out a huge exasperated and annoyed sigh, then looked at Barney.

'You deal with it,' she said, and stormed back up the stairs.

'Mummy!' wailed Ella, as her mother disappeared from view. 'Mummy!'

Barney looked down at this scene of child carnage and felt glad that these spawn were not, and never would be, his.

Hoagy shrugged his shoulders.

106

'Mum's on,' he said. 'That's what dad used to say. Not sure what it means.'

That, my grown up little friend, thought Barney, is something that will never change.

'Can you explain it to me?' he asked.

'Wee man,' said Barney, raising his voice over the general tumult of Ella's rejection issues, 'you must be joking.'

The front door was knocked and then Miranda Donaldson bustled in, looked at Barney with grave suspicion, ignored Hoagy and headed straight for the greeting wean.

'What's the matter with you, darlin'? she said, bending down next to Ella.

'Mum got mad, 'cause Ella called me a little fuck,' said Hoagy.

Miranda Donaldson turned and looked at her grandson, raised the old grandma eyebrow at him and then look back at Ella.

'Well,' she said, voice very low and comforting, 'what was your mother thinking? It's not like you were wrong, now, is it?'

Barney surveyed the scene of domestic ecstasy, turned away, wandered into the sitting room, parked himself in a big comfy chair and began the long wait for Garrett Carmichael.

✂

Bartholomew Ephesian twitched. Took another long drink of Lagavulin. Grip on the glass so tight it was in danger of breaking. Head full of the kind of bloody, dark thoughts that always came to him when things were not going according to plan.

Jacobs had passed onto him Ruth Harrison's reluctance to share the required information, as well as the unexpected intervention of the Barbershop Duet. He hadn't known Barney would be trouble the instant he'd arrived but any able-bodied man, when none was required, was liable to be a problem. That Igor had stood up for Ruth Harrison was a complete shock to him but that was because he expected little of Igor. What he did not need at this stage, however, were two more people to be dealt with.

Then there was the matter of the amateurish set-up at the George Hotel, leading to the incarceration of Tony Angelotti.

107

He was incensed by the fact that Gainsborough had thought he could deal with any problem himself but much more concerned that there were Italians on the island. Ephesian did not doubt for one second where they had come from and who had sent them. And there was one of them at large, which meant that the necessary phone calls would be made and the one who was currently locked up in the tiny cell behind the police station would be out before Gainsborough had had time to write his stupid name in crayon across the top of the arrest report form.

There was also the matter of inducting his son into the brotherhood, something else which was getting him more agitated. As was the arrival of the corpulent Ping Phat.

'I can't trust Randolph to commit the murder,' said Ephesian suddenly, addressing the other problem that was aggravating him. 'I can barely trust him to go to the toilet when he needs to.'

'Don't worry,' said the voice behind him. 'I'll take care of it.'

Ephesian knew he could trust Jacobs with everything and when he was unable to achieve an objective, such as that afternoon at the house of Ruth Harrison, Ephesian would never blame him.

'Good,' said Ephesian. 'And perhaps it would be appropriate to take care of Randolph at the same time. He knows too much.'

'Yes, sir' said Jacobs.

Ephesian turned round, away from the dusk and the dying of the day over the islands to the west.

'Ping Phat,' he said, beginning to rattle off the list of problems, 'the item in the possession of Ruth Harrison, the two bloody barbers and the Italians. We can hardly just kill them all, however convenient it would be. I don't like mess,' he concluded.

'Yes, sir,' said Jacobs.

Ephesian drained his glass, held it out for Jacobs to take from him and refill with three fresh ice cubes.

'Tonight,' he said, 'we need to collect the item from the cathedral. No messing about, you go there, you remove it. We need to get it up here. The Italians will be all over the place. Take care of it.'

'Yes, sir,' he replied, handing over the refilled glass.

'Before that, though, you should see Ruth Harrison. Be brutal. Short, swift, vicious. Don't mess around. Thomson is seeing the lawyer tonight, so we need only worry about Igor. Just take him out. I'll have a word with Gainsborough in case anyone gives him a call.'

'Yes, sir,' said Jacobs, dutifully.

'We'll need to put the word round about the Italians. It'll almost be worthwhile releasing the one we have, as he'll lead us straight to the other one. It might be all right just to keep an eye on them, we can see how close they're getting. Make a few calls.'

'Yes, sir.'

Ephesian took a sip from his third whisky of the late afternoon and held his hands out to the side.

'Businesslike. We need to be businesslike. The problems are mounting, we need to address them and put them to bed.'

'Very good, sir.'

'Ping Phat will need to wait until tomorrow.'

'Very good, sir.'

'And the same for the small matter of the murder. Tomorrow night, but you know all about that.'

The two men stared across the room, wondering how bloody it was all going to become. It was always so much easier when you could take care of things through gentle persuasion. Money talked, of course, but Ephesian never liked to talk with money. A little intimidation was the best option and it was always regrettable when he had to go further.

Needs must, he thought to himself. The only way to deal with Ping Phat was violence. And a murder had to be committed for the ceremony to take place. They were the necessary acts of bloodshed. The other work could be kept low key but if that wasn't possible then Jacobs would do what he had to.

'It'll be a pleasure, sir,' said Jacobs.

Of that, at least, Ephesian was certain. Jacobs may have had the whole Jeeves vibe going but the man was a sadistic, callous bastard. Who could nail a Lagavulin with ice.

109

He took another long drink from the well and his head twitched involuntarily as his thoughts turned back to Gainsborough and his clumsy attempts to detain the Italians.

21

The Third Constant

'So, there are three things, not two.'

Barney forked another piece of *chicken in strawberry yogurt with a mythology of thyme*, took a sip of a curious Italian white with insinuations of lavender and an aura of Vatican II, and raised the universal eyebrow of curiosity.

'You see,' she said, finishing off a mouthful of *cretaceous beef on a platter of sangfroid*, 'the common philosophy is that there are two principles. Right wrong, yin yang, equal opposite, good evil, black white, you know how it is.'

He nodded. Amateur philosophy. Can't go five minutes in the world without coming across it. Everybody thinks, after all.

'And your theory is?' he asked. Impaled a piece of broccoli which had been cooked to perfection. (The broccoli had been termed *100% steamed alleviated legume verte*.)

'There's a third thing,' she said.

'The grey,' suggested Barney.

'Not exactly,' she said. 'I call it the Garrett.'

He paused with the fork on its way to his mouth.

'The Garrett?' he asked.

'Yeah,' she said. 'The Equal, the Opposite and the Garrett.'

'You named this thing, whatever it is, after yourself?'

'Why not?' she said, no hint of shame. 'They all do it. Einstein's Theory of Relativity, Newton's Laws of Physics. What's the difference?'

'Come on,' said Barney, 'that's totally different.'

111

'How?' she said, a little aggrieved. She was used to people happily sucking in her Garrett theory without question because she was the hottest woman in town and most of them weren't listening anyway. Barney was forlorn and stuck somewhere down a pit of gloom and just wasn't buying into the allure of Garrett Carmichael which fascinated most of the men on the island.

'Einstein,' he said, 'was a guy with an enormous moustache who came up with a theory of relativity. He just said, you know, this is my theory, what d'you think? Everybody else said, well that sounds like a good theory and started talking about it, and other people said, yeah that is a good theory I like that, whose is it, and the first people said, it's Einstein's, so it became known as Einstein's theory.'

She looked at him as if he was talking in strange tongues.

'Same for Newton,' he continued, ignoring the strange tongues look. 'It wasn't like either of them named some *thing* after themselves. Newton didn't call the apple Newton.'

'A newton is an amount of force,' she said, with a bit of a duh-huh look about her.

'Aye, but it wasn't flippin' Newton who named it that. It was scientists later on.'

'Well, Einstein then,' she said. '$E=mc^2$, what about that?'

'You think the E in $E=mc^2$ means Einstein?'

'Of course it does,' she said sharply, heading swiftly onto the defensive.

'Einstein$=mc^2$? You think Einstein's theory of relativity was about him personally. That he was equal to mc^2? What d'you think mc^2 actually is? Muscle times colon squared? Mince times cheese squared? What exactly is it you've always thought the guy was made of?'

'Are you finished?'

He lanced a piece of chicken and nodded. There was a feisty spark to the conversation but not in a Katharine Hepburn/Cary Grant kind of a way, where you knew they were going to get together at the end of the movie. This was edgier and meaner, genuine annoyance behind the acerbity.

'The equation is not about Einstein himself,' she said. 'Einstein, as a term, refers to a unit of energy or something. Just because I'm not a physics expert doesn't make me a total idiot.'

Barney stared at his plate. Not entirely trusting himself to look at her, although it wasn't as if he was laughing.

Women. Had this been a guy in the shop he would have let him away with anything. Einstein, Newton, whatever. He would have let him say that the moon made a massively elliptical orbit of the earth and at times was further away than Mars. But he couldn't sit here and let Garrett Carmichael away with it.

'E,' he said, 'means energy. M is mass, c represents the speed of light in a vacuum.'

A passing waiter, on his way to another table carrying two plates of *customised pork fillets in a clingfilm of four cheeses*, caught Garrett's eye and nodded.

'He's right,' said the waiter. '2.997925×10^8 metres per second.'

Barney gave him a glance, thinking that that hadn't really helped. Garrett looked straight through him, the waiter moved on. She turned back to Barney, a little put out. There was one of the fundamental building blocks of her life laid bare. Like finding out about Santa or the tooth fairy.

'I'm still calling it the Garrett,' she said.

'Very well,' replied Barney. 'I mean, I'm not saying you can't, because it's not like there aren't examples of guys who have done that. Although, usually people who name things after themselves are like weird dictators and stuff. Pol Pot named a cooking implement after himself for example.'

She was hurt. He smiled at his own joke, but it wasn't that kind of discussion.

'Thanks,' she said.

'So what is it?' he asked casually, in order to move on.

'What d'you mean?' she asked, although she knew. She felt like the entire evening's conversation was drawing to a close, even though they still had *caramelised profiteroles with a sea cow of raspberry custard* to come.

'The Garrett,' said Barney. 'What is it? The thing that is neither equal nor opposite?'

113

'Well I'm not telling you now.'

'Come on,' he said, although he knew they were well past the point when she would be prepared to discuss anything.

She had moved on to that place where words were no longer needed. Barney shrugged, took another drink, and wondered whether the evening would ever recover.

✂

Jacobs knocked on the door of Ruth Harrison's house. Had not been at all concerned about dealing with Igor, yet had been happy enough to see him walking on Shore Street, having left the Harrison house a few minutes earlier. She had hoped he might stay the night but things had taken an uncomfortable turn after his condolences had turned from the sympathetic to the erotic, and the new widow and the deaf mute hunchback had made love very passionately. Once the dust had settled and all the required clothing had been put back in place, the atmosphere had been a little uneasy and Igor had excused himself to go and get a nice cup of tea, ignoring the inference that Ruth was incapable of making one.

That the door opened at all was a surprise to Jacobs. He had expected that she would look to see who was waiting and then pretend to be either out or dead. And having opened the door he expected her to be intimidated and wary.

'Mr Jacobs,' she said, instead, 'come in, come in, quickly,' and she stood back to let him enter.

Jacobs walked cautiously into the house. All the lights were on, and he felt very warm in his overcoat and scarf. She closed the door behind her and stared at him, standing at the foot of the stairs.

Suddenly he realised why she wasn't as fearful as he'd been expecting. She was not alone in the house, as he had presumed she would be. The barber must still be here.

Jacobs glanced at the stairs, his mind whirring into action. That presented a whole new set of problems. He believed, wrongly, that Barney Thomson was of much greater metal than Igor. Believed, correctly, however, that there would be far more notice paid if something should happen to the new barber than if

114

it happened to his hunchbacked sidekick. You know, if Batman ever got killed, complete uproar. But Robin? Who'd care?

'Listen,' said Ruth, indicating the landing above.

'Imagine you have protection, do you, Mrs Harrison?' he said coldly.

'What?' she asked.

Above them, footfalls padded back and forth, a few in one direction, a pause, then the same number back. Another pause, and then once more into the routine. A few steps, pause, a few steps, pause.

'What is he doing?' asked Jacobs.

He was a prosaic man. As with his employer, he liked things straightforward, everything laid out in front of him, so that problems could be seen and dealt with.

'I don't know,' said Ruth, 'that's the thing that's scaring me.'

She hesitated, staring at him as if she was looking for Jacobs to protect her, rather than being in need of protection from him.

'Before,' she continued, 'he was just going to the toilet. Now, Jesus, I don't know! It's driving me insane. God, what is he doing? He's been at it since just after Igor left.'

The sentence trailed off at the end, as the possibilities dawned on her. Jonah had been restlessly padding back and forth since Igor left. He knew! He knew what she and Igor had just done.

'Have you spoken to him?' asked Jacobs, flexing his fingers, frustrated at her curious behaviour.

'No!' she said, and she took a step back, so that she was pressed up against the front door. 'I can't do that. I don't know if he can speak anyway, you know. I haven't heard him.'

Jacobs studied her. Her face was drawn and pale, she looked far more intimidated and frightened than before.

'I thought you said Igor had left?' said Jacobs, questioning in his mind the fact that he'd seen Igor ten minutes previously.

'Igor did leave,' she protested.

'So it's the barber upstairs? He can talk, can't he?'

'What?' said Ruth, still not attuned to the fact that Jacobs had no idea what was going on.

'I'll go and have a word,' said Jacobs with much irritation.

She looked at him wide-eyed, but said nothing. More fool you, she thought, and her only concern was that something would happen to him up there and he'd never come back down. Then she would once more be left alone, at the mercy of her dead husband.

Jacobs turned and ran up the stairs. No messing, straight in for the fight, hackles raised, ready for action. He stopped at the top of the stairs, looked around. The barber must be hiding.

And then, in his two second pause, he heard it. He heard *them*. The slow pads of the footfalls on the carpet. He listened to them go up to the bathroom door, pause and then turn back to the door of Jonah's office. He stood there for a full minute, as the feet minced forlornly back and forth. The pragmatist in him studied the floor, wondering what was making the noise, although he did not venture forward. Hairs stood on the back of his neck.

He turned and walked slowly back down the stairs. Ruth remained where he had left her, back pressed against the door.

'What is that?' asked Jacobs. 'Some pathetic trick you've got set up to make me think there's someone else in the house?' He knew it wasn't that but he needed a rational explanation.

'It's Jonah,' she said. 'He's haunting me.'

Jacobs stared coldly at her. A large part of him wanted to deny what she had said but he knew she was telling the truth. The ugly sensation which had crawled all over his body told him so. He had been standing listening to the spirit of Jonah Harrison.

Bartholomew Ephesian wasn't going to believe any of that.

'Where's the hand, Mrs Harrison?' he asked.

She appeared surprised that he would change the subject.

'The hand?' she said.

'We need it back. It's not yours to keep.'

'Someone's stolen it,' she said, as if Jacobs ought to have known that already.

'What do you mean?'

Jacobs could feel the anger rise inside him, the anger which he always managed to channel. You had to use anger well or it worked against you. This was his strength. He had the temper and the passion but he knew how to use it.

116

'It's gone. I found it this morning in the freezer. Well, I didn't know Jonah kept anything like that. I panicked a bit…'

She stopped and listened as there was a temporary pause in the noise from above, and then inevitably it started again, one slow padding footstep after another.

'I hid it at the bottom of the garden. Besides the roses. After you came earlier, I took Igor and that barber out to show them. It was gone. No idea where it went.'

'Is there any way they could have got to it before you showed it to them?'

Ruth Harrison tried but she wasn't really capable of any kind of clear or concise thought.

'I suppose,' she said.

Jacobs wondered if there was any point in pressing her further. However, he had been given enough of an idea to draw the conclusion that the hand was now in the possession of one of the barber shop employees. He moved towards the door.

'Whose hand is it anyway?' asked Ruth, realising he was about to leave and not wanting him to.

'I'm leaving now,' he said. 'Could you stand away from the door, please?'

She moved slowly.

'Don't go,' she said. 'Please, you can't leave me with that.'

Jacobs turned and stared back up the stairs at the gentle, horrible pad of Jonah Harrison's footsteps, felt a shiver curse its way down his spine, and then he gave her another look of cold contempt, pulled open the door and walked out into the night.

22

Archimedes & The Dog

'You sure this is wise?' asked Chardonnay Deluth.

'I know what I'm doing,' said Romeo McGhee.

She glanced at him in the way that she usually did. That looking at him like he was an idiot way that most women in relationships with men quickly perfect.

'Romeo,' she said, 'you never know what you're doing.'

'It's cool, baby,' he said, words just a little incongruous with the meely-mouthed west of Scotland accent.

'The man is going to tear you to shreds,' she said, as they opened the unlocked gate and began walking the short distance up the driveway to the big house.

Bartholomew Ephesian would have loved a huge driveway, snaking its way through trees and past lawns but there just hadn't been the ground available. Certainly not on the west side, with the view out over Bute and Arran, and if there had been space on the east side, why bother when all you had to look at was dull mainland, a large dock and a nuclear power station?

'He can't tear us to shreds,' said McGhee. 'He tears us to shreds, he doesn't get the stupid hand, does he? We have him in our power. We have total dominion over him.'

Chardonnay Deluth gave him another idiot look, then unconsciously began to hang back as they approached the front door. He was the definite salesman here. She had no idea what she was supposed to be, other than the stupid patsy who had allowed herself to be talked into coming along.

McGhee gave her a smile, acknowledging the fact that she was hanging back.

'It's cool, babe,' he said. 'Totally cool.'

✂

Bartholomew Ephesian looked down on the bleak waters of the firth. Checked his watch and wondered how Jacobs would be getting on with his list of errands. A man he could count on but still the overall responsibility was his, he was the one charged with changing the course of history. And history was what mattered.

The doorbell rang and he turned quickly and suspiciously away from the view. No one ever came to his house in the evening. The night before his destiny, this would be no coincidence and he suddenly wondered if this might be Ping Phat himself.

He rested the whisky glass on the desktop and walked through the house. Visitors were rare and when they came they would be greeted by Jacobs. This was the first time in over three years that Ephesian would actually be answering his own door.

He stopped at the door, breathed deeply, cracked his fingers, settled the nerves and opened up.

He stared at the necks of his visitors. Recognised the man as the son of one of their former members; did not know the woman.

'What?' he asked brusquely.

'We need to talk,' said Romeo McGhee, and presumptuously made a forward move.

Ephesian made a movement to cover more of the doorway, nervousness having been replaced by scorn. McGhee stopped just short of touching him. Ephesian hated people touching him.

'I doubt it,' said Ephesian. 'I'm a busy man, Mr McGhee.'

'Not too busy to see me,' said McGhee.

'On the contrary,' retorted Ephesian, and he took a step back and began to close the door, his annoyance far outweighing any vague curiosity. McGhee automatically stuck his foot forward, crossing the boundary into the house.

Ephesian's head twitched.

119

'I'm going to count to five, Mr McGhee,' he growled, 'and then I'm calling the police.'

Another twitch, an intake of breath as he controlled his temper.

'One...,' he began.

'I have the hand,' said McGhee quickly, cutting off the drama of the count. 'Jonah Harrison's frozen hand.'

Ephesian was, sure enough, stopped dead in his boots. He eased the door away from McGhee's foot.

'Now I'm beginning to understand why you pitched up at my place the day after my old man croaked.'

Ephesian stared hard at McGhee's chin, let his eyes move on to Chardonnay Deluth and the smirk on her lips. Always funny, she was thinking, to see an over-stuffed balloon like Ephesian get put to the sword. Maybe McGhee wasn't so stupid after all.

'What is it you want?' asked Ephesian.

McGhee hesitated, enjoying the moment. For all the bluster he'd been showing his girlfriend, he'd been walking up the hill to Ephesian's house full of anxiety and completely lacking in confidence. Had surprised himself by being able to balls it out. But now the anxiety had disappeared in smoke and his self-confidence had arrived with an $89billion Senate-approved budget. Time to stop and smell the roses.

Ephesian recognised what he was doing, was happy for McGhee to be so full of himself. Gave him time to think, knew that McGhee's guard would drop as his self-assurance increased.

'First of all,' said McGhee, 'I would appreciate it if you would invite myself and my good lady here into your house and have your man attend to us. I think a single malt would suit me just fine. Chardonnay, what can the man get you?'

Ephesian turned his eyes on her, the gaze staring right through the centre of her face. Mind turning, already formulating how he would deal with them.

'I'm not sure,' said Chardonnay, warming with every second to her boyfriend.

For Ephesian, however, nothing had really changed. Two minutes earlier he'd been in a position of needing to extract the

120

package from Ruth Harrison. Now he was needing to extract it from Romeo McGhee.

'Come in,' said Ephesian, looking directly at Chardonnay Deluth's nose, 'and we'll see what we can do for you.'

✂

Igor sat on a green bench across the lawn from George Street, looking out at the dark sea. Coat wrapped tightly around himself, but still feeling the cold. Needed to be inside but didn't yet want to go back to the small room that had been his home for five years. Old and worn green carpet, wallpaper of a rich maroon, faded to an unattractive brown, battered lampshades, a frayed rug, and a small television in the corner, which was perfect for watching *It's A Wonderful Life* and *Mrs Miniver*, but hopeless for *Independence Day* and *The Return of the King*.

There was something in the air, something more than the smell of the sea and the wind which worked its way through the islands from the Atlantic. The town was about to change in some strange way which he could not foresee. But suddenly things seemed to be happening, in a place where months and years could go by with barely any incident of note.

Maybe it was time to leave, something he had thought before, even in less troubled times. But for him, it hardly seemed an option. He was accepted here, the people were used to him, he had his job, however mundane. To go someplace else, would be to walk into a new town and start all over again, people staring and muttering and judging and talking about him, not behind his back but right there in front of him. The way that the people of this town had not done for a long time. He at least appreciated that, no matter how low the regard in which he was held by many of the townsfolk.

'You look lonely.'

He didn't turn immediately. Recognised the voice. Gently Ferguson, barwoman at the Kendall.

He finally looked at her and shrugged in that uncomfortable way of his.

'Arf,' he said. It's all relative, he thought. A person sitting on their own looking out at the sea need not be lonely; he had never

121

once in his life been in a large crowd of people and not been lonely. Maybe I exude loneliness.

'I hear you,' said Gently Ferguson. 'I can stand in the bar every night and feel that I'm the loneliest person on the planet.'

Igor turned towards her. Felt aware of his hump. She looked out to sea, felt his eyes on her, although it was different to all those evenings in the bar when she was aware of the eyes of men.

'Sometimes I think it's impossible to be lonely when you're surrounded by nature,' she said. 'You don't need people to feel part of...,' and she hesitated, then indicated the sea and the rocks and the islands in the bay and said, 'this.'

Igor followed her gaze back out to the water, felt her shiver next to him.

'It's cold,' she said.

'Arf,' said Igor.

'I know,' she replied, 'I need to get inside.'

Igor didn't want her to go yet. When she goes, he thought, I'll be lonely, where I wasn't two minutes ago. Such is the way of the poet.

'You shouldn't sit out in this,' she said, and then, still without looking at him asked, 'would you like to come back for a cup of tea?'

Igor stared at the pale profile in the chill night air.

'Arf,' he said.

She smiled, turned and embraced him with a look.

'Lovely,' she said. 'Let's go.'

23

Æs Triplex

Jacobs turned the key in the lock, opened the large wooden door and stepped into the small cathedral porch, closing the door behind him. Paused for a second, enjoying the still darkness. Checked his watch. Wasn't sure what Roosevelt would be doing but no need to trouble him with this. It wasn't as if Ephesian didn't possess a key to every lock on the island.

He opened the inner door and walked through to the nave. He let his eyes become adjusted to the dark, enjoying the stillness. Took a few steps into the nave, his footsteps sounding clear and sharp, unlike the dull pads of the ghost of Jonah Harrison. Then the thought of the ghost had him looking over his shoulder into dark corners, before the pragmatist in him was able to dismiss it.

He was about to collect the greatest, most sought after artefact of the last two thousand years. This was no time to be afraid of the likes of Jonah Harrison, even if Fatman was dead.

He stopped at the font, which stood in the bottom corner, opposite the door. The instructions had come from Lawton, the one who had finally been able to crack the code. That it had been Lawton who had achieved the momentous breakthrough was of the utmost regret to Ephesian and Jacobs but at least he had proved to be as pliable as Ephesian had required him to be.

They had concentrated so much of their searching on the more elaborately decorated chancel, rather than the naïve and simplistic nave. It had seemed obvious since the search had begun in 1976 that this was where the object of glory would have been hidden. The chancel with its beautifully enriched walls of encaustic tiles, the wonderfully painted and raftered ceiling, the Bishop's Chair, the beautiful stone screen separating it from the nave.

Or if the original members of the *Prieure* had been intent on the chancel as cover, distracting from the more obscure hiding place, surely they would have chosen the small ante-chapel, with the organ and the small stained glass windows. *I am Gabriel, that stand in the presence of God.* Or the original Chapter House, now the Lady Chapel, tucked away at the back.

Even when they had allowed themselves to search the nave, somehow the font had seemed too obvious and had not drawn them in. The three part painting in the middle of the nave, the worship of the lamb, that had interested them. As had the painting above the pulpit, a dying Christ on the ground below the cross, supported by two chubby little cupids, the desperate Mary imploring the Lord at his side. They seemed to hold some clues, as the font never did. The font, beautifully carved and craving attention, seemed to deny secrecy.

Not that it had never been subjected to investigation but when it had, it had not yielded any answers.

Jacobs shivered again, glanced once more over his shoulder. He had been in the cathedral many times, he had searched for the answer possibly more than any of the twelve. Yet had his examinations of the font ever been more than rudimentary?

He shook the shiver away. Back in the real world, back to doing what had to be done. It was Lawton who had discovered the answer, it was Lawton and Ephesian who had come to the cathedral to establish that he was right and to, at last, uncover the Holy Grail itself. They had left it in the cathedral, however, intent on collecting it on the evening of the ceremony. The presence of the two Italians had forced Jacobs down here to collect the Grail earlier than anticipated.

He ran his hands over the body of the font. Eight sided, on every second side a carving of one of the apostles. St Luke, the bull; St Mark, the lion; St John, the eagle; St Matthew, the man. Many who had looked at it had thought it peculiar and many were those who had pressed and prodded and shoved and tinkered. The carvings had seemed solid, however, none had really believed that this would be the way in.

Jacobs was aware of the sound of his breathing in the cold stillness. He took the torch from his pocket and looked over the carvings.

The clue had been in an innocent section of *Virginibus Puerisque*, by a former Grand Master of the *Prieure de Millport*, Robert Louis Stevenson. *Æs Triplex*. Triple brass, a strong defence. No clues within the text, just the nature of the piece and the title and the well known association between the author and the society. When it had occurred to Lawton it had been instinctive and had easily fallen into place.

Doing as instructed, Jacobs placed the torch in his mouth, shone the light on the font, reached round the sides and pressed the wings of John and Mark, and with his knee, pushed at the wings of Luke. In the still darkness he heard the small click in the inner workings of the font. His heart quickened.

He walked round to the other side, to the carving of St Matthew, a man amongst three beasts. Even now it still wasn't evident, but Lawton and Ephesian had worked it out eventually so Jacobs knew what to do. He pressed down on St Matthew's head and then, with a sudden small jerk and a grinding of stone, the carving moved out of the body of the font, revealing the hidden drawer.

Jacobs, throat dry, hands shaking, shone the torch into the little niche which had opened up before him.

It was empty.

He stuck his hand in, felt around the tiny space.

'Shit,' he muttered. 'Shit!' Nothing.

The lights came on behind him.

Jacobs turned, the shock of the interruption showing, heart beating wildly. An instant, however, and he had himself under control. Closed the drawer and walked forward.

'Father Roosevelt, I looked for you,' he said calmly.

'How did you get in here, Mr Jacobs?' asked Roosevelt.

'I had something to collect for Mr Ephesian,' answered Jacobs, ignoring the question.

'You won't find it,' said Roosevelt calmly.

125

'Why not?' asked Jacobs, not bothering with any pretence as to why he might have been there. Roosevelt was part of the brotherhood, he knew what was required from here.

'Because it has already been removed,' said Roosevelt.

'What d'you mean?' demanded Jacobs. 'Who by?'

'Mr Lawton,' said Roosevelt. 'He came about an hour ago and informed me that he had to collect the article for Mr Ephesian. In light of that, perhaps you would like to explain your actions.'

'Let's get this straight,' said Jacobs, with no intention of explaining anything. 'Lawton came here, he told you that Mr Ephesian had sent him, he removed the artefact and left?'

'Mr Jacobs, I'm not sure I appreciate your manner.'

'Did you see him take it from the font? Did you see him?'

Roosevelt hesitated but he was intimidated by Jacobs, as were most people on the island.

'He allowed me to open the hidden drawer,' said Roosevelt. 'I held the Grail of Christ in my hands, I touched the very cup that held the wine and the blood of Jesus, I felt the...'

'Whatever,' said Jacobs. 'But you gave this to Lawton and he left saying he was going to give it to Mr Ephesian? That's it?'

'Yes,' said Roosevelt. 'That's it.'

Jacobs looked at his watch. It could be that Lawton had taken the chalice round to Ephesian's house but he knew he wouldn't have. Ephesian, as Grand Master of the Brotherhood, had given Lawton a direct order not to remove the Grail from the cathedral.

Jacobs had been sent out to collect two items and he would be returning with neither. Ephesian would be unhappy but he needed to speak to him before making a move on Lawton. He must return, give Ephesian the facts, and take further instruction.

He pushed past Roosevelt and walked quickly from the cathedral.

126

24

Archie Gemmill

The Holy Grail. The cup used by Christ at the Last Supper, the same cup in which Joseph of Arimathea caught Christ's blood. Taken by Joseph to France and then to England. The object of the great quests by King Arthur's knights. Or perhaps the Grail is something more intangible, a more ethereal concept. There are those who say the Grail is the bloodline of Christ himself, that it was not just the goblet that was taken by Joseph to France, but the very family of Christ. His wife, Mary Magdelene, and who knows how many offspring? This theory has Jesus not as the son of God but as the descendant of the kings of Israel, with the secret protected by knights and societies through the ages, waiting to explode the myth of Christ's divinity and to restore his descendants onto the throne of, well, who knows exactly. Maybe Israel, maybe a united Europe, maybe any old dodgy African republic they can get hold of.

The Grail, by these standards, is not a single item but a mass of documentation and artefacts and people. And yet, for all the museum of articles that make up the existence of the Grail, there is still at the heart of it, the small wooden cup. As seen in *Indiana Jones & the Last Crusade*.

And, whatever the truth of the nature of the Grail, the small wooden cup at its centre was exactly what had been hidden for one hundred and fifty years in the small compartment in the Cathedral of the Isles in Millport. It had been moved and then placed in the middle of the heavy mahogany table in Augustus

Lawton's dining room. However the cup was no longer there; it had been stolen from Lawton, shortly after he himself had taken it from the Cathedral of the Isles.

Lawton had devoted years to the search and when, just a week earlier, he had made the breakthrough, it had been the defining moment of his life. A sense of duty had foolishly made him report his triumph to Ephesian, something which he'd quickly regretted. He had wrestled for a few days with the instruction not to remove the Grail but finally he had found the desire too great, the need to bring his life's work to fruition too pressing and he had visited the cathedral and taken the Grail back to his home.

Which was where he now remained, even though the Grail itself had been removed. He had not relinquished it lightly but eventually the blows which had rained down on his head had overcome him, he had collapsed, and his attacker had lain down the implement, a large brass sculpture of Archie Gemmill's goal against Holland in the 1978 World Cup Finals.

So, as Lawton lay unconscious, blood caked to the side of his head and pooled on the parquet flooring, the Grail was gone.

✂

Barney Thomson closed the door of the shop, turned the key, crossed the road to the shore side of the street and began walking along beside the white sea wall, face turned towards the breeze and the salty smell of the waves.

His night might have been considered a disappointment but he hadn't known what he was looking for. To end up in Garrett Carmichael's bed? Not at all; that was for others on the island, not him. Interesting conversation and a nice bit of food? That, generally, is the best you can expect from any dinner. The conversation had been curious and had muddled almost to a standstill after the Einstein incident; the food had been adequate. Barney had slid into some strange non-specific gloom and had lost interest. Consumed by thoughts of his impending mid-life depression, he'd suddenly found himself in need of time alone, to contemplate the great beyond.

So, as the evening had progressed towards dessert and coffee, he had felt the desire to talk gradually constrict within him, until his humour and sociability had disappeared into an angry and tight little ball at the centre of his stomach. Had been barely able to mutter a goodbye as Carmichael had left, saying that she needed to release her mum from the kids.

I'll probably need to apologise for being a miserable bastard, thought Barney, as a wave crashed against the wall beneath him, catching his face with the spray. He had stayed in the restaurant for more than an hour after she'd gone, drinking a further three cups of coffee and eating an *execution of kiwi fruit on an echelon of baked Alaska*. After that he had answered the pull of the barbershop, to do nothing more than open up and inspect the premises, turn out the lights, sit in one of the chairs and stare morosely out of the window.

Now he was walking forlornly along the front, heading back to his house for the night, wondering for how long this was going to be his life.

He took a last look at the sea, arrived at the door, checked his watch – still an hour before Mrs Donaldson's curfew – and walked in. Listened to the stillness for a second, then removed his shoes and coat and walked through to the kitchen. Didn't want anything else to eat, just thought he ought to report in to the camp commandant before retiring.

There was a man in the kitchen making himself a savoury snack. Caviar and cream cheese on Jacob's Cream Crackers. He looked up as Barney padded silently into the room in his socks. Rusty Brown, on whom Barney had bestowed the magnificent *Kobe Bryant* the day before.

'Barney,' said the old fella.

'Mr Brown,' said Barney. Didn't feel like talking.

'The lady of the house is just getting changed,' said Brown. 'One of the kids puked on her.'

Barney looked at the old man for a second, then started to turn.

'Look at this,' said Brown.

Barney turned back, the mother of all fuck-off expressions on his face. Brown ignored it.

'What colour would you say this was?' he asked, holding up the small 100g jar of caviar.

129

Barney stared at the jar.

'Black,' he said. 'It's caviar, it's black.'

'Come here,' said Brown, and he rose from the table and walked over to one of the work surfaces, which had a light attached to the kitchen unit above. 'Take a closer look.'

Barney ground his teeth. There's something about company that makes you realise that when you're so depressed your guts feel black and wasted, that it's not just that you're miserable; you're pissed off and miserable.

'Look at it,' said Brown. 'Come on.'

Barney stared into the jar. The caviar wasn't black. For no reason that he could establish he felt a wash of light.

'It's beautiful, don't you think?' said Brown.

Barney nodded. Brown was right. The caviar was a rich, dark, delicious purple. Black from a distance but on closer inspection it had so much more colour and warmth.

'Isn't that just the most wonderful metaphor for so many things in life?' said Brown, smiling, looking at Barney's face.

Barney just stared at the deep purple, strangely captivated.

'Don't you leave that jar open any longer, Rusty Brown, or the place'll be stinking of fish! That's the last thing we need!'

Neither man turned. Brown looked at Barney, a little smile came to his lips and he winked, for all the world like he was Burt Lancaster.

'Good night, Mr Brown,' said Barney. Rusty Brown smiled.

Barney looked at Miranda Donaldson as he walked past, she glowered in return. Neither said anything, until he was out of the room and walking through the hall to the stairs.

'Newton was an arsehole,' she muttered at his back.

He stopped, he didn't turn, he decided to ignore all the replies that automatically came to mind, then he started walking, the weight of the world on his shoulders, up the stairs.

130

25

Two Dumb Animals

Tony Angelotti smirked stupidly at Police Constable Gainsborough, who had taken his seat once more behind his desk and was contemplating a pot of Harrods No.372 *Late in The Evening & Pissed Off Blend*. The call had come through from a higher power to release the Italian, as most everyone who hadn't been stupid had known it would. The higher power who'd actually made the call had been part of the Strathclyde Constabulary, taking instructions from descending echelons of higher higher powers.

'You can leave now,' said Gainsborough.

The smile broadened, Tony slowly lifted his closed right fist and then raised the middle finger with deliberate panache. Or what he thought was panache, but clearly wasn't.

'Fuck you.'

There are moments as a police officer, although not too many in Millport, when you want to take a tight hold of your truncheon and bludgeon some muppet to a bloody pulp. Usually when these moments occur, you take a tight hold of your truncheon and you bludgeon the muppet to a bloody pulp. Sometimes, however, your hands are tied.

'You're free to go,' said Gainsborough coldly.

'I know,' said Tony. The smug smile began to take over his entire face, like some conceited and self-righteous cancerous growth. Gainsborough couldn't take it any more, turned away

131

and walked into the small kitchen off the back of the outer office to put the kettle on.

Tony laughed, opened the door and stepped out into the sea breeze cold of late evening. Closed the door and stood looking at the small scene before him. Tiny, rocky bay, playing field beyond, street lights in an arc for two hundred yards or so to his right, running alongside the row of houses that included Miranda Donaldson and Randolph Grey and the Millerston Hotel; to his left, the sea stretching out to the dark islands across the firth. He pulled his jacket closer to him, felt the wind on his face. He breathed deeply and there was something in the smell of the cold air that reminded him of the smell of the warm Mediterranean of his childhood.

'What the fuck am I supposed to do now?' he muttered.

He was a little over a hundred and fifty yards away from his hotel but what with him being a single cell stupid shit, he just didn't know whether to turn left or right. Briefly considered walking back into the police station and asking for directions but the manner of his departure precluded that as an option.

He turned at approaching footsteps and tensed, wondering if this would be another stupid attack by way of the stupid policeman. It's what he would have done himself, after all.

'Hey,' said the new guy, 'you must be like, the Italian, yeah?'

Tony attempted to broaden his shoulders even more.

'So what?' he replied belligerently. 'What does that make you?'

'You're Tony, right?' said the guy, smiling. 'That is so cool.'

'Why?' said Tony, thinking that yes it was cool that he was Tony, but who was this presumptuous little shit to say it?

'Because, Dude-o,' said the guy, 'that's my name too. Totally cool. People call me 2Tone,' he added, and held out his hand.

Tony regarded his hand with the same disgust as the nickname and folded his arms. 2Tone was oblivious to the body language and turned his unanswered extended hand into some sort of gesture of solidarity.

'Cool,' he said.

'What is?' asked Tony.

'I like spoke to some other Italian guy, you know? A friend of yours, asked me to like, give you a message.'

Tony regarded 2Tone with suspicion.

'What friend?'

'Didn't, like, give me his name or anything. The guy seemed a little wired, kinda creeped me out a little, you know. But he gave me a couple thousand to pass something on and another couple of thousand in it for me if I keep my mouth shut. Just like, grabbed me in the street, you know. So, here I am, dude.'

Tony was trying to work everything out. Of course, there was no way he had the intelligence to work *anything* out, never mind everything. In fact, when he finally thought to say, 'So, what is it you've to tell me?' it was a small moment of triumph.

2Tone nodded. This was his moment to pass on the two thousand pound message.

'All right. He says he's checked out of the hotel. He said you'd know what he meant by that.'

After grabbing 2Tone off the street, and with no knowledge of the fact that he was dealing with the son of his principal adversary, Luigi had realised that the conversation which would unfold with his Tony was going to be between two idiots. However, having already dragged 2Tone into it, he hadn't wanted to ditch him and explain the story to someone else.

'That means he's moved to another hotel?' said Tony.

'That's the thing,' said 2Tone. 'He's not gone to another hotel, he's incommunicado, you know, underground. He's like a fox.'

'Why?' asked Tony.

'He thinks you'll get, like followed when you leave here. Like, there'll be some dude following you and all. He's worried they'll lead you to him. Then he wouldn't be a fox, he'd be, you know, like a rabbit or some stupid waiting-to-get-eaten animal like that.'

Tony shook his head and stared at the damp road. What kind of idiot did Luigi think he was? And what if he had been followed? What were these pointless islanders going to do about it?

'So won't you be followed the minute you leave here?' said Tony, giving 2Tone the look that he usually received from Luigi.

'Like, it doesn't matter, dude,' said 2Tone, smiling stupidly. 'Firstly, he's like totally going to pay me to keep my mouth shut. And secondly, it completely doesn't matter, 'cause I like can't tell anyone anything anyway. And I'm not going to see him again.'

'So how the fuck is he going to pay you?'

2Tone still smiled. He wasn't entirely sure about that but it felt like an effort to think about it, so he wasn't about to. He also still had some of the message to deliver, so he needed to focus.

'He also said you should like keep checking out the cathedral.'

'And what the fuck's he going to be doing?'

2Tone did a kind of rapper thing with his hands.

'Don'no, Dude,' he said. 'I'm just a guy, I don't know shit.'

Tony nodded at that one. It wasn't often he got to feel intellectually superior when in conversation with even the most marginally sentient of lifeforms.

'Anything else?' he asked.

2Tone nodded sagely, using a thoughtful face.

'Think we're done, Dude,' he said.

'Good,' said Tony. 'I can go back to the hotel, you can go back to being an idiot.'

'Like, yeah, total, man. Oh yeah, wait a minute,' said 2Tone, shaking his head, 'there is something else. I'm such a dork.'

He fished around in his pockets and dug out a small piece of paper. Tony took it roughly from him and read it quickly. He squinted, he looked up at 2Tone, he thought to inquire what the hell it was supposed to mean and then decided that there was little point in asking. He turned to go before remembering that he didn't actually know which way that was supposed to be.

'Which way to the George?' he asked, expecting 2Tone to be too stupid even for that.

'Like it's totally that way,' he replied, pointing him to his left.

Tony looked along the road and wandered off without any further inane discussion. 2Tone watched him go then stood contemplating what he was going to do with the next few minutes of his life, not being one for long term plans.

He noticed a movement in the police office and looked in. Gainsborough was watching him. 2Tone waved, Gainsborough nodded and then lifted the phone to Bartholomew Ephesian.

26

And Who Shall
Be Able To stand?

Jacobs returned to the house at a little after eleven o'clock. His evening had, for the most part, been completely unsuccessful. No Grail, no hand. He had already spoken to Ephesian on the phone, before completing his final errand of the day, so he knew that McGhee and Deluth had the hand and he knew what they wanted; and he had also passed on the news of Lawton's theft of the Grail, which he had then immediately regretted. Ephesian had difficulty handling situations that seemed to be spiralling out of his control. Jacobs did not yet think that that was what was happening here but equally it wasn't going smoothly. And he knew that his definition of out of control wasn't going to be the same as Ephesian's.

He stood in the large hall, listening. He had first gone to his own quarters to remove his coat and scarf and now had come through the short corridor which connected his spacious apartments to the house.

Sometimes his employer would be in bed by this hour but not tonight. Still too many things to discuss, the list growing rather than diminishing. He walked through to the dining room, with the small office off to the right, wondering if Ephesian would be standing in the dark, staring down on the dark grey of the firth, small tumbler of single malt in his left hand. Surrounded by quiet and darkness and solitude, the way he spent so many of his late evenings.

The two rooms were empty and Jacobs got his first feelings of unease. He went to the window and stood, as Ephesian usually did, looking down at the water. Did not see the same things that Ephesian saw. Then he turned and walked through to the study across the hall.

The room was illuminated by a small desk lamp but Ephesian was not in the large comfy chair by the window, which was where he always sat when he chose to take his sanctuary in here. Jacobs walked over to the book shelf which contained the complete works of Robert Louis Stevenson, pulled gently on the small hardback second edition of *Virginibus Puerisque*, then stepped forward through the doorway as it opened up before him.

He walked carefully down the stairs because he had not, after all, been a young man for some decades now and his eyesight was verging on the dysfunctional. Bottom of the stairs and the cellar room was in complete darkness. He flicked one in the row of six light switches and stood looking into the dim corners of the room. There was no one there; none of the thirteen chairs around the table occupied. He must have been wrong, he thought. Ephesian must have gone upstairs, perhaps for the first time in his life, dealing with stress by going to bed and trying to sleep on it.

As he was about to flick the light off, he heard the most meagre of sounds. He stopped, held his breath. This was a dark creepy room in the bowels of one hundred and fifty year old foundations, but it had never before spooked him in any way. However, today was the day he had for the first time in his life encountered a spirit of some sort, even if it was one who was stuck for eternity trying to get to the toilet, and his heart skipped, he felt his skin tighten. Yet he did not throw any of the other light switches. Swallowed, deep breath, banished the feelings of unease and stepped forward. He bent down and looked under the table.

When he saw what was there the feeling of unease vanished completely, to be replaced by instant determination. Another problem to be sorted out, another glitch to be added to the list and dealt with as summarily as possible.

137

It had been a long time since he had seen his employer in this state. Thirty years maybe, although there had been occasions in all that time when he had wondered if it had happened and he had just not been there to witness it.

When the stress became too much for him and Ephesian's brain could not cope with it, his only retreat was to fold his body and his mind up into a small black ball, to make himself as insignificant as possible, to lock himself up in darkness and silence, surrounded by nothing, to reduce sensory input to virtually nil.

And so Jacobs was kneeling down, looking under the table, where Ephesian was lying curled foetally up as small as he could make himself, his head resting on the cold stone floor at an awkward angle.

'Mr Ephesian,' said Jacobs.

No response. Jacobs breathed steadily and checked his watch, knowing that this was something which would take a while.

'Mr Ephesian,' he said again. 'We need to talk. I believe I have solutions to most of our difficulties,' he added as an enormous lie, yet with the kind of assurance which he knew would be required for the next two or three hours, in order to coax Ephesian out from his protected world.

27

Craterous Skin

Barney lay in his bedroom, contemplating some of the great matters. Why is it, he was thinking, as he stared at the orange light cast from outside, that woman are so adept at spotting cellulite in other women? A man can look at a woman in a bikini for months and not notice if she has cellulite. He'll notice what her breasts are like for the first few weeks, then he'll move on to noticing the bum, legs and stomach. But if you were to quiz him on whether or not she had cellulite he wouldn't have a clue. He probably wouldn't even be able to tell if he was asked to establish it as a specific task. Women, on the other hand, seem to be genetically trained to notice cellulite within the first quarter second of visual contact, and everything else later. They have a specific part in their eyeball, missing from men, which sees only cellulite on thighs. This means that when they see some fantastically attractive woman on a beach or by a pool, it doesn't matter if she's slim and gorgeous with long legs and amazing breasts. If she's got cellulite, the other woman thinks, 'okay, we're level.' For men though, it's relegated to somewhere in the far far distance behind breasts and an ability to keep the fridge adequately stocked with the right kind of beer.

He shuffled over in bed, lay on his left side and stared out of the window. Eyes wide open when he should have been asleep. Having been Bill Murray in *Ghostbusters*, he'd now progressed to being Bill Murray in *Lost In Translation*. And wasn't his entire life, he pondered, an extended version of *Groundhog*

Day? From one barbershop to the next, one series of murders after another.

'I'm Bill flippin' Murray,' he muttered into the orange darkness. 'How sad is that?'

And he wondered if he could go down and make himself a cup of tea and whether it was worth invoking the wrath of Miranda Donaldson, for although there hadn't been a specific *Thou Shalt Not Make Cups Of Tea In The Dead Of Night* commandment, he wouldn't be surprised to find her standing erect in the kitchen clutching a rolling pin and ready to blatt him soundly over the head.

He lay like that for a few minutes and then turned onto his back once more.

'Johnny Depp,' he said to the empty sky. 'Why couldn't I have been Johnny Depp?'

✂

Normally the cathedral door would be locked at this time of night. It certainly had been earlier, when Jacobs had had to use Ephesian's spare keys to gain entry. However Father Roosevelt had realised that on a night such as this, the penultimate day before the world changed forever, the Cathedral of the Isles was likely to be in demand. There were only a few people in the world who realised the significance of this place – although the number would be astronomically high by Thursday morning – but the number was enough, all the same, for there to be a potential stream of visitors. And so Roosevelt had decided to leave the door open for the night to allow anyone who thought there might still be something to find here, entry to the nave. That the thing for which they all searched had already been removed, was known only to him, Lawton, Ephesian and Jacobs. And, of course, to the man who had bludgeoned Lawton to unconsciousness using Archie Gemmill.

There was a window high up on the wall of the chancel, behind which was a small room, part of the college buildings, formerly the infirmary in the Canon's house. Here it was that Andrew Roosevelt had set himself up for the night, perched on an uncomfortable wooden seat, accompanied by two flasks of

140

coffee and a packet of Jaffa cakes, to spy from behind a thin curtain on whoever might come to visit.

For years he had watched tourists and worshipers at the cathedral, wondering whether they were there simply to marvel at the intricacies of the interior or whether they knew more than they appeared to. That while they gazed with the interest of a tourist, that in truth they searched for the clue which might lead them to the Grail. Tonight, however, he could at last relax and watch with curiosity rather than anxiety.

Slowly and silently he unscrewed the lid of the first flask and poured some more coffee into the small white mug – the one he'd received a few years previously from a Maryhill rabbi, the words *Have A Kosher Christmas!* written in pink around the rim – and then he leaned forward and peered round the edge of the curtain.

Tony Angelotti had been in the cathedral for just under half an hour. He still had the strange feeling of some level of intelligence about him after his earlier discussion with an even bigger idiot than himself, but it was beginning to wear off as he minced around the nave and chancel.

He stopped just below the pulpit and looked up at the scene of the stricken Christ, post-crucifixion and in need of *Nurofen Extra Strength Nails in The Hands*. He stared for a few seconds, then turned round and looked at the rest of the small space, then he held his hands out before him, shaking his head, in a *how the fuck am I supposed to work this out* gesture.

Roosevelt smiled. He had spent the previous half hour wanting to toy with the man, calling out hot or cold depending on how close he'd come to the font. It had reminded him of the time a few years earlier when one seemingly innocuous and very corpulent American tourist had started intimately studying the carvings of the gospel saints. Growing worried, Roosevelt had then called out to the man from his hiding place, warning him off.

The man had then turned and begun a conversation with the empty cathedral, thinking that he had been talking to God Himself, a part Roosevelt had rather enjoyed playing. Telling the man he had to lose three hundred pounds by that Christmas or he was going to have a heart attack and die had probably been a little unnecessary and self indulgent, but Roosevelt liked to think that he had saved his life.

This time, what with the general seriousness and enormity of the occasion, Roosevelt chose to say nothing, but sipped silently on his coffee and munched on his fourth Jaffa cake of the evening.

'Fucking piss,' said Tony shaking his head. 'Fucking Scotland.'

✂

Luigi had blended seamlessly into Millport life, part of the furniture. He had needed somewhere to hide out for a few hours, to spend the night undercover, before he would emerge the following day, find Tony, which would be like finding a cockroach in Thailand, and then go about his business of finishing off the matter which had brought them to this Godforsaken island in the first place.

'You'll be having another glass of wine before you go to bed,' said the old woman, more as a statement of fact than a question.

'Thank you, Nella,' said Luigi. 'You are a kind and beautiful woman.'

The old woman shook her head at the compliment but she was smiling all the same. Her friend looked up from her knitting and tutted silently but she was still feeling good from the fact that Luigi had told her how graceful and elegant she was just a few minutes earlier, so she parked the petty jealousy to one side and smiled at Luigi as he glanced round at her.

'I am a lucky man tonight,' he schmoozed. 'And to think I could have been stuck in Rome.'

✂

Igor lay in bed and stared at the ceiling. Two women in one day. How often did that happen to him, he wondered, at around the same time that Barney was considering his personal transmogrification into Bill Murray. Well, actually this was the third time this year, but hey, that's not so many compared to some other deaf mute hunchbacks.

Gently Ferguson snuggled her chin closer into the soft fat of Igor's upper arm and sleepily caressed the hairs on his chest.

142

'Thank you,' she said drowsily, 'I needed that.'

Igor looked down at her and kissed the top of her head. Her hair smelled of apple shampoo and he breathed in the smell of it for a few seconds before resting back on the pillow and looking up once more at the ceiling.

'Arf,' he said softly, and she burrowed her face even further into the cushion of his arm.

✂

Augustus Lawton still lay in the pool of his own blood, the merest breath of life about him, destined to lie in a vegetative state for some years to come. Sometimes the penalties of greed can be harsh, and sometimes you don't get the chance to learn your lesson.

✂

The other woman whose company Igor had had the pleasure of that day, was still sitting on her kitchen floor, back pressed against a cabinet full of cleaning fluids, eyes permanently pointed upwards, as if she could see the noise upstairs through the floors and the walls.

Ruth Harrison was terrified.

28

The Monstrous Mind
Of The Psephalopod

It all becomes too much. You break down, fall to pieces, return to a collection of millions of individual cells, almost as though they are completely unrelated to one another. All sensory perception closes down, it's as if you are no longer a sentient being. You barely exist on any level, the world is drawn into you so that there is nothing else, nothing outside the confines of the tiny space into which you have withdrawn. You try to bring your body into the space, and although it doesn't have a chance of fitting, you draw it in as tightly as you can. Everything is minimised, as if someone is shooting at you and you are reducing the target to the least possible area. There are no guns aiming at you, no bullets coming your way, but it feels like there are. You need to be in control and the only thing of which you are certain is that you're not. When you realise that you have control over nothing, that events and people and situations are dictating your life and not the other way round, the only thing you can do is withdraw as far as possible, retreat to the place where nothing and no one dictates to you. And if that place is so small, it is a dark, untouchable point in the pit of your guts, your body wrapped tightly around it and all mental functions shut off, then that is where you go.

However, there's always an out, there's always a recovery. Strength of character. You don't retreat to that place to give up. You retreat to convalesce. You break down, let all the molecules disperse, and then gradually they come back together. You're at the bottom of the dark ocean, then suddenly you're shooting up through the depths towards the light. But there are no bends to be had, you never come up too fast. You have retreated to where you are in control, so no one can drag you from the place before you want to leave. And then, when you return, you are ready. Ready to acknowledge what you control and ready to address those things which still lie outwith your power. Maybe the reaction looks odd, maybe to others you are peculiar and unbalanced, but it serves you well. It's one of the things which makes you a stronger person than so many of those who would mark you down as unbalanced.

Ephesian took another sip of sparkling water. 2:35am. No time for alcohol this. There was too much to be sorted out. He had retreated, he had regrouped. Jacobs didn't understand, not really, despite having had a life of dealing with his employer. When you hide away in the tiniest, darkest place you can find, you don't do it to seek reassurance from others. The hours Jacobs had spent believing he'd been talking Ephesian out from his hiding place had been completely ineffective. Jacobs could have been saying anything. His words had been meaningless, Ephesian had heard none of them. Destruction and recovery had come from within, as had always been the case.

'We'll need to use the money in the morning,' said Ephesian. 'Lawton is a spineless toad, McGhee just as unimaginative. He holds what he does and all the ignorant little runt can think to demand is money.'

'He doesn't know what he holds,' said Jacobs.

Ephesian grunted.

'It wouldn't make any difference. An idiot holding the riches of the world is still an idiot.'

'But Lawton knows the power of what he has,' said Jacobs. 'He might well not be so easily dealt with.'

Ephesian nodded, took another sip.

'Yet he is as shallow. That's why we need the money. Of promises he may well be mistrustful, but a suitcase full of money, enough money to take him anywhere he wants to go, he will not be so foolish as to turn his back on that.'

145

Jacobs did not reply. He stood with his hands behind his back, following Ephesian's gaze out to the west and the dark night. Ephesian belched softly, the back of his hand at his mouth.

'I can speak to Anthony in the morning,' Ephesian continued. 'It may well be that with him also, all I will have to do is to show him some money. I will certainly dispense with the initiation, he need know nothing about what he is participating in.'

'And the matter of his dealings with the Italians?' said Jacobs.

Ephesian did not reply. He did not think that his son would be openly working against him. He would have been used as some kind of unwitting pawn. However, it meant little, and he was confident that the Italians would know nothing of the nature of the ceremony which would take place that evening at midnight. The secret that had been guarded all these centuries remained just that. The Catholic Church were here to stick their noses into the situation because they knew they would not like what came out of it. However, even they did not have any conception of the magnitude of what was going to happen. And so, as part of his controlling process, Ephesian was convinced that the Italians just needed to be watched for the time being. Or, at least, the one at the hotel could be watched; the other, now acting discreetly, needed to be found.

'We just have to give Ping Phat his head,' said Ephesian, after a short gap. 'He cannot usurp us at this stage, there is too much knowledge he does not have. If he must become involved, if he must be some sort of observer to the ceremony, then perhaps it would be pragmatic of us to accept what must be. At least that way we can keep an eye on him.' He waved his glass.

'You should get some sleep,' said Jacobs.

Ephesian didn't turn. He glanced at his watch without taking in the time. He did feel tired but he wasn't yet ready for sleep.

'There will be ample time for that,' he said vacantly.

Jacobs recognised the tone. Their discussion was over. His boss might not feel the need to lie down but he himself needed a few hours before the rigours of the day ahead. Ephesian might have been able to work his mind around to a positive state but all Jacobs could see were problems and obstacles.

He turned and walked silently from the room. Ephesian did not even notice him go.

><

Barney's mind rambled on. Three o'clock in the morning, he'd been in bed for almost four hours and not once had he even come close to getting to sleep. Eyes wide open, head full of the banal and the mundane, mixed with the occasional matter of weight.

At the end of *It's A Wonderful Life*, how come everyone is so full of smiles? If the bank investigator bloke was about to arrest Jimmy Stewart for fraud or embezzlement or whatever it was, surely just because everyone in the town shows up and says, 'Here, we'll pay back all the money you think he stole,' doesn't mean he wasn't guilty. Okay, we know he wasn't guilty, but surely there still has to be a trial? You can't let a guy off completely just because everyone thinks he's nice. And then in that final scene, in amongst all the cheerful, weepy people, there's old, miserable-as-shite Mr Potter. Why's he looking so chipper? Because he's got the flippin' $8000, that's why. You don't see him handing it back, do you? And what has his journey been in movie terms? After decades of misanthropy and money-grabbing, he turns into this jovial old buffoon, 50% smile, 50% heart of flippin' gold. How did that happen? Because Jimmy Stewart met an angel? Or maybe there was a parallel story with old man Potter, removed from the final cut, where he met Lucifer and was shown how even more wonderful the town would have been without him in it and it cheered him up to think that he'd ruined at least a few lives.

Barney, shut up! he thought. Get some sleep. Count sheep. Think of how to describe cricket to an American. Calculate all the prime numbers under one million. List the world's airlines. Think of a cellar full of cockroaches and count them.

They say cockroaches would survive a nuclear attack. Urban myth? It's accepted fact but how do they know? Maybe the cockroaches survived Hiroshima or on all those ex-beautiful islands in the middle of the Pacific. Maybe that was part of the tests; they took a variety of lifeforms – cockroaches, locusts, white tigers, dodos, snow leopards, a couple of Mormons –

147

bombed the stuffing out of them and then bimbled back across to the island a few minutes after the mushroom cloud had cleared. *It's all right, Chip, you can wear a protective suit if you want but you probably won't need to.* Of all the animals and bugs on the island the only ones to survive were the cockroaches, albeit they'd all been converted to The Church of Jesus Christ of Latter-Day Saints. Or maybe it'd been mentioned in a Disney film once and out of that the urban legend had grown. Maybe the cockroaches will just get squished with the rest of us.

Finally Barney poured his legs over the side of the bed and stood up. He walked to the window and looked out to the dark sea and away to the east. The first hint of dawn was beginning to make an appearance on the horizon, another early morning about to kick off in another small town.

He felt the slight lift that he always got when he was up with the dawn of the day. His mind meandered through the Far Side cartoon of *The African Dawn*, the animals sitting around drinking coffee, took a swing through Calvin & Hobbes and the beautiful clean canvas of their final snowy day, and then juddered to a halt at the reality of a life built on walking aimlessly from place to place, of relationships made and squandered, and of another day when he knew that life's beauty – no matter how many old men talked about the simple pleasures of the sound of the fizz when opening a bottle of tonic or the feel of sea spray on your face or the excitement in a child's eyes when discovering something that as an adult you've taken for granted for decades – would only briefly touch him, before being banished by the general darkness of the suffocating gloom that he could not seem to shake.

He sat down in the large comfy chair by the window, the high ledge partially restricting his view of the sea, and for the first time in over four hours his eyes felt heavy and he was finally able to close them with intent.

29

Augustinian Predestination

'And would you like fries with that, sir?' said Barney.

Well, that wasn't what he actually said but sometimes he felt like saying it. The fast food counter that is a barbershop.

'Tapered or square at the back?' asked Barney.

The man in the hot seat, old Seth Bagan, brought the universal frown of inquisition into play.

'How d'you mean that?' he asked.

'A taper,' said Barney patiently, 'is where the hair at the back is shaved to a gradual end. A square cut is where the hair is all the same length at the back and cut in a straight line at the bottom.'

'Oh,' said Bagan, who had somehow managed to get to the age of one hundred and ninety-three without ever finding this out.

'Isn't a tapir an odd-toed, South American ungulate with a flexible proboscis?' said the other old fella, parked on the bench behind them.

'Well I don't know,' said Bagan, 'I thought that was a sloth?'

'The sloth's an edentate,' said Barney.

'Eden Tate? Was that the guy who was married to Sharon Tate?' said one of the old men.

'You're thinking about Roman Polanski,' said the other one.

'The Romans,' said Bagan, 'they knew a thing or two.'

'Arf!' said Igor forcefully, getting a bit fed up with it all.

'You're thinking of alfresco,' said the guy on the bench. 'The Romans loved that style of wallpapering.'

'Wasn't Al Fresco the guy who won the F1 World Championship five times in the 50's?'

'Fangio,' said Barney, despite his own determination not to be sucked back into the general level of absurdity, 'that was Fangio.'

'Fangs!' said one of the old guys, 'don't sloths have fangs?'

'*No!*' Igor wanted to scream, '*they're flippin' edentates! That means they don't have any flippin' teeth! No incisors, no molars, no pre-molars, and definitely no flippin' fangs!*' However, it came out as, 'Arf!'

'You said that already,' said one of the old guys.

'So, Igor,' said Barney to change the subject, 'Ruth was all right last night?'

He hadn't really wanted to ask the question in front of the customers but he'd needed to say something before the conversation disappeared up any more blissfully stupid tangents.

Igor guiltily looked at Barney, mumbled something that sounded suspiciously like *arf*, then lowered his head and started sweeping up, even though no hair had yet fallen on this day.

'Igor?' said Barney.

Igor swept.

'Igor?' he repeated.

Igor swept, this time turning his back on Barney, his brushstrokes growing a little fiercer.

''Scuse me a minute,' said Barney to the old guy about to be the beneficiary of a splendid *A River Runs Through It*.

'No problem,' said Bagan. Then he added, as Barney laid down the scissors and walked to the rear of the shop, 'You probably want to ask him about Gently Ferguson.'

Barney looked at the old guy, then caught Igor's guilty eye and gestured to the back room. Igor threw old man Bagan a zinger of a look and then followed Barney into the rear of the shop. He left the door open, only for Barney to close it.

The two men stood staring at each other, Barney waiting for an explanation.

'Arf,' mumbled Igor eventually.

150

'I left you to look after her,' said Barney. 'I thought you two had, I don't know, a thing or something. I thought you were going to stay the night. What happened?'

Igor looked Barney in the eye but couldn't hold the gaze. He stared at the floor.

'Who's Gently Ferguson?' asked Barney. 'If you had another date last night, why didn't you say?'

'Arf,' muttered Igor.

'That's not good enough,' scolded Barney. 'The woman was scared and she's got those two cowboys after her. You should've stayed.'

Igor looked up again. Held his hands out in an Italian gesture of self-explanation.

Barney studied him, trying to work it out. There is one sure thing, he suddenly realised, that will drive a man and woman apart before their time.

'You slept with her,' he said, not even asking the question. 'You slept with Ruth and after that things got awkward and you left.'

Igor looked uncomfortable and then dropped his gaze again.

'Igor!' said Barney. 'For crying out loud, man, the woman needed someone. Jings, her husband died the day before.'

Igor's head plummeted another few inches.

'Igor, I know you've got that whole silent but sensitive thing going on that women love, but you've got to control the old pecker, mate. Restraint is what marks the man, my hunchbacked friend. She needed you and you completely abused that. And then you left her alone with the ghost of her dead husband and easy prey to those goons from the big fella at the top of the hill.'

Barney shook his head. Igor mumbled apologetically.

'And who's this Gently Ferguson comedienne?'

The deaf mute was silent.

'You shag her 'n all?' asked Barney.

Igor looked up, answered with a seriously guilty face and then stared out the window at the grey morning.

'Igor!' said Barney, 'you are something else. I mean, I'm impressed, and given that you'd already left Ruth's place, I

151

don't suppose it matters, but you've got to screw the nut, chief, you know what I'm saying?'

Igor nodded. Barney stared at him for a while, then turned and followed Igor's apologetic gaze out of the window.

'Right,' said Barney, 'I take it you're going to be uncomfortable going round there again this morning?'

'Arf,' said Igor.

'Okay, here's what we're going to do. We'll stick the *Closed* sign on the door, I'll finish off the two old geezers, then I'll go round there and see how she's doing. You can stay here and, I don't know, just try not to sleep with any women or anything.'

'Arf.'

'Good.'

The black BMW pulled into the short driveway. The green posts were a testament to the gate that had once stood at the entrance, but it had come off its hinges several years previously and Augustus Lawton had not been someone who ever did much about the small jobs around his house.

Jacobs parked the car by the front door, got out and walked round to open the door for Ephesian. Ephesian was still doing mental exercises to keep his thoughts positive and took half a minute to be aware that they had stopped.

He got out, Jacobs closed the door, then Ephesian stood back and let his man ring the doorbell. Jacobs was holding a case containing exactly one million pounds in clean, crisp fifty pound notes. Ephesian had stood and stared at the contents, taking in the smell, for almost an hour that morning.

'You'll let me do the talking, sir,' said Jacobs deferentially.

Ephesian was aware of the vague feeling of discomfort in his stomach. Nerves. Stupid nerves. They just needed to get in there, get hold of the Grail and leave Lawton to his money. As long as he went nowhere until after the ceremony that evening.

Jacobs rang the bell again. Ephesian looked at his watch. Jacobs turned away and looked down the short hill to the little of the sea which was visible in between the sides of buildings. The day had dawned with one of those strange flat calms that you know are never going to last. Not off the west coast of Scotland.

'No wind,' said Jacobs.

Ephesian didn't hear him. He was aware that Jacobs had spoken but the words had not penetrated.

Without looking to his employer for permission, Jacobs tried the handle and then, finding it locked, he fished out the large set of keys, identified the couple for Lawton's house and opened the door. He walked in quickly and silently, Ephesian following with hesitation, that part of his brain which dictated to him that he himself should never break the rules, holding him back from entering with the confidence of Jacobs.

The house was a shambles but they both knew that the house was always a shambles. This was not as a result of a random trashing of the property. The dining room was just off the entrance hall, so there was no extended period of searching for the man. Within ten seconds of walking in, Jacobs was standing over Lawton's body, the head bashed bloody, puffy and swollen around the face.

Ephesian entered the room slowly in Jacobs' wake, stopped suddenly on seeing what was before them, stared at it for a few seconds, then turned quickly away from the blood. Not for a second did he feel anything for Lawton. No compassion. That the man had been attacked was entirely of secondary importance. The thing which mattered was that the Grail was obviously gone and very possibly the other item which would have been kept in Lawton's freezer.

'Fuck,' Ephesian muttered, standing in the doorway to the dining room, his back turned to the mess on the carpet.

Jacobs bent down, quickly and closely examined the body.

'He's not dead, sir,' he said. 'We should get the ambulance up here, maybe they'll be able to revive him. He might be able to tell us who did this. You go back out to the car, sir. There's no need for you to be here. I'll see if the item in the freezer is still there, and search for the Grail. Then I'll call Gainsborough and let him sort out the rest.'

Ephesian didn't move. Jacobs waited for a few seconds and then walked quickly through to the kitchen. Ephesian listened to

153

his footsteps, as he felt the first vultures of uncertainty begin to pick at the fragile confidence and self-assurance which he'd built up through the long night.

When, in the bleak silence, he heard the tiny fizz of the freezer door opening, he walked back to the front door, then down the driveway and back out onto the road for the walk back up the hill to his house. He didn't want to sit in a car waiting to find out just how bad it had all become. He needed to be at home, surrounded by everything that was familiar.

Inside the house Jacobs was rummaging through the freezer, and he finally found what he was looking for, hidden under the rubble of *Iceland* goods.

He hauled out the small package, studied it for a few seconds then laid it down on the kitchen table. Then he looked around the room, eyes quickly taking everything in.

Was it likely that the Grail might still be here? He had to assume that Lawton had been attacked for the Grail but it didn't mean that he hadn't already hidden it and that his assailant had been unable to find it in the house.

He made his decision. The Grail would not be here. He took one last look at the kitchen, walked around each room of the house making a quick search in case there was anything else obvious about which he needed to know, took a last look at the body of Augustus Lawton, placed an abrupt call to Constable Gainsborough, and then walked quickly out of the building.

As he closed the front door behind him, and a slight breeze was blown through the house, the mugs in the small wooden stand beside the kettle gently swayed. Two plain shiny purple cups, a blue mug from Lapland, a *Best Dad In The World*, a Glasgow Rangers, a contraband Calvin & Hobbes and, resting silently on the counter beside the stand, an odd-shaped Wallace & Gromit, a small chip out of the rim.

30

Wraithwreckers

Barney first knocked, waited and then tried again. No answer. Knocked again, waited a short while and then stood back and studied the house. Looked over his shoulder, wondering if any of the neighbours were watching him although not really being bothered if they were, and then he opened the gate to the right of the house and walked into the back garden.

He thought he saw a movement in a window across the back wall. Perhaps he was being watched from up there.

Knocked at the back door, left it only a few seconds and then round the back of the house and looked in the kitchen window. Immediately he saw her sitting on the floor, back up against a unit, eyes wide and fearful, staring back out at him. He went around to the back door again, tried the handle then knocked.

'Ruth!' he called out. 'It's Mr Thomson. The barber.'

Nothing. Barney felt in tune with the woman inside. She was clearly terrified and there was likely no one on the planet who could've turned up at this point and been gladly welcomed.

'I'm here to help you, Ruth,' he said, pitching his voice at just the right level, between sympathy and audible volume.

He stood back and looked at the door.

'Complete empathy with the female mind, Barney,' he muttered.

There is no female mind, wrote Charlotte Perkins Gilman in 1898. *The brain is not an organ of sex. As well speak of a female liver.*

Well, what had *she* been smoking?

'You don't need to be scared, Ruth,' he said, raising his voice. 'If you can still hear your husband, come with me and I'll take you away from it. And don't worry about Ephesian's men. They won't do you any harm while you're with me.' Pause, time to play the sensitive man card. 'I know about Igor and I know he let you down. You'll be safe with me. You don't even have to let me in, just come out and we can go to a café somewhere.'

Another pause. Needed to see her face to know if he was making any progress. For all he knew she could be paralysed in some trance-like state of fear.

'I know about the insincerity of men, Ruth,' he began again. *'Men are vile inconstant toads*, wrote Lady Montagu, and she was right. Igor took advantage of you but he's that kind of man. He's Julio Iglesias, he's Don Juan. Women love him and he can't help himself.'

Pause, let that all sink in a bit. *Igor is Don Juan*, he repeated to himself, and he smiled.

'And the goons from up the hill, they're nothing, Ruth. Whatever their game is, they're not getting past me. Really.'

Another pause.

'And I'm sure there's something we can do about your husband.' A further hiatus in his smooth talk, while he considered what that might be. 'We could get the house exorcised.' Hesitated again, while he thought about what he'd just said. *Get the house exorcised, Barney? What the fuck is the matter with you?* 'One of the ministers on the island or we could get someone in from outside.'

He leant against the door frame. How long before he broke the door down? Looked at his watch, glanced up quickly as he caught another movement in the window above the garden wall. Stared up for a few seconds then turned back to the door.

'Or maybe there's like a Ghostbusters type of thing up in Glasgow. There's all sorts now. We'll look in Yellow Pa...'

The lock clicked, the door opened slowly. Ruth Harrison appeared, staring wildly at Barney. Her face, her posture, everything about her bore the mark of someone who had spent a night haunted by terror. Her face was a grisly pale grey, lined

156

and wan and tired, the face of a woman at least twenty years
older than the one Barney had seen the day before. Her hair was
as dishevelled as her clothes. Barney grimaced when he noticed
the large damp stain around her crotch where she had peed in
the middle of the night. Her spirit had been laid waste.

'Jesus,' he said.

She caught his eye for the briefest of seconds and then stared
at his chest. She seemed barely to be breathing. Barney stepped
forward, across the threshold of the kitchen and put his arms
round her. At first she flinched although she did not pull away,
and then gradually, as Barney held onto her, she relaxed into it
and slowly she lifted her arms and put them around him.

Barney said nothing for a while and in the silence the noise
came to him. He had been aware of it as soon as the door had
opened but the sight of the decrepit woman before him had
distracted his mind from the sound. But now he heard it.

Coming from upstairs. A constant pad and shuffle. Feet
walking and in turn being dragged across the floor. A horrible
sound, designed almost to crawl under your skin, to bleed into
your consciousness. And accompanying the noise, barely
audible in amongst the gentle padding and scraping, a much
lower and more sinister sound. An evil and malicious laugh.

Barney was aware of the hairs on his neck and then he was
gripped by a sudden shiver. Ruth pulled away from him, feeling
the shudder in his body, the scared eyes looking up at him.

'An exorcist?' she said, her voice tiny and frail.

'Let's get you out of here,' said Barney, and he reached
behind her, took the key from inside, pulled the door over and
locked it.

And just before the door closed he heard another, louder
explosion of laughter, as if Jonah Harrison could see everything
that was happening in the kitchen, could see into the head of his
terrified widow and into the head of Barney Thomson.

✂

'It'll have to be a woman,' said Ruth Harrison, frowning across
the top of her cup of tea.

Barney raised an eyebrow at her but nodded. There were few
enough of these people in the Yellow Pages without them

157

having to be so prescriptive as to need to choose their sex, but he understood Ruth's resentment and distrust of men. Even though she was currently putting her trust in one.

He looked once more at the small advert, the only one listed under Exorcists.

✠ GOD ✠

Troubled by ghouls, spectres, poltergeists, mischievous spirits, apparitions or other unexplained phenomena? Call the Lord God Almighty on 0816 666 666, and watch evil spirits disappear.

GOD – FOR ALL YOUR EXORCISM
REQUIREMENTS

Tel./Fax: **0816 666 666**
Catering For The Religions Of The World

✡ ॐ ✝ ☺ ☠ ✌ 〠

'He may be a divine, omnipotent all-powerful being,' said Barney shaking his head, 'but He's male nevertheless.'

'Who is?' asked Ruth.

Igor looked up from where he was sheepishly and unnecessarily washing the scissors. *How many divine, omnipotent, all-powerful beings are there, for crying out loud?* he wanted to ask bitterly. Igor was feeling a little sore at being made the scapegoat for Ruth's long and terrifying ordeal.

'Doesn't matter,' said Barney.

He stared at Igor for no particular reason as he tried to think of what other categories an exorcist might come under. *Ghostbusters*, he thought. He hummed as he thumbed. Reached the page, nothing.

He turned quickly to the section on churches and read through the full list to see if any of them mentioned exorcism in their entries. Again, nothing. There were a few desperate cries for a decent sized congregation, including one church which stated that it showed MTV and served beer and peanuts throughout the

158

service, but a complete lack of exorcism services. He looked up at Ruth, who was watching him intently, her lips poised at the rim of her mug.

'How are you getting on?' she asked.

'Struggling to find a specialist,' answered Barney.

She slurped noisily at her tea. Igor gave her a scything look.

Maybe, thought Barney, they'll have done that thing where they put the words ghost and busters into a thesaurus and come up with something completely different, yet the same.

He started thinking of names and flicking through the book. *Spectrerupturers. Spookbursters. Spiritbreakers.* (There was indeed an entry under *Spiritbreakers* but it turned out just to be an advert for the Labour government.) *Phantomthrashers. Phantasmsmashers. Apparitionbashers.*

He closed the book and looked at Ruth and Igor, who were both staring at him. She's depending on you, Barney, he thought, you need to come up with the goods. Of course, all the woman needed to do was go along to one of the local ministers on the island. But they were all men.

'Arf!' said Igor suddenly, eyes wide.

Barney stared at him and for some reason that neither of them could explain, immediately understood what he had just said.

Wraithwreckers!

Barney turned quickly through the pages to the W's, and there, as if by some sort of divine intervention, was the small advert, the only listing in the section headed Wraithwreckers.

---

www.wraithwreckers.com
Lose all those annoying
ghosts today!
Call the Reverend Merlot Tolstoy!
Tel.: 09988 888 8888

'Merlot?' said Barney, looking up. 'That sound like a woman's name?'

'Arf!' replied Igor in the affirmative.

'I think so,' said Ruth Harrison, suddenly looking a bit more positive.

'Okay,' said Barney, 'I'll give it a try.'

He reached over to the phone and dialled. Igor watched him intently, Ruth stared at him, her mouth slightly open, letting in flies. Barney felt bizarrely like a presenter at the Eurovision Song Contest, dialling up Moldova or Serbia & Montenegro to find out how their judges had voted, while the audience waited with breaths stalled.

A couple of rings.

'You're through to *Wraithwreckers.com*, this is Merlot Tolstoy speaking.'

'Hello,' said Barney, 'my name's Barney Thomson.'

'Mr Thomson,' said Merlot Tolstoy, 'how can we be of help to you today?'

The words spoke of American customer service values, the accent was very soft west of Scotland.

'Can I take from your advert,' said Barney, 'that you're in the business of getting rid of ghosts?'

'You certainly can,' said Merlot Tolstoy. 'We originally called ourselves *Ghostbusters* but we got sued for $17billion dollars by Columbia Tristar. So we've been through a few names since then, but we kind of like this one. Course, you're our first call in five months.'

'How many of there are you?' asked Barney.

'Only me,' she replied, no hint of embarrassment. 'I like to refer to myself in the plural to suggest a level of conglomeraticy.'

'That doesn't really fit with telling me I'm your first call in five months and that you work alone,' said Barney.

'We're still trying to get me on my customer service course.'

'To teach you how to lie convincingly?'

'Absolutely,' she replied.

'Isn't that a bit of a thing for a minister?' asked Barney.

Merlot Tolstoy giggled.

'You sound like my parishioners in Shettleston, but we always say, well the church has been lying for centuries about all sorts of things, so what are a few wee fibs over the phone?'

160

'Fair enough,' said Barney.

'So, how can we be of assistance to you today?'

Barney paused, thought of how this was going to sound.

'My friend's husband died on his way to the toilet two days ago. It seems he's trapped for eternity needing to pee and keeps padding back and forth to the bathroom.'

As he spoke, Tolstoy punctuated his words with *uh-uh's* and *yes's* and *mmm's*, and an *'oh yes, urino-poltergeistation,'*

'Then yesterday evening my friend inadvertently had sex with another friend of ours who had gone round to comfort her,' continued Barney, and both Igor and Ruth gave him a serious amount of eyebrow.

'Common,' said Tolstoy. 'Very common.'

'So now her husband's spirit isn't just dying to take a piss, he's also super pissed off and seriously haunting her, you know?'

'Yes, we understand,' said Tolstoy. 'We've read about cases like this in *Sport on Sunday*.' A slight pause, which Barney did not fill as he sensed there was more coming.

'We just have a few questions,' said the Reverend Tolstoy.

'Fire away,' said Barney.

'Has she sold the film rights?'

Barney smiled. It is the new millennium after all.

'Not as far as I'm aware,' he replied.

'Good,' said Tolstoy. 'We need a stipulation in our contract that in the event of a film being made with due regard to the story of the haunting or demonic house possession, that my character can only be played by Uma Thurman, Angelina Jolie or Kate Beckinsale. Any other actress being considered for the part has to be approved by me before the script can be shown to the said actress.'

Barney didn't immediately reply to that one.

'Do we have your friend's agreement?' asked Tolstoy sharply.

'I think you can make that assumption,' said Barney.

'It'll have to be firmer than an assumption,' she said.

'We'll sign the contract.'

'Good. Now, are you the friend?' she asked.

161

Barney looked at the phone again, shared his slight confusion with the other two.

'I said I was,' he replied.

'Aye, but are you the actual friend who slept with your friend?'

'Ah. No, there are an actual three of us, sitting here right now.'

'Does the house have a history of demonic possession?'

'Not as far as we are aware.'

'Have any brutal acts of malevolence ever taken place in the house?'

'Not that I know of.'

'Was the deceased interested in any way in the occult or any supernatural phenomenon of any description?'

'He was pretty straight, as far as I can tell.'

'Where are you?'

'Millport.'

Slight pause as Merlot Tolstoy checked her watch.

'We can be there in about an hour and a half, depending on the ferry crossings. Give me your number and we'll call when we arrive. You can direct me to the appropriate site of operations.'

Barney gave the number, the Rev Tolstoy *mmm*ing constantly.

'We'll need the widow plus four others,' she said crisply.

'Why?' asked Barney, wondering who he was going to rope in for this. Did Ruth Harrison have any real friends?

'We use a 5th century Aramaic exorcism ceremony, which itself evolved from an earlier Babylonian model. Of course, we've adapted it to comply with modern Christian theology but the point is that we require a circle of six. Is that a can-do?'

'No problem,' said Barney, on the basis that if the worst came to the worst, he'd always be able to rope in a couple of the old fellas from the shop, who could come along and stand drooling in the circle with no idea whatsoever about what was happening.

'Cool,' she said. 'We'll see you in around ninety minutes.'

'Cool,' said Barney, as usual going with the flow.

She hung up. Barney turned to the others and shrugged.

'She'll be here in an hour or two, depending on the ferry.'

Ruth dissolved in a pile of relieved mush and reached out to hold Barney's hand.

'Thank you,' she gasped.

'Right,' said Barney, 'we'll need to get you cleaned up and into a change of clothes.'

'I'm not going back to the house,' she said quickly.

'It's all right,' said Barney, keeping hold of her hand and settling her down. 'We'll go round to Igor's place, won't we Igor?'

'Arf,' muttered Igor, frowning.

'You can have a shower and we'll get you some clean clothes.'

He paused to think about whether he wanted to visit Ruth's house and face the spirit of her dead husband on his own, or whether he could just nip along the front and buy her a new outfit from the shop on the corner of Shore and Newton.

'We'll get you a new set of clothes,' he repeated, deferring the decision. 'Finish your tea and we'll get going. Igor, is your place all right or do you need to go home and clean it up before you have a female guest.'

'Arf!' barked Igor.

Barney held up his hand in apology.

'Sorry, my hunchbacked friend,' he said.

'Arf.'

Barney nodded a further apology for casting aspersions on Igor's cleanliness, looked at Ruth, then walked through to the front of the shop to do some thinking about who they were going to get to assist in the exorcising of Jonah Harrison.

31

Pushing The Blue Sky

Two minutes back in the shop and Barney had two customers. James Randolph, no less, come to have his hair sorted out in the strange hope that it would also help him think more clearly, and another one in the endless line of old fellas who had retired to Millport some time in the previous thirty years.

After an initial wariness between the barber and customer, following their meeting the previous day at the house of Ruth Harrison, Randolph was now just struggling to stay awake. You know that thing which comes with getting your hair cut? The warmth of the shop, the murmur of low noise, the gentle hum of the razor, all on top of a late night and a glass or two too much wine. He didn't stand a chance. Still, he was preoccupied with murder and killing and death and had begun to wonder if there was some way that was used to kill animals which could be applied in some novel way to humans.

'Lambs,' he said suddenly, even though he was struggling to keep his eyes open, following on from a brief discussion on the fate of calves. 'How do they kill them?'

'Do they kill lambs?' asked the customer from the bench, a look of concern on his face.

Barney looked at him, then turned back to Randolph.

'Had a customer once,' said Barney, continuing to engage Randolph in conversation, 'a farmer. Here's what they did.'

Randolph caught his eye in the mirror. Barney could tell he was on the verge of falling asleep.

'You know those things you get in DIY stores to dispense Polyfilla and grout and stuff? A long tube, you push a plunger down from the top. It's a spring-loaded one of them. Metal. Pull it back, stick it at the back of the lamb's napper, let it go. The next thing the lamb knows it's snuggling up to some mint sauce.'

Randolph closed his eyes.

'That's why they call them spring lambs,' added Barney.

'They don't do that to lambs, do they?' said the voice from the back. 'They don't kill lambs? Not really?'

Barney and Igor glanced at each other.

'How do you think they get the lamb from the field onto the plate?' asked Barney.

'But lamb,' he said. 'I mean, I never really equated the two.'

'What did you think lamb was? Some sort of processed meat extract, which they just called lamb to give it a name?'

'But lamb! They don't call pig, pig. They don't call cow, cow. So why do they call lamb, lamb? I always thought, well I don't know, that it was something totally different.'

'Some other less cute animal?' suggested Barney.

'Yes.'

Barney stared at Thomas Petersen, gave a look to Igor and then turned back to James Randolph.

'Well,' he said, 'does that answer your questi....' and he stopped when he saw that Randolph's eyes were closed and the man had drifted off to sleep. Barney smiled to himself and lapsed into silence. The customer asleep, he could go about his business without prejudice or interruption. The ideal situation. So he snipped quietly away at an area behind the left ear and wondered why the man had bothered to bring up the subject in the first place.

✂

Ten minutes later, James Randolph awoke with a start. He straightened up and looked in the mirror, established his bearings, realised that he'd fallen asleep in the middle of a haircut, then got his head around the fact that the very vivid dream from which he'd just emerged was exactly that. A dream. A dream in which someone had just been murdered.

165

Barney dabbed at the back of Randolph's jumper with a brush. Randolph rubbed his hands roughly over his face as he hurried through the dream, committing it to memory before it faded.

He started to smile. He had been an observer in the dream, standing outside a lone house on the side of a hill. Dusk, the sea below, the last gulls of the day crying to the departed sun, the sound of the wind bustling around his head. He had looked in through the sitting room window into a house he did not recognise. And there he had watched a killer and his victim, and he had watched the victim die a most singular death.

The smile broadened. Was it a new kind of murder which he had just witnessed? Probably not, but it was interesting and it was different. Different enough, he felt sure, to impress Bartholomew Ephesian for the first time in his life.

Still, he would have to do a little research, and where better to start than the barbershop?

'Everything all right for you, sir?' asked Barney, administering the final brush down.

'What d'you know about stomach acids?' said Randolph suddenly, looking at Barney in the mirror.

Barney recognised that the wheels were turning, that here was a man with a plan. He himself had developed a nose for murderous intent and this was what he was seeing in James Randolph.

'Nothing,' said Barney. 'Nothing at all.'

'There are acids in your stomach?' wittered the concerned customer from the back.

Randolph took in Barney's gaze for another couple of seconds, and then turned away and stared into the mirror. A fine haircut, the hair of a man who was about to mean business for the first time in his life. Get home, a cup of tea, and then he could spend a short while on-line as he established exactly what he needed in order to commit the crime which he had just witnessed in his dream. And then he would be set to execute the murder as laid down by Bartholomew Ephesian.

James Randolph had not, after all, been informed of the change of plans.

✄

166

'Well, that's a lot of money,' said Romeo McGhee, smiling. He looked round at Chardonnay Deluth who was smiling back, her eyes wide with greed. One million pounds. For a piece of bony meat. Easiest money either of them would ever make. McGhee, however, was about to get a lot greedier. 'You guys must be pretty desperate to get a hold of Jonah's hand.'

He flicked his eyebrows at Jacobs, smiled some more.

'You as desperate as you look?' he asked cheekily.

Jacobs had a sudden vision of leaping across the coffee table and pounding McGhee's face. He closed his eyes, composed himself, closed the case and straightened his shoulders.

Ephesian was at home battling his demons. Jacobs had not had to persuade Ephesian to allow him to undertake this particular task on his own. Ephesian's humour and confidence were fragile enough for him to retreat at the first sign of trouble. More regrouping. What he required was for something to go right, yet the closer they got to the culmination of decades of work, the more problems there seemed to be.

Despite his excitement at what lay ahead, Ephesian had begun to think that perhaps they would have to postpone. It didn't have to be this evening and perhaps they had rushed into it following Lawton's discovery. And it would be a wonderful way of pissing off Ping Phat, the fat Chinese bastard having dragged himself onto a plane for the first time in decades.

Jacobs favoured pressing ahead. Did not believe that any of their problems were insurmountable, regardless of the missing Grail. Assumed, wrongly, that whoever had attacked Lawton would appear McGhee-esque from the woodwork to levy some trivial blackmail demand.

'You've seen the money,' said Jacobs indifferently. 'Let me see the hand.'

'Not so fast, bucko,' said McGhee stupidly.

Jacobs' face remained expressionless. This was not unexpected. Even the lowest form of life always thinks it can get more than its due. Chardonnay Deluth, on the other hand, slung him a look of horror. She was about to get her hands on one million pounds.

'Rome!' she ejaculated. 'What's with you?'

'It's cool, babe,' he said, eyes never leaving Jacobs. 'We're still going to get our million. Aren't we, Mr Jacobs? Or should I call you Cream Cracker?'

He laughed at his own joke. Jacobs, who hadn't heard the joke since he was seven or eight, stared deeply into McGhee's core and imagined injecting him with a vial of some flesh-eating virus and watching his body rot and die over the ensuing few weeks.

'What do you want?' Voice hard as marble, dull as dust.

'Rome!' repeated Deluth.

'Well,' said Romeo McGhee, 'I've been thinking.'

'Romeo, don't be a fucking idiot,' she said, leaning towards him, her voice lowered, as if Jacobs wasn't going to hear her.

'What do you want?' asked Jacobs again, ignoring the woman.

'Well,' said McGhee, 'as far as the talk goes around here, you cowboys have a right little brotherhood between you all, with your tasty little clandestine meetings on a Tuesday evening. Donut Jonah was a member of your wee cabal and presumably the frozen hand is all tied up with the same business.'

He paused, asking the question of 'hot or cold' with his eyebrows raised. Jacobs remained impenetrable. McGhee was slightly disarmed by Jacobs inscrutability but managed to keep up his confidence, or at least, the appearance of it.

'So, what I'm thinking is that you'll need someone to take Donut Jonah's place, am I right?'

Jacobs said nothing.

'For fuck's sake, Romeo, don't be an arsehole!' said Deluth.

He waved her down with a calm hand.

'You've turned up here with a million quid, exactly as I asked for. No attempt to negotiate me down, no attempt to strong-arm, you just want the hand so that you can get on with whatever you're doing. So I'm thinking, chief-o, that you must be doing something pretty soon. Now I want to be a part of it.'

'Do you?' said Jacobs coldly, speaking at last.

'Aye,' said McGhee, 'I do.'

They held each others' gaze across the coffee table, Deluth simmering on the sidelines.

Jacobs breathed deeply. The urge to leap across the table and tear him to pieces was strong. He glanced at Deluth but she was playing her part in the Mexican stand-off by staring at McGhee.

If he killed McGhee with his bare hands right now, Jacobs thought, would it terrorise Deluth into telling him where the hand was hidden?

Jacobs abruptly stood up, clutching onto the bag.

'I'll need to speak to Mr Ephesian,' he said, then turned and started to walk away.

It would mean returning empty-handed once more to see his boss but he could sense the anger within him about to come bursting brutally to the surface, and it is rare in life for such an explosion of rage to ever achieve anything positive. At least allowing McGhee into their forum would guarantee the hand being there and it wasn't as if they had a queue of decent applicants lined up. And, now that Lawton was in hospital and not showing any signs of waking up, they were looking for two new members of the brotherhood, rather than one.

'You can leave the money,' said McGhee, his voice oozing slime even without trying.

Jacobs stopped but did not turn. Counting to ten.

'No I can't,' he said eventually without turning, then he opened the door into the hall and was gone.

They listened to the front door closing, and then McGhee and Deluth looked at each other. McGhee smiled, suddenly having disappeared several miles up himself.

'Cool, eh?' he said. 'We are so kicking their butts.'

'You,' said Chardonnay Deluth, 'are a complete fucking twat.'

And she walked brusquely to the bathroom to install herself and seethe.

32

The Barbershop Quartet

'I'm not sure, really. What do you think?'

Barney looked at the back of the customer's head. The man was in his late eighties, weak-jawed, sallow-skinned and irresolutely-eyed; the customer who had been waiting behind Randolph. Had a good head of grey hair on him, however, demanding a straightforward short back and sides.

'I think a short back and sides would do you fine, sir.'

'Do you think?' said Thomas Petersen, studying his hair in the mirror, as if coming across it for the first time.

'Aye,' said Barney.

Igor looked suspiciously up from his sweeping.

'I had been thinking more of a *Keanu Reeves* type of affair. You don't think I'd suit that at all?'

The door opened and another old fella, his face hangdog all the way down to his knees, minced in, huddled against the cold as if it was minus fifty outside. He closed the door and regarded the occupants of the shop.

'Aye, it's all right for you lot sitting in here, with your heating and your fancy double glazing,' he muttered.

Igor rolled his eyes.

'If you'd just like to take a seat, I'll be done here in about ten minutes,' said Barney.

'Is that all?' said Thomas Petersen. 'Are you sure?'

'All right, all right, I'll sit down,' said the newcomer, 'but God knows what havoc that old bench is going to play on my haemorrhoids. I'd be better standing, but then if I do that my varicose veins'll pop and my hip replacement'll seize up. Can't sit, can't stand and Christ knows what it would do to me if I tried to kneel. Christ knows.'

'Igor,' said Barney, 'get the fella another cushion, please.'

Igor nodded a resentful acceptance and disappeared into the back room. The old fella tutted and looked out of the window.

'They say it's going to be this cold until the autumn and then it's going to snow for six months,' he said to no one in particular.

'So,' said Barney, deciding to ignore the ray of sunshine in the corner, 'a short back and sides all right for you, sir?'

Thomas Petersen looked doubtfully in the mirror.

'Well, if you're sure,' he said.

Barney lifted the electric razor, flicked the switch and swung the razor down onto the back of the customer's neck. Igor emerged and handed the new boy the cushion.

'I suppose technically that's a cushion,' he mumbled, as Igor trudged back to his sweeping, 'but it'll probably cause complete mayhem with the trapped nerves at the base of my spine.'

And then he sat down with a great deal of puffing and muttering, as Igor lifted the broom and imagined himself a Ninja.

And so, everybody in their place, the shop settled down. First customer getting his hair cut, second customer waiting on the bench, barber at his position, razor buzzing away in his fingers, barber's deaf, mute, hunchbacked assistant sweeping at invisible particles on the floor. The natural order of things.

Ruth Harrison had been dispatched for a walk along the front to get some fresh air. She was sitting on a green bench beside the crazy golf course, fingers crossed in her lap, jumping every time she heard footsteps on the pavement behind her. Trying to lose herself in an intimate world of seagulls and waves and rocks and sky, to wrap herself into a cocoon of all she had ever known. Return to some childhood place where the world could be blocked out and she could play and be in her own imaginary world for hours on end.

She was aware of the cars passing behind her every now and again but many of them slipped by unnoticed. So it was that, when the cavalry from *wraithwreckers.com* arrived in their twenty-four year-old red Peugeot, she did not see them. The car pulled up outside the barbershop, not too far from where she was sitting, as Barney had directed.

Merlot Tolstoy stepped out of the vehicle, put on her _1.99 Woolworth's shades, looked up and down Shore Street checking for possessed spirits and demons and any other agents of malfeasance, turned and looked out on what she saw as a godless, cruel sea, and then walked into the barbershop.

The four male occupants of the shop turned. The maroon shirt with white dog collar attachment was a bit of a giveaway, so that Barney and Igor immediately knew who had come into their presence. Thomas Petersen and old miserable-as-shite Jack Monroe regarded the newcomer with some concern.

'We're here,' said Tolstoy, authoritatively.

'Thanks for coming,' said Barney, not stopping the cut.

'No problem. Got here as fast as we could. Boat was running ten minutes behind schedule.'

'Ten minutes?' chimed Monroe. 'You're lucky it wasn't ten hours. And you call that a boat? It's a bath with an engine.'

Tolstoy hesitated then turned back to Barney.

'Are you ready to show us the infected property?'

'Give me another couple of minutes to finish this off, then I'll need to do the other gentleman, which won't take long...'

'Are you saying I don't have much hair?'

'...then we'll go. Ruth is waiting just along the front.'

Tolstoy glanced out the window and made a positive identification of the forlorn and scared woman on the bench.

'We saw her on the way by. Have we got a complement of six?'

'Well,' said Barney, 'there's you and me. There's Ruth, whose husband is the problem. There's Igor here behind the brush.'

'Igor,' said Tolstoy with a nod.

'Arf.'

172

'Then I thought we could ask these two gentlemen if they might help,' said Barney, giving them both a quick glance.

'Ask us what?' asked Thomas Petersen, sounding concerned.

'Typical,' said the old fella from the bench, 'that's what today's society's all about. Always asking, never giving. No doubt I'll end up doing it, whatever it is you want, but I won't like it, I'm telling you that now. Not one bit.'

'What is it?' asked Petersen, 'I mean, you're not saying much, but already I don't like the sound of it.'

'Exorcism,' said Tolstoy. 'We need a gathering of six.'

'Exorcism!' said Petersen, and fortunately Barney felt the explosion of worry and restlessness coming and knew enough to back away from the cut for five seconds, as Petersen's head swivelled round. Although, not all the way round.

'Standard procedure,' said Tolstoy. 'We do it all the time.'

And she gave Barney a bit of a *don't blow my cover, we need these people* look. Barney kept schtum.

'Who is 'we' exactly?' asked Jack Monroe from the bench.

'But exorcism,' worried Petersen, whose head had at least calmed down enough for Barney to restart the cut, 'how do you mean that? Are we talking demonic possession? Green vomit and bile and really bad language? I don't like bad language.'

'If there are more of you,' continued Monroe, 'why do you need us two to make up the six? Sounds like there's some sort of ecumenical insurance scam going on. You church people are only ever interested in money. Did you know the Catholic Church owns 51% of *ExxonMobil*? What is the matter with these people? Used to be the church was about values and decency. Not now.'

'Do we need overalls?' asked Petersen, interrupting.

'Arf!' barked Igor from behind his brush.

'Aye,' said Barney. 'Enough talk. I'll finish these cuts, then the five of us are picking up Ruth and heading over to her house to see what's what. We cool?'

'We're cool,' said Tolstoy.

'Arf,' said Igor.

'I think so,' said Petersen with no conviction whatsoever.

173

'So Ruth's getting haunted by old Jonah, eh?' said Monroe. 'Serves her right for all those lovers of hers. I always said no good would come of it. Always said it.'

And he shook his head disapprovingly.

'Arf.'

33

The Postman Always
Brings Mice

'Psst! Psst!'

Tony Angellotti stopped and looked around. He had walked up Cardiff Street, had kept going up the hill past the farm and was approaching the top of the town with the graveyard and golf course beyond.

He thought he'd heard something but decided he probably hadn't, and started to walk on again.

'Psst! Tony!' Louder this time. Tony turned, as ostentatiously as Luigi had hoped he wouldn't.

'Luigi?' he said, looking into woods, up and down the road. 'Luigi?'

'Not so stinkin' loud, you idiot,' said Luigi. 'Try and look inconspicuous.'

'Where are you?' asked Tony, louder this time, because he was confused and annoyed.

'Stop looking like you're talking to someone, you moron. Lean on the post box beside you and try to look casual.'

Tony looked at the box and suddenly wondered if that was where the voice was coming from. Then he leant on it, looking as conspicuous as an Italian Vatican-sponsored hoodlum in Millport in the middle of April was going to.

'Are you in the freakin' post box?' he said, looking down in through the hole.

'I said don't be conspicuous, you idiot. Do not look in the fucking box!'

Tony straightened up, still looking at the box, doing the full Italian hand gesturing routine thing.

'So you're in the box?' said Tony.

'Of course I'm not in the box! What's the matter with you?'

Tony stared at the box and then finally settled down and stopped looking like a blot on the landscape. He leant against the box, tried to look relaxed and stared super-casually up the road.

As it was, he was not being watched as Luigi had presumed he would be. Bartholomew Ephesian's mind had been on other things and the Italians had slipped through the net of his concerns. That Jacobs had also let the problem escape, was indicative of the pressures he too was feeling, despite his efforts to be the rock for his employer's fragile self-belief.

'So where are you then?' asked Tony.

'I'm on the hill above the golf course,' said Luigi. 'Don't look up here!' he added with a stage whisper, at exactly the point that Tony turned and looked up at the hill above the golf course.

'So are you, like shouting?' he asked, turning and looking back into the woods. 'How come I can hear you?'

'Cause there's a microphone in the freakin' post box,' said Luigi, with exasperation.

Tony looked back at the post box, nodding his appreciation.

'This is some fucking post box,' said Tony. 'Maybe this country isn't as backward as it looks.'

'I put it there you idiot. Jesus, how did I end up with a partner this stupid?'

'Yeah, well, the guy you sent to talk to me last night was even more stupid than I was, so what does that make you?'

Luigi started to object in the usual manner but actually saw his point, so instead made an abrupt change of subject.

'Did you find anything in the cathedral?' he asked.

Tony shook his head and turned and looked up at the hill.

'I can't see you up there, are you sure that's where you are?'

'I'm hiding behind a stinkin' bush. Stop looking up here and tell me if you found anything in the cathedral.'

176

Tony shrugged, glancing at a passing car, while attempting to appear even more casual than he already was.

'I couldn't find nothin', but then, I'm an idiot. Go figure.'

He smiled at his ironic self-deprecation.

'You still there?' he asked, looking at the post box.

'I'm thinking,' said Luigi.

And while he was thinking, he was lying down on the cold grass, on top of approximately thirty-seven individual little pieces of rabbit droppings, looking through the bushes behind him to where the big house of Bartholomew Ephesian sat austerely staring down over the golf course, down to the Firth of Clyde.

'Big house, big problems,' he muttered quietly.

Ephesian's house had been the number two location on his agenda, after the cathedral. From where he now lay, concealed in the bushes and grass, he had a clear view of the road leading up to the house, as well as the two main windows at the back, which overlooked the westward view. So he had already had several sightings of Ephesian and Jacobs, although had decided not to try to follow them about the town. Tony would have to be his eyes and ears, no matter how blind and deaf that made him.

'Mouse?' said Tony. 'Did you say something about a freakin' mouse? I hate mice.'

✂

'Do you think we should postpone?' asked Ephesian, finally voicing what he had been thinking.

Jacobs stared at his employer's back, well used to his crumbling confidence in the face of setbacks.

'I think that would be unwise, sir,' said Jacobs. 'The longer we leave matters, particularly now that the Grail has been moved, the more chance there is of something going wrong.'

'Of something going wrong?' said Ephesian strongly. 'You don't think enough has already gone wrong?'

'We're almost there, sir,' said Jacobs soothingly, 'we must hold our nerve. The Brotherhood are forewarned and will be in attendance. McGhee's foolishness plays into our hands. I no more want him as part of the *Prieure* than do you, but if he comes, he is coming straight back with the hand which is all we

177

need. One of our two main problems solved. The money means nothing and we have a replacement for Jonah Harrison.'

'And Lawton?' said Ephesian. 'And the Grail? And bloody Phat, who will be turning up here any minute?'

Jacobs hesitated, sorting out how to order everything, to minimise the concern.

'With McGhee replacing Harrison, Lawton's injuries just leave us where we were to begin with, needing to find a willing participant to the ritual. Your son Anthony is likely still that person, despite his brief association with the Italians.'

'And they're another thing! Jesus.'

'But we have the package which was held in Lawton's freezer, his replacement is a formality, however unwanted. Ping Phat? All the more reason to insist on conducting the ceremony tonight. What if we postpone and he decides to stick around? He could cause all sorts of trouble.'

Ephesian's head twitched.

'The Italians we can do nothing about, until it is time and we see what moves they are likely to make. Despite his previous ham-fisted attempts to negate the problem, we can probably count on Constable Gainsborough to deal with them as they arise.'

Ephesian grunted.

'Having thought ourselves in trouble, suddenly we are left with one real problem,' said Jacobs. He paused.

'The Grail,' said Ephesian.

'Yes,' answered Jacobs.

He checked his watch then looked round at the clock. Almost one o'clock in the afternoon.

'We have just over eleven hours in which to find it,' he said, and Ephesian blurted out a bitter laugh.

'We should postpone,' he muttered, shaking his head.

He turned and glanced at Jacobs' waistcoat, then turned away and looked down once more at the slight wind ruffling the flags on the golf course away to his right.

34

Et In Arcadia Ego

'Is there anything else we should know before we go in?'

The strange collective of six, about to embark on their mission to send Jonah Harrison on his way from the house, were standing outside on the front lawn. The Reverend Merlot Tolstoy was leading the way but had stopped with her back to the front door to address her troops. She looked each of the five members of the company in the eye, searching their souls. She had been told about the manner of Jonah's death and the reason he hadn't been able to enter the shrine of eternal urination in the first place. She had been told of Igor's use and abuse of the fragile Ruth. She had not been told of the severed human hand in the freezer, as neither Barney nor Ruth had considered that relevant.

Her look lingered longest on Ruth, as she was obviously the one who would have something to tell. Long enough, in fact, that Ruth felt compelled to say something.

'I'm scared of spiders,' she blurted out uncomfortably.

'That's all right, madam,' said Tolstoy, 'We doubt that that will come into play. Anything else?' she added, broadening her scope around the group once more. It was intended as a final remark, to be ignored, before they entered the temple of doom.

'I'm afraid of the dark,' said Thomas Petersen nervously.

'Oh, for pity's sake,' muttered Monroe. 'It's two o'clock in the afternoon. Course, the way this weather's closing in, it'll be dark by half past. Have you seen those clouds?'

179

'Not a problem,' said Tolstoy. 'We don't require darkness.'

Final look around the crowd. Ready to roll.

'I'm scared of wide open spaces,' Ruth Harrison chipped in at the last second.

'We'll be inside,' replied Tolstoy quickly.

'I can get claustrophobic in a small room with too many people,' said Petersen. 'And sometimes the light bothers me. You know, if it's too bright.'

'We believe we're doing this on the upstairs landing, so it'll be nice and open, with plenty of room for the six of us, and with this cloud cover the light shouldn't be too bad.'

'I hate flying,' said Ruth.

'Me too!' blurted Petersen hurriedly.

'You know,' added Ruth, 'not the actual flying part, just the take off and landing and when it gets bumpy.'

'Aye,' said Petersen, 'that's what gets me too. I think.'

'Really, folks,' said Tolstoy, retaining her patience, 'we're walking up the stairs, not taking a helicopter.'

'Helicopter?' said Petersen, perturbed, 'I wouldn't even go near a helicopter.'

'I don't think I'll ever be able to walk up a flight of stairs again after this,' said Ruth. 'I'll be traumatised for life. Like Agnes from number eleven. Couldn't walk up stairs again after the time she found her old man in bed with his best mate, Brian.'

'I think we could do with some focus here,' said Barney.

'Absolutely,' chirped Tolstoy. 'What the man said. It's time.'

'I hate Des O'Connor,' said Petersen.

'Arf.'

'Let's go,' said Tolstoy, and she turned, opened the door and took the first step into the house.

She stopped, she listened. Barney came in behind her and stood at her shoulder, examining the silence, whilst the others waited outside.

'Nothing,' said Tolstoy after about thirty seconds.

'Maybe he's waiting for us,' said Barney.

'Maybe.'

'For pity's sake,' said Monroe, 'if I stand out here much longer my sciatic nerve'll go, then I'll never see the last of it.'

Tolstoy turned and addressed her troops once more.

'We're going up. Everyone come into the house and stay close together. If anyone starts to drop off the back, call out for assistance.'

'I thought we were only going upstairs?' said Petersen.

Ruth Harrison suddenly grabbed hold of Igor's hand. He winced slightly but squeezed her hand all the same, and then this bizarre collective minced into the house and began to trudge heavy-legged up the stairs.

'I bet I end up missing the snooker,' muttered Monroe.

✂

The magnificent six were holding onto one another's hands, although this was making a majority of the men feel a little uncomfortable as there weren't enough women to go around. Their discomfort was being added to by the general feeling of unease in the house, a feeling of evil and of some unseen possessed spirit. Ruth was shaking with fear and anxiety, delighted to be holding onto Barney and Igor.

'We must all put our faith in the Lord God,' said Tolstoy, and Barney wasn't sure if she was referring to the group or just herself.

'Oh for crying out loud,' muttered Monroe.

'Are you sure?' asked Petersen.

They had been in the house for just under twenty minutes and had so far yet to bear witness to the shuffling footsteps of Jonah Harrison. Barney and Igor were curious as to what had happened to the old fella. Petersen was growing increasingly nervous. Monroe was having his high level of scepticism duly rewarded. Tolstoy was beginning to think that it was all a complete load of nonsense but knew she had to go through with the whole shebang in order to justify her fee. Ruth was beginning to feel like you do when you call the TV repairman and the flippin' thing starts working fine the second he walks through the door.

'I am the man that hath seen affliction by the rod of his wrath,' began the Reverend Tolstoy, embarking on the odd bit

181

of *Lamentations* because she thought she ought to be saying something. That thing she'd said to Barney earlier on the phone, about basing her exorcism on a 5th century Aramaic ceremony had been a complete load of mince. She was just plain winging it. 'He hath led me, and brought me into darkness, but not into light. My flesh and my skin hath he made old; he hath broken my bones.'

'I know how that feels,' said Monroe in a low mutter, still aggrieved that he was between Petersen and Igor.

'He was unto me as a bear lying in wait, and as a lion in secret places. He hath caused arrows of his quiver to enter into my reins. I was a derision to all my people; and their song all the day.'

'Oh, aye?' mumbled Monroe.

'Where are you going with this, exactly?' asked Petersen.

'He hath filled me with bitterness, he hath made me drunken with wormwood. He hath also broken my teeth with gravel stones.'

'Well, you wouldn't want to go to a dentist around here,' muttered Monroe.

'O Lord!' exclaimed Tolstoy, upping the tempo, 'fill us with your grace and your munificence. Come amongst us and be one with our circle of faith. My heart is fix'd, Lord; I will sing, and with my glory praise.'

That ought to do it, thought Barney.

'My God! Moab's my washing-pot,' she blurted on, quoting any old part of the Bible she could get her hands on, 'my shoe I'll over Edom throw.'

'Are you sure you've done this before?' asked Petersen.

'My Beloved Jesus, there is a darkness in this house that rends its very spirit. We beseech you, come into this dark land and free the haunted and accursed souls and let them go on their way to Heaven! Not unto us, O Lord, not unto us, but unto thy name give glory, for thy mercy, and for thy truth's sake.'

She paused. She looked upwards at the badly needing painted white ceiling, with a very unpleasant purple floral border. The scepticism around the circle was growing and she was getting the vibe. Time for some more Old Testament, she thought.

'O Heavenly Father, the flesh that toucheth any unclean thing shall not be eaten; it shall be burnt with fire: and as for the flesh, all that be clean shall eat thereof. But the soul that eateth of the flesh of the sacrifice of peace offerings, that pertain unto the Lord, having his uncleanliness upon him, even that soul shall be cut off from his people!'

'She's talking about lunch now,' said Monroe.

'Dear Christ!' she ejaculated.

Took the words right out of my mouth, thought Igor.

'Dear Christ!' she repeated, going off wildly on any tangent which came to mind, 'For there was a deadly destruction throughout all the city; the hand of God was very heavy there. And the men that died not were smitten with the haemorrhoids: and the cry of the city went up to heaven!'

'Don't talk to me about haemorrhoids,' said Monroe bitterly.

'Sshh!' said Barney suddenly. The crisp sharp sound immediately heightened the tension around the circle and brought back the nerves and the adrenaline which had begun to subside. Hands were squeezed more tightly, a couple of them threw anxious glances over their shoulders. It was coming at last. The first noise from Jonah's office.

A chair was pushed in at the desk. The footsteps strode hurriedly across the floor, the door opened. At least, there was the sound of the door opening; the gentle creak of the hinges, the door being dragged across the carpet. The assembled company stared at the door but it had not moved.

Now there was a pause, as if the ghost of Jonah Harrison was standing in the doorway, looking at this absurd circle of six. They couldn't see him but they felt him, they all knew he was there. Even the miserable Monroe could tell there was another, even more miserable, presence in their midst.

'Jonah!' cried Ruth Harrison, looking at the doorway in fear and awe. 'I'm sorry, I'm really sorry! I should have let you into the bathroom. Can you forgive me?'

They held tightly onto one another, each one wary of the unseen manifestation of one man's need to pee.

'And Igor,' she added. 'I'm sorry about Igor!'

183

'It's hardly your fault he's a hunchback,' said Monroe, whose wariness, to be fair, was bordering on weariness.

'Arf.'

'Cast out this spirit from within these walls, Dear Lord,' burst forth the Reverend Tolstoy, almost in song. 'Allow him at last to relieve the ache within his innermost flesh, allow him to release the burning glory of his bladder, allow him to free his most divine pee from the prison of his urinary tract, and let him travel on once more, through the path of life unto death!'

Barney slung her a look but her eyes were closed, her face pointed upwards, aiming pleadingly at the Lord.

'Cry freedom! dear Christ, and unleash the dogs of waste water!'

Barney smiled ruefully and looked back at the door. Ruth Harrison, however, was fearfully gripping onto his hand, her heart racing, her nerves strained far more tightly than they had been over the previous two days. And, on the other side of her from Barney, her nails were digging into Igor's palms.

Thomas Petersen was even more scared. The Reverend Tolstoy, had she had a second to be honest with herself, would have had to admit to also being consumed by terror, which was why the tone of her voice was becoming more and more agitated with each fervent shout.

'And when he was come into his house, he took a knife, and laid hold on his concubine, and divided her, together with her bones, into twelve pieces, and sent her into all the coasts of Israel!'

'Lost her bleedin' marbles,' said Monroe.

'And in this way, Dear Jesus, divide the eternal urine of Jonah Harrison into twelve pieces and send it into the waste pipes of the land and down to all the coasts of Scotland!'

Just as everyone else in attendance was about to turn upon her, castigate her for being a complete idiot and strike her down with great vengeance, there came another sound from the doorway. Once more blood froze, hearts skipped beats and fingernails dug viciously into the clammy palms of others.

A first, tentative footstep, as if Jonah was unsure whether or not to stride purposefully along the corridor to the bathroom.

184

'Oh my God!' yelled the Reverend Tolstoy, in such a manner that the meaning was not entirely clear.

'Come on, Jonah,' said Barney, thinking that at least one of them ought to retain some grasp on sense, however bizarre the circumstances.

'Aye,' said Monroe, 'I've missed my afternoon cup of tea because of this, and you know what happens to my kidneys when I do that.'

'My God forbid it me,' wailed the minister, 'that I should do this thing: shall I drink the blood of these men that have put their lives in jeopardy?'

'You're not drinking my flippin' blood,' said Monroe.

'Arf!'

Another footstep and then another more quickly followed. They could not see him, but they knew he was almost upon them. Ruth gasped, Thomas Petersen was terrified and contemplating making a break for it.

'Stand firm!' barked Barney.

'Come amongst us, Jonah!' cried the minister, 'and feel the hand of the Lord upon you!'

Another step and suddenly Jonah was in their midst. As one, each of the six, these hardy four men and two women, could feel his presence, as if his soul was passing straight through them. And each of them suddenly felt the most burning desire to go to the toilet.

Ruth gasped, Tolstoy ejaculated strangely, Petersen whimpered.

'Jesus,' said Barney.

'Good thing I wore my incontinence pants,' said Monroe glumly, even though he had for once found the positive in a situation.

And then, as instantly as it had come, the feeling of intense, bladder-bursting need had passed and Jonah's footsteps trudged on in the direction of the bathroom. Relief swept through each of the six as the sensation of need disappeared, yet they were each left with a great comprehension of Jonah's bane.

'Free him, Lord!' howled the minister, 'now that we have each shared in the anguish of his urinary torment. Free him! Free his soul! Free his urine from its eternal prison!'

Petersen finally cracked and pulled his hand away from Tolstoy. On his other side, Igor held tight and would not let him away.

'Do not break the circle!' shouted Tolstoy, flailing around for Petersen's hand.

'I want to!' he wailed back.

'Hold her hand!' barked Barney authoritatively. 'Do it!'

Petersen swallowed, big wide nervous eyes, and allowed Tolstoy to grab onto his cold and damp fingers.

'Girl,' said Monroe gruffly.

They heard the sound of the bathroom door open and close and then lock, although they did not see it move.

'Here we go, Lord!' screamed Tolstoy, as if Jonah was clean through on the goalkeeper in the last minute of the World Cup Final. 'Freedom!'

She paused, she gripped tightly onto Barney and Petersen. There was a silence, as they stood and waited, bodies tense, every sense strained and directed towards the bathroom.

And then it came. A dribble at first, then quickly a free-flowing stream of gold. And although the burning desire to pee had passed through each of the assembled company and was now gone, they each felt Jonah's enormous relief as finally, with the helping hand of the Lord God, he was able to substantively pee.

'Thank God for that,' said Petersen.

'We must!' exclaimed Tolstoy.

Ruth's shoulders dropped, her head dipped an inch, her grip on the others relaxed, as the strong stream of pee gradually began to wear down after almost a minute.

'But this is just what I've heard before,' she mumbled. 'He's done this a hundred times. He's still here.'

Barney gripped her hand more tightly, as did Igor.

'This is different,' said Tolstoy, her voice suddenly quiet, having lost all the qualities of the TV evangelist which she'd had for the previous ten minutes. 'Feel it, Ruth. It's not just

Jonah who is here. God is also amongst us. Jonah will be free, Ruth, believe me.'

'But how will I know?'

She stared at Tolstoy, eyes wide with hope and fear and desperation and a hundred other conflicting emotions.

The toilet flushed. They heard the unmistakable sound of a zipper being pulled up.

'Does the toilet usually flush?' asked Tolstoy.

'Yes,' said Ruth, quietly. 'There's no difference.'

The door to the bathroom opened. Ruth turned quickly to look, her heart suddenly in her mouth.

And there he was. Jonah Harrison. Or, at least, the spectral wraith of Jonah Harrison. They could see through him, back into the bathroom, but he was definitely there, in all his former hugeness.

'Oh, fuck,' said Petersen.

'Dear God,' said Tolstoy. 'Dear God,' she repeated.

'Jonah?' said Ruth. 'Jonah?'

But he was not staring at her. He stood in the doorway for a second, eyes looking nowhere in particular, but with a comforted and fulfilled appearance about him. Then he rubbed his hands together and started to walk towards the circle.

Petersen recoiled, the others held firm.

One, two, three footsteps and he was almost upon them. They tensed, Barney and Igor held firmly onto Ruth, and then the ghost of Jonah Harrison walked through the entwined hands of his widow and Barney Thomson.

'Jonah!' she exclaimed.

But still he did not look at her, there was no acknowledgement from him of the small band of exorcists. He stopped in the middle of the circle, so that each of the six was no more than two feet away from the ghost.

'Dear God, take his soul,' said Tolstoy, thinking she ought to say something.

'Jonah?' said Ruth.

At last he turned and looked directly into the eyes of his widow. He smiled, a look that seemed to forgive her everything.

187

All her mistakes and foibles of the last two days, and all her faults and errors from the previous thirty years.

'Oh, Jonah!' she said, and she pulled her hand away from Barney and held it out towards him.

He stood still. He embraced her with a smile once more, and then slowly his vague appearance, his thin apparition, began to fade.

'Jonah!' she said again, more loudly.

One last smile, one final look between husband and wife, and he was gone and Ruth Harrison was left staring into the face of old Jack Monroe.

'Oh, God,' she said, and then suddenly she was on her knees, her hand slipping free of Igor, great wells of tears suddenly coming from the pit of her stomach.

Barney was about to make a move to comfort her but the Reverend Tolstoy nodded at him and then she bent down beside her and put an arm around her shoulder. Barney and Igor stared at one another and then shivered, as they felt the same footsteps across their graves.

Now that it was over, Petersen backed away from the small crowd and leant against the wall, eyes still wide with fear and awe.

Monroe surveyed the scene for a few seconds.

'Suppose you think that went well,' he muttered.

And, as Ruth Harrison finally wept for her husband, the assorted men of the strange little exorcism turned away and left her and the Reverend Tolstoy alone, to at last submit to her grief.

Barney turned at the top of the stairs and looked back at the two women, kneeling on the floor. He caught Tolstoy's eye and she nodded at him. Barney returned the look and then followed Igor down the stairs and back out of the small house, which was no longer haunted by the ghost of Jonah Harrison.

35

Satan & Sally

Father Andrew Roosevelt was giving a brief interview to a young couple, who had ventured into his presence to ask him to marry them. They had arrived with an appointment a little less than thirty seconds before Jacobs and Ephesian had also arrived to see Roosevelt. Jacobs had wanted to barge in, push the young couple aside and get on with business. Ephesian had instructed that they wait their turn.

And so the two most important men on the island sat outside the small office in the college buildings beside the cathedral, while Father Roosevelt took a short consultation with Sauvignon Medoc and Buster Mack.

Roosevelt looked up from their birth certificates and smiled.

'Everything seems to be in order,' he said. Mind completely distracted by the not unexpected arrival of the Dark Knight and his henchman. Roosevelt was very, very nervous. He could, when the mood took him, be very scathing with young people whom he thought were getting married for the wrong reasons. Medoc and Mack, however, were about to get an easy time of it. Roosevelt's mind was a mess and whatever small part of it was saved for day to day parish business, was submerged under layers of anxiety.

'Cool,' said Mack.

'And when is it you'd like to get married?' he asked.

'This Saturday,' said Medoc quickly, then she smiled at Mack and they giggled.

189

Roosevelt frowned but the objections which should have been there were not in attendance.

'That's, em…' he stumbled, 'that should be fine.'

'Cool.'

'And why have you chosen the Episcopalian Church for your wedding?' asked Roosevelt, the words tripping out because that was what he always asked. And the answer to that question was one he would usually treat with the utmost scorn and derision. In eleven years of asking he had yet to discover anyone under the age of thirty who could explain to him what marked the Episcopalians out as different from the Church of Scotland.

'This is the Episcopalian Church?' asked Medoc.

'Like, I don't even know what that is, dude!' said Mack.

'Simplistically,' said Roosevelt, 'it refers to church government by bishops.'

'Bring it on!'

'Yeah,' said Medoc. 'Does that mean we get, like, married by a bishop?'

'No,' said Roosevelt, his mind pouring over all the different things which Ephesian was potentially about to throw at him. Principally, he assumed, the fact that he had allowed Lawton to remove the Holy Grail. 'I'm not a bishop.'

'Whatever,' said Medoc, 'we'll still let you do it.'

Roosevelt looked from one of them to the other, mind a thousand miles away. Or, more to the point, actually only about seven yards away. At least the presence of Ephesian meant that there was a lot less likelihood of bloodshed.

Medoc and Mack smiled curiously, recognising the priest's pre-occupation with other matters.

'Everything all right?' asked Medoc.

The words drifted into space and floated around for a while before Roosevelt realised that they'd been directed his way.

'Yes,' he said, 'sorry. Yes, everything's fine.'

He smiled at them.

'When did you two meet?' he asked.

'Last night,' said Mack.

'It was magic,' said Medoc.

190

They could have told him they hadn't met until that minute, or that they were brother and sister, and he would have gone for it.

'Last night?' said Roosevelt. 'That's lovely. Really lovely.'

'I know you must be very surprised,' said Medoc, despite the fact that Roosevelt looked as though he'd been injected with two litres of Valium, 'but do you believe in love at first sight?'

Roosevelt just heard something about love and nodded. The happy couple held hands and smiled revoltingly at each other.

'We do,' said Medoc. 'And I know what people will think. We're only seventeen, it's too early to make these decisions, but we know, deep down. This is the real thing. I feel like I've known Simon all my life.'

'Buster,' said Mack.

'Buster,' she repeated, and squeezed his hand a little harder. 'But you know, sometimes you just know, don't you?'

'Wicked,' said Mack, and Medoc giggled.

'Wicked?' she laughed. 'No one says wicked anymore. That is *so* ten years ago.'

She took her hands away and smiled at Roosevelt, as if trying to draw him into the joke.

'Are you dissin' me, bitch?' said Mack.

'You can't call me that,' said Medoc.

'If the straightjacket fits,' replied Mack, which wasn't entirely appropriate but was what his father always said to him.

She gave him the finger and then turned back to Roosevelt.

'It's a good thing I love you,' she said, without looking at him, and at the mere mention of the *L* word, Mack once again disintegrated into a pile of mush and snuggled up to her shoulder.

Roosevelt watched this little display of love, anguish and reconciliation and then suddenly decided that he couldn't put the others off forever.

'Saturday, one o'clock,' he said quickly, looking at Medoc, as it was apparent she was the brains behind the operation.

'You'll do it?' she asked, surprised.

'Whatever,' he answered. Which probably wasn't the appropriate response under the circumstances, but his mind had moved even further away from this business. 'Come and see me

191

on Friday morning and we can sort out all the details.' And the words *if you're still together by then* came to mind, which was surprising given how little he was concentrating on the two people across the desk.

'Awesome,' said Mack and stood up.

Medoc giggled.

'No one's said *awesome* in six years, David.'

'It's Buster,' he said bluntly.

'Yeah, I hear you,' she said. 'No one says awesome. It's so, like, last millennium.'

And off they went, out of the door, to argue and make up and argue again, past the waiting Ephesian and Jacobs and on out into the cold grey afternoon of an April day by the Clyde.

As soon as they had opened the door to the office, Roosevelt could see the two men waiting outside. And now he sat and waited as they slowly rose from their uncomfortable chairs, walked into his office unbidden, and closed the door behind them.

'We need to ask you some questions,' said Jacobs.

Roosevelt anxiously looked from one to the other. Jacobs' eyes burrowed into his head. Ephesian looked at the white collar of Roosevelt's yellow shirt.

'Tea?' suggested Roosevelt pathetically.

36

Artistic Distemperament

They were back in the shop because Barney wasn't entirely sure what else to do. He had offered Igor the chance to finish for the day but had recognised that, as much as he himself, Igor probably craved some normality. A few hours in the place where they both belonged, that was what was required.

They were standing together, as they often seemed to do, at the window looking out on the waves in Millport Bay. The day was getting colder as it progressed towards late afternoon, emphasising the safe comfort and warmth of the shop. Barney glanced at the clock. They had been reopened for just under an hour and, as yet, no customers had come in. Wondering if word had got around that the two of them had been involved in strange dealings of the paranormal.

'Arf,' said Igor quietly, knowing what Barney was thinking.

'Aye,' said Barney.

O wild West Wind, thou breath of Autumn's being; thou, from whose unseen presence the leaves dead are driven, like ghosts from an enchanter fleeing, yellow, and black, and pale, and hectic red, pestilence-stricken multitudes, thought Igor.

'Aye, but it's supposed to be spring,' said Barney.

'Arf,' said Igor nodding. *The seasons are all to cock these days.*

'They certainly are.'

The door opened. They turned and looked to their left. A customer had arrived just as they had been expecting there not

193

to be one. Such is the nature of things, after all. Always expect the unexpected...

'Afternoon,' said Barney.

The customer, a dour looking chap in his early forties with hair that was already short, said nothing, although he did nod uncomfortably.

Barney indicated the chair, the bloke took off his coat, handed it to Igor because Igor was waiting to take it from him, and then took his place in the big chair.

'What'll it be?' asked Barney, as Igor hung up the fellow's coat and then lifted his broom and started to sweep something up.

'Haircut,' said the man brusquely and without any hint of humour or impending elaboration.

'Number one at the sides, finger length on the top?' asked Barney.

The guy caught Barney's eye in the mirror and nodded. Possibly smiled awkwardly but it was hard to tell. Barney made his usual quick three second assessment of the napper before him, draped the cape and the towel around the bloke's shoulders and then lifted the electric razor and clipped on the number one.

'It's getting cold again,' he said casually, as he got the razor up and running and started to make smooth majestic sweeps along the side of the customer's head.

Igor glanced up. *You've more chance of getting me to talk*, he thought.

'Igor was just saying it's like autumn, and he's right,' said Barney as his next gambit.

The man stared into his own reflection.

Barney waited a few seconds, started to bring the razor round to the back of the head, then continued with, 'We were at an exorcism this afternoon. Igor and I. Pretty weird but glad we did it all the same, I think. Eh, Igor?'

'Arf.'

Barney caught the customer's eye in the mirror but he wasn't biting. He was, however, shuffling around under the cape trying to dig something out of one of his pockets. Barney, while not switching off the razor, at least took it away from the immediate

194

vicinity of his head, while he looked curiously at the man to see what he was going to produce.

Eventually, through the folds of material, the bloke came up with a small card which he held aloft. Barney took it from him, finally turning off the razor.

**University of Michigan
Department of Psychology**

This man is a writer. As such he suffers from severe artistic temperament and is consequently unable to conduct himself appropriately in even the most basic of social situations, including this one. Please do not talk to him.

Hans Elzinga

April 29th 2003   Professor Hans Elzinga PhD

He read it, thought about how wonderful it would be to have something like that and to have the balls to use it, and then offered it to Igor. Igor didn't take it but gave him a rueful smile.

'Seen it before, eh?' said Barney.

'Arf.'

Barney handed the card back to the customer, switched the razor back on, waited until the bloke had returned the card to his pocket and then began again on the back of his head.

Then he thought, bugger you, you cheeky bastard.

'Could do with one of them, myself sometimes,' said Barney. 'Must be pretty handy thing to have. I mean, does it work if you're in court or the police come to your door?'

The customer stared stony-faced at himself in the mirror.

'Are there other cards in the series? I mean, do you have positive cards which actually say something, to save you asking a question?'

He looked at Igor, who sort of smiled back.

'That'd take the hassle out of all sorts of tricky conversational situations, eh, Igor? First time you meet a woman in a bar. You

195

could just hand over your card which says, *I'm weird so I can't talk to you. However, I'd like to buy you a drink and have sex later. Nod once if you're in agreement.*'

Igor laughed. The customer didn't.

'Still, you're a deaf, mute hunchback and you manage fine without that, eh?' said Barney, catching Igor's eye in the mirror.

Igor smiled again, this time a little more sheepishly, deciding that he probably wouldn't ever let Barney see one of his *This man is a deaf, mute hunchback. Please take pity on him and let him buy you a drink and have sex* cards.

'Funny old world,' said Barney.

The customer said nothing.

'I mean,' Barney continued, intent on a rambling soliloquy, 'had this guy in the other day, who'd said he'd visited every country on the planet. Listed them all, as well. Apparently he was born in Uganda. And every time a country splits into two, or changes its name even, he has to go back. Quite fascinating. Where was the last place he'd been again? Aye, Belarus. Visited a friend in Minsk. And here's the thing about Minsk...'

✂

Jacobs cracked his knuckles. It was a primitive gesture but he could tell that the sound went straight down Roosevelt's spine. Ephesian glanced to his side, hoping this could be as painless as possible.

'Why?' said Jacobs coldly.

'I've told you,' Roosevelt answered quickly. 'He said he'd been sent by Mr Ephesian. This has always been an honest brotherhood, I had no reason to think that the bond would be undermined at this stage.'

'You knew the Grail had been uncovered,' said Ephesian, before Jacobs could interject more forcefully. 'You knew that the Day of Days is almost upon us. The Brotherhood is made of mortal men, Father, and as such itself has the characteristics of mortal men. Jealousy and rivalry and hate. You cannot see the heart of the beast without looking beneath the surface.'

'I am sorry,' said Roosevelt. 'I am a man of God. I have put my trust in the Lord and in his people, my fellow man. I cannot allow suspicion to rule my life.'

Ephesian stared at Roosevelt's chest. He liked the man, he even liked his argument. Life would be easier if everyone could be trusted. It was also his own basic instinct, one which had had to be suppressed as he had progressed in his business life. If you wanted to get ahead in almost any line of work, there was no place for honesty and trust. He had often found that out to his cost in the early days and thank God he'd always had Jacobs on hand to bail him out.

'Very well,' said Ephesian, 'what's done is done. We must move on. Have you any idea where the Grail is now?'

'I don't know!' blurted Roosevelt. 'Why don't you ask Lawton, it was he who took it.'

Ephesian glanced at Jacobs, who managed to acknowledge his boss without distracting his eyes from the interrogation of Roosevelt.

Ephesian paused, Jacobs stared, Roosevelt wilted. Felt the eyes of the other two men strip him bare down to his soul and then set him on a spit to roast over a fire.

'What?' said Roosevelt.

'He's in hospital,' replied Ephesian. 'He was assaulted.'

'With Archie Gemmill,' added Jacobs brutally. 'He's in a coma, might never get out.'

'Oh, dear God!' said Roosevelt, and his hand clutched at the small cross which he wore around his neck. 'Dear God,' he repeated, heart racing, eyes wide.

'We must be strong, Father,' said Ephesian quietly. 'We must.'

Roosevelt leant back, his hand still clutching the cross, staring at the ceiling. Tears started to form in the corners of his eyes. Jacobs looked at him with complete contempt.

'If you hadn't given him the Grail, it wouldn't have happened,' he said bitterly.

'Simon!' barked Ephesian. 'Enough.'

Roosevelt tried to choke back the emotion and the guilt, yet his tears began to flow and become more audible.

'Father,' said Ephesian gently, 'you have to control yourself. You acted in good faith, you have nothing for which to chastise yourself. Lawton has no one to blame but himself. It was he

197

who chose to extract the Grail prematurely, it is because of this that he paid the price. No one will ever blame you for the attack.'

The words went as far over his head as had the earlier words of Sauvignon Medoc and her trusty new boyfriend, Buster.

'We need your help now, Father,' said Ephesian. 'Now is our time of need and now is when you can play your part in the greatest event to happen in the world in two thousand years.'

'The man is in a coma!' exclaimed Roosevelt without looking down.

'That others may live their lives in harmony!' responded Ephesian strongly, a more apt phrase than his original thought of *It's only Lawton*. 'Let not Lawton's ordeal be in vain, Father. The Grail is no longer at his house. Whoever attacked him, took the Grail. You must tell us everything you know, everything about what happened when Lawton came to the cathedral to collect the Grail. We need clues, Father, and you are all we have at the moment. You must tell us everything.'

Roosevelt finally lowered his head and looked into Ephesian's eyes, even if those eyes were not staring directly back. He could feel the brutal gaze of Jacobs upon him.

'I have nothing to tell, Grand Master,' he said eventually, the tears streaked down his face. 'I am sorry. I saw nothing.'

Ephesian twitched and in an instant could feel the temper rise within him. He needed to be in control and this just sent him much further away from where he wanted to be.

'Fuck,' he blurted out, the only manifestation of his wrath.

Jacobs glanced at his boss, then cracked his knuckles once more and looked back at Roosevelt.

37

The Eponymous Phat

Luigi Linguini stood by the window in Ephesian's office, looking down over the long sweep of the hill, the golf course to his right, the dull firth beneath him, the dull hills of Bute and Arran beyond. Almost recognised the stark beauty of a grey afternoon in Scotland but his natural cynicism about the place prevailed and he quickly turned away, a cold shiver rippling down his body.

'You'd think he'd have the heating on. In Italy, we'd have the stinkin' heating on. Of course, the stinkin' sun would shine for more than two minutes at a time in Italy.'

He checked the time then turned and examined the room. He had been all over the house in the hour or so since Ephesian and Jacobs had gone out. Having no idea how long they would be, he was prepared to be walked in on at any moment, but his basic confidence allowed him to not worry about that. It would be dealt with if and when it happened. And it might just be that he would take up residence somewhere in the house until the evening.

The house had nineteen rooms, most of which were obviously rarely used. Classic bachelor's large house. Kitchen, bathroom and Jacobs' rooms aside, only four rooms were actually ever occupied. The bedroom, the office and dining room overlooking the west coast of the island, and the study at the front of the house. It didn't mean that whatever he was looking for – and he wasn't entirely sure what that was – would not be kept in one of the other rooms, but he knew men and their simplicity. If there was anything significant in the house, it would be in one of the three rooms downstairs.

He had just spent twenty minutes in the office going through the drawers, examining the artefacts on the shelves and the pictures on the walls. It was time to have a closer look at the study.

He pulled his jacket more tightly around him, began to wonder what his helpless idiot of a colleague was doing, and then dismissed the thought and walked back out into the hall.

✂

'So, who else would know about the Grail?' wondered Ephesian, as Jacobs drove the car slowly away from the cathedral down to George Street.

Jacobs gave Ephesian a quick glance then turned back to the road. He was well used to his employer's inability to think laterally, his continued trust on face value, no matter how obvious it would seem to others that there was a lie staring him in the face. It was that which had made him a constant butt of practical jokes in his school days, something else which had forced him to retreat further into the dark realms of diffidence.

'It must be one of the Brotherhood,' Ephesian continued. 'My God, that they should choose this moment.' He began to run through the members of the cabal in his head, wondering which one of them was the most likely to jeopardise their magnificent enterprise. And not for a second did the thought occur to him that it would be for any reason other than money.

'Lawton must have spoken to one of the others,' he said, as Jacobs took the car past the tiny St. Andrews church and along towards the grounds of the Garrison. 'Greed can do the most brutal things to the minds of men.'

He looked at Jacobs for the first time since leaving the cathedral buildings.

'Which of them...' and he let the words tail off. Rubbed his left thumb into the palm of his right hand. 'We need to speak to them all,' he said, feeling strangely discomfited by Jacobs' silence. 'In whom was Lawton most likely to confide of our number?'

200

'Mr Ephesian!' snapped Jacobs suddenly.

Ephesian turned sharply, lowering his gaze and fixing his eyes on the cigarette lighter. Jacobs gripped the steering wheel, trying to control his impatience. Fifty-seven years of servitude had made him quite used to his employer's closed mind but sometimes he needed to be brought sharply to heel. Not everything was black and white, not everyone could be taken at face value. People lied.

Ephesian said nothing, Jacobs turned right and drove up the road towards East Farm.

'We need look no farther than Father Roosevelt.'

'What do you mean?' asked Ephesian quickly.

'He's lying.'

'He's a priest!'

Jacobs snorted.

'He's a priest,' Ephesian repeated, more forcefully.

Fifty yards short of the farm, past the woods where the ground opened out with fields on both sides, the cathedral now up on the small hill to their right, Jacobs pulled the car into the side of the road. Ephesian stared straight ahead, eyes on the flattened and dried out remains of a long dead roadkill.

'Sir, he's lying.'

'Why? Are you saying that he attacked Lawton?'

'Yes!'

'Why? If he had the Grail, if he wanted money, then why not mention it there? He had us in his office, why let us go without making his demand? He knows we need the Grail by tonight.'

'It's not about money!'

Ephesian turned. This time their eyes connected, a quick flash, Ephesian's head twitched violently and he looked away.

'What d'you mean? What else is there?'

Jacobs kept his eyes on Ephesian, daring him to look back.

'I've monitored the movements of the Brotherhood ever since we arrived on the island, Grand Master,' said Jacobs. 'You know I have. And particularly this week.'

He paused, eyes still narrowed and demanding. Ephesian's head spasmed again, twice, sharp jolts. Struggling to keep

201

control, but he didn't want to erupt in violent temper. He wanted to curl up, he wanted the problems to go away.

'Lawton had no friends,' said Jacobs slowly. 'He kept no association. There is no way, no conceivable way, that he shared his secret with others in the Brotherhood. I know he told us, I know he was foolish enough to approach Ping Phat, but that was taking the secret up the chain, to see what he could get for himself. There is no way he would have taken it sideways.'

'Why take it to anyone? Why not just blackmail us?'

'Because he was impetuous. He was stupid. He told you and he told Ping Phat because he could not contain himself. But he quickly realised how foolish he'd been. That was why he decided to retrieve the Grail for himself.'

Ephesian breathed deeply, staring blankly up the road. Feeling his head was about to explode, information overload. Not yet seeing that this simplified everything. If Roosevelt was the culprit, if it was that straightforward, then their problems could be resolved much more easily than he'd been anticipating.

'So why did Roosevelt give Lawton the Grail?' asked Ephesian.

Jacobs stared sharply at Ephesian, teeth clenched. Look at me, he thought, just look at me for once in your fucking life!

'He didn't give him it! He didn't know where it was until Lawton took it. He must have followed him to his house and retrieved it for himself.'

'But he said he didn't know where it was.'

'He was lying!' shouted Jacobs, then he stopped while he brought himself under control. It was years, maybe even decades, since he'd lost his temper at Ephesian. 'He was lying,' he repeated, his voice struggling with rage. 'He does not want the Grail to be found! As soon as it had been taken from the Cathedral he retrieved it and took it out of our reach.'

'But why?'

'I don't know. Perhaps, now that the day has come, he is against our goals. He would not be the only one of his kind to feel that way, were it the case. This thing that we have all worked so long to achieve, this bane that has been passed down through the generations, this truth that binds us, it will split the churches of the world. That is why the Italians are on the island. But it is not just Rome who will be offended or disbelieving. Every church, every single one will be rent asunder. Who knows for whom Roosevelt is working. It might be the Episcopalians, he might just be doing it for himself.'

'We need proof.'

'We have the proof,' said Jacobs. 'The facts are there before us, sir. The only people who knew about the Grail find were us, Ping Phat and Roosevelt.'

He stopped, he looked at Ephesian. Ephesian turned and stared at Jacobs. Suddenly this time their eyes locked. Ephesian felt sucked in by it, although he found the feeling of looking directly at someone horribly disconcerting, until, with a shake of the head, he managed to pull himself away and look out up the road.

'He can't be on the island already,' said Ephesian.

Jacobs stared along the same stretch of road, the sudden little moment of epiphany turning his convictions about Roosevelt to dust.

'I don't know,' he said.

Silence descended on the car. Ephesian could feel his insides begin to churn and grind, could feel the sickness at his core worsen by the second. Jacobs was suddenly aware of nervousness, the final piece in the jigsaw having seemed to be about to fall into place, now once more out of reach.

He angrily put the car into second gear and screeched quickly away from the kerb.

✂

The doorbell rang. Luigi Linguini sat in the leather chair looking out to the far end of the golf course. He had seen the people arrive at the front gate and had ducked down into the chair, its back turned to the window overlooking the driveway.

Sit it out, presumably whoever it was would leave in a short while, and then he could continue his search of the room. So far he had been in there for ten minutes and had yet to uncover anything. His task was undoubtedly hampered by the fact that he had no idea what he was looking for.

The doorbell rang again. Suddenly he leapt out of the chair and walked through the room. Balls, he thought to himself. Balls!

Into the hall, switching into character and he opened the front door with a flourish, ready to greet his visitors.

'Good afternoon,' he said, smiling. 'How can I help you?'

There were five people before him, arranged in ascending order so that the most important was clearly at the back, currently turned away and looking down across the island.

'You will be Mr Jacobs,' said the woman at the head of the queue.

'Yes,' he said smoothly. 'And who can I say is calling?' he added, playing the part.

'We are Ping Phat,' said the woman.

Luigi nodded. He had heard the name before after all and looked along the row of Chinese men and women until he reached the face at the back, now turned expectantly towards him. Ping Phat might have lost out on a few doughnuts to Jonah Harrison, but he was at the very least eating at the same bakery bar.

'Mr Ephesian is home, no?' asked the woman.

Luigi smiled.

'He is home, no,' he said. 'Just stepped out for a short time. Perhaps you would like to wait.'

The woman bowed her head and said, 'That would be most delicious.'

Luigi took a step back and ushered the communion of Chinese into the house, before closing the front door.

'In here if you please,' he said, directing them to the west wing of the house, into Ephesian's office.

The Chinese filed into the room, Luigi walking serenely after them, wondering where it was all going to lead. Once assembled they all stood looking at him with some anticipation, Ping Phat himself in their midst, regarding Luigi with expectant eyebrow.

'Can I get you...' Luigi began to say, and then let the sentence drift off as he wondered what exactly would be appropriate to offer these people at this time of the day.

204

'It is wonderful you to meet, my brother,' said Ping Phat suddenly.

Luigi found himself putting his palms together and bowing. *Luigi*, he thought to himself, *get a fucking grip!*

'And you, Mr Phat,' said Luigi.

Ping Phat burst into a ridiculous laugh.

'Ping! Ping!' he said. 'Let us not be formal after all this time.'

'Ping,' said Luigi, warily.

'Strange that the works of Robert Louis Stevenson we have to thank,' said Ping Phat. 'After such a long search we had.'

Luigi nodded. *Jesus*, he thought, *this guy sounds like stinkin' Yoda for Chrisssake.*

Robert Louis Stevenson!

'Close we are,' said Phat. 'Delicious it is to be here at such an auspicious time. Delicious, yes.'

Robert Louis Stevenson...

Luigi nodded, smiled again. Time to get out of Dodge before they cottoned on to the fact that he wasn't Jacobs. Which they already would have done if Ping Phat had not left his PA behind in Paris, choosing instead to travel with two bodyguards, a personal trainer and his Principal Private Secretary.

Tea, he thought, that's what these people drink.

'Can I offer you some tea?' he asked, attempting as much formality as possible.

Ping Phat smiled. Recognised, he thought, a butler's inherent need to serve.

'Kind of you that is,' he said. 'Tea we will all take.'

'Very good, sir,' said Luigi, then he backed off quickly, left the room and closed the door behind him.

He breathed a sigh of relief at having managed to escape, took a second or two to compose himself, and then walked quickly back into the study, not entirely sure what he was going to be able to unearth but at least with some idea of where to look.

38

Bunglestiltskin

'So I'm on a ski lift, you see, suspended in mid air, nowhere to go. Suddenly, out of nowhere, a snake appears at my side, in the unoccupied half of the chair.'

'What kind of snake?'

The guy shook his head.

'Don't know. Know nothing about snakes, not my line. I'm in women's toiletries.'

'Cool.'

'So what did the snake do?' asked the customer from behind.

Igor looked up from behind his broom so that he could more clearly see the bloke's lips in the mirror. Usually he didn't need to because he had heard all these customers' stories a hundred times, but this one was new. For most of these old geezers, all the interesting things had happened decades previously. Dreams were just about the only way for them to update their lives.

'He bit me,' said the guy, currently under the razor and receiving the benefit of a fantastic *Jude Law*.

'Snakes are as snakes do,' said Barney.

'Exactly,' said the bloke.

'Was it poisonous?' asked Garrett Carmichael, who had come into the shop to establish the progress of Barney's paperwork.

'Viciously,' said the guy. 'The minute it bites me I can feel myself start to ebb away.'

'What happened to the snake?'

'I don't know,' he replied lightly. 'It vanished or something. Anyway, the chairlift gets to the end and there I am, running around like a lunatic looking for the antidote. I can feel myself dying. I'm stopping people, grabbing at them, asking for their help. Jings, I'm stopping small children in the street asking if they know what their mother keeps in the medicine cabinet.'

'In the street?' asked Barney. 'Thought you were at the top of a chairlift?'

'It was a dream,' he said casually, 'locations come and go.'

'Got you.'

'Did you die?' asked the old geezer at the back.

'Nah,' said the Jude Law.

'They say if you die in your dreams you really die in your bed,' chipped in Garrett Carmichael from behind.

'So what happened?' asked Barney.

Jude Law shrugged.

'I woke up with the missus sticking her elbows into my ribs. Said I'd been chuntering. Jings, if I'd had a million pounds for every time I could've elbowed her for chuntering,' and he shook his head, then paused when he thought about how that had just come out, and then he shook his head again.

'Snake dreams are pretty serious,' said the old guy behind.

Ain't that the truth, thought Igor in agreement.

'Just a rehash of the day's events,' muttered Jude.

'What happened to you yesterday?' said Garrett Carmichael.

'The snake symbolises fears and worries that you might not yet be aware you have,' said Barney. 'That's what they say.'

'It's phallic, isn't it?' ventured Carmichael. 'It represents dangerous sexual desires, something like that. Must be someone you want to sleep with who you shouldn't, eh?'

Jude grunted.

'Aye,' said the old codger from the back, 'and someone with a phallus at that. I've always wondered about the way you combed your moustache.'

'Ach, bugger off,' muttered Jude.

'But then,' offered Carmichael, who had happened to stumble upon one of her favourite subjects, 'the snake also signifies that there is someone in your life you don't trust. Who's that then?'

207

'My lawyer,' he said quickly, catching her eye in the mirror, and she laughed.

'Arf,' said Igor, looking at Barney.

Barney nodded.

'Igor reckons that the snake implies that you're going to attain an arch enemy, and only if you overcome the snake in your dream will you be able to overcome the enemy.'

'Jings, I'm ninety-one for pity's sake, I have trouble overcoming my two shredded wheat in the morning. And where am I going to get an enemy at this stage?'

'I reckon it's the race-against-time factor that's the more worrying for you,' said the other old guy.

'He might have a point,' said Carmichael. 'It means you're stressed and can't cope with the pressures of modern life.'

'Modern life? I spend my day sitting in a near comatose heap in front of the television! The only stress I have is whether I'm going to have enough cotton hankies to mop up my drool. That and all the other weird and disgusting gunk and fluid that emanates from your body by the time you get to this age.'

Barney hesitated as he steered the scissors around the left ear. It's just plain better not to be reminded of some things.

'Turned cold again,' he said mundanely.

'Aye,' said someone in agreement.

'You had a chance to look at those papers, Mr Thomson?' asked Carmichael.

Barney looked at the clock. Glanced at the waiting customer, back at the Jude Law, took a quick look out onto the near-deserted street along the sea front.

'Can I deduce from the prevaricative essence of your rejoinder that you have yet to scrutinize the portfolio?'

'If I can deduce from the question that you're assuming I haven't read them yet, aye, you're right.'

'And the other lawyers?' she asked. 'You've contacted them?'

Barney turned fully round, remembering to lift the scissors from the Jude Law as he did so, and said, 'I used to watch *Petrocelli* when I was younger. I'll be all right.'

She gazed at him thinking that here was another man who thought he knew better than a lawyer. And even though she

208

knew he was not going to be caught out in any way on this, it would serve Barney Thomson right if he were to get shafted by some manner of means.

'Be it on your head,' she replied bluntly.

Barney smiled at the motherly tone, then turned back to the Jude.

'See you later,' he threw over his shoulder as an invitation for her to leave.

She shook her head, rose from her chair, glanced and then smiled at Igor, who muttered something that sounded like *arf*, before bowing to his brushwork. Garrett Carmichael then left the premises and the status quo of the bastion of manhood was once again regained.

'The night before,' said Jude Law, 'I dreamt I was going to a new school. What's that all about?'

'Unresolved childhood anxieties,' said Barney and the other customer in unison.

Arf, thought Igor in agreement.

✄

The car slowed as it pulled into the driveway. Jacobs and Ephesian glanced at each other as they saw the Renault Scenic parked to the left of the house. Ephesian twitched.

'D'you recognise it?' he asked, as Jacobs brought the car up behind the Renault.

'No,' he said. 'I don't.' Then he quickly got out and walked round to open the door for Ephesian.

Ephesian hesitated and then stepped out into the chill of the afternoon. He took a moment to taste the sea air, something which he always did. A few deep breaths, fingers tensing and relaxing. Jacobs waited impatiently, recognising his need for routine, but thinking that this was one time when it would be wise to forego it. Forgetting, in a time of crisis, that for a man such as Ephesian, the more stressful things became, the more necessary routine became.

'Ping Phat?' said Ephesian eventually.

'Quite possibly,' replied Jacobs. 'Nice that he feels so at home that he let himself in.'

'What are we going to do?'

209

Jacobs stared at his boss. There was no point in trying to second guess Phat because neither of them had any insight into how his mind worked. They knew his routine, they knew the people who worked for him, they knew some of his goals, at least. But in their long association, Ping Phat had continually surprised them, beginning with his involvement with the Brotherhood in the first place.

'We go in, we talk to him, we see what he wants and if he has anything to demand of us. Try to establish if he has the Grail. We had our little moment of epiphany back there but it doesn't mean we were right. My initial premise might still be accurate. Roosevelt could be the man.'

Ephesian breathed heavily through his nose.

'Perhaps Roosevelt and Phat are working together,' he said in a low cold voice.

'Perhaps,' said Jacobs. 'Perhaps it is not even Ping Phat who awaits inside. We should stop making assumptions, go in, find out everything we can in as short a time as possible and then retreat somewhere to establish our strategy.'

'Yes,' said Ephesian.

And with determination mustered as much as possible, they marched into the house.

39

Who Built Thebes?

They walked into the office to be greeted by the five faces pregnant with expectation, waiting for a nice cup of tea. Neither Jacobs nor Ephesian had ever met Ping Phat before, but here they were walking in on a Chinese sea; there was no doubt whose company had descended upon them, and in the midst of the five, there was no doubt which one of them had the presence, the charisma and the authority. The short stocky figure in the middle, his back turned to the door as they entered, looking down on the cold grey sea far below.

Ping Phat turned and stared at the two men. As he presumed that he had already met Jacobs, he had no idea who the man standing next to Ephesian might be. Ephesian himself, however, was instantly recognisable. Ping Phat knew far more about Ephesian than Ephesian realised.

'Mr Ephesian,' he said, 'delighted I am.'

And he strode forward, hand outstretched.

'Ping,' said Ephesian without the requisite level of enthusiasm, as usual his voice betraying every negative feeling that coursed through his body. Ping Phat laughed.

'This is Simon Jacobs, my man,' said Ephesian, nodding minimally in his direction, hoping that this introduction might lead Ping Phat to introduce the other four characters who he'd brought with him. Stopped himself saying what he considered to be the more appropriate *So you let yourselves in then?*

211

Ping Phat regarded Jacobs with curiosity, ignoring for a couple of seconds the outstretched hand. Eventually he accepted it and smiled inquisitively.

'I believed Mr Jacobs I had already met,' he said. 'An individual most helpful.'

'We have not met before, sir,' said Jacobs, shaking his head and doing the Jeeves thing. Although by now, after a couple of days of full-on stress, Jacobs had more of the Jeeves-by-way-of-Hannibal-Lecter look about him.

'Know that do I,' said Ping Phat, who was sticking to his Yoda-by-way-of-Yoda-with-a-dash-of-Yoda routine.

Ephesian stared at Ping Phat's nose wishing that something would just make sense. His head twitched, he began to feel the pressure build inside his skull. Deep breath, then another, determined not to betray the agonies to anyone else.

The woman stepped forward to Ping Phat's right and nodded deferentially at Ephesian.

'I believe that Mr Phat's confusion comes from our earlier meeting some ten minutes ago with your butler, who allowed us to enter the house and is currently brewing a pot of tea for our consumption. He led us to believe that he was Mr Jacobs.'

'I'm the butler,' said Jacobs. 'I'm Jacobs.'

He stared between Ephesian and Phat, didn't even glance at the woman, then muttered, 'Shit,' and headed quickly to the door. Stopped in the doorway and turned back.

'What did he look like?' he asked, directing the question at Ping Phat.

Ping Phat raised an eyebrow at the tone, unused to anyone talking to him in that way.

'He had black hair, quite a dark complexion,' said the woman. 'Mediterranean perhaps.'

Jacobs glanced quickly at Ephesian, who almost returned the look, but his eyes had now dropped to the floor. He desperately needed to retreat from the room and from these people.

'Fuck,' said Jacobs, fully aware of who it was who had been in the house, and he ran out to start the search, slamming the door behind him. As if it was all Ping Phat's fault.

212

Ephesian turned and stared at the door. He was going to have to get out. He needed to lie down or fall down or drop down. Anything.

'Abrupt Mr Jacobs is,' said Ping Phat, the right level of admonition in his voice. Had expected more from Ephesian and his staff.

Ephesian did not answer.

'Is there a problem about which Mr Phat should be told?' asked the woman.

Ephesian twitched again, this time his whole body seeming to spasm.

Head down and he was on his way out. There were some words of apology on the tip of his tongue but they never fully formed. Some strange sound escaped from his lips, and it may even have been a variation on the syllable *arf*, and then he opened the door and quickly walked into the hall and turned up the stairs, leaving the Phat collective to themselves.

Ping Phat looked at his watch, then at each of his team in turn, and then finally his gaze fell on the drinks cabinet.

'Well,' he said, 'fuck this. If they're not going to bring us tea, we may as well help ourselves to some of the single malt he has there. Sam,' he said to one of the bodyguards, 'find the kitchen and bring us some ice.'

'Yes, sir,' said the bodyguard and off he went.

Jacobs had already visited the kitchen, as he had done every room on the ground floor in less than a minute, before thumping upstairs marginally behind Ephesian. The more thorough search would come after he had established on the first quick viewing that Luigi Linguini was nowhere to be seen.

However, when in time he had taken the more methodical approach and gone through every hidden corner in every room, there would still be no sign of the Italian who had dared to impersonate one of the Brotherhood. Luigi Linguini had left the building.

40

A Needle Pulling Thread

The old fella beneath Barney's scissors was not at all responsive, but it was nearly the end of the day and Barney felt like talking. Half way through an elaborate *Red Hot Chilli Pepper* and flowing nicely, Barney was in the groove. Igor was sweeping up behind, there were no other customers waiting. A curious day was drawing to a close, although Barney had no idea of the drama and downright excitement which had still to happen.

'And here's another one,' he continued, some way into a monological dissertation on bad song lyrics. '*Ray, a drop of golden sun. A drop* of golden sun?' All right, so Barney wasn't exactly being this century, but it was his shop and he could talk about what he wanted. 'A ray of sunshine can hardly be described as a drop. A drop? Seriously, a drop's a tiny thing. A rain-*drop*. Tiny. A ray isn't a drop. Why didn't they use beam or streak or shaft or stream? They're all good words, and they're all one syllable 'n all. *Ray, a beam of golden sun!* What's wrong with that? They could've used any of those words. What were they thinking?'

Barney looked at the customer in the mirror, his face going along with the *what were they thinking* line. The customer, an old fella with grey hair and a look of sagacity in his eyes, stared at Barney for a while, then slowly reached inside the cape and produced a card, which he held up for Barney to take from him. Barney smiled and took it as offered, wondering what

214

profession this guy was going to have which would excuse him from conversation. The card, however, offered no profession, only philosophy.

> He who knows does not speak.
> He who speaks does not know.
>
> *Lao Tzu 604-531 BC*

Barney stared at it for a second, nodded appreciatively and then handed it to Igor. Igor read it, nodded appreciatively and then slipped it into his pocket.

'Might start using that myself,' he said, although it disappointingly came out as *arf*.

'You should,' said Barney.

He looked at the customer again. The old fella held his gaze for a second or two and then looked down at the shelf in front of him, believing his point to have been made.

'I always used to think that Stipe sang *Don't blow your head off* in the middle of *Everybody Hurts*,' said Barney, at least bringing his chat a little up to date, even if he was completely ignoring the centuries old Chinese philosophy.

✂

James Randolph sat on a bench along the sea front not too far from the barbershop. Legs crossed, jacket buttoned up, the wind blowing the invigorating smell of the sea into his face. Feeling more relaxed than he had in a long time, the fact that he had to kill someone that evening notwithstanding. The principal defining factor in his mood was that he had his method of murder. He was, for once in his life, about to pleasantly surprise his employer.

He had left the barbershop that morning with an idea in mind, which he had then spent three hours on the internet perfecting. It seemed so simple, yet he felt sure it had a glorious originality to

215

it. All the best things in life have simplicity in them, of course. He should have known that right from the start. After having spent three days thinking up more and more elaborate plans to commit murder, he should have known that the idea when it came to him would be beautifully austere.

He had followed his few hours on the internet with a quick trip up to Glasgow and now he was back in Millport armed with all the necessary ingredients to commit the crime.

His relationship with Ephesian was peculiar and not one which was formally laid down on any contractual basis. He was nominally a part-time casual employee, yet one who was required to do something on Ephesian's behalf around the town on most days. Rarely, however, did he ever impress his boss. He would carry out his tasks with the minimum of fuss and little imagination, but as long as he achieved his goals to some degree, he knew he could rely on Ephesian's loyalty. Tonight, however, for the first time in as long as he could remember, he really was going to impress him.

He had no idea, of course, that Ephesian had moved on into a thick morass, a sea of troubles like he had never imagined, and that he had already relieved Randolph of his duties. Jacobs had now been tasked with committing the murder to drain the blood that was required for the ceremony. Jacobs had also been tasked with getting rid of Randolph.

Ephesian, however, had never done his two-week personnel management course on an island in the middle of a Welsh lake, living on worms and beetles and Fruit Loops, running over hot coals in his bare feet, and masturbating himself into a frenzy in a mass polyglot of chanting, cannibalistic sub-mutants. He wasn't versed in business best practice of passing information down the chain of command. And so Randolph had not been kept abreast of the decision making process and was unaware of how Ephesian envisioned things panning out.

James Randolph, happy in his ignorance, turned round on his bench every now and again and looked at the short stretch of the shopfront along Shore Street, which encompassed both the barbershop and the small solicitor's office of Garrett

Carmichael, checking that his prey was still at work for the late afternoon.

He looked back out to sea then picked up the plastic bag which had been sitting on the bench beside him and held it in his lap. It was plain yellow, good quality, no supermarket advertising on the side, something in which Randolph always took a strange pleasure. This evening, however, it was the contents which were much more important.

Across the water, above the hills of Arran, the sun was, for the first time that day, beginning to force its way through the clouds, so that long, translucent drops of golden sun were streaking from the clouds down onto the sea.

'Drops?' said Randolph quietly to himself. 'You can hardly call them drops.'

✂

Jacobs walked into the bedroom. The late afternoon sun, which James Randolph was watching smother the sea in new light, was also shining brightly into the only room upstairs in the big house which was ever occupied. He stood in the middle of the room staring at Ephesian, waiting for the man to turn and look at him. Knew that he would not but thought that he ought to give him the opportunity.

Ephesian was aware of the presence in the room. Knew it would be Jacobs but could not bring himself to turn. His world was unravelling before him. Every time he attempted to get things into some kind of order, every time Jacobs managed to persuade him that the pieces were falling into place, they immediately suffered another setback.

He was sitting at his window seat, another vantage point from where he frequently watched the firth below, although now his head was in his hands and he was swaying very slightly from side to side.

'Sir,' said Jacobs quietly but with urgency and annoyance.

Ephesian twitched. He wasn't turning, not yet. He had another couple of hours to sit here at least, head down. He wanted Jacobs to go away and sort everything out, before returning later in the evening to tell him that all the problems had been taken

217

care of. And he wanted Jacobs to tell him that Ping Phat was on his way back to fucking China.

Ping Phat! He had a sudden and very uncomfortable thought that Phat might have come up the stairs with Jacobs and be at this moment standing in the doorway, laughing silently at him. So some strange fear of embarrassment it was that suddenly roused him from his mental prison and he stood up quickly, his heart beating wildly, staring at Jacobs.

Ping Phat wasn't there but Ephesian's breaths still came in short stabs, he still felt the unnerving touch of a cold sweat.

'The Italian is gone,' said Jacobs. 'We can't worry about him. He's taken nothing, he will have found nothing.'

'Are you sure?' asked Ephesian, looking at the carpet.

'Yes,' said Jacobs. 'Now that Ping Phat is here we must use it to our advantage. Establish what he is after, establish whether he has the Grail.'

Ephesian's head twitched, his entire upper body seemed to accompany the movement.

'He is a straightforward man,' continued Jacobs. 'If he has the Grail, he will not hide it from us, he will make demands. That is how he works. If he does not possess it, we can return to our original assumption. Then we target Father Roosevelt and we should be in possession of the Grail before late evening.'

Ephesian trembled again, a more minor tremor.

'Let's go, sir,' said Jacobs. 'Once we have the Grail, I can commit the required murder, you can speak to Anthony about indoctrinating him into the brotherhood, and then we can relax for the last couple of hours before the rite. We are almost there.'

This time Ephesian managed to listen to him and to accept the words without the accompanying facial spasm. Jacobs had done it again. Smoothed over the worst of the events, put as good a spin on the facts as possible.

Ephesian felt a shiver course its way through his body, he stared at the door and breathed deeply. Time to meet Ping Phat, fragile self-assurance currently intact.

'Right, come on,' he said, as if he felt some basic need to at least act like he was in charge.

'Very good, sir,' said Jacobs, falling nicely back into the old Jeeves routine.

41

Fortune Cookie
Philosophy

Another day done and dusted, the third in the shop. Everything
already felt very familiar, mundane almost. Today, what with
experiencing an exorcism and the general weirdness of having
had someone else's soul walk through his body, had been a little
different to the norm, but the afternoon had in the end taken an
accustomed turn, the usual series of old guys requesting
inappropriate haircuts.

Barney and Igor were standing somewhat forlornly at the shop
window, looking out over the sea. They had yet to put the
Closed sign on the door but it was now into early evening and
they were sure no more customers would come. The brief
excitement of the day having passed, Barney had lapsed once
more into the melancholic solemnity of his mid-life crisis.

Maybe he could go on a walking tour of Africa. Visit every
country on the continent by foot; that would be a suitably grand
British piece of insanity to mark the complete lack of
achievement in his life up to this point.

Did he have the survival skills to handle the jungle, the desert,
the savannah, the townships, the leach-infested rivers, the
market places selling masks to tourists, the marauding, pot-
smoking machine gun-toting teenagers in northern Congo, the
land mines in Western Sahara? Did he know enough about
Africa to last ten minutes in any one of the forty-three
countries? Course he didn't.

So, Africa it was then. That would be a grand old few years out of his life. He could come back, should he survive, and appear on Richard & Judy and BBC Breakfast. He could write a book and do celebrity get-me-out-of-here shows.

'Arf,' said Igor, by way of telling Barney to tuck it in.

'Aye,' muttered Barney, 'I'd be lucky if I could walk through flippin' Greenock without getting taken to the cleaners.'

The door opened and an old geezer stuck his head in. Barney was beginning to wonder if anyone ever died on Millport or if this was where people were sent to exist for all eternity.

'You're not still open?' said the old guy.

Barney looked at Igor, glanced round at the clearly still open shop and turned back to the old fella.

'Aye,' he said, 'we are.'

The old guy snorted.

'I don't believe it,' he said, then he closed the door and minced unconvincingly away back up the street.

Barney and Igor stared out the window.

'Pub bet,' said Barney.

'Arf.'

A movement across the road caught his eye. James Randolph had finally risen from his vantage point on the promenade. Barney had been thinking about the vague strangeness of his manner in the shop that morning, wondering what he was up to. How do they kill lambs?

'You close up, will you?' he said, touching Igor's arm.

'Arf.'

He grabbed his jacket, opened the door, turned the *Closed* sign round as he went, then passed silently out into the cold of early evening. Igor watched him go and then hurriedly began to tidy everything away.

Barney paused. There were a few others abroad but nowhere near enough for Barney to be able to blend into the crowd. Fortunately, however, Randolph was entirely distracted by following his prey and had not noticed Barney leaving the shop.

And along the road, less than a hundred yards ahead, Barney saw the object of James Randolph's intent. Garrett Carmichael had just left her office and was walking quickly along Shore

Street in the direction of her house, hurrying to get home after a late afternoon at the office.

Barney started walking after them, as Randolph crossed the road and casually approached Carmichael. They both worked for Ephesian, they knew each other well, there was nothing strange or menacing in his approach. Had James Randolph seen Garrett Carmichael in the street on any other day he would have spoken to her. This was no different. Apart from the fact that he was carrying with him an unmarked plastic bag containing the world's most dangerous cheese sandwich.

Barney was close enough to hear the greeting that passed between the two as Randolph came alongside. He had no idea why he was suddenly worried but he found himself quickening his pace to catch up.

In the shop, his well-developed sixth sense screaming at him, Igor also realised the impending danger to Garrett Carmichael and was even more concerned than Barney.

✂

'If tea you are now in position to make, grateful I would be.'

Jacobs nodded at Ping Phat, managed to keep the contempt from his face when looking at the drained whisky glass, then looked around the rest of the gang to enquire after their tea needs. The female assistant caught his eye.

'Mr Phat is very particular about his tea, something about which I did not inform the previous Mr Jacobs as I sensed he was not an expert.'

Jacobs took the compliment and smiled.

'Particular?' he asked. Ephesian stood a little to the side, staring at his desk, wishing they could ignore the formalities.

'He takes twenty-three sugars,' she said.

'Ah,' said Jacobs.

'In order to facilitate this,' she continued, 'he requires the boiling water to be placed directly into the cup. There must be no intermediate teapot stage. The sugar should then be added to the hot water, while the water as yet remains uncontaminated by tea of any description.'

Oh, Jesus Christ! thought Ephesian, *will you just get on with it!*

222

'The teabag, which will be of a mild green tea, should then be placed in the sweet water for two minutes, stirred once with a silver teaspoon and then withdrawn.'

Jacobs' face sagged into a withering Jeeves.

'Mr Ephesian does not keep teabags of any description in his home. We have *Sir Thomas Lipton Chinese Green Tea no.14*, if that would be appropriate, but I would then require further instruction on the preparation process.'

The assistant glanced at Ping Phat who slowly nodded.

'Mr Phat finds that acceptable,' she said to Jacobs. 'Do you have a small tea-retaining device which can be placed in the cup and then removed?'

'Do you mean a metal bag?' asked Jacobs.

She thought about this for a second and then nodded.

'Yes, I believe you might call it a metal bag.'

'Then, there is your answer,' said Jacobs, who was veering horribly into pomposity, such was his way. 'We have no teabags in the house, metal or otherwise. We have tea leaves, we have a pot, we have a strainer and a holder in which to place the strainer once the tea has been poured.'

'Very well,' she said, 'in that case Mr Phat would like the same procedure to be followed as previously outlined, and then the leaves placed loosely into the cup and left to brew. He does not like loose leaves in his cup, but if that is how it is to be...'

'Very well,' said Jacobs.

'Indeed. Now,' she continued, 'would you like me to once again outline Mr Phat's specific requirements in relation...'

'Oh for God's sake,' blurted Ephesian, finally unable to contain his frustration and annoyance. 'Do you have the Grail?'

Jacobs looked sharply at Ephesian, close himself to blurting out something he shouldn't. They had needed to quietly assess whether or not Ping Phat had the Grail without letting him know that it was not in their possession. Now Ephesian, in five simple words, had completely shown his hand.

Ping Phat stared at him and he himself gave a slight tense shudder, as if controlling some instant emotive response to Ephesian's words. He gave Jacobs a quick glance and then with

223

a nod to his assistant, his Elvis entourage began filing dutifully from the room.

The door closed behind them and then there were three. Jacobs and Ping Phat were making brutal eye contact, each trying to read the mind of the other.

'Leave us alone, Jacobs, please,' said Ephesian suddenly.

Jacobs turned quickly round, looking angrily at his boss.

'What?' he said sharply.

'Leave us alone,' said Ephesian. 'Mr Phat and I need to talk. You must go and attend to our other guests.'

Jacobs glanced at Phat hoping for some support but Phat was never going to be interested. Ephesian was the only one who mattered to him. He had also realised that Jacobs was the more malignant half of the double act and it was as well to have him out of the way.

'I think it would be advisable if I stayed, sir,' said Jacobs.

Ephesian stared out of the window, just to the right of Ping Phat's head, his jaw set angrily.

'You must attend to the other guests,' he repeated blankly.

Ping Phat had kept his eyes on Jacobs all the way through and now there was a contemptuous smile. Jacobs saw it, wondered if it was at his dismissal or at the obvious disarray in the camp.

'Very well, sir,' he said quickly and then he turned and walked hurriedly from the room, Ping Phat watching every step.

Ephesian waited until the door had closed and then he walked around Phat to the large landscape window and looked down at the darkening firth. Phat came up beside him and for a short while they stood and watched two small yachts which were visible mid-channel.

'You do not have the Grail?' said Ping Phat eventually, in this moment of crisis deciding to drop the ridiculous Yoda business.

Ephesian breathed deeply, trying to control the ever-increasing spasms which wracked his head every time he came to the slightest point of calamity.

'You think I have it?' asked Phat, without any hint of condemnation or accusation.

'You were one of the two people who knew that Lawton had made his discovery,' replied Ephesian quickly.

'And what has become of Lawton?'

Ephesian wanted to look Ping Phat in the eye but that desire only really manifested itself as wishing that Jacobs was in the room to do it for him.

'He removed the Grail before Jacobs or I could retrieve it. When we went to his house to deal with the problem we found him knocked unconscious and the Grail gone.'

'You have seen the Grail?'

Ephesian glanced round at Phat's shirt buttons.

'Yes,' he replied, abruptly.

'Then you searched thoroughly? Just because something is not visible, does not mean it is not there.'

Bloody centuries' old Chinese wisdom, thought Ephesian. Reduce everything to fortune cookie standards.

'Whoever took the time to leave Lawton in a coma was not going to leave the Grail hanging on a mug stand. Nevertheless, Jacobs made a search of the property. It has been removed.'

Ephesian had spoken forcefully but Ping Phat was not at all convinced. Nothing in the world is obvious, nothing can be taken for granted.

'And will Lawton emerge from his coma?' asked Phat.

'Not any time soon,' said Ephesian.

Ping Phat nodded his head slowly in a judicious, eastern kind of a way that Ephesian found very irritating.

'I do not have the Grail,' said Ping Phat eventually. 'I arrived on this island only an hour ago. I assume that post-dates Mr Lawton's unfortunate accident?'

Ephesian did not answer. Now that they were meeting in the flesh he disliked Ping Phat even more than he thought he would. Years of subterfuge, years of keeping the Faith and keeping the secrets of the Brotherhood hidden from the world, had cost money. When he had taken over as Grand Master in the nineteen-eighties, they had been struggling for finance and he had felt that the organisation and its links around the world might collapse. They had needed an input of capital and it had come from Ping Phat. Somehow he had always hoped that his own business empire would become strong enough to support

225

the *Prieure de Millport* on its own, allowing him to discard Phat, but it had never happened.

'You said there were two who knew about Lawton. May I assume you refer to Mr Jacobs?'

Ephesian coughed, his face and neck tensed. Clenched and unclenched his right hand.

'Jacobs and I are one,' he said coldly. 'I was referring to Father Roosevelt, the keeper of the cathedral.'

Ping Phat raised a sage eastern eyebrow which Ephesian felt rather than saw.

'Then you have a suspect list of one,' he said.

'It would appear so,' said Ephesian.

'The Brotherhood did not know?'

'Roosevelt was the only one,' said Ephesian.

'Then it would seem that you have a simple solution to your dilemma,' said Ping Phat, with further Asian simplistic Tao-like theorising.

Ephesian did not reply. The yachts in the firth toiled against the wind and away to their left a small cargo vessel appeared from behind the island of Lesser Cumbrae.

If only everything could really be reduced to soundbite philosophy, thought Ephesian. If only these people could see that all the problems of the world can be reduced to soundbite philosophy, thought Ping Phat.

42

Cheese Sandwich

James Randolph had not thought it through, which was not entirely unlike him. He had waited until Garrett Carmichael had left the office, so that when he came to murder her she would be with her children. If he had gone to see her in her office, then he would have found her alone. Some strange logic had dictated, however, that he couldn't disturb her at work.

He thought that Garrett Carmichael had a soft spot for him and to an extent he was right, but only in that she had a soft spot for every man on the island.

'Garrett,' he said, by way of introduction.

'James,' she said, nodding. 'You've been waiting for me?'

Randolph seemed embarrassed, as if the thought had not occurred to him that Carmichael would have seen him.

'You should have come in,' she said smiling, which was when it occurred to him how much better that would have been.

The incomplete nature of the plan was the measure of the man. He had not thought it through beyond the initial cause of death. Assuming she died in the manner he was anticipating, he was then going to have to collect some of her blood for use in the ceremony that evening. How exactly he was going to achieve that with her two children running around in complete ferment, he wasn't at all sure.

'What can I do for you that you've been waiting for me so long? Are you not cold?'

'I, eh...' he started to say, before realising that what he was about to say was absurd. Up until this point it had seemed like a decent approach, but now, in the flesh, he was realising it was one of the lousiest chat-up lines in the history of civilisation.

'Aye?' she said, amused by his nervousness. Assumed that he was looking for a date of some kind.

'I've invented this new kind of cheese sandwich,' he said hurriedly.

Had he intended it as an actual chat-up line he would have died in his boots, as she burst out laughing. In fact he died in his boots anyway because, even though he was intending to try to kill her, he was aware that the proposition had taken on a date-like feel.

She let the laugh die down and smiled at his pallid cheeks and the general gormless stupidity of the man.

'And would that be one of them in that bag there?' she asked, nodding at the plain yellow bag which he clutched in his fingers.

'Aye,' he replied.

'Well, that's nice of you to bring one for me. Would you like to come in for a cup of tea?'

Instant relaxation, having successfully made the breakthrough.

'The kids can try it out as well,' she added.

'No!'

She turned at the curious tone.

'I mean, I've only got two,' he blustered.

'We can break a couple of pieces off,' she said. 'My mother's already fed them anyway, so they won't be too hungry.'

Randolph momentarily closed his eyes. Another possibility of the plan which he had not considered. Beginning to see his great strategy unravel, beginning to think that he was bound to screw this up as much as he screwed up everything he did for Ephesian.

As they reached the front door and Carmichael took the house keys from her bag, footsteps approached quickly from behind. The cavalry.

'Garrett,' said the voice.

They turned, Randolph's heart sinking even further.

'Mr Thomson,' said Carmichael, 'come to bring the papers? I'm done working, maybe we could talk in the morning.'

He hesitated, recognised the brush off, looked at Randolph.

'Just wanted to talk a couple of things over about them, if that's all right. Thought now might be a good time.'

She stared at him for a second, considered her options and then shrugged.

'Whatever,' she said, and opened the door. 'You can come in if you like. James has brought us a revolutionary sandwich. Cheese. I'm sure he wouldn't mind if you tried it.'

The two men looked at one another, Randolph guiltily assuming that Barney would see right through him. They had mentioned stomach acids before in the shop, now here he was arriving with a cheese sandwich. Wasn't it obvious?

'Sure,' said Barney, 'that'd be great.'

The children appeared, to herald the further sinking of Randolph's confidence. Upon seeing Barney, Hoagy completely ignored his mum, stood to attention and saluted.

'Lieutenant Carmichael reporting for duty, sir!' he said, barking out the *sir* and pronouncing *lieutenant* the American way. Ella grabbed onto her mum's legs and tried to rugby tackle her. Barney stood in front of Hoagy to inspect him, pointed at something on his chest and then flicked his nose.

'At ease, lieutenant,' he said, pronouncing it correctly.

'It's loo-tenant!' said Hoagy. 'I want to be an American!'

And off he charged to subvert the Third World.

Miranda Donaldson appeared at the kitchen door, coat already buttoned up to the neck, steel breeches fastened down with rivets and bolts under a heavy plaid skirt.

'Well, I see you've come here for your dinner Mr Thomson,' she began, her voice the quality of salt on open wounds.

'No, he hasn't,' butted in Carmichael.

'Which is good, because there'll be no dinner at my house this evening. Been here all afternoon.' She stopped beside her daughter and regarded her with maximum parental contempt. 'They're fed but not bathed. I don't care what the time is. If you want to retain any attachment to them whatsoever, you're going to have to take some part in bringing them up.'

229

'Mum!' said Carmichael.

But Miranda Donaldson had said her piece and she was off. Glanced viciously at Randolph, reducing him to a pile of festering mush in the process, as she bustled down the corridor, and then she was out into the evening, the door slammed shut.

'Is Gran on too, Mum?' asked Hoagy, from the top of the stairs.

'24/7,' said Carmichael and she walked into the kitchen, her daughter still draped around her leg. 'Ella, can you let go?'

She didn't. Carmichael stopped just inside the kitchen door, breathed an enormous sigh, the good feeling of a reasonably successful day at the office immediately and instantly flushed away by her mother, then she dragged Ella over to the fridge, took out a box of white wine – an *Anstruther Sauvignon* 2005, fishy with hints of golf – and poured herself a glass. She looked at the two men standing either side of the kitchen doorway.

'Gentlemen,' she said. 'Help yourselves. James, you've got five minutes to do your cheese sandwich then I'm running the bath. You pair can hang out in the kitchen if you like, I don't care.'

'Don't drink the wine!' exclaimed Randolph suddenly, for no reason that anyone else in the room knew anything about.

'Why?' she said, looking at the glass, thinking he must have seen something floating in it.

'You know,' he said, grasping for any kind of explanation, 'you might, you know, adulterate the cheese sandwich.'

She looked at him strangely. Barney was even more suspicious, neither of his previous encounters with Randolph having inspired any trust or liking for the man.

'Give me the bag,' he said suddenly, walking past Randolph into the kitchen and taking the bag out of his hands as he went.

Randolph, now completely adrift, let him take it, staring helplessly as Barney opened the bag and removed the murder weapon.

Barney, suspecting poison, removed the sandwiches and held them in his hands. Two slices of plain white bread, diagonally sliced. He opened them, checked the contents. They looked,

230

more or less, like regular cheddar cheese sandwiches. He glanced up sharply at Randolph.

'What's with the sandwiches?' he said.

'Nothing. They're just cheese. Nothing.'

'I thought you said they were some kind of breakthrough sandwich?' said Carmichael. No longer in the mood to play.

'No,' said Randolph helplessly.

Barney sniffed the sandwich, could detect nothing other than an aroma of mild Scottish cheddar.

'Are they poisoned?' asked Barney.

'No!' said Randolph, taking a step back. 'No.'

'Poisoned?' said Carmichael, looking at Barney with incredulity. 'What kind of books have you been reading? Why would he want to kill me?'

'Aye,' said Randolph.

'He works for Ephesian, doesn't he?' said Barney.

'So do I,' she retorted.

Barney stared at her, then Randolph.

'So, it's all right to eat this, then?' he said.

Randolph stared at the sandwich. Shook his head, then nodded. Had no idea what to do. Wanted to grab the sandwich and do a runner but realised how much that would implicate him now.

'So, it's all right to eat this, then?' repeated Barney.

'Yes,' Randolph muttered in reply.

'Fine,' said Barney, holding one of the sandwiches forward. 'Let's see you eat it then.'

'This is insane,' said Carmichael. 'James, just tell us what's so special about the sandwich.'

'Can I have some sandwich, mum?' said a wee voice from the floor.

'Ssh.'

Randolph took the sandwich from Barney and stared at it. It wasn't poisoned. It was worse than poisoned. Now, however, he felt trapped in a corner and was just too stupid to know how to get out.

He put the sandwich up to his mouth.

43

A Stupid Kind of Murder

Jacobs did not even bother knocking. He had business to take care of. All formality was out of the window, including the formality of checking with his employer that he wanted him to do what he was just about to.

He had not waited to hear Ping Phat's protestation of innocence. He'd seen the man, looked at his small entourage of goons and spooks and sycophants, factored in his sudden arrival at the house and had made the instant judgement that this was Phat's first appearance on the island. Which left only one option.

'Father?' he called, standing in the hallway of the large house attached to the cathedral grounds. Very trusting of Roosevelt to always leave his door open, he'd often thought.

'Father?' he repeated. Give it five seconds and then he would check the cathedral. Maybe the man was making some last ditch attempt to pray to his God.

The hallway was illuminated only by a small lamp. No other lights had yet been turned on in the house, despite the gloom of early evening. It should have been light for another hour or two, but the low, grey cloud was making short work of the afternoon. The walls were hung with uninspiring watercolours of cold Scottish seas, and an old etching of the cathedral, badly framed.

Jacobs was about to leave when he heard the quiet pad of footsteps, and then the door to the kitchen opened and Roosevelt was standing in the dark at the end of the hallway. They stared at each other for a while, the meagre light of the small lamp illuminating Jacobs' face. Roosevelt was in shadows, his nervousness and discomfort protected by the dark.

'Where is it?' said Jacobs bluntly. There would be no artifice here. He was sure Roosevelt had taken the Grail, he didn't want some stupid, protracted argument resulting in him having to do any more bodily harm to the man than he already intended.

'I am protected by the Lord,' said Roosevelt, the nerves tumbling out with his wavering voice.

'You have the Grail,' said Jacobs coldly.

Jacobs could hear the ticking of the large grandfather clock which dominated the front room of the house. A floorboard creaked underneath Roosevelt's anxious feet.

'Where is it?' Jacobs repeated, this time taking a step along the hallway. The first coercive step, knowing that success would likely come from measured intimidation.

'I don't have it,' said Roosevelt.

'Who does?' asked Jacobs sharply, although he did not believe Roosevelt for a second.

In his way, Roosevelt was as incompetent at this game as Randolph. These were not criminals who were playing games of murder and assault and theft. They were ordinary people, dragged out of ordinary life by extraordinary circumstances. And they were rubbish at it. He did not respond to the question, and his silence spoke volumes of his guilt.

Jacobs this time took several strides quickly along the hall, stopping a few feet short of the priest, close enough now so that his own face was in shadow with the lamp behind him, and the worried and tortured features of Roosevelt were clear to him.

'These are dark times, Father,' said Jacobs harshly, 'and times that are short. We need the Grail, and we will not be stopped by your pusillanimity and faintness of heart.'

'What you are planning is wrong!' Roosevelt ejaculated.

'How can you of all people think this is wrong?' snapped Jacobs. 'We have waited two thousand years for this.'

'It is wrong!' protested Roosevelt again, becoming stronger as Jacobs took another step nearer to him.

'Who are you working for?' asked Jacobs.

233

'No one!'

'Who are you working for?' he repeated, face curling.

'I don't need to work for anyone,' replied Roosevelt, discovering some hidden reserves. 'I can see the blasphemy of this act of my own accord. I work for myself, yet I work for the Lord and for Christians everywhere.'

Jacobs lost control. Took one step forward, grabbed the priest by the white collar and brought his head violently down onto the bridge of his nose. With a muffled gasp, Roosevelt dropped to his knees, hands to his face.

'I work for the Grand Master and for the Brotherhood,' said Jacobs. 'As should you. You swore an oath. Tell me where I can find the Grail or you will find that you have yet to feel the full force of my God-sent brutality.'

Roosevelt looked up from his knees, then swayed to the side until he was leaning against the wall. He stared into the blackness of Jacobs' eyes then slowly shook his head.

'It is not here,' he said. 'I do not lie.'

'But it was you who dealt with Lawton,' said Jacobs, a statement rather than a question.

Roosevelt closed his eyes, remembering the feel of Archie Gemmill as he had crunched into Lawton's head. The sound of cracking bone and the guilt of drawing blood in the Lord's name.

'Yes,' he mumbled.

'Then where is the Grail?' demanded Jacobs.

'It is not here,' mumbled Roosevelt, and his head dropped.

Once more Jacobs could not contain his wrath. He kicked Roosevelt viciously in the face, sending him backwards, his head smacking on the frame of the kitchen door. Then he stepped over him, bent down and picked him up by the collar.

The priest's face was covered in blood, his head lolled easily to the side. He was unconscious. Jacobs had lost control too quickly. He may have been innately brutal, but he was in his way as unused to doing this as Randolph and Roosevelt were inept in their chosen fields of crime. His sensible and measured intimidation had lasted barely a few seconds before rude violence had taken over.

234

He held Roosevelt's head close to him for a second before letting him fall back to the floor, then he straightened up and looked down at the crumpled heap of the bloody cleric.

'Shit,' he muttered.

Revive him and try to get more information, or work it out himself without any further recourse to violence?

He looked at his watch. There was the other matter to take care of, the murder of Garrett Carmichael and the collecting of her blood, which he had correctly decided was no job for James Randolph. That was just as important as finding the Grail. He could take care of that, while he gave thought to the problem of locating the holy chalice.

He took a last look at the stricken priest and then walked quickly into the kitchen in search of the man's freezer.

✂

James Randolph was in bits, in the space of a few minutes having quickly descended into the kind of pointless mush that Ephesian and Jacobs would have expected of him in such trying circumstances. Made to feel awkward by Carmichael, discomfited by her children, embarrassed by the clumsiness and lack of aforethought in his plan, subjugated and demoralised by the presence of Barney Thomson. The man could not have felt more like a child and, although he did not suffer from the complex condition that haunted the behaviour of Bartholomew Ephesian, he wanted nothing more now than to curl up into Ephesian's foetal ball.

'Eat the sandwich,' said Barney harshly, insomuch as you can utter the words *eat the sandwich* harshly.

Randolph looked like he was having to force back tears. All mental functions breaking down. His spirit had been crushed and he genuinely suspected that if he ate the sandwich he would die.

'I can't,' he sobbed, dropping the sandwich. 'I can't.'

'James?' said Carmichael. Wondering, incredulously, if Barney hadn't been as far off the mark as she'd first thought.

'Need to pee, Mummy,' said Ella from the floor.

'Go to the bathroom, then,' said Carmichael on auto-pilot.

'Why can't you eat the stupid sandwich?' said Barney.

He took a step forward as some sort of intimidatory gesture. There would be no violence to follow, however.

'I'll explode!' ejaculated Randolph loudly. 'I can't, I can't!'

There was a brief intermission while all the other adults in the room looked at him strangely.

'I need to pee!'

'Go to the bathroom!'

'What are talking about?' said Barney. 'You've already eaten your dinner?'

'No!'

'You're Mr Creosote? You don't look like him.'

'No!'

'What then?'

'I need to pee, I need to pee!'

'Go to the bathroom!'

'I'm scared!'

'I'm talking!'

'Eat the sandwich!'

'No!'

'Need to pee, need to pee!'

'For God's sake!' exploded Garrett Carmichael, and she grabbed Ella by the hand and hauled her rudely from the kitchen. On up the stairs to the bathroom they went, where she was able to gently sidestep Hoagy's question of, 'Has she peed in her pants?'

The men were alone. Barney waited until the general mother/daughter kerfuffle had died down and then he pulled a seat out at the kitchen table and sat down. Could see the state Randolph was in, recognised that he would be easy to get information out of.

'Tell me everything while she's out of the room,' he said.

Randolph nodded, not quite able to look Barney in the eye.

'The Brotherhood...Mr Ephesian...' he began, stumbling. He had to talk, but felt a horrible, clawing self-loathing for doing so. 'They need to kill Mrs Carmichael.'

Barney raised an eyebrow. His life was so plagued by murder and death, the fact that he had stumbled upon another sordid little crime in another little town seemed hardly surprising.

'Why?' was all he said.

'I don't know,' replied Randolph, head bowed. 'There's something going to happen tonight, some ceremony. With body parts. I'm not sure of all the details, but they need blood. I don't know why it has to be Mrs Carmichael's, but those were the instructions.'

Barney paused as he listened to a further stramash from upstairs. Then he heard the sound of convoluted and ancient plumbing and realised she had started to run the bath. She had sensibly chosen to withdraw from the absurdity of the discussion.

'So you were intending to kill her with a cheese sandwich?' ventured Barney. 'And it wasn't poisoned?'

'No,' he said sorrowfully. 'No poison.'

'Well, that's something,' said Barney. 'Poison's for girls. You, on the other hand, made an exploding cheese sandwich.'

Randolph nodded. He began slowly.

'In the shop this morning,' he said, and drifted off, his eyes wandering around the fallen sandwich. 'In the shop, when I fell asleep, I had a dream. A new way to commit murder.'

'By giving someone a lethally explosive cheese sandwich?'

'The cheese had nothing to do with it,' answered Randolph prosaically, Barney's tone going several miles over his head. 'It's what I put in the sandwich spread.'

Another pause, which Barney did not push to fill.

'A blend of enzymes, acids and metal shavings, which would react with the hydrochloric acid in the stomach to generate an explosion.'

'Excuse me?' said Barney, with some curiosity.

'I created a potion which would react with the acids in the stomach to create an explosion.'

'Are you a chemist?' asked Barney, thinking that while he had never actually known a chemist, every single chemist on planet Earth had to be more intelligent than this guy.

'No,' he said, looking up. 'I dreamt it.'

'You dreamt all the ingredients of this mixture which would make someone's stomach explode?'

'Aye.'

'And did you test it on anything? A mouse or something?'

'Didn't have time,' he replied.

Barney stared at Randolph for a while.

'What?' said Randolph, edgily.

'Have you done this before? I mean, tried to kill someone?'

Randolph shook his head.

Barney held his insipid gaze for another couple of seconds and then suddenly bent down and lifted the cheese sandwich.

'No!' cried Randolph again, as Barney put it to his mouth and took a large bite.

'You...what...?' stuttered Randolph.

Barney swallowed.

'When is it I'm going to explode exactly?' he asked.

Randolph began to back away out of the kitchen.

'Now,' he said. 'It should be instantaneous.'

They looked at each other for a while. Barney did not explode.

'You are such an idiot,' he said eventually, and then he reached over the table, took a long swallow from Carmichael's wine glass and then walked quickly past Randolph and out of the kitchen.

'Rotten cheese sandwich, by the way,' he said, and then he strode up the stairs two steps at a time.

Poked his head round the door of the bathroom, where Hoagy and Ella were both submerged in bubbles and Garrett Carmichael was sitting bored on the toilet seat.

'We need to talk,' said Barney.

'I might know why they want to kill me,' she said quietly.

Barney leant against the door frame.

'Who wants to kill you, mum?' said Hoagy.

'No one,' she replied. 'We can talk when the kids are in bed.'

'Bad guys or good guys?' asked Ella.

'The good guys aren't going to want to kill her, are they?' said Hoagy mockingly. 'You're a stupidhead!'

'Am not!'

'Stupidhead, stupidhead!'

44

The Wash

'My husband was part of the brotherhood that has existed on this island for nearly a hundred and fifty years. The *Prieure de Millport* they call themselves.'

Barney took a sip of wine. Randolph looked on from the corner, eyes as wide as Gollum.

'I don't know, I suppose it's a secret society like any other, that's what I always thought. They only ever have twelve members at one time, and whenever a member dies, they take an age carefully selecting the replacement.'

She took a deep breath, drank some wine. Barney sat in silence giving her the space to talk. Upstairs the children bounced around the bedroom.

'The members have to swear on their lives and the lives of their family that they will never divulge the society's secret. I always used to tease Ian about it. I mean, I didn't really know what he was doing when he went off on a Tuesday evening. Anyway, he was as good as his word, never told me a thing. There was a bit of talk around the village, but not much. Most people have always just left them to it, really.'

Another pause, another sip of wine, another slight cringe as a great thump came from the bedroom. She glanced aloft and smiled ruefully at Barney.

'My mother's right, isn't she? I don't need to go to work every day, not really.'

'You don't have to justify yourself,' said Barney softly.

She smiled again, took her eyes away from his. Lifted the wine glass, didn't take a sip this time, placed it back on the table.

'Then Ian found out he had cancer. It didn't take long. I don't know, five months in all. Quite lucky, I suppose. Better than being dragged out for years and years like some people.'

'When was that?'

'It started when I was six months pregnant,' she said, and she paused again. Barney was quiet. 'So at least he got to see Ella for a few weeks.'

'I'm sorry,' he heard himself saying.

'The last couple of weeks he was pretty out of it. Drugged up, had the occasional moment of clarity. He told me everything a few days before he died. He had about half an hour when he'd just been drugged, he felt a bit better but the side effects hadn't kicked in.'

She breathed deeply, swallowed, held back the tears. Barney put his hand across the table and she reached out for it, as she transported herself unwillingly back to the small room in the Victoria in Glasgow. Randolph glanced up, then immediately dropped his eyes.

'It's the Holy Grail,' she said, smiling awkwardly. 'That's what this is all about. The stupid Holy Grail, can you believe it?'

'The cup?' asked Barney.

She shook her head.

'No. Well, yes, partly. The chalice that caught the blood of Christ. Apparently it's hidden in the cathedral.'

'In Millport?'

'Go figure,' she said, shrugging her shoulders. 'Has to be somewhere.'

Barney let out a low whistle.

'I'm super sceptical about that, if I'm honest.'

'I know,' she said. 'So was I. Always have been.'

Barney turned and looked at Randolph.

'You know about this?' he asked. 'You one of the brothers?'

Randolph shook his head, Barney turned back to Carmichael.

'Who else is there?' he asked.

'I'm not sure. Ian didn't tell me that. There are rumours about the town. I'm pretty sure Jonah was one of them.'

That was not entirely unexpected, thought Barney, given Ephesian's interest in the widow.

'Anyway, the chalice is only part of it. There's something else. He told me about the chalice first, by the time he got around to the rest of it, he was becoming garbled. Couldn't tell how much of it was true, by their standards at any rate, and how much was hallucination. It wasn't like I was searching Ephesian or his freak servant out to discuss details.'

Barney glanced round at Randolph, wondering how much of this he already knew, wondering if he should have ejected him. However, it seemed sensible to retain him on the premises for the time being until he had some idea of what was happening.

'There've been books about it recently, in the last twenty years or so. I've read them all since Ian died. None of them mention Millport, though. The story of Christ's life and death.'

Another hesitation, this time because she didn't believe what she was about to say. Barney left her to it. Took a sip of wine, waited to see what was coming. All to the background of the general mayhem upstairs. Two kids and no immediate parental authority. How wars start.

'You know, it's that thing where Mary Magdalene was Christ's wife. They had children. When Joseph fled to France with the Grail, as the legend goes, he also took Jesus' wife and weans.'

'Family ticket,' said Barney glibly.

'Exactly. So, to really shorten two thousand years of history, there were descendants of Jesus back then, and there still are now, two millennia later.'

'A direct lineage to Christ?'

'Aye.'

'Fan-tastic,' said Barney. 'There's no one not going to buy into that when he makes his debut on Parkinson or Letterman.'

'Well, whatever, but you can see the problem, you can see why it's a secret. Jesus is supposed to be divine, son of God and all that. If it turns out he was an average guy, wife, kids, mortgage, game of darts down the Horseshoe on a Friday night,

241

it punctures a whole bunch of religious beliefs, doesn't it? Kind of conforms to my theory of the Garrett, but I expect you don't want to go there.'

'Let's stick to the facts,' said Barney.

'Aye, well, that's about it, without a whole bunch of unnecessary details.'

'So who is it, then? The descendant of Christ. Is he on Millport? Is it Ephesian? Ephesian is the descendant of God? That would explain his attitude.'

'I don't think it's him, but this is the point. Jesus wasn't the son of God, he was just a guy.'

Barney turned once again to Randolph, who was watching Carmichael, taking it all in.

'So, what's happening tonight then?' asked Barney, looking back to Carmichael.

'Don't know,' she said.

'Why should they want you dead?'

'Don't know,' she said.

'Why should they want your blood?'

'No idea.'

'So why did you say you thought they might want you dead?'

She shrugged.

'I never thought they knew that Ian had told me what he did, but who knows? I know at least Jacobs, and maybe Ephesian, went to see him in the last few days.' The image of her dying husband came back to her and she paused. Let herself see him lying there for a few seconds, remembered taking her new baby into the hospital to see her father, lying in some strange world that only he inhabited. A dying man and a new baby. Both of them inscrutable, both of them seeing things and understanding things like no one else can.

'So I don't know,' she said eventually. 'If they know that I know, they might well want me dead.'

Barney watched her for a while. Studied her, evaluated whether or not she was telling him everything that she could, decided she was. Turned back to Randolph after a short while.

'You got anything to say?' he asked.

Randolph didn't even look up. Shook his head.

'You know none of this?' said Barney.

'Why would he?' said Carmichael. 'He's nothing to them. Ephesian just throws sticks for James to run after.'

Randolph continued to stare at the floor. Confidence shattered. Garrett Carmichael was not wrong. He never knew anything worthwhile. And when Ephesian threw a stick, he ran after it.

'Mummy!' came the cry from upstairs, accompanied by uncontrollable wailing. 'Mummy! Hoagy said I'm a zombie!'

'I did not! She's lying!'

'I'm not a zombie!'

'I didn't say that!'

'He did!'

More tears from the bottomless well.

Garrett Carmichael laid her hands on the table and engaged both of the men in the room.

'I'm away to turn out the light. If, in my absence, anyone arrives at the door asking to kill me, tell them I'm unavailable.'

She smiled in a certain way and rose from the table.

Barney watched her go, and then took another drink of wine when she was finally out of view and he could hear her wading into the morass of her two children. Turned to look at Randolph, but he was too occupied with his own failings and foibles.

Life, he thought, is like a dodgy stomach after a big dinner. It never throws up exactly what you think it will.

The doorbell rang.

Barney laughed and looked at Randolph.

'The next assassin,' he said, and rose from the table.

Randolph waited until Barney was gone from the kitchen before looking up. As he slowly recovered his composure, he was beginning to wonder whether he should have said everything he had. Ephesian, if he should find out, would be furious, although it would be Jacobs he would have to answer to.

Barney opened the door.

'Arf.'

Barney smiled and opened up for Igor to enter, then stuck his head out of the door and checked along the street for anyone nefarious, before retreating from the cold. Igor was standing in the kitchen doorway looking suspiciously at Randolph. Barney walked through and put his hand on Igor's shoulder.

'Thought you might make an appearance,' he said.

Igor nodded. He may have made himself available to the likes of Ruth Harrison and Gently Ferguson, but he was in love with Garrett Carmichael, and at some stage over the previous three days Barney had managed to work that out.

'Today on the news,' said Barney, 'on the orders of Ephesian, Randolph here was going to try to kill Garrett by use of some cheese, but has failed. Meanwhile, there's a secret society on this very island protecting the descendants of Christ, and tonight they will be carrying out some weird ritual which will involve blood. Garrett's blood, so they were thinking, but we're going to not let that happen.'

Igor, with his muppet-like face and hunchback contorting in an exaggerated manner, looked shocked. He turned and snarled at Randolph. Barney once again placed his hand on Igor's shoulder.

'It's all right, Igor, she's safe. We're here, we can look after her until they've finished whatever it is they're up to tonight. And I don't think we have to worry about heid-the-ba' here anyway. The only problem will be if that psychopath Jacobs shows up, but we can deal with that if we have...'

The doorbell rang. Once. Somehow managed to sound ominous, as if the inner workings of the bell knew that it was Jacobs outside, come to collect the blood of the unwilling victim.

'Oh for crying out loud,' came the voice from upstairs, 'did you lot hand out party invitations. I'm trying to get the kids to sleep.'

Barney and Igor exchanged a glance. Barney was unconcerned, but the mute hunchback of the two of them could be a little thin-skinned sometimes when it came to women, and took it personally.

Barney trudged along the corridor and opened the door. Sure enough, there in the pale, creeping flesh, stood Jacobs, all brooding malice. As the day had progressed and Ephesian had

244

retreated more and more into his dark, impenetrable shell, Jacobs had sunk further and further into bleak malevolence.

'Why am I not surprised?' he muttered darkly.

'I could say the same thing, cowboy,' said Barney.

Jacobs stared cruelly into Barney's eyes and then looked over his shoulder. From where he stood he could make out the outer reaches of Igor's hump.

'The gallant crime-fighting double act has moved on,' he said caustically. 'Aren't there any other women you need to protect?'

'I don't know,' said Barney. 'Are there any other women whose blood you want to use in some weird ceremony this evening?'

The anger flashed across Jacobs' face. He stared back over Barney's shoulder, mind racing, trying to work out how Barney could already know such detail.

Igor? Could Igor know that much?

'Randolph!' he suddenly exploded, and then with two quick strides he pushed passed Barney and stormed into the house. Barney, for his part, allowed him access as he wanted him in there. An identifiable enemy like this was better within.

Jacobs stormed into the kitchen.

'Randolph!' he shouted again.

Randolph cowered in the corner. Barney appeared in the kitchen. Jacobs turned and looked bitterly behind him. Igor stared at the intruder.

'Where is she?' barked Jacobs.

'Arf,' muttered Igor, threateningly. *Keep your stinkin' hands off her*, he wanted to say, something which he managed to communicate reasonably well, even to a man such as Jacobs.

Jacobs scowled at Igor and Barney in turn, then looked round at Randolph.

'Where is she?' he repeated.

'Upstairs,' said Randolph, eyes attached to the floor. 'Putting the kids to bed.'

Barney moved across the door, blocking the way. Jacobs glared at him and then pulled out a seat at the table.

'I'll wait,' he said.

More angry glances were thrown around the room, and then slowly the tension settled and the combatants relaxed into the temporary lull of a bizarre situation. Jacobs had come round to murder Garrett Carmichael, and was sitting in the kitchen waiting for her to appear, with two men who knew that that was what he wanted to do and were intent on not letting him do it. It was absurd, and Barney was of a mind to open up a discussion about it. However, he chose instead to stand by the door and wait to see what moves Jacobs intended to make.

Footsteps behind him and he stood back to let Carmichael enter the room, confident that there were plenty of things to be said before anyone tried to do anything stupid.

Carmichael looked around the room, taking in each of the men in turn.

'Well, isn't this nice?' she said, acerbically.

'We need to talk, Mrs Carmichael,' said Jacobs.

'Whatever,' she said. 'But make it fast. I'm pissed off. The kids are pissing me off, my mother's pissed me off. I had an all right day at work, then I've been home for five minutes and my confidence is shattered, I feel like a crap mum and a crap person and a crap lawyer and I could kill someone. And looking around this room there appear to be four stupid men as candidates, so make it fast and then fuck off.'

There's nothing scarier than a woman on the edge.

She was met with silence.

246

45

Spilled Blood

Ephesian pulled gently on the copy of *Virginibus Puerisque* and watched as the large hidden door in the library wall slid inwards. He gestured for Ping Phat to go ahead of him, Ping Phat reciprocated the gesture. Ephesian accepted the innate lack of trust which was bound to exist between them, flicked the switch for the dim lights down the steep stairwell and walked in ahead of Phat. Once inside, he closed the door and the two men began to walk downwards in silence.

Ephesian felt backed into a corner. Problems seemed everywhere and all-consuming, and in this particular problem he had quickly accepted his fate. Ping Phat was pushing for as much involvement in proceedings as he could get; Ephesian had still to speak to his son about replacing Lawton in the Brotherhood, something which he had been reluctant to do in any case. So Ping Phat was about to be admitted to the Brotherhood, with none of the usual checks, with no consultation between Ephesian and his senior lieutenant.

They reached the bottom of the stairs, where the cellar opened out to the large room with the thirteen-seated table at its heart. Now Ping Phat walked ahead of Ephesian, his eyes open in awe. He turned and smiled at Ephesian, although the man was staring at the chair at the head of the table, wondering if they would ever have the opportunity to fill it.

Finding himself ignored, Phat turned back to the table, pulled out one of the chairs and sat down. His hands ran up and down the old wood, feeling the grooves and marks which had accumulated over the years.

'So this is the very table at which Christ took the Last Supper,' he said.

Ephesian looked at the back of his head.

'You misunderstand,' he said.

Phat turned sharply, Ephesian quickly lowered his gaze.

'Joseph fled Israel with Christ's family. He took with him the chalice from which Jesus had taken wine at the supper. He was in no position to take any of the furniture.'

'I see. And you have lost the Grail?'

Ephesian did not respond. They had already spent half an hour talking about the lost Grail.

'And this table?' said Phat, accepting that his cheap Grail jibe had been ignored.

'It was made in the mid-nineteenth century and was initially placed in the cathedral. When this chamber was constructed a few years later, the table was disassembled and brought down here.'

'Ah,' said Ping Phat. 'Not the table of Christ, but auspicious nevertheless.'

Ephesian did not reply. He didn't want to be down here with Ping Phat, he didn't want to be making small talk. He wanted to know that Jacobs was carrying out his tasks and if he had retrieved the Grail from Roosevelt. Instead he was stuck holding the hand of the visitor, like some five pound an hour tour guide.

'So,' said Phat, 'there is the business of my initiation into the Brotherhood, no?'

Ephesian stared at the ground, and then he walked to the back of the room, opened the drawer at the top of the small cabinet, and took out the long thin piece of maroon cloth, three candles, a bowl of rose petals and the large ceremonial dagger.

✄

'So, you,' said Carmichael, pointing to Jacobs, 'you first. Is it true you want to kill me? And don't bullshit, because I've had enough of that in the last half hour.'

Jacobs stared at her for a few seconds, then glanced at Barney. The situation was insane and here he was, push coming to shove, and he was proving to be as small-town inept as everyone else.

'The Society has a meeting of the utmost importance tonight,' he replied, going off on a politician's tangent, addressing a question he had not been asked. 'There are certain items which we need to collect for the ceremony to take place.'

Carmichael put her hand on her hip.

'Like my blood,' she said.

Jacobs did not reply. Igor scowled, although he made sure to replace the scowl with a look of dog-like affection when he stared at Carmichael. But although she too was secretly in love with Igor, she was in no mood for dog-like looks of affection from anyone, even from a little guy with a roguish hump.

'How much do you need exactly?' she asked, looking witheringly at Jacobs.

This one caught him off guard a little.

'What?' he said.

'You need all six pints or just a cup? Do you freaks up there want to bathe in it or are you just after a quick drink?'

Jacobs had been thrown firmly on the back foot. Felt a bit like a criminal who'd just been asked by the police what kind of vehicle he'd like them to provide for his escape.

'What?' he repeated.

Barney stared at Jacobs and asked, 'Why Garrett?'

'I'm doing the talking, Bucko,' said Carmichael, who was flowing and enjoying the power that a full on fucked-off woman has over men. Barney held up his hands in a backing off gesture. 'So, aye,' she said, turning to Jacobs, 'why me?'

Jacobs gritted his teeth. He'd been sucked into the mess. Without saying a word it was already acknowledged that he was here with the intent to kill her. And, despite the knife in his pocket, he wasn't sure how he was going to do that, surrounded by three other men, at least two of whom would try to stop him.

'The blood needs to come from a woman, to represent the Sacred Feminine.'

'You've been reading too much pulp fiction,' interrupted Carmichael, rolling her eyes.

'She needs to be a mother,' continued Jacobs unabashed, 'she needs to be someone who is versed in the way of the society.'

'You know that Ian told me,' she said as a statement of fact.

Jacobs looked into the weary eyes of a widow whose heart died every time she thought of her husband in the hospital.

'We ordered him to,' he said coldly.

The sadness went, she shook her head, smiled ruefully.

'You knew he was dying, you took advantage of him, and you thought it wouldn't matter if his wife also died some day.'

'Exactly.'

'Did you tell him why you wanted me to know?' she asked, the thought troubling her as soon as she'd asked the question. Had her husband knowingly set her up?

'We told him we'd decided to take on female members and that you'd be taking his place. He thought he was doing you a favour.'

She laughed bitterly, pulled a seat away from the kitchen table and sat down. Stared at the table top for a few seconds then looked up at him. Waved her hand dismissively.

'And if the kids are orphaned, who cares?' she said. Could feel her emotions swinging wildly all over the place. Igor wanted to reach out and hold her hand.

'Yes,' said Jacobs, 'if you want to be brutal about it. There's a higher purpose here.'

'And what would that be?' she asked sharply.

Jacobs began to drum his fingers on the table. He needed a plan, he needed to get out of this situation, he needed to get away from Barney and Igor.

'Come up to the house with me and we can speak to Mr Ephesian,' he said.

'No!' said Barney.

'Arf!'

'And who's going to look after the kids?' she replied. 'Tonight, and for the next fifteen years after you've slit my throat?'

'We can talk,' said Jacobs, wittering on. 'Maybe we can make some kind of arrangement.'

'Arrangement? That would be where you only killed me a bit? Or maybe you'd just hack off a limb? Would that give you enough blood?'

'Mr Ephesian can be very accommodating,' said Jacobs.

'Whoop-de-doo.'

'Get out,' said Barney quietly.

Jacobs looked brusquely round at him.

'I'm discussing matters with Mrs Carmichael,' he said.

'You're discussing how you're going to kill her. This is insane. Get the fuck out of her house.'

'Arf!'

'It's all right, Barney,' said Carmichael, holding up her hand. And she looked round at Igor and gave him the kind of look which made his heart dissolve into mush, and she mouthed *It's all right* silently to him.

'So,' she said, turning back to Jacobs, her wildly fluctuating mood having settled into some sort of resignation, borne of the unreality of the whole thing. Just could not take seriously that they were sitting in her kitchen matter-of-factly discussing her murder. 'Why do you have to actually kill me?'

Jacobs drummed his fingers some more, a rhythmless beat as he was a rhythmless man.

'People give blood donations, don't they?' she said. 'You don't die the second you hand over your pint to the blood transfusion service. At least, I didn't the last time I went.'

Jacobs drummed on. Not yet considering what she was saying, barely listening, trying to work out how he was going to be able to do this without killing everyone in the room.

'You are, surely,' she continued, 'a Christian society. It doesn't sound very Christian to have to sacrifice someone. Is it actually laid down by the hand of God somewhere that you need to kill the person? If you just ask nicely, you can have some of my blood for your stupid ceremony, I don't care. Take it.'

Barney looked at her as if she was insane, as did Igor, who this time did reach out and take her hand.

'It's cool,' she said to them.

The words finally sank in for Jacobs. He stared at her, everything not yet really computing. Trying to decide if this was

251

just another diversionary tactic and if he should even be allowing himself to consider the idea.

He and Ephesian had thought all along that she would have to die. Just asking for her blood had never even crossed their minds. But was it actually laid down anywhere in the old teachings, the documents first written down by the Knights Templar over nine hundred years previously, that there had to be a sacrifice?

'Garrett,' protested Barney, 'really, shouldn't we just get this comedian out the house? Why are you even entertaining this guy? Call the police.'

'Arf!'

'And say what?' she said. 'There's a secret society who wants my blood? Are you kidding me? And the police around here means Gainsborough, and I suspect he's probably one of the flippin' brothers.' She looked at Jacobs, who said nothing.

'Call the police on the mainland,' urged Barney.

'Same question,' she said. 'What do I say to them?'

Barney did not reply.

'So how much blood do you need?' asked Carmichael again.

'Half a cup, maybe,' said Jacobs, a little non-plussed.

'Cool,' she replied. 'I'll get a bottle and a knife. Any of you practiced in medicine in case I faint?'

Barney and Igor looked shocked.

'I'm kidding,' she said. 'I'm not going to faint. I'll make a cut in my hand and see how we're getting on, all right?'

'This is stupid,' said Barney. 'You owe them nothing.'

She thought about it, who she owed and who her life belonged to.

'I owe Ian, and he'd want me to do this. And if it gets you lot out of my house, then we're the better for that. And when you're gone, I'm going to go upstairs and sit and watch the children sleeping, because I'm never angry with them when they're like that. And tomorrow and the day after tomorrow and the day after that, I'm going to try to keep that feeling of not being angry.'

They exchanged a glance, Barney appreciated the thought, even though he would never truly appreciate the wonderful hell that it is to have children.

'And you,' she said, turning to Jacobs, 'do we have a deal? I presume for all your brooding malevolence, you don't actually want to have to kill anyone. I'll give you credit for that, even if you don't deserve it. I give you the blood and you can toddle off back to your master up the hill.'

Jacobs wondered if he'd been backed into a position which he didn't want to be in, but all the while she'd been talking, he'd been calculating the odds, deciding what Ephesian would say, deciding what effect it would have on the ceremony. All along there had never been any acknowledgement that there required to be any sacrifice as part of the rite. The death had purely been as a means to get the blood.

'Very well,' he said cautiously.

'Lovely,' she said, with lyrical sarcasm. She stood up. 'Right,' she said, 'you can have your blood and leave. James, you can just leave. Barney, thank you, I appreciate your help, and I'm sure you'll want to stay until Mr Jacobs has his pound of flesh, but once he leaves, so can you.'

Barney nodded guardedly.

'Igor,' she said, turning round, and then she hesitated. 'I'm still going to go up and sit and watch the children, but you can stay if you like. I'd like you to stay. You can be the guard against old bloodsucker here coming back.'

'Arf!' said Igor.

'Lovely,' she said again, and then she walked to the cupboard to get a beaker into which to drain some blood.

It's a funny old life.

46

Where Are They Now?

The door closed behind them and Barney Thomson and Simon Jacobs walked quickly away from Garrett Carmichael's house. Jacobs had his cup of blood; Randolph had already been summarily dispatched; Carmichael was spending quality time with her children, now that they were fast asleep; Igor was guarding the tea and biscuits; and Barney Thomson wasn't exactly sure what he was going to do for the rest of the evening, although he was beginning to feel a bit peckish. However, he wasn't entirely convinced that he ought to leave Jacobs to his own devices. Which, strangely, was exactly how Jacobs was feeling about Barney Thomson, and explained why he was about to make what seemed on the surface to be a strange proposition.

'Would you join our fellowship, Mr Thomson?' he asked out of the blue, just as Barney was taking a look out to sea and enjoying the chill breeze.

Barney raised an eyebrow and studied Jacobs' face for any sign of sarcasm or some sort of twisted humour.

'Now why would you ask me that?' he asked.

'I'm a logical man, Mr Thomson. You may have been my adversary up until this point, but you are clearly a man of some quality. A vacancy has arisen and I feel you are the appropriate man to fill it. After tonight there will be no requirement for the secrecy of the past.'

'Jonah Harrison?' asked Barney.

'That position has already been filled. This is a slightly more recent matter, although not due to any fatality.'

'Go on.'

Jacobs directed Barney up Hill Street, intent on visiting Lawton's house to search for the Grail. Confident that Barney would be curious enough about the whole business to enlist.

'I had a slight disagreement with Father Roosevelt this evening, the cleric at the cathedral. I doubt he will be in attendance.'

'You nailed him?'

Jacobs threw Barney a glance, did not immediately reply.

'He may require some hospital treatment,' he said after a few steps, 'but nothing that won't heal with time.'

Barney smiled. Thugs are as thugs do, no matter who they're working for or what class they come from or which side of the right/wrong fence they think they belong to.

'And what's the big event?' asked Barney.

Jacobs genuinely considering telling Barney, even though none of the brotherhood knew apart from him and Ephesian. However, he remained cautious on this matter and shook his head.

'You are either in or out, Mr Thomson,' he said. 'Join us and be part of history, or walk away and wake up tomorrow morning to read about it in the papers.'

You're going to miss the early editions, thought Barney, but decided against out and out flippancy at this stage.

'Where are we going now?' he asked instead.

'To search for something, the exact nature of which I will reveal as soon as you commit to the cause.'

'Very intriguing,' said Barney. 'All right, I'm in.'

'Good,' said Jacobs. Another two of his problems squared away in one go. Roosevelt replaced, Barney Thomson struck off the list of antagonisers. He would now just be another bloke standing around the table in awe of what would be unfolding before him. 'We are going to the house of Augustus Lawton to search for the Holy Grail.'

'Ah,' said Barney. 'Cool. You don't have the Grail then?'

'Not yet,' replied Jacobs.

Barney checked his watch. Almost ten-thirty. No wonder he was hungry. The evening had whizzed by.

'When's your ceremony supposed to take place?'

'Midnight,' replied Jacobs.

Barney let out a low whistle.

'Cutting it fine.'

Jacobs checked the time, although he already knew.

'I should call Mr Ephesian,' he said. 'Excuse me.'

And he took the mobile from his pocket and made the call, wondering if Ephesian would even answer. Barney turned and looked back at the sea, through the houses at the end of the street, breathed in the sea air and wondered if he was about to spend the rest of the evening with a series of old men whose hair he had cut in the previous three days.

✂

Many others amongst the combatants of the story had drifted off into quiet, small town oblivion for the night.

Ruth Harrison was back where she belonged, standing in front of the bathroom mirror, squeezing spots, applying make-up, imagining that the Reverend Dreyfus might have a change of heart and be round to see her the following morning clutching a large bouquet and a box of *Terry's All Gold*.

Tony Angelotti was standing beside the post box at the top of the town, staring at the stars, wondering when Luigi Linguini was going to make another call, so that he could tell him that he had uncovered absolutely nothing at the cathedral. Luigi Linguini, however, was in hiding and was not yet due to emerge for another hour or two. Tony was wasting his time, something which he was finally beginning to realise. Wondering vaguely if his colleague had been murdered.

Luigi, however, was currently huddled up, cramped, hungry and very, very keen on finding a bathroom.

Father Roosevelt had recovered from his head-butting and was sitting in his kitchen, a bag of frozen peas on his face and a glass of medicinal whisky in his paws. He had thought of going to Lawton's place to remove the Grail, but couldn't face leaving the house. Imagined that Jacobs would be waiting for him, wherever he went, to inflict further pain. Nevertheless, he had Faith that the Grail would not be found.

Augustus Lawton remained in his hospital bed, a small machine blipping beside him. No visitors, no get well soon cards, no flowers. An eternity in true purgatory for stealing the Holy Grail.

2Tone was hanging with a couple of buds watching *High Society* on DVD for the eighteenth time. *High Society* is the new *Lock Stock*; Bing Crosby is the new Vinnie Jones.

Marion and Nella were arguing over whether to watch a repeat of *Where The Heart Is*, or *Big Brother – Uncut!*

Many of the other players in the piece were girding their loins for the big event of the evening, the ultimate meeting of the organisation of the *Prieure de Millport*. Few of them, however, realised the significance of what was about to take place. All they knew was that they had been called to an extraordinary meeting and that each of them had to bring along the sacred item which they had kept in their freezers since the first day they'd become a member of the society. With the exception of Ephesian and Jacobs, however, none of them had any idea of the momentous and earth-shattering event that they were about to witness.

Nothing less than the re-birth of the direct lineage of Jesus Christ himself.

All in a day's work for Barney Thomson. If he could help Jacobs find the Holy Grail, of course, without which the evening was going to redefine *damp squib* for the new millennium.

47

The Pain of The Silent Phone

Barney smiled as he watched Jacobs jangle the huge set of keys, before finding the correct one for Lawton's front door.

'In a position to do that with every house on the island?'

Jacobs didn't reply. Unhappy about allowing Barney so much access to his working methods, but he knew that tomorrow the day would dawn differently from any day of the previous two thousand years. The *Prieure*'s work would be over and their secrets and working methods would no longer interest anyone.

Jacobs opened the door, stepped inside and turned on the hall light. Barney followed, closing the door behind him.

The house was large, Victorian and lived in by a single man. Clutter and dust everywhere. The stairs, which led directly up from the front door, were lined with piles of books and clothes and miscellaneous junk on nearly every step.

Barney took it all in. Jacobs saw none of it, concentrating on possible places where Roosevelt might have hidden the Grail.

'What does it look like?' asked Barney.

'The Grail?' said Jacobs. 'No idea. Haven't seen it. A wooden cup apparently.'

Barney idly looked at piles of rubbish, lifted things up and looked underneath, then followed Jacobs into the dining room.

'How do you know it's wooden if you haven't seen it?'

Jacobs started moving around the room, looking in cupboards, a cursory search.

'Mr Ephesian has seen it.'

'You'd think it'd be gold,' said Barney. 'Encrusted with jewels. Isn't part of all this malarkey that he was the king of Israel?'

'Whatever,' said Jacobs, disinterestedly. 'But then, he worked as a carpenter. Who knows?'

'The whole yin-yang thing again,' said Barney. 'On one hand, king, on the other, helping people put up their Ikea furniture.'

'Exactly.'

Jacobs stretched to look on top of a series of cabinets, his hands coming down caked in dust and cobwebs.

'You know for sure it's here somewhere?' asked Barney.

'No,' said Jacobs, 'we don't. I'm guessing.'

Barney let the pile of clothes he'd been looking under topple over. Straightened up, studied Jacobs' back.

'You want to explain that?' he said.

Jacobs breathed heavily and turned. Acting like he was tired of the questioning, but he knew Barney was right to ask.

'The Grail was kept hidden in the cathedral. Lawton discovered its whereabouts and took it for himself. He brought it back here. Father Roosevelt knew he had taken it and, for his own purposes, decided that he did not want the ceremony to take place. He came round here, he put Lawton in a coma. Now we have to find the Grail.'

'Surely he would have taken it with him?'

'You have to understand the minds of men, Mr Thomson,' he said, suddenly sounding like some master criminal. Barney took a seat on the arm of the chair.

'Enlighten me,' he said.

'Father Roosevelt is a very limited man. He had just burst Lawton's head open, something which one must presume would have shocked him. He finds himself standing over an unconscious man, blood everywhere. He panics. What to do with the Grail? The Holy Grail. He's a man of God, he can't destroy it, yet he knows he can't take it back to the cathedral or we'll get it. He can't take it back to his house, because if we work out it's him who attacked Lawton, we'll come looking for it. Maybe he thinks Lawton is dead, maybe he thinks this is the

259

last place anyone is going to think of looking for the Grail. He hides it here.'

'In plain sight?'

'Very possibly.'

Barney nodded and pursed his lips.

'That's some convoluted thinking there,' he said.

'On the contrary,' said Jacobs. 'Very simple, to accompany a simple man such as Father Roosevelt.' He checked his watch, felt an increase in the nerves that he was doing so well to hide. 'And we have a little over an hour to find it. We should get a move on.'

✂

The Brotherhood of the *Prieure de Millport* began arriving in ones and twos shortly after eleven o'clock in the evening, each with their large or small package in hand. They were each surprised, however, to be greeted upon their arrival by a member of the entourage of Ping Phat, rather than the expected Jacobs. They were then ushered into the dining room, to wait until the appointed hour and to meet the legendary Phat himself, who took the opportunity to revert to Yoda-ism and to regale the members of the society with tales of eastern business shenanigans.

First to arrive was Romeo McGhee, frozen hand in a bag in tow, but having managed to shake off the close attentions of Chardonnay Deluth. The latter had been as difficult as he'd been expecting, and in fact he'd had to sign a paper which she'd hurriedly drawn up on some _12.99 legal document software, attesting that he would share equally all money which came their way as a result of his involvement with the *Prieure*. Carried away with his new status in life, he was already beginning to think of ditching Deluth and felt sure any lawyer worth their weight in mince would be able to make exactly that of the stupid document.

He was immediately out of his depth, as Ping Phat began to elaborate on a story of share dealing in Shanghai, but he nodded and said *cool* and smiled enough to get by.

Next in line was Philip Luciens, the paramedic, clutching a much bigger package than McGhee, and who was also quickly

260

subsumed into the conversation on the Shanghai stock exchange. By eleven-twenty, the old buffers Matthew 'Rusty' Brown and Simon 'Ginger' Rogers had also made an appearance and the gathering was well underway.

Upstairs, keeping away from it all, imagining events to be out of control and heading towards disaster, Bartholomew Ephesian stood in the darkness of his bedroom, looking down over the sweep of hill to the dark sea below. Wondering if this was the end to all his dreams.

He checked his watch for the thirty-eighth time since eleven o'clock, looked round at the bedside table. There is nothing more painful than a phone which does not ring.

Without the Grail there would be no ceremony, not tonight, not ever. Perhaps they could postpone this evening, unearth the Grail, and go ahead at some later date, but would he still be Grand Master after this shambles? Ping Phat, for all the smiles and Asian formality, was a formidable man who would not stand for things going wrong.

He looked at his watch again, he glanced round at the phone. His stomach curled and twisted with nerves. Bartholomew Ephesian's world was falling apart.

48

Honty Grython And
The Moly Pail

'It's not exactly the great Grail quest that they talk about in books, is it?' said Barney.

Jacobs looked up quickly from a kitchen cupboard, his face red. With midnight approaching, Barney had grown more and more forlorn and hungry, accepting that they were on a wild goose chase. Searching for a needle in a haystack, when there probably weren't any needles or wild geese in the haystack in the first place. Jacobs, on the other hand, had swung dramatically in the opposite direction, his searching becoming ever more fevered.

'No fighting or dragons or beautiful women. Just scrabbling round a filthy old house, looking under year old newspapers.'

Jacobs tried to control his temper.

'This is not a lost cause, Mr Thomson,' he growled. 'Don't sit there making glib comments. Look for the bloody thing!'

Barney had had enough. Curious enough about the business to hang on for a little longer, rather than go home and do the hunter-gatherer thing in Miranda Donaldson's fridge, having forgotten in any case that her front door would already be bolted; not quite curious enough to get back down on his hands and knees.

'Think I'll have a cup of tea,' he said. 'Would you like one?'

Jacobs snarled, then started tossing things out of kitchen cupboards. Barney smiled, filled the kettle. Checked the fridge for milk, which there was, smelled it and set it up on the counter.

'Mugs, mugs,' he muttered to himself, looking around. The kitchen had gradually fallen into ever increasing disrepair, under the onslaught of Jacobs' pursuit. He found them behind a discarded breadbin.

'Glasgow Rangers or Wallace & Gromit?' he asked, the sentence trailing off with a sudden realisation.

'Fuck's sake,' muttered Jacobs in response, standing up and looking at Barney like he was going to strangle him.

'Wait a minute,' said Barney.

'What?'

Barney put the Rangers cup down on the kitchen work top and held the odd-shaped Wallace & Gromit in both hands.

'It's a wooden mug,' said Barney, not taking his eyes off it.

'What?' said Jacobs, clearly annoyed.

'The mug, it's wooden.'

'It's a stupid mug, for crying out loud!' barked Jacobs.

'Look!' said Barney, and for the first time engaged Jacobs' eyes, instantly quelling the man's rampant ill-humour.

'What?' Jacobs repeated, but this time more inquisitively.

'Look at it,' said Barney. 'It's been painted to look like a regular mug, it's got this Wallace & Gromit sticker on it, wherever the guy got that from, but who makes wooden mugs in this day and age?'

Jacobs slowly took the cup out of Barney's hands. He studied it for a second and then looked at Barney. They held each others' gaze and then Jacobs quickly swivelled, removed the sticker, turned on a tap and held the cup under running water. A couple of seconds and then slowly the paint began to come off, revealing the bare, two thousand year old wood beneath.

Jacobs had no immediate feeling of awe at holding the cup of Christ, such was his enormous relief. He looked round at Barney, checked the clock as he went. Quarter to midnight. Ephesian was going to be in bits.

'Take this and finish washing it down,' he said, 'I'm going to call Ephesian.'

Barney saluted and said, 'Yes, boss.'

Jacobs no longer minded the flippancy. They were almost there. He dried his hands and pulled the phone out of his pocket.

✕

Back at the ranch the collective had gathered. As time had worn on, the font of stories that was the rotund and Yoda-like Ping Phat had dried up, as he had grown ever more concerned that nothing seemed to be happening. He had no idea where Jacobs had gone having not seen him now for almost five hours. And after his initiation into the Brotherhood by Ephesian, and the slow climb back up the steep stairs, he had seen nothing of him either.

Ping Phat was once again standing at the window, although unlike Ephesian directly above him, he was unable to look out into the dark as the lights were on behind him.

And as with the conversation of their unexpected host, the chatter from the collective had slowly dried up.

So now, as midnight approached, the room was silent. Ping Phat, plus eight members of the Brotherhood, as well as Phat's happy little band of four followers, each sitting in peace, with whatever thoughts they allowed themselves in this company.

Silence, bar the small clock ticking on the mantleshelf and the vague murmur of the central heating.

Heads turned at a new sound, the rush of footsteps down the stairs.

'Ah!' said Ping Phat, with the exhibitionist's need to attract attention to himself. 'At last the news!'

To the bottom of the stairs, the footfalls padded quickly along the hall and then the door was opened with a flourish. Ephesian, for all his complicated peculiarity of character, was not averse to a little showmanship. Not that he engaged anyone in the eye. Instead he presented himself to the Moroccan carpet.

'I'm sorry to have kept you waiting, gentlemen. I believe everything is now in place to begin. If you would like to follow me downstairs.'

Amid great shuffling, the rustling of packages and the gentle hum of relief, the collective began to rise. Ping Phat jumped quickly to his feet, nodding at his entourage to stay where they were. He clapped his hands and approached Ephesian.

264

'Time it is, my friend, history to create!'

'Indeed,' said Ephesian, flinching a little at the hand which was placed on his shoulder, but with the call that he had just taken from Jacobs, the knots and twists and pains in his stomach had been instantly removed, to be replaced by exhilaration that they had finally arrived at this great day.

He twitched, he almost smiled, he turned and walked quickly from the room, across the hall towards the library, his band of happy thieves behind him.

✂

Jacobs and Barney walked swiftly up the road, out of the town towards Hill Farm and the turning up to the big house. Jacobs was clutching the Grail, Barney was carrying the small bag which Jacobs had had with him since he'd left Roosevelt's house.

'You need to be initiated into the Brotherhood before you can sit in on the ceremony,' said Jacobs, very business-like. 'Usually it's a ceremony in itself, but these are exceptional circumstances.'

'Cool.'

'I'm going to tell you some facts, you must accept them, no matter how much they might challenge your current beliefs. If you need a time for reflection, you can do it tomorrow.'

'I'll pencil it in,' said Barney.

'This is all about Jesus and his heirs. He may have died on the cross, but he left a wife and children.'

'I know.'

Jacobs slung him a sharp look.

'What d'you mean?'

'Garrett told me.'

Jacobs grunted. Well, it wasn't as if it wasn't his fault that she'd found out in the first place.

'She won't, at least, know about Azarael Corinthian?'

Barney shook his head, Jacobs strode on, voice rapid-fire.

'The history of the descendents of Christ is long and rich and will be told soon enough. The work of the *Prieure de Millport*, the society of which you are just about to become part, has involved documenting and protecting the lineage from the time

265

of Christ himself until the present day. It has involved many great dynasties and many public names down the centuries.'

'I'm believing every word so far,' said Barney, a cheap remark which Jacobs pretended he hadn't heard.

'The impetus for much modern political movement, such as the European Union, has come from the Society or its partners. It was all leading to the day, New Year's Eve 2000, the dawn of the new millennium, when the descendants of Christ would be revealed, and the heir to the throne of Israel would step forward and take his place as king, not only over that country, but over the realm of Europe and over Christians and Jews everywhere.'

Barney gave him the old eyebrow.

'Sounds like rank imperialism to me, but go on.'

'The problem was that by the mid-nineteen seventies, there was only one remaining survivor of the line.'

'Azarael Corinthian,' said Barney.

'I shan't dwell on detail, but certain aspects of his lifestyle were questionable. He died of a heart attack at the age of thirty-six.'

'Bummer.'

'Quite.'

Jacobs turned up the road through the farm, the smell of the farmyard embracing them, together with the sound of the shuffling of cows in the night.

'So why d'you keep going?' asked Barney. 'The guy have a love child?'

Jacobs snorted at that remark, although extensive investigations had been carried out at the time to establish whether or not that might be the case.

'The Society has long had this cup in its possession. We believe it to possess magical powers, including the greatest power of all, the power over life and of death. To drink from the cup is to restore and to be reborn.'

Barney walked on at his side, thinking that if it wasn't for all the other baloney and out and out nonsense he'd heard in his life, this would be the most ridiculous mince he'd ever been told. It was, however, in the top twenty.

'I'm intrigued,' he said instead.

266

'The Society has worked in the past thirty years or so to preserve the legacy and the life of Azarael Corinthian.'

'I thought you said he'd died?'

'We have preserved his body.'

Barney said nothing.

'In order that no one member of the Brotherhood be burdened with the responsibility, Azarael's body was carved into twelve pieces. Each one of us was tasked with retaining one single part, keeping it safe and keeping it, well, frozen, until such times as we were in a position to resurrect the last descendant of Christ.'

Barney looked down at the bag he'd been carrying for the past ten minutes. The look did not change on his face, he didn't drop it or anything, it wasn't as if he hadn't handled frozen body parts in the past, but he was curious as to what exactly it was. There are parts of another man's body, after all, that you just don't want to have too close to your hands.

'The left foot,' said Jacobs, reading Barney's mind.

'Ah,' said Barney, relaxing. 'I can handle that.'

'Tonight,' said Jacobs, and now his voice took on greater weight and solemnity, as if he was announcing some major event on the ten o'clock news, 'Azarael Corinthian will be reborn!'

Barney looked at him out of the corner of his eye.

'By drinking Garrett's blood from the Holy Grail?'

'Indeed. And tomorrow the Society, using its extensive contacts around the world, will announce the return of the heirs of Christ, and change the political map of the world forever.'

Barney had begun to wonder if he'd inadvertently walked onto the set of a movie.

'Why didn't you just use the Grail when he died in the first place? More dignified than keeping him in a freezer.'

'Alas, Azarael took the secret of the Grail's location to the grave.'

'Or to the fridge.'

'We have searched desperately. We knew it was in the cathedral, and we had many long arguments about whether we should demolish the building in our search. However, certain members of the Society held sway and we searched in vain for

267

many years. The millennium came and went. Two weeks ago, however, one of our number made the breakthrough.'

They walked on in silence for a short while, as Jacobs thought of the glory to come and Barney thought of how the monstrously absurd was becoming more and more monstrously absurd as they went along.

'So,' he said, 'tonight you're going to do what, exactly? Arrange the frozen body parts as a kind of jigsaw, pour some of Garrett's blood into the mouth, and the body of Azarael Corinthian will magically reassemble, the fella will get up and tomorrow he's going to be king of the world?'

Jacobs smiled in a determined manner.

'Exactly,' he said.

'Were you drinking at all before you came out tonight?'

'And now, Mr Thomson,' said Jacobs and he took a small knife from his pocket. Here we go, thought Barney, takes all his time to explain his deranged plot to take over the world and then he stabs me. Typical. 'Give me your left hand.'

Ah, thought Barney. Blood brother baloney. Perfect!

He offered up his left hand, Jacobs took hold of it and quickly ran the sharp knife across the palm. Barney winced slightly but the cut was not a deep one. Then Jacobs cut into his own hand and offered it up for Barney to shake. He hesitated a moment at this part of the equation, but then held out his hand and took the hand of Simon Jacobs, so that Barney Thomson joined forever the society of the *Prieure de Millport*.

The brothers were once again twelve; the Grail had been found. Everything was in place for the resurrection of Azarael Corinthian.

49

The Ceremonial Big Bang 1

The table was occupied. The ten brothers of the *Prieure de Millport* were sitting in place, waiting to see the two empty chairs filled and ultimately the large chair of office at the head of the table taken by the reborn Azarael Corinthian.

Corinthian himself, or at least his collected body parts, was lying out on the table. Only the left foot, currently being carried by Barney Thomson, and the head, the responsibility of Jacobs, were missing. The brothers now all knew why they were there.

The room was illuminated by twenty-three large white candles, and for the first time in a hundred and fifty years, the fireplace had been lit and the long flue leading up to the surface was finally being made use of.

To the left of the empty seat at the head of the table sat Ephesian, the Bible open in front of him. He was reading over the words, although there was not one of them which was not engraved on his heart. Opposite him sat Ping Phat, who had cheekily taken the place which had for years been reserved for Jacobs. Phat was more than happy to have a childish bunfight over status, even at this late stage.

They heard the movement at the top of the stairs and each of the collective turned and looked up at the approaching footfalls. Most of those in attendance were completely unaware of the drama surrounding Father Roosevelt and were expecting him to be accompanying Jacobs.

The footsteps grew louder and closer, until Simon Jacobs and Barney Thomson stepped out of the dark into the yellow light of the small room. Barney winced at the sight of the roughly put together body on the table top, reminding him as it did of his own questionable past.

There were a few surprised faces around the table, as there had been at the attendance of Romeo McGhee and Ping Phat.

Ephesian nodded at Jacobs, who accepted the instruction.

'Gentlemen,' he began, 'we have one final new initiate this evening, as Father Roosevelt has decided that he no longer belongs with us. This is Barney Thomson, a local businessman.'

The group as one looked in his direction and intoned, in a prescribed chant, 'You are our brother.' All except one of them, who tried to say those words but all that came out was *Arf*!

Barney looked at Igor in surprise, Igor gave Barney a *glad to have you aboard* nod.

Around the table, starting from Bartholomew Ephesian, sat Philip Luciens the paramedic; Simon 'Ginger' Rogers, old buffer; Romeo McGhee, young buffer; Igor, deaf mute hunchback; Thomas Petersen, slightly concerned old man; Rusty Brown, old buffer; the Reverend Judas Dreyfus, Judas by name, Judas by nature; Thaddeus Gainsborough, police constable; and Ping Phat, overweight, over-ambitious Chinese golfer.

Such was his general excitement and state of ferment, a minute or so had passed without Jacobs noticing that Phat had taken his seat beside the soon to be reborn king. However, as he looked around the table, having joined with the brothers in welcoming Barney to their midst, he realised the two empty chairs were at the bottom, between Igor and Petersen.

He breathed deeply, he gritted his teeth. The crowning moment of all their lives was just about upon them. This was no time for petty boardroom politics. Yet in ten minutes' time, the new ruler of half the known world would be sitting at the head of the table and Jacobs would be a mile away at the far end, having been usurped.

Ping Phat glanced at Jacobs, let his eyes rest upon the man, let the malaise that existed at his heart sink in, let the new order sink in. Jacobs was no longer number two in the organisation, just as Ephesian was no longer number one.

Ping Phat's eyes drifted away, his face expressionless. Jacobs clenched his fists and looked at Ephesian. Ephesian stared at the Bible.

The other members looked down at the table before them, or at the bizarre assemblage that was Azarael Corinthian, and nervously awaited Jacobs' reaction. Jacobs looked at each of them in turn, deciding whether to pick one of them up and forcibly move them, having already made the judgement call that he couldn't do it to Ping Phat.

At last his eyes settled on Igor, a man with whom he was already unimpressed. Not at all happy that Igor had stood up for Ruth Harrison and Garrett Carmichael. Yet Igor was next to last at the bottom of the table and hardly worth the effort.

Barney watched Jacobs for a few seconds, smiled at what he imagined was running through his head and then took the seat next to Igor. The two men nodded at one another, then Barney opened up the small polythene bag he'd been carrying and, doing his best not to actually touch the item in question, pushed the frozen left foot along the table top into position.

Barney's movement had broken the moment and now Jacobs decided to assert some sort of authority over proceedings. He laid the three bags he had brought down the stairs with him on the table and looked around the room. From the first bag he produced the small wooden cup which he and Barney had retrieved from Lawton's kitchen. He held it aloft for all to see, his face beaming with pride that it was he who had brought the Grail.

'Behold!' he said magnificently, 'the Cup of Christ! Brothers, I bring you the Grail!'

It was a moment and a proclamation that demanded a fanfare, a John Williams-esque melodic cinematic theme or at least a round of applause and a bit of cheering. However, none of the assembled company had ever been in an actual seeing-the-Holy-Grail-for-the-first-time situation, so they were a bit vague on the etiquette. Instead they looked on in awed silence.

271

Jacobs waited for the reaction, decided that he had received the right blend of fear and wonderment, then slowly took out the small vial of red liquid.

'The blood,' he said, 'with which the king shall be reborn.'

A little less awe this time but still his audience were hooked. They waited nervously for the final package to be opened, the one which Jacobs had retrieved before coming down the stairs.

He looked around his audience, all of whom stared back, anxious and excited. Except Ephesian. And Ping Phat, who was being superior. And Barney, who was slightly bemused by it all. And Igor, who was still angry with Jacobs and with himself for being part of an organisation that would have harmed Garrett Carmichael.

Slowly Jacobs unwrapped the heavy parcel, tiny fragments of ice pinging from it onto the table as he did so. And then, with one final sweeping flourish, the frozen head of Azarael Corinthian was revealed, and Jacobs dramatically held it aloft in his hands, the head high above his own.

'I bring you the King!' he exclaimed, and the pallid frosty blue features of Corinthian looked grotesquely down on the company of men.

Barney shivered and looked away.

Jacobs was breathing heavily, exhilarated by his moment of grandstanding.

'The King!' he said again with vigour, and then he lowered the head and walked slowly round, looking each of the men in the eye as he went. And when he reached the head of the table, he glowered at Ping Phat in triumph, as if this moment actually meant something. Ping Phat ignored him, the glower turned to contempt. And then Jacobs leant across the table and placed Corinthian's head triumphantly at the top of the torso.

'Behold the King!' he said this time, as a variation.

'It is time,' said Ping Phat suddenly, once again dropping the Yoda business. 'Mr Ephesian, let the ceremony commence.'

Jacobs had once again been usurped.

'Yes,' said Ephesian, not taking his eyes off the frozen face of Corinthian.

Jacobs gritted his teeth, slowly straightened up and minced grudgingly back down the length of the table and sat down opposite Barney. He glowered across at him and then turned and looked up the length of the table towards Ephesian.

Ephesian took a deep breath, composing himself. At last the moment had arrived and his nerves were gone.

'Behold!' he began, 'he cometh with clouds; and every eye shall see him, and they also which pierced him: and all kindreds of the earth shall wail because of him. Even so, Amen. I am Alpha and Omega, the beginning and the ending, saith the Lord!'

Without instruction the men around the table began to join hands, the new initiates going with the flow; Ping Phat reaching across to Ephesian, Barney reaching across to Jacobs.

'Be thou faithful unto death, and I will give thee a crown of life!' exclaimed Ephesian.

And then it happened. Suddenly, with no warning, the doors to the small cabinet at the top of the room, little more than four feet from where Ping Phat was viewing the beginning of his next great marketing opportunity, burst dramatically open, and out sprang Luigi Linguini, filled with all the hubris and devotion of the Catholic Church, intent on destroying the most unholy and un-Christian of ceremonies which was about to take place.

'Not so fast, you stinkin' Pagan scum!' he cried.

50

The Ceremonial Big Bang 2

The Catholic Church is a pretty big organisation. One pope, one hundred and fifty-eight cardinals, four hundred and seventeen archbishops, over thirty-seven billion dollars in the bank, over seventy-three thousand chapels and cathedrals and other religious buildings, owning over five million, nine hundred thousand acres of land, with nearly two billion practicing members. And yet, here they were, the entire future of their faith at stake and they were completely dependant on one little guy, who'd been sat scrunched up in a tiny cupboard for the previous seven and a half hours. He was tired, sore, hungry and desperate to go to the bathroom. All that, and it felt like his legs had been asleep forever. Which didn't fit well with suddenly leaping out of the cupboard and trying to sprint across the floor to disrupt the ceremony in whatever way he saw fit.

First big movement onto the floor, the *pagan scum* remark having just left his mouth, and whack, his legs gave way. Couldn't feel a thing, right leg first, tried the left but there was nothing there either and suddenly he was pitching forward, arms and legs flaying dramatically.

Smacked his head on the end of the one hundred and fifty year-old wooden table. Tried to stop himself, right enough, but he had little feeling in his arms either. Forehead to wood, a loud crack, and he collapsed onto the floor, the blood immediately oozing from the small cut.

Somebody said, 'What the…?' and let the question drift off.

'Just like the bloody Catholics to screw up,' muttered Jacobs, who still had the humph.

Ping Phat bent down to shift Luigi's head away from his feet. Felt for a pulse and under his nose for a breath.

'Still alive, but unconscious. We can proceed.'

Ephesian nodded, he and Ping Phat once more joined hands, and again there was nothing to stand in the way of the return of the King. That was that for the Catholic Church. If only they had chosen to deploy a thermo-nuclear device to obliterate the entire island, as some of the cardinals had argued.

'Dear Lord!' proclaimed Ephesian, although he didn't quite have the TV evangelist's voice that Jacobs had down pat, 'we gather here today, not to bring back your son, but to restore the line of Jesus, who was king, and who served you as prophet and teacher. Behold, we stand at the door and knock! With the blood of the sacred feminine, we revive the line that was lost. I am he that liveth, and was dead; and, behold, I am alive for evermore, Amen; and have the keys of hell and of death!'

He looked up the table and, for the second time in two days, magically managed to look Jacobs straight in the eye. There passed a look of knowledge and understanding between them, a bond that would not be shaken by the presence of the usurper.

'The blood,' said Ephesian softly.

Jacobs nodded, then lifted the vial of Garrett Carmichael's blood. He removed the top and slowly poured the contents into the Grail, letting the last few drops drip mesmerically. The audience was spellbound. Only Igor found this a little distasteful. Some of the others assumed that someone must have died for this blood, but thought it a reasonable price to give life to the man who lay disjointedly before them.

'Full circle,' said Ephesian. 'We must each drink the blood.'

You're kidding me! thought Barney.

That's part of my bird! thought Igor.

Are you sure? thought Petersen.

Nothing none of us haven't done before, thought Luciens.

Just like the Ardennes in '45, thought Rusty Brown.

Didn't even have to do that in the Ardennes in '45, thought Ginger Rogers.

275

Three billion dollars by the end of the week, thought Ping Phat.

I'd prefer a nice cup of tea, thought PC Gainsborough.

Knew I should have sent Chardonnay instead, thought McGhee.

Not again! thought the Reverend Dreyfus.

However, they were all silent with their thoughts. Jacobs took the first sip, a tiny amount, his tongue flicking out to remove the excess from his lips and then he passed the cup to his left, to Thomas Petersen. And as the cup was passed around, Ephesian recited slowly from Revelations, pausing only to take a sip of blood when the cup was passed to him by Ping Phat.

'His head and his hairs were white like wool, as white as snow; and his eyes were as a flame of fire; And his feet like unto fine brass, as if they burned in a furnace; and his voice as the sound of many waters. And he had in his right hand seven stars: and out of his mouth went a sharp two-edged sword: and his countenance was as the sun shineth in his strength. And when I saw him, I fell at his feet as dead.'

Barney Thomson tasted another person's blood for the first time and then laid the cup, still half-full, down on the table. He swallowed quickly, did his best to rinse the taste out of his mouth with saliva. Tried not to think about what he was part of. Suddenly felt a bit nervous about the freakishness of it all, of this absurd chopped up body lying frozen before them.

'Pass the cup to the head of the table,' said Jacobs quietly, and Barney wondered how long he'd been lost in morose contemplation.

He passed the cup onto Igor and then through Romeo McGhee, Ginger Rogers and Luciens, it reached Ephesian.

'By the pouring of the blood onto the lips of our King, and by the laying of our hands upon him, the line of Christ will be reborn!' cried Ephesian, who was just about beginning to get the hang of the Jimmy Swaggert routine. 'We must stand!'

As one the brotherhood rose. Every heart was thumping at the thrill of the moment, even the hearts of the new initiates who had come along curious rather than faithful. Ping Phat saw investment and marketing and money; Romeo McGhee saw newspapers and marketing and money; Barney Thomson saw none of that, but still his heart raced at this bizarre and grotesque ceremonial creation of life.

'And I saw heaven opened, and behold a white horse; and he that sat upon him was called Faithful and True. And he hath on his vesture and on his thigh a name written, KING OF KINGS, AND LORD OF LORDS!'

And Ephesian lifted the Holy Grail, the ancient wooden cup of Christ, and poured the remainder of the blood slowly into the frozen mouth of Azarael Corinthian. The first small amount entered the mouth and then quickly it filled the frozen space and began to spill over the sides and run down his cheeks and to collect in two pools on either side of the table.

When he was finished pouring, he placed the Grail on the table and laid both his hands on Corinthian's head.

'Join me, Brothers!' he said, his voice breaking with the strain.

They were almost there, their king was about to be reborn. He closed his eyes and allowed himself a sudden image, a dream of the next few minutes and of the next day, when the glory of God's kingdom on earth would once more be reinforced to a needy and desperate world.

Ping Phat also placed his hands on Corinthian's head and then, in turn, down the table the brothers of the *Prieure de Millport* pressed their hands against the frozen flesh of the naked heir to the throne of Israel and of Europe. Barney Thomson lightly touched the left foot, noticing that no one was bold enough to lay their hands on the royal genitals.

The fire flickered with some draught down the long flue, there was not a man amongst them who was not shivering with nerves, or wracked by anxiety, every sinew strained, every muscle rigid.

'And he shewed me a pure river of water of life, clear as crystal, proceeding out of the throne of God and of the Lamb!' declared Ephesian.

'Return to us, oh Lord!' cried Jacobs.

'Return to us!' cried Ephesian.

277

And then the cry was taken up by six more, 'Return to us!' and then ten of the brothers of the *Prieure de Millport* began to exalt in unison, 'Return to us! Return to us! Return to us!' Barney raised an eyebrow and wasn't chanting anything.

'Arf!' chanted Igor.

'Be reborn, my King!' ejaculated Ephesian, breaking ranks. '*De profundis clamavi ad te, Domine; Domine, exaudi vocem meam!*'

They all felt it; they felt the power and the majesty of the Lord coursing through their veins. They pressed their hands more firmly against the cold body, they each closed their eyes and lifted their heads to heaven, waiting to be touched by God, waiting to feel the warmth return to the frozen body of Azarael Corinthian.

Ephesian felt a shiver pulse down his spine, his fingers itched and twitched, but the spasms in his head were gone forever. His moment had arrived and not just the heir to the king of kings was about to be reborn.

'Arise! Arise!' he called.

'Arise!' cried a few of the others.

'Arf!'

'Drop down dew, heavens, from above, and let the clouds rain down righteousness; let the earth be opened, and a saviour spring to life!' ejaculated Jacobs, getting in on the act.

And the great love and strength and power of the Lord flowed down from heaven as a raindrop on a tiny leaf, and they all felt bathed in the wondrous glory of God's light. This was the moment of resurrection when their king would be reborn!

Ephesian dared to open an eye and look at what had been the jigsaw of Azarael Corinthian.

Nothing had changed.

A few others dared open an eye as they had imagined the heat of the Lord's blessing surging through the stricken and chopped up body of their king.

Nothing.

Slowly, around the circle, one by one, they all opened their eyes, the taste of blood still on their lips, and looked at their king. Still frozen, after all these years.

278

'What's happened?' asked Rusty Brown.

Ephesian said nothing. Suddenly the twisting discomfort which had plagued his stomach for the previous two days returned.

'What's gone wrong?' asked Jacobs, looking at Ephesian.

Ephesian had once again lost the ability to look Jacobs in the eye and was suddenly on the point of returning to the shell he had occupied all his life. It should have happened by now, the resurrection should have come with the pouring of the blood and the laying on of hands. Ephesian felt scared and nervous, wondering if he had done something wrong, wondering if he had not followed the ancient *Prieure de Sion* parchments correctly. Had he just let down generations of knights and monks and grand masters? Mouth open, breath beginning to come in short stabs, eyes wide and locked on Corinthian's blue and frozen face.

There was a stunned and suddenly melancholic silence around the room. There was not a man there, amongst the permanent members of the society, who had not believed that the Grail would bring their revered leader back to them. Instead, they were standing flat and dejected, confronted by nothing more than twelve individual body parts, assembled in approximately the right order, and still frozen.

'Maybe we could stick him in the microwave,' said Rusty Brown.

Jacobs was the first to move, walking round the table and picking up the Grail. The affront of Ping Phat, the hubris of the man in trying to appropriate the organisation for his own ends, was now forgotten. All that mattered was that the Grail had not done what they had thought it would.

'Dear Lord, how could you let us down? How could you deny us the divine powers of the Grail, the cup of Christ?'

He held the Grail aloft, so that one or two of the others looked up at it, as if raising their eyes up into the face of God. And one or two of them, it must be said, took a look at their watches and thought, I have to be up early in the morning.

'I think I'm seeing a problem here,' said Barney Thomson.

279

Jacobs stared angrily at him, as if equating the fact that Barney could see a problem, with Barney also causing the problem.

'Problem, yes, there is,' said Phat, who was looking most disconcerted at the disappearance of a host of marketing opportunities. For example his extensive range of *Cup of Christ Kitchenware*, which was at that very moment being manufactured by six year-old children in Malaysia, would all be for nothing.

Ephesian did not even hear Barney. He was slumped in his chair, eyes locked on the frozen face, yet seeing nothing.

'You're saying that the Grail has divine power,' said Barney.

'Yes,' snapped Jacobs angrily.

'Yet, your whole argument here, all your society is about, the secret it has been keeping all this time, is that Jesus was the descendant of the kings of Israel, a mortal man, that there is a direct lineage him to this frozen piece of disassembled meat before us. A king perhaps, but not born of God.'

'Yes,' snapped Jacobs again, but he had begun to see where Barney was going.

'So the Society claims that Jesus was mortal and not divine. He was not born of God. Therefore, if he's not divine, why would the cup he had his last drink out of, be divine?'

There were a couple of nods around the table.

'You didn't seriously think that this,' he said, indicating the grotesque array of parts before him, 'was ever going to come back to life? And if it had, that it wasn't going to scare the absolute hell out of you?'

He let the words sink in. There was some low murmuring around the table. Jacobs looked incensed but it was impossible to tell who or what he was incensed at.

'I suppose,' someone muttered.

'I've seen some weird stuff in my time,' said Barney, 'but it's usually being done by weird people. You lot are too normal for this.'

He looked around the table, at all the embarrassed faces.

'Who would've believed you anyway? How can you prove or disprove anything that is born of faith? It comes from the heart

280

and the soul. Two thousand year-old parchments aren't going to tell anyone that what they feel inside isn't true. And this…,' and he waved his hand at the table, letting the words drift off. 'Go home, go to bed,' he added, then he took a last look around the collective and turned to Igor.

'Come on, mate,' he said. 'Let's go.'

'Arf.'

Jacobs looked angrily at them but had no words to stop them. The rest of the collective watched them turn to go, thinking about what Barney had said and wondering just how weird they were being exactly.

Barney took a last look at the absurdity of what had just taken place, and then he and Igor began heading up the stairs.

'You going back to Garrett's?' asked Barney.

'Arf.'

'Cool. Maybe I could sleep at yours, 'cause I've just realised the time.'

They were gone, and then there were ten.

Around the table the low mumblings grew, the shuffling and the rustling and the glances at watches. A few looks were thrown the way of Jacobs and Ephesian, but no longer was anyone concerned with Ping Phat. Ten minutes ago they had accorded the man some respect, the monied businessman from the east. Now he was a fat foreigner who'd been stupid enough to get involved in an extremely bizarre business with a bunch of no-hopers in provincial Scotland.

'I should probably be getting to my bed,' said Ginger Rogers. 'Up to Glasgow in the morning. Getting the 7.50 from Largs.'

'Aye,' said Rusty Brown. 'I'm having a lie in tomorrow, but I'm keen to start it now.'

Chairs were pushed back, tired bodies were raised up onto tired legs, and the last ever meeting of the *Prieure de Millport* was in the process of being dismantled.

'Someone should probably do something with that,' said Luciens, pointing to the frozen corpse.

'I'll come back up in the morning,' said Gainsborough. 'Need a cup of tea and my bed.'

'It's not like he's going anywhere,' added Luciens, and Gainsborough laughed.

And then, walking around the table, Luciens stumbled across the prone figure of Luigi Linguini and the paramedic in him took over and he bent down to try and revive the man, considering it a better option than trying to haul a dead weight up the stairs.

And so, in a quick succession of ones and twos, the members of the collective were gone, including Ping Phat, already on the make, already running through in his head what merchandise had been manufactured up to this point and how best it could be marketed around the world.

And in the end, after Luciens had raised Luigi groggily to his feet and told him not to keep calling him pontiff, only Simon Jacobs and Bartholomew Ephesian were left.

Jacobs slumped down into the seat next to Ephesian, and he too locked his eyes on the blood covered face of Azarael Corinthian. Years of planning and dreams all for nothing. The lineage of Christ was dead. They still had the documentation, but they knew that Barney had been right. What did any of it matter?

'Dear Christ,' said Jacobs, the words a low and humble mumble.

Bartholomew Ephesian said nothing, but stared morosely at the top of the head of the last king of Israel, as he began the long night's drift into the long early morning of the first day of his descent into insanity.

Epilogue

A New Dawn

It was a fresh day, mostly blue skies peppered by occasional strings of white clouds, the wind which was blowing in off the sea a delicious cool breeze, smelling of salt and adventure and faraway places. A spring day, still demanding a jacket and a robust pair of trousers, but a spring day as it used to be before global warming weirded out the planet's weather systems for the foreseeable future. Middle of April, bit of sun, bit of chill in the air, winter over, hint of summer, the wonderful smell of the grass and the earth from a little rainfall in the middle of the night.

Barney had left the door of the shop open so that he could fully savour the aroma of morning. He had stopped at the bakers on the way along the road and had bought four fresh rolls, two each for him and Igor. Intended to wait and see if any customers arrived first thing, before establishing exactly when he was going to ask Igor to grill the bacon out back. Cup of tea, beautiful morning, bacon roll.

Today he could let his mid-life crisis pass. It would be back, presumably, on its pale horse, to wreak whatever havoc it chose with his mental well-being, but today the world seemed all right. He could get the paperwork signed, commit himself to this place and to Igor, and maybe he'd take his first look at houses along the front. See if there were any available round the west side of the island. Something near the boatyard.

283

He was standing in the doorway, resting against the frame. Igor was inside the shop, leaning on the brush, following his gaze across the road and the white promenade wall, out to sea. The waves were low, occasional white horses breaching the swell, a few small boats bobbled around in the bay.

Barney vaguely wondered if the secret society would continue its work, even without a figurehead. Or perhaps they would have decided in the middle of the night to keep the figurehead they had frozen, until such times as science had found a way to successfully resurrect him. After all, hadn't he himself once been reduced to just a brain in a jar?

Barney did not know, never would know, and would not have cared had he known, that Ping Phat and his entourage had departed that morning, having spent the remainder of the night plundering the *Prieure de Millport*'s secret documents and its secret frozen body parts. They had taken it all, while Ephesian and Jacobs had stood by and let them, so lost were they in disappointment. Not that Ping Phat had any grand motives involving lineage and the denunciation of two millennia of Pauline beliefs and dogma. He had no idea what use he would make of all the material, yet he knew that leaving it behind benefited him not. Better to take it with him and establish later how much money he could make from it. Even at a basic level, perhaps the Catholic Church would be willing to pay for it.

Ping Phat was gone, the *Prieure de Millport* had been split asunder, Ephesian and Jacobs were broken men who would never recover. Barney Thomson was just a guy who was about to buy a barbershop and settle down into life by the sea, and who cared not at all for the plots and schemes of clandestine societies and Asian businessmen.

'I got a right roasting from Miranda this morning. Felt like a kid,' said Barney, turning his head into the shop. 'How was Garrett?'

Igor nodded, couldn't keep the hint of a smile from his face. Certainly there was a relaxed serenity about him, which Barney recognised as coming from the realisation of true love.

'Smashing,' said Barney. 'You know what a Garrett is, as in the third divining force in life?'

'Arf,' said Igor.

'You'll have to explain it to me sometime,' said Barney.

'Arf.'

'Thanks, mate.'

'Excuse me!' said a cheery voice.

Barney turned, a customer on the doorstep. And one of the twelve, no less. Luciens, the paramedic.

'Hello,' said Barney, stepping back. 'Come in.'

'Thanks,' said Luciens.

Igor nodded at him, the spell of early morning had been broken, and he returned to the back of the shop, his hunch a little less marked than before, and began to carefully and dutifully sweep away at whatever was left of yesterday's hair. Luciens removed his jacket and took his place in the chair before the mirror.

Barney took a quick last look out at the sea before the work of the day was due to begin, then walked over to the chair and draped the cape and small towel around Luciens' neck and shoulders.

'Morning off?' asked Barney.

Luciens nodded.

'On call, to be fair,' he said, 'but it's not as if anything much ever happens around here, you know.'

Barney smiled.

'And even when it threatens to,' added Luciens, 'it usually goes wrong, eh?'

'Aye,' said Barney. 'Seems to be that kind of place.'

'Aye, that's what so good about it.'

'Arf.'

Luciens paused, a wee smile came to his face as he thought about something.

'Funny that, when the Italian fella leapt from the cupboard and immediately splatted his head against the table,' he said, laughing. 'Wanted to have a bit of a giggle at the time.'

Barney shared Luciens' laugh, the wonderful light-heartedness of it being infectious.

'But hey,' Luciens continued, 'I had a cracking idea for that lot the other day when I was talking to the weans.'

285

Barney started the cut as Luciens talked, aware without asking that he would be after a *Hugh Jackman - Van Helsing*.

'Which lot?' he asked to show interest although he knew who he meant.

'Rome,' said Luciens. 'The Vatican. I was attempting to put into words the difference between Coke Lite and Pepsi Lite, which wasn't easy by the way, and I got my words mixed up and said Pope Lite.'

He raised his eyebrows to Barney in the mirror.

'Pope Lite, what d'you think? Doesn't it have a fantastic ring to it? Catholicism with half the guilt. Think how many more people they could interest in the whole religion thing if they offered a kind of fast food version, you know what I'm saying? A ten minute, pray 'n dash service; shorter hymns, soundbites instead of sermons, maybe a *commit one sin, get one free* offer. They'd be queuing up. Fan-tastic!'

Barney studied the back of Luciens' head and snipped carefully around a patch which 2Tone had obviously got his hands on at some time in the past.

Another strange little episode of his life was over. Maybe he would stay here for a while after all, let something other than wandering and loneliness become normal.

'You could give away little plastic, moveable figures of Christ with every confession,' suggested Barney.

Luciens nodded.

'Top!' he said. 'You know, I really think we could go somewhere with this. You know, maybe we could draw up a blueprint over a pint tonight? You on?'

Barney thought about it but not for long. What was there to think about?

'Sure,' he said. 'We can put together a portfolio and present it to the Archbishop in Glasgow.'

'Top,' said Luciens. 'You in Igor?'

Igor raised his head from his serene dreams of Garrett Carmichael. He had no idea what they'd been talking about.

'Arf,' he said.

'Cool,' said Luciens. 'The more the merrier.'

Barney looked at Igor and nodded.

286

'The Kendall tonight at eight, it is then,' said Barney, so that Igor picked it up. 'Although, Igor might have other things to do.'

Igor nodded and then returned to his sweeping. Barney watched him for a second, took another glance out at the unflustered sea, took a moment to be aware of the smell coming in on the breeze, and then turned back to his customer.

'But you wouldn't sell burgers!' said Luciens, coming up from another thinking session. 'Or soft drinks for that matter. No sir, that would be like blasphemous, and you can't have that.'

'Not in this life,' said Barney.

'No way,' said Luciens.

'Arf!'